WILD

WILD

GEESE

Eilis Dillon

SIMON AND SCHUSTER

NEW YORK

For Vivian,
whose ancestors were fleeing from France to Ireland
at the same time as mine were fleeing
from Ireland to France

Copyright © 1980 by Eilis Dillon
All rights reserved
including the right of reproduction
in whole or in part in any form
Published by Simon and Schuster
A Division of Gulf & Western Corporation
Simon & Schuster Building
Rockefeller Center
1230 Avenue of the Americas
New York, New York 10020
SIMON AND SCHUSTER and colophon are trademarks of
Simon & Schuster

Designed by Eve Kirch
Manufactured in the United States of America

1 2 3 4 5 6 7 8 9 10

Library of Congress Cataloging in Publication Data
Dillon, Eilis, date.
   Wild geese.
   I. Title.
PZ4.D579Wi 1980   [PR6054.I42]   823'.914   80-15630
ISBN 0-671-22852-8

PART ONE

1

When James Brien inherited his father's estate near Moycullen, a few miles west of Galway, he went at once to Paris to look for a wife. He had been led to expect that he would find one among his many cousins there but the search proved not to be so easy. The year was 1736, only forty-five years since the Irish aristocracy had fled to France after the disastrous siege of Limerick, but already they had settled down to a cheerful, pleasant life there. The welcome they received at court, and the titles restored to them by Louis XIV, compensated to some extent for the wealth and position they had left behind. It made Frenchmen of them all, and their first rage and despair at their exile had settled into a pragmatic acceptance of their new condition.

James had written in advance to Count de Blezelle, who owned an estate not far from Tours as well as a house in Paris, in the rue du Bac. His wife was the daughter of Count Richard de Lacy, who had fought with King James against William of Orange and had left Ireland in 1691 with the Dillon regiment. Arthur Dillon, who owned the regiment, married Christine Sheldon, whose father had brought another regiment to France, and over the following forty-five years Dillons, de Lacys, Butlers, Sheldons, Brownes, Lallys and Briens married each other. More and more families kept coming from Ireland as the laws against Catholics were tightened. Some tried going back for a while or went for short visits to their decaying estates, but they always returned with horrifying tales of life there. In the end there were more cousins in France than James had ever met at home. They never forgot their origins but now it seemed that none of them wanted to go back to live permanently in Ireland.

The only one of all the young cousins who gave James any encouragement was Sophie de Blezelle. She was the youngest of the Count's eight children, sixteen years old, with a liking for independent thought which her mother and sisters considered highly dangerous. Old Cousin Marie, who had charge of James, was told privately by the Countess that he might be the answer to her difficulties. It was not that Sophie was short of offers of marriage. From the age of twelve she had been noted as eligible, inquiries even coming from England where Catholic brides were in short supply. Sufficiently powerful people were untouched by the laws—her cousin Henry Dillon, the eleventh Viscount, was married to Lady Charlotte Lichfield and they were known to be interested in Sophie for one of their friends' children. Great things could be done for her, if only she would keep silent and accept life as it was.

But she would not. Even at ten years old, when her two older sisters were about to marry men who served with the family regiments, Sophie said to them:

"You have never seen those men. What will you do if you look at them on your wedding day and don't like them? Won't it be too late then? Perhaps you won't be able to love them."

They were shocked. Hélène, who was the older one, kept her head and said patiently:

"Now, little Sophie, it's time you learned a few useful things. When you're our age, Papa will find you a husband and you'll be married just like us. That's how it has to be."

"But why? Why can't you see him first? Why can't you marry someone you know? What would happen if he turned out to be really, truly horrible?"

Hélène flushed angrily and said:

"Oh, then you could protest, but it would be dangerous."

"How, dangerous?"

"You know quite well, Papa would put you into a convent and he would tell everyone it was your own choice, or else you would be an old maid for life."

"I won't be an old maid, and I won't go into a convent either. I'll marry for love and be happy."

"You'll see," they said. "It's not so easy."

When all the other girls avoided James, Sophie was sorry for him. She forced herself to listen to his endless accounts of himself and his property. He was twenty-seven years old. He had a fine château, restored by his father in 1710, thousands of acres of land and a great river, the Corrib, flowing under the windows, like Chenonceau. He pulled a miniature out of his pocket to show a great white house with trees on rising ground behind it, and the river flowing past, not exactly under the windows but near enough to make the comparison with Chenonceau possible. There was a little stone harbor in the foreground, with several boats, and he said that the river was alive with salmon. Sophie peered at the miniature, then went to get a reading glass to examine it properly. When she came back he told it all to her again, and about his plans for improving the land on the lines begun by his father.

Later the cousins asked:

"How can you put up with him? He's such a bore, going on about his trees and his sawmill. That house of his is miles out in the country. The nearest town is Galway and it's a poor little place. Even in Dublin there's hardly any life, no king, no court, only a Lord Lieutenant, a kind of Governor, who opens a season in Dublin Castle with one levée and then goes back to London as fast as he can. Cousin James lives on his estate all the year—imagine it!—among the cows and hens. And he says it's against the law for a Catholic to keep good horses, even for farm work, and only for our powerful English cousins he would be displaced from his fine house and land altogether."

Uneasily Sophie answered this tirade:

"There must be other great houses around. His can't be the only one."

"There are others but most of them are empty, no one in them but servants and stewards. Most of the Catholic gentry have emigrated and the Protestants spend their time in Bath and Cheltenham and London, just as we come to Paris. If Cousin James was not such a bore he would do the same."

"How do you know all this?"

"We ask the right questions."

"I think you're all being very nasty about him," Sophie said, with the fellow-feeling she would have had for a despised cat.

9

"Watch out," they said. "Your Mama has noticed you."

"What do you mean? Everyone said we were to be nice to him."

Too late, Sophie realized what she had done. A day or two after this conversation her mother sent for her and said:

"Sir James Brien has made an offer for you. Your father and I think he will do very well. He says he finds you an inspiring companion. I've seen you tête-à-tête with him more often than was proper but if you're going to marry him that won't matter."

"Only because the others were laughing at him, only because no one would talk to him—"

"You have been told how a lady behaves. Well, once you're engaged to him all that will be forgiven."

"But I'm not engaged to him!"

"Are you objecting? Are you refusing "

"Couldn't I have more time? I don't know him at all."

"You've had plenty of time. In fact you are probably already compromised. It would be quite improper to refuse him now."

"But I don't love him," Sophie protested for the last time.

"You know nothing about that. You must never say that." Her mother's voice sharpened and her little bony fists clenched with fury. "You should be glad to have him, a fine handsome man, ten times too good for you, with a title, a cousin too. What did you think you would get? A royal prince, perhaps. Do you think we could have bought you one of those? God knows you're no beauty. A girl with your coloring can't pick and choose."

Sophie gave up, through a mixture of physical fear and despair, but she never forgot that scene, going over and over it during her worst times in the following years.

In a gesture possibly inspired by guilt her mother gave her Amélie, her own maid, to go with her to Ireland. She also provided a minimum of silver and linen, since in spite of what James said she could not believe that an Irish household could have enough of such things already. Now and then she said:

"It will probably be all right. You're young enough to deal with whatever turns up. They must have put some good things into a house of that size. We always hear of the great houses they had before the flight of the Wild Geese." This was the name by which the emigrant aristocracy was known. "The Irish are a good-hearted people. Amélie will take good care of you when things go wrong. A Frenchwoman is what you need. And remember that it's your own choice. You must never complain afterwards. Papa won't allow it."

They were married within a few weeks, just after Easter, by the Archbishop of Paris, with dukes and princes at their wedding. Afterwards turned out to be even worse than she had imagined. Her sisters would tell her nothing and in the light of that scene she dared not ask her mother what was expected of her. After the evening banquet Amélie brought her to the main guest room, dressed her in one of her new nightdresses and a lace cap and then deserted her, squirming with embarrassment when Sophie held on to her hand to make her stay. Long ago the maid used to stay in the room with the bride, she said, closing the bed curtains sharply around her, but this was gone out since her mother's time. Sophie said:

"You can stay in a dark corner. He won't see you. The curtains are heavy. Please, please don't leave me alone with him."

"I can't stay. He's a foreigner. They're different. Now be a good girl. I must go—I can hear him coming." She ran out of the room.

James tried to have patience but after two hours of attempting to make love to Sophie he exclaimed:

"Did your mother tell you nothing at all? I thought French girls knew everything."

He lit the lamp and gazed at her with big, disappointed eyes, sulky with his grievance, so that she became sorry for him again and encouraged him to begin once more, concealing her terror at what was happening to her. In the morning, at their first encounter she gave her mother such a stare of pure hatred that she saw her cringe away. It was her only revenge for the torments she had suffered, all the worse because she felt that it need not have been at all like that. If only he were not so dull and humorless—he had been quite offended when she had giggled at the ridiculousness of what they were doing, and indeed had taken all the fun out of it. Nevertheless she found herself becoming almost fond of him. He was indeed a dreadful bore but he was handsome and attentive. At first she found it pleasant to be envied by the cousins who had come to the wedding but soon she found that they had learned from her family to despise him, and therefore her. She was glad when after less than a week it was time to set out for Ireland.

They traveled by way of England where they visited more cousins and received more presents, which were piled into a new coach. They drove through the gloomy mountains of north Wales and waited at Holyhead a miserable three days until the Captain of the packet boat decided that it was calm enough to sail. He was almost wrong. Thirty hours later, weak and frozen, they disembarked at Dunleary, the little port outside Dublin, and immediately started for Galway. Sophie wanted to see something of Dublin but having been away so long, more than six months, James said that they must go home. Rather than endure a long lecture from him on his responsibilities she agreed. His own traveling carriage and coachmen, as well as two footmen and two outriders, had been with him in France, but fresh horses had been brought from Galway and had waited at Dunleary for more than a week, with two more grooms and coaches for the baggage.

Sophie was charmed at first with the journey. The weather had changed and the whole country was glowing in the May sunshine. Near Dublin it was as fine as anything she had ever seen in her life. There were good cottages and walled demesnes, sometimes glimpses of large, well-kept houses, but the farther west they traveled the poorer everything became. Hovels on the very roadside housed swarms of ragged peasants who followed the carriage with cries like birds, their skinny hands stretched out for the handfuls of small coins that James sometimes threw from the windows. They stopped at inns three nights on the way, the servants riding ahead to give warning that they were coming and to order dinner. They were received like kings, rooms were cleared so that they could dine in private, the landlords escorted them upstairs bowing all the way, while the dispossessed crowds of ordinary customers peeped at them through half-open doorways and around the corners of passages. James said that it was no use calling at the great houses that they passed because the owners would all be absent at least until June, if they returned at all. There seemed to be a great many new houses building or just built, standing huge and stark among unmade lawns and gardens, but there were older houses as well, most of them apparently falling to pieces. There was a fashion for building new houses, James said, because everything was so cheap just now. Sophie remembered the miniature but couldn't bring herself to ask questions about Mount Brien Court.

On the afternoon of the fifth day they passed through Galway. Miserable thatched cottages were huddled in groups, right in the town, and there were some large dark stone houses with windows as narrow as in a fortress. The main street was crammed with wretchedly ragged peasants who had come in to sell their eggs and fish from deep willow baskets which they laid on the ground at their feet. Not one woman seemed to have a bright ribbon or a piece of lace to wear, as they would have had in France. A fair green at the top of the main street was a mass of donkey-carts, the smallest she had ever seen, halted nose to tail, used to pen in calves and chickens and pigs. The air was filled with loud voices, speaking a language she had never heard before. It was fair day, James said, looking on the scene casually as the carriage nosed its way through. The coachman cracked his whip high in the air so that she feared he was going to strike the people with it but he was only indicating that he wished to pass with his team. Many people recognized the carriage and ran along beside it, waving and shouting. Sophie asked softly:

"What are they saying? Do you know their language?"

"Of course. I use it to speak to the laborers. They're saying a welcome to both of us, to you especially. You should wave back to them."

Though some of the faces did not look welcoming at all, she put her head out of the window and waved and bowed and smiled as if she were not frightened out of her wits of them. The carriage passed through another, smaller market where potatoes were being sold, and by thatched hovels so filthy that even the sunny day could not make them palatable. Then they crossed a bridge over a shallow, wide, fast-flowing river and presently came out on a long windy road with a river almost as wide as the Loire off to the right and on the far bank some pleasant rolling country but with scarcely a single tree. On that far bank she saw a stone castle by the river and she feared that this was how her new home would be, a keep, a fort, an outpost in the wilderness. Half an hour later they drove through a pillared gateway and across a wide, treeless park, by a curving avenue that followed the contours of the land. No house was visible yet, only the pale sky and pale grassland, and the white graveled avenue which seemed to go on for miles. As they reached the top of the last hill a long white house came into view, with a little harbor below, exactly as it was in the miniature. She turned quickly to James, saying in English:

"This is beautiful."

Amélie poked her head out of the window and gave the house an approving look, the first she had managed for anything since they had touched the shores of Ireland.

Later James conducted Sophie all over the house, explaining every detail as if it really were Chenonceau, until her feet were sore and the muscles of her face stiff from smiling at dozens of servants, not one in livery, and from praising hideous second-rate statuary in niches and on pedestals everywhere. James's father had bought them on the grand tour, mostly in Italy. There was one good picture of an Italian lake, and a small marble faun that looked out of place among all the other rubbish.

The house itself was beautiful, with bright, well-furnished rooms and good kitchens and yard buildings and coach houses. She was disappointed at first that there were only five bedrooms for guests. In spite of everything, at sixteen years old she still wanted her mother, and she would have settled for some of her sisters instead, if only for the pleasure of showing them all her new possessions.

Gradually she discovered that no one would ever come. It was too dangerous, they wrote, with the fierce laws against Catholics and Jacobites. When she reassured them that there was never any trouble at Mount Brien, they said they were too busy with their families. As time passed, she no longer wanted to have them. She had learned enough Irish to talk to the servants and teach them French manners but she could not possibly get them all into livery. James said they couldn't afford it because he was spending so much on new cottages and on drainage and fertilizers to improve the land. French people would find her way of life outlandish, or conclude that she had come down in the world. And they would never understand why a clutter of wandering poets and singers and musicians had to be entertained, sometimes for weeks at a time, in the servants' quarters and in the kitchens. James said that this was a family tradition and that they must always feel welcome.

Sophie's eldest son, Maurice, was born when she was seventeen, then three more sons with a year between each. Her two daughters, the last of her children, died when they were two and three years old, of an epidemic of smallpox which also killed her husband. Now at last she was free. She was only twenty-six years old. She could abandon the estate and go back to France, taking her surviving children with her, out of this accursed country, as her forebears had done before her. Plans and ideas chased each other through her head as the three terrible funerals went on. James's, the last one, was the worst. At least he had never known of the deaths of his two daughters. When the family vault was opened yet again, she clutched her eldest son's hand and shut her eyes, unable to bear any more sorrow. Some of the neighboring landlords, who happened to be at home, had sent their empty carriages. She recognized Mr. Flaherty from Moycullen House and Mr. D'Arcy from Woodstock, and John Nugent who was their nearest neighbor, and she knew it was very kind of them to come in person, terrified as they were of the smallpox.

The poor people for miles around came in hundreds, people who had known James and his family all their lives. Many of them wept and moaned prayers in Irish, swaying up and down on their knees. She knew their grief was real. James had been their friend, making a point of knowing the details of everyone's family life, and his improvements to his estate were famous throughout Connaught. One by one they approached her to offer their sympathy but she saw the fear in their faces. At last a man named Colman Quin, who had charge of all the farm horses, said in careful English, his soft drawl more pronounced than usual:

"We're thinking, my lady, that you'll be wanting to go back to your own place after this disaster. Why wouldn't you? Ireland is a bad country for all at this time."

"I don't know," she said uncertainly. "I've thought about it, I suppose." He was a short, bow-legged man who had once been a jockey. She had to look down into his face, rather like looking at a child. This impression was emphasized when at her answer his face wrinkled up as if he were about to cry. Quickly she went on: "I haven't had time to make up my mind about anything, Colman. There's no hurry. We'll go on as usual for a while, at least."

He looked more cheerful at this lukewarm encouragement and later she saw him circulating among the other farm workers, obviously telling them what she had said.

Two reasons combined to make her stay. One was that she knew she was necessary to the tenants and farm workers, that even if she managed to sell the estate the new owner would almost certainly clear them off the land to make room for the more economically sound policy of grazing cattle and sheep. The second reason was just as strong, perhaps stronger: she would not be welcome in France. Her mother, widowed for several years, made little effort to pretend that she was interested in Sophie even now. Her annual letter, usually written at Christmas, was very short, ending always with a cold inquiry about the health of "all those little children." Sophie guessed that her mother would blame her for the deaths, using this evidence of her worthlessness to justify the way she had treated her. And she guessed too that her mother had not been entirely able to stifle the voice of conscience, and that this was why she never wanted to see her daughter again. But she had some obligations and Sophie insisted on her rights. As soon as they were old enough she sent the three youngest boys to France to join the family regiments. They were named Arthur, Theobald and Henry after their Dillon godfathers and were soon off serving in different parts of the colonies. Maurice she educated herself to take over the estate, remembering with great profit the long boring lectures she had endured from her husband. She found him a priest as tutor, as she did later for her grandchildren, and then sent him to a cousin's estate in England for two years, before arranging a visit to France for him in 1758, when he was twenty-one years old, to find a wife. One thing she was certain of, that there was not a single girl of all her acquaintance among the gentry in Ireland that she would welcome into her house as a daughter-in-law.

2

Maurice's bride, Cécile, was never happy in Ireland. Sophie would not admit that she was dissatisfied with her. Bitterly she remembered her own despair at the poverty and ruin she had seen on her arrival, and wondered at herself for luring another woman into the same trap. She had done it automatically, almost without thinking, and Maurice because of his youth had followed her instructions unquestioningly. The alternative was to look for an English girl who would have been at least as miserable, and who would probably have refused to live at Mount Brien Court all the year as Cécile was willing to do. Sophie had wanted another Frenchwoman about the house to ease her own homesickness and to speak her language. The main trouble with Cécile was that she was not healthy. She managed to have two children, Robert, born a year after the marriage, and Louise three years later. Seven years after that she died of a difficult birth, and her infant son died with her.

Maurice had always seemed to Sophie to be something of a weakling but this time he surprised her. Within a year of Cécile's death he brought Fanny Warner to the house for the first time. Sophie took him aside afterwards and said:

"Maurice, I hope it's not too late to advise you not to marry that ignorant woman."

It was too late, and he did marry her, and his mother was proved quite right in her judgment that he would regret it, but there was not much that he could do about it. After Cécile, delicate, over-refined, so sensitive that she sometimes seemed almost to stop him from breathing, Fanny had certain compensations as a wife, but daily life was mortifying and coarse compared with what it had been before. And Fanny was rough with Louise, because she looked exactly like her mother though she was perfectly healthy. Fair, slender, delicate Cécile was a legend in the whole neighborhood, all the more so as she had died so young and so far from home. Maurice had heard that there wts a ballad about her.

Sophie counteracted some of the worst of Fanny's ignorant ways but she could not do everything. Neither could she conceal her distaste for Fanny's three sons. They were all black-haired Briens, all healthy, which should have pleased her, but Sophie almost seemed to forget that they were her grandchildren as much as Robert and Louise were. Fanny resented this, as well she might, and at times a cold civil war in the house made everyone's life painful, from the servants upwards. Sophie kept her grip, reluctantly supported by Maurice, daring Fanny to oust her from the position she had gained during the interregnum, indeed during the whole of Cécile's time at Mount Brien Court. Even when Fanny brought her sister to live in the house, their combined efforts were never a match for Sophie.

One of her triumphs was getting Father Burke as tutor to the older children. His family came from Ennis, fifty miles away, and he was home from Bordeaux on a visit to his cousins, who were the Briens' nearest neighbors, when Sophie met him. He had not wanted to stay, since he was a parish priest in France, but Sophie used her influence with some cousins in Bordeaux to get him on loan for several years. Fanny complained that his presence in the house was a danger to the family. It was against the law to harbor a priest, she said, hissing in her terror and looking over her shoulder in a ludicrous way, as if she thought a spy was at the door behind her. Then she broke into Irish, her first language and still the one she used when she was agitated, until she saw Sophie's eyebrows lifted in disapproval. She quickly reverted to English. Everyone for miles around knew the priest was there. Sooner or later someone would inform on him and they would all be arrested, deported, burned out, dispossessed—she didn't know what misfortune would fall on them. Sophie said scathingly:

"None of those things will happen to this family. You are a Brien now, my dear. A gentleman's family must have a tutor."

The last statement was made as if it would be news to Fanny. She stuttered furiously and went off, not daring to scream at Sophie. She knew it was true that no one could touch the Briens even though they were Catholics in a country where that in itself was to break the law. Fanny screamed at Maurice later, however:

"Your mother—she despises me. She looks at me as if I was something the cat brought in. The Briens! 'You are a Brien now, my dear.' " She mimicked Sophie's French accent, a trick she had learned almost at once, and Maurice turned away in anger. "I know all about the Briens, the cutest able-dealers in four counties, always making out when everyone else is being hunted, cute enough to change their name too. O'Briens they are but no one dares to call them that. I should be glad, to be sure I should be glad now that I'm one of them, but she sneers at me and laughs at me. She treats me like an upstart or a tally-woman, instead of her son's wife. I'm as good stock as she is any day of the week, for all her fine airs."

This was pure bravado. Fanny was descended from a minor officer in Cromwell's army, left behind in Ireland with a grant of land instead of his pay, in 1650. He had lowered himself by marrying a poor Catholic girl and deserting his Protestant heritage, so that Fanny's family was despised by the displaced Irish gentry as well as by the Protestant aristocracy. Maurice sometimes admitted to himself secretly that he deserved what had happened to him, since he had chosen her deliberately because her lowly background would make her obedient and undemanding. She had good country skills and a brisk way about her but this turned into aggression and violence as time went on. Even her native prettiness evaporated in a few years, leaving her dried up and disgruntled, with a watchful, peevish expression.

Fanny's sister Sarah was like one of those cats that are never plainly seen, always disappearing through doorways or between bushes, only a slow tail betraying them. She spoke little, always in a low voice in contrast to Fanny's shrillness, so that people felt grateful to her for being easier. The children noticed that she always appeared silently when there was trouble or an argument. Any misfortune drew her. Then her round, pale eyes rested without expression on the person most affected, and though she said nothing then or later, one had the impression that she fed on the pain of others. Maurice tolerated her because he thought she siphoned off some of Fanny's complaints. Sometimes he asked impatiently:

"Why can't you keep out of my mother's way?"

"How can I do that, in my own house?" Fanny demanded.

"Or try to please her."

"There's no pleasing her. If I do a thing the way she does it, she lifts her eyebrows as much as to say 'So you think you'll be as good as me, do you?' If I do things my own way, she looks at me as if I came in off the bogs and was past praying for. It's all in her looks."

When his eldest son, Robert, was nineteen years old, Maurice arranged with Father Burke that he should go to Paris to study at the Sorbonne. It was the end of a long battle with Fanny, who had been agitating for years to get him and his sister out of the house.

"They're a pair of little foreigners," she hissed maddeningly, again and again. "They'll never do here. They'll be better off in France, where they came from."

It was reasonable to send Robert away but an excuse had to be found for sending his sister with him. It came easily, since her French inheritance had found its way into the charge of Cousin Charlotte in Paris, and the only way to gain possession of it was to go there in person. Then began the battle with his mother, so that by the time all the arrangements were concluded Maurice was made to feel a criminal by all sides.

The first time he broached the subject to his mother was on an afternoon in September 1779. He had barely reached the point of telling her that Louise had asked to go with Robert to France when Sophie stood up and walked out of the room without a word. An hour later, becoming uneasy, he searched the whole house, upstairs and down, the dairy and the buttery and the pantries, and was finally directed to her sitting room by Sarah, who said with a knowing smile:

"I think you'll find her in her own little retreat."

"Retreat? Retreat? What are you talking about?"

Exasperated as usual by Sarah, Maurice went to his mother's sitting room on the first floor. It had been arranged for her when Maurice first married, with rose-patterned chairs and curtains, and touches of gold paint to keep up with the French furniture. It was kept dusted, and in wet weather Sophie sometimes brought Robert and Louise up there to tell them stories of her early life in France, a thousand years ago it seemed to them. Maurice came abruptly into the room and said:

"Mother, in the name of God what are you at?"

Sophie turned to look at him, her face invisible against the light, then said in an unnaturally high tone, too fast:

"Don't blaspheme, child. And don't call me 'Mother.' I've asked you a thousand times. I'm making lace. Why shouldn't I? I made lots of lace when I was a girl. I was brought up to it. We did it for an hour every day in Paris, in the afternoon, in Hautefontaine too, when we went to visit, embroidery and tapestry and lace." Her forehead wrinkled with irritation at the memory of it. He said:

"But here! You've never done it here."

There was no need to ask why she had to resort to lace making. Maurice said:

"You always knew that Robert would have to go to France some day. We've talked about it hundreds of times."

"Yes, hundreds of times. I must have thought some miracle would happen to prevent it. And you never told me about Louise. You only mentioned that an hour ago, when you said you had written to Cousin Charlotte."

Maurice said uneasily:

"She has asked to go. I've agreed to it. Father Burke will go with them and see them safely into Cousin Charlotte's house. It's the only way that Louise will ever get her mother's money. If she doesn't go herself, Cousin Charlotte will never give it up."

"You think she will give it to Louise?"

"She must. I've heard she's hoping that Louise will never come to claim it."

"That she'll die, like her mother. That would be convenient for Charlotte. But Louise is very healthy, thank God."

Relieved at this practical comment Maurice said:

"She will have plenty of friends among the cousins. There's nothing to worry about."

"I wish she didn't have to go at all. Surely you could see to it for her."

"Mama, you know I can't possibly leave everything here. She

is a sensible girl. And Robert wants her to go with him. He says she'll get no more education once he's gone."

He stopped then, realizing that he was on the verge of enlarging the argument unpleasantly.

It was January of 1780 before a letter came from Cousin Charlotte to say that Robert and Louise could set out for Paris at once. This time Maurice knew where he would find Sophie, who seemed nowadays to keep a permanent watch on the avenue from her sitting room window. Sure enough, she has seen the carrier ride up with the letter. She knew what was in it before Maurice opened his mouth. He stood at the door, looking at her, so that she had to speak first.

"Well? When can they go?"

"As soon as possible, Cousin Charlotte says. She has arranged her daughter's engagement and she says she's ready now to receive them. She doesn't sound very friendly but perhaps that's just her stiff English. Her daughter's name is Teresa. I'd forgotten."

"Who is the man?"

"One of the de Lacy cousins. He's away in America in the army, she says. She wants Robert and Louise to be settled in before the wedding."

"Will the wedding be soon?"

"She doesn't say. Who knows when the bridegroom will come back? If they leave in a week they may avoid the gales at the equinox."

"Yes, the sooner the better, then."

"You sent my brothers there, all of them."

"I would not have sent your sisters."

"They will come back."

"You think so? I doubt it."

"It will solve the problem of Celia Nugent."

"I had thought of better ways of solving that."

"You could visit them."

"You know perfectly well that I'll never go to France again. I'll go and tell Biddy at once. There's a great deal still to be done."

"Yes."

It would keep her busy. Biddy was Louise's maid, trained by

old Amélie who still took care of Sophie. Biddy had even learned a little French from Amélie, asking her questions and trying to find out about the strange country that everyone seemed to find so important. She was wild, almost sick with excitement these days at the prospect of her journey to France with Louise, and at the possession of four new dresses.

Sophie was so calm that evening at dinner that everyone watched her in trepidation. Towards the end of the meal she turned to Father Burke and said in an unnaturally sweet tone:

"So, Mr. Burke, soon you will be leaving us."

The long oak dining table was lit by three splendid branching candlesticks that Sophie had brought from France. Each carried six candles whose light glittered on the silver and on the polished wood. It lit up the expressions of the family all too well, Fanny already bridling, Maurice looking irritated, Sarah's eyes traveling from face to face, the three small boys shrinking against the backs of their chairs as if they expected to be attacked. They had been brought in for dessert but their looks showed that this would not be much of a treat today. Robert and Louise were blankly polite but they moved their pale blond heads a fraction of an inch closer together. Father Burke's face twitched and wrinkled, his agitation showing tactlessly and clearly. Sophie watched him with amusement while he tried to find words to save the situation. He was a huge man with wiry black hair which he tried to keep tidy by tying it back in a pigtail. He looked very fine this evening, in a black suit that Maurice had had made for him in Galway, but already the first stains of snuff were beginning to spot the front of the coat Fanny said:

"He will be coming back to us, of course. Hasn't he three more coming up to him any day now?"

"Ah, yes." Sophie turned to gaze at the three little boys as if they were pieces of furniture that she was appraising in a shop. "You think they will be able to learn Latin and Greek and mathematics? I didn't know you believed in such things. And perhaps it is already too late. Hubert must be almost ten years old."

"Mama!"

Maurice sat forward, one fist on the tablecloth. Sophie subsided with a satisfied smile and a long-drawn-out sigh. Maurice knew that in another moment she would have added that Fanny should be pleased at the prospect of getting rid of the priest since she was always so frightened at keeping him in the house at all. For the last two years, since Fanny had wanted him to begin teaching Hubert, Sophie had managed to prevent it by one ruse or another, even threatening to send away the governess who was teaching the younger children, saying that without Hubert she would not have enough to do. All this would be gone into if Maurice allowed them to speak to each other. Afterwards he followed her out into the hall and steered her into his rent room, holding her by the elbow, saying when the door was shut:

"Mama, you must not tease Fanny like that in company."

"Tease her?" Sophie's large blue eyes were innocent but she let slip a snort of contempt. Maurice tightened his grip and she said: "Are you threatening me?" She shook herself free. "I won't tease her, if you say so, but how is she to learn?" Seeing his look of despair she turned away saying: "Very well, I'll let her alone. But what am I to do without Louise? Why should she go too? We could bring her out here, in Dublin, or in London, and abandon the legacy. We could find her a good husband somehow."

"You know she will be much better off in France." Seeing Sophie's uncertainty he went on: "And besides, Louise is too French for an Irish or an English husband." Now she was glaring at him furiously and he said softly: "Cécile was not happy here. We must learn by experience."

"What nonsense! Cécile was born in France. The climate, the language, the whole way of life—everything was strange to her. Louise is Irish."

"It hurts me too, as you know very well."

"Don't forget that I was happy in Ireland, as long as your father was alive."

In all the thirty years since his father's death she had insisted on this story and he could not bring himself to argue with her further.

3

During their last week in Ireland, Robert and Louise escaped every afternoon for several hours with the excuse that they must pay farewell visits to the tenants. They kept to the home estate, though part of the property was twenty miles away, near Cong, where Maurice had bought two adjoining farms twelve years ago when their owners sold out and went to America. He took Robert there once or twice, long rides through mountain passes descending at last to the upper shores of Lough Corrib. Here there were smooth fields, prepared for grazing sheep. In spite of having cleared off most of the tenants, the former owners had not been able to make a success of things. No sooner had the farms been stocked with sheep than the English parliament enacted new laws against the export of wool from Ireland and they lost everything. Maurice with his mixed farming, and especially because of his sawmills, was doing better but the estate in Moycullen was still heavily burdened, to keep the Cong one on its feet until times got better.

Robert had no pleasant memories of these expeditions. Maurice explained to the people that it would take time to get things back into condition but they hardly believed him. All landlords were enemies, and besides Maurice was a Catholic who might lose everything at any moment. They knew he had powerful relations in England who had saved him from destruction so far, but if some Protestant informed on him the Dublin parliament might hand over all his property to the informer without consulting the English one at all. That was the law, and it was discussed endlessly over turf fires throughout Connemara whenever his name came up. How could you put your trust in such an uneasy vessel? It would take years for him to prove that his goodwill was genuine and not just another trap, though his reputation had preceded him from Moycullen. Black looks followed them as they rode around the property, hairy faces glared from smoky doorways, the agent put on an imperious tone when he addressed the cottagers and Robert saw the murderous looks of hatred in their eyes. This was ignored by his elders though they must have noticed it.

Maurice, who was often described as a true Brien, was tall and broad and black-haired, and Robert felt ridiculous for being so light and pale and fair-skinned, like a changeling. In every house that he and Louise visited during that last week, the old people commented loudly and admiringly on their appearance. This was all right when they were near home, with people they had known all their lives and who had reason to be grateful to Maurice, but on the last afternoon, on a distant mountain road, taking what they thought was a short cut to visit Robert's old wet nurse, they came to an unfamiliar village. It was a cluster of thatched hovels set haphazardly on a stony patch of ground, surrounded by a wasteland of bog and mountain. From up here there was a magnificent view of the lake, the hard wind intermittently ruffling its water to the color of lead. Their horses' hooves rang on the stones as they picked their way among the cottages. Old and young women came trotting out, barefoot, to stand on their doorsteps and hoot compliments in Irish, not addressed to anyone in particular:

"They're like a little king and queen. Look at their white skin like snow, and their gold hair. The girl has a neck like a swan. Her waist is slender enough to get your two hands around it."

This raised a laugh from a small group of men who were sitting motionless on a rock a short distance from the houses. It was clear that no one realized their words were understood. Robert turned in his saddle and called out in Irish:

"Will this road bring us down to Creevagh?"

All the people went silent but stood there, staring, apparently without embarrassment. Then a woman in a ragged red flannel skirt and a torn blue blouse came forward, pushing her wild hair back from her forehead with both hands. She said quickly:

"It will do that. Who do you want down in Creevagh?"

"Katta Folan, that's married to Matthias Crowley."

"Isn't that a fine tongue of Irish he has! Where did you learn to speak it so well? Would you be a Brien from the Court?"

"I am Robert Brien. I learned my Irish from Katta when I was small."

"You drank her breasts?"

"Yes."

"She's a Barna girl. Her son Colman is the one age with you. He's your brother."

"Yes."

"And this is your true sister. We heard you'll be going away."

"Tomorrow morning."

"You look happy when you say that. Why wouldn't you, and you young and the world before you? All the gentry are going away. That's why we are the way we are, so they say. They take their guineas and they go away."

"My father is not going away."

"Don't be angry, little son. I know well he won't go. He's a good man like his father before him. I wish we had the like of him here."

"Who have you here?"

"A man called Mr. Herbert." She pronounced the foreign name very carefully. "But if he walked up to me and pulled my nose, I wouldn't know him. He never comes here, only Mr. Ross, his agent. Do you know Mr. Ross?"

"No."

"I thought you would know him because he's a gentleman." She said the word with heavy contempt. "He comes for the rent, and for his potatoes and chickens. He's fat and heavy, from all the chickens. He'd smell out a pig or a young calf a mile away." Suddenly she seemed to remember that she was talking to one of the same caste and stopped, but in a moment went on hurriedly: "When we saw you coming we thought you might be of the family of Mr. Herbert, coming to look at your land and property. Let you go straight on there and turn down the hill where you'll see a fork in the road. It's a steep hill but you'll be all right with the horses. You'll take the left-hand turning. Tell me now, have you never been to Creevagh before?"

"No. Katta comes sometimes but it's a long walk for her."

"It is, little son, a long walk. You'll come back by the low road if you're late. It's not good on the mountain after dark unless there's bright moonlight. Katta will put you on the right road."

"Thank you a thousand times."

"Does your sister speak Irish too?"

"Indeed I do," Louise said quickly, glad to prove herself.

"God bless you, the two of you. Tell me, boy, are you going to be a soldier in France?"

"No. I'm going to France to be a scholar."

"That is much better. I'm very glad to hear that, and the whole country will be glad too. Come back to us some day with all your learning."

"We will come back."

She walked a few courteous steps with them, a hand on the rump of each horse, stepping along easily between them on her bare feet. Then she stood and waited while they rode off. As the track wound downhill they turned in their saddles and waved to her. For a while they were able to ride side by side, talking now and then when the sound of the wind and the movement of the horses allowed it. As soon as they were well out of the village Robert said:

"I do mean to come back. Papa doesn't want it. He's been driving me crazy, telling me I'm a Frenchman. Yesterday I reminded him that I'll be his heir some day and he got quite agitated. He said I'm never to say that—I was only joking but he took it so seriously. I wish I knew what is going on in his head. He seems so anxious to be rid of us, and still I think he doesn't want us to go at all."

"Aunt Fanny is tormenting him in private. Biddy told me that."

"I might have known," Robert said bitterly, then went on as if he wanted her to continue with her revelations. "Biddy seems to know everything."

"Biddy told me that Aunt Fanny wants Hubert to be a Sir some day. She even suggested that he could turn Protestant and cut you out. She has been talking about Celia Nugent too."

"What has she been saying?"

"All sorts of things. You know Aunt Fanny."

Louise was desperately interested in her brother's friendship with Celia but had never had the opportunity to discuss it with him. Now she was warned off by his reluctant tone, though she knew he was waiting eagerly for her answer. Even a year ago she would have bounced into the most personal conversation but lately she found that something she could not understand impeded them both. Their old natural friendship seemed to have gone forever. She sensed that Celia had something to do with it, though Celia herself was always very friendly to Louise. Everything had become so unpleasant lately that she had welcomed the news of going with Robert to France like the reprieve of a death sentence.

His face was flushed now and his mouth twisted angrily as he said:

"Aunt Fanny has the mind of a hen woman. How does Biddy hear all this?"

"From Aunt Fanny's Nell, of course. What else have servants to talk about? Aunt Fanny has no discretion. She talks away, but Papa tries not to answer her while Nell is in the room, just walks around and looks miserable, Nell says. And she says no man could be a match for that old bitch—"

"Louise! If you use words like that I'll tell Grand-mère that Biddy is not fit to look after you."

"You wouldn't! Robert, that was a nasty thing to say. Anyway I was quoting. Don't you want to hear any more?"

"All right. Go on."

"Things have been so awful for so long, I can't be sorry to go away. I'm not sure that I ever want to come back. Only for you, Robert, I would be left here forever. Do you know what Aunt Fanny was planning?"

"Something stupid, I'm sure."

"I was to learn to keep house. My books were to be taken away because they distract me from the proper business of a woman and make me unattractive. I was to learn to cook, from Molly Davis in our own kitchen, and how to keep chickens and make butter from Patty in the dairy, to get rid of my high notions. I've learned all those things already from watching. Nell said Papa was furious when he heard that. He might have agreed to some of it later, though. I told you this when I asked you to take me with you but I think you hardly heard me then."

"I did what you asked, didn't I? I hate gossip. It's lowering."

"Any port in a storm. I'm very glad to hear gossip if that's the only way to save my skin. I didn't think you would succeed with Papa."

"It's all settled now."

"Perhaps. She'll still be working on him, trying to make sure we're gone for good. That's why she's not looking like a cat in a tripe shop these days—"

"Louise, you must not use expressions like that. If you do that in France, it will ruin you."

"In France there will be other ways of saying things. We won't speak English much."

"When we do, they will expect us to speak good English. They'll be watching to see if we're *farouche* from living in Ireland. Please remember to be careful. Papa says the French love everything English just now. It's the fashion." Suddenly he changed his tone to one of false hilarity which made Louise look at him anxiously. "When Mama was alive she sang for me:

> *'Marie Madeleine, veux-tu te marier?*
> *Non, non, non, non, non, je ne veux pas ça —'*

I've forgotten the words. I don't think I have them right. I wonder if they still sing that song for babies—'*Ni avec un prince ni avec un roi —'* "

"Why do you sing: *Veux-tu te marier*?" Louise asked sharply. "Have you been told about plans for marrying me?"

"There is nothing serious."

"But there is something. Tell me, tell me!"

"There is nothing to tell."

"I know there is something. Grand-mère has been giving me advice, just in case, she said, but I can see it's more than that. Have they told you something? Who is it?"

"No one at all, really and truly. And whatever happens, you will be better off than if you were with Fanny."

"I wish we knew more about Cousin Charlotte. Papa doesn't like her, I'm certain."

"I'm glad to go," Robert said firmly. "Grand-mère will take care of Papa. Aunt Fanny won't win, even with Aunt Sarah to spy for her."

"I'm sorry about Aunt Fanny. When she came first I liked her. I stopped missing Mama so much. Fanny had a warm feeling about her, and she played with me and took me for walks in the garden. I used to hide behind the box hedges and run out at her, and she'd pretend to be frightened. Do you remember that? Then when Hubert was born and Aunt Sarah came, she got cross and nasty, and pushed me away when I went near her. She didn't begin to beat me until Hubert was three and she began beating him. I remember the first time. She said it would make up for all the times when she hadn't beaten me —"

"Do you have to remember things like that?"

"How can I forget it. It's not so long ago," Louise said impatiently.

"No, I suppose one can't forget."

"She might have done better if she had brought a woman in to nurse as Mama did for us. A servant would stand up to her better than Aunt Sarah does."

"I don't want to think about them at all," Robert said, kicking his horse's flanks so that it plunged forward.

Louise knew that it was a mistake to speak to Robert of their mother. He said once that when someone was dead it was stupid to think about them again. Death fell and cut off, and that was that. One day Maman was there, the next she was not, though her beautiful body, stiff like a doll, was laid out in one of the bedrooms for all the country people to come and see and pray over. Louise could still hear those murmuring prayers, like waves of the sea, rising and falling on the edge of her mind. Before she could prevent it, a sharp sob escaped her. Robert seemed not to hear and they rode on in silence.

The track had narrowed and now they could no longer ride side by side. After the fork Robert went in front, the horses placing their hooves cautiously, testing every sliding step before putting their weight down. Lying back in the saddle to keep their balance, they watched the white clouds sweep through the huge sky, whose blue was sometimes reflected in patches on the waters of the lake below. Several boatmen were fishing among the islands. A cluster of mud cottages on the edge of the lake was Creevagh, part of the Burke estate, huddled together in a crazy bunch without form or pattern. Some green showed where the land had been drained to make cultivation of potatoes possible. Most of the sheep on the hillsides around belonged to Burke of Moycullen but close to some of the cottages a small piece had been fenced off to keep a pig, which usually had to be brought into the house on cold nights and at farrowing time. Goats and donkeys were tougher and they could be left out for a large part of the year, or in a lean-to shed at the gable of the cottage. Katta owned a pig but she had made Matthias build her a shed for it. Robert had been told that they would recognize the cottage by the pig shed, the only one in the village.

They did not need this. She had seen them coming, away off on the mountainside, and she was waiting for them at the other side of the small stream that clattered beside them on its way to Lough Corrib. She had been expecting them for days, having had a message that they would come, but no date had been mentioned. They put the horses to the stream, then dismounted at once and ran into her arms, Louise first, then Robert. She looked them over carefully, a hand on the shoulder of each. She smelled of turf smoke, the sweetest smell they knew, since she was the only person who had ever held them close. Louise's wet nurse, the wife of one of the gardeners, had died of pneumonia before Louise was a year old, and Katta had adopted her as a second foster child whenever she came to visit. She was a handsome woman with curly black hair in which several snow-white streaks were beginning to appear, and large, beautiful, dark-blue eyes. Her face had been too strong to be pretty when she was young. She was much taller than either of the Briens, and she said as she walked with them towards the cottage, the horses trailing behind by their reins:

"You must grow, Robert. You must eat well and get fat when you go to France, and be as big as your father when I see you next."

"I'll never be as big as my father, Katta. You know that well."

"How long will you be gone?"

Of course she would ask that question first, the one they could not answer. Robert said:

"It won't be too long. France is very far away. We're going to study."

"Both of you?"

"Louise will study too. She will have her books at Cousin Charlotte's house. I'll see her every week."

"The whole world is changing. She'll marry a Frenchman and I'll never see her again."

"Even if I marry a Frenchman, I can come back."

"Of course you can," Katta said hurriedly, then shook her head like a restive horse and went on: "And you're going by Cork, we heard."

"By Kerry, with Father Burke. His cousins have ships that go from Cahirdaniel. We can't go through England—we might be stopped because of the war with France."

"Sure you know all about it. Father Burke is going all the way with you—that's good news. Will he be coming back?"

"Not for a while."

"Perhaps he'll send a message. I'll go to the Court and hear news of you."

"We'll ask him to send you a special message—we'll write to you ourselves."

She looked more cheerful then. Suddenly she lifted her chin and gave a long call, like a sea gull's cry, echoing along the mountainside. People came to the cottage doors to watch them pass, and she said:

"We'll visit the neighbors afterwards. Colman will come down from the mountain now."

The clean January air blew into the cottage, sending the smoke from the hearth whirling around the room to find its way out over the half-door. There was no chimney. The floor was a sheet of natural rock, which was why the cottage had been built in this exact place. Out on the coast where rocks and stones were plentiful, they were used to build the houses. Here by the lake they had to be built of mud and scraws, the sod with the grass still attached to it to give it substance. The whole house was no more than twelve feet square. A bed propped on stones filled one corner and served for the whole family. Two flat stones had been arranged for sitting, one at either side of the fire, but there were also four stools for visitors. When Katta had gone to meet them, Matthias had built up a huge fire of turf, a circle of sods around the remains of the old fire in the middle of the room. A staggering heat came from it. Cut and dried by their own labor, turf was the one luxury of the people, unless the landlord forced payment for each basketful brought from the bog. Mr. Herbert's agent had not yet begun to do this, so the magnificent hospitality of the fire was possible. Knowing that Robert hated hot fires, Katta placed them both on stools where they could breathe the air from the open door. Matthias came forward to greet them, using English as a compliment to them. He barely waited for them to be seated before asking eagerly:

"Do you think, sir, will the French be coming?"

"It's said they will," Robert said, "unless they have been frightened off by the Volunteers."

"Will you be a soldier?"

"I asked him that," Katta said, "and he says he's going to be a scholar."

"Thank God. Then you won't have to fight your own people. It would be a strange thing to be sent to Ireland wearing the uniform of a soldier of France and to have our Volunteers shooting after you."

He laughed with a sound like a bark.

"Are you joined?"

"I'm too old," Matthias said, "but Colman is thinking of it though he has no taste for soldiering. He'll have a gun in his hand anyway, but he says it's not Frenchmen he'll be shooting. The English think we'll defend the country from the French and the Americans but aren't they our best friends at this time? The recruiting sergeant was around this place last month and he looking for men to go to fight the Americans but he was beaten by a grand Frenchman that came the week before him. He enlisted a few of the boys in the American army. It's a mad world and there's no one rightly able to understand it. Colman says there's good times coming and we'll own our own land, and sell our own sheep and wool and cattle—I don't believe that day will ever come."

"Things are better than they were."

"What way are they better?"

"The Protestants are saying the Catholics must get a fairer deal. The parliament in Dublin is saying we must have free trade or we'll break away from England altogether."

"Free trade for Protestants is what they mean."

"There's talk of a declaration of Irish rights."

"Is there any talk of priests for the people? Is there anyone saying they can come home to us and not go in fear of their lives?"

"My father says there will have to be an end of the laws against us."

"Sure there's no laws against the gentry," Matthias said, his mild tone removing any suggestion of bitterness.

"That's not true! The reason I must sneak off to France to be educated is that I'm a Catholic. I can't go to Trinity College in Dublin. My father could lose his land at any time. The Volunteers are the beginning of a change—now that the Catholics are allowed to join, the whole country is armed. In Belfast the Catholics and the Protestants are saying they'll work together and soon we'll have a free country."

Robert found that he was speaking almost hysterically, shocked as he was at the condition in which Katta lived. The bare rafters and the underside of the thatched roof were thick with soot. The walls were an ugly yellow from the smoke of the fire, and were cracked and broken from continually shrinking and expanding according to the degree of their dampness. Matthias said calmly:

"Everyone is full of new ideas. Everyone is saying something. I wonder is it all only talk."

"A lot of things can be done by talking."

"Only if you have the guns behind you as well. Colman says we have the guns now and there's nothing to wait for. Like yourself, he says it's time to do something new."

"I didn't say that."

"It's what you meant. We've been quiet too long. And what do we care for the German king? If they had kept the right king it would be a different story."

Colman appeared in the doorway at this moment and gazed at the visitors with pure delight. He had to look down on them even when they stood up—at nineteen he was over six feet tall but skinny from work and hunger, with his mother's black hair and dark-blue eyes. His clothes were a collection of rags, several sizes too small but extended in essential places by the insertion of pieces of cloth of other colors. Robert recognized them as the remains of clothes of his own. Colman spoke in Irish.

"You're going, brother?"

"Yes, but I'll come back."

"Don't go at all. Stay with us here and help us. All the gentry are going. We'll be needing you when the French land. We'll fight side by side and we'll shoot the English with their own guns."

"I'll come back."

"Leave him alone," Matthias said. "You have no right to ask him. He'll go to France and to all those countries where the gentlemen go, Italy and Greece and Turkey, and he'll come home a match for all the talkers of Ireland."

Colman was silenced at this rebuke though he remained as cheerful as ever. He went to sit on the floor close to Robert, his knees drawn up to his chin. They had the attachment to each other of twins, each having always been a part of the other's life though they met only twice a year now, when Colman accompanied his mother to Mount Brien Court. They had lain together in her arms, one at either breast while she fed them, until they were two years old. With one of those odd picture memories that remain from infancy, Robert remembered how she had wept when her husband came and demanded her back. She had come to visit him in the spring and autumn of every year as she had promised, even when she was pregnant with her other children. She usually stayed the night, sleeping in one of the servants' rooms, and she always took home presents, a piece of cloth to make a dress, some cast-off clothes for the children, flour or meal, fruit from the garden. Robert had taken it for granted that his father gave her money now and then too. Or had he thought about it at all?

He could not be sure. Throughout the rest of that afternoon, while they made the rounds of Creevagh to be shown off and to say a few words to every family, to listen to songs and watch some dancing, he felt a mounting sense of disdain for himself. He had never asked how Katta lived. He had never come to Creevagh to find out. In all his life he had never seen so many idle, sickly people as there were in that village. There was nothing for them to do. Most of them looked half-starved. All were in rags, even Katta's family, in spite of their patrons. Robert knew that when the other landlords came home from England, they laughed at his father for spending so much on unprofitable improvements to his tenants' cottages, and Robert had assumed that Katta was taken care of too. Father Burke's cousin, James Burke, was the loudest of the critics, always saying it was cheaper to throw the cottages down than to rebuild them. He could see Mr. Burke now, whiskey glass in hand, standing in front of the drawing-room fireplace the last time he came home, listening with a sardonic expression while Maurice said that the only hope for Ireland was a contented peasantry. Dirty, shiftless, little better than cattle and just as stupid, Burke said contemptuously, and they multiplied like vermin. Maurice could have answered every one of his comments but he made no attempt to convert him.

He did have one convert, in Celia's father, John Nugent. His land had a common boundary with Mount Brien on the Oughterard road, so that he was able to watch with envy what went on there. Maurice had given him seedlings and encouraged him to plant trees on his waste land but some kind of mental inertia prevented him from cultivating them and the little trees died. He accepted this as an inevitable fate, but it did not stop him from walking to Mount Brien on summer days to watch the sawmills working and to make suggestions for improvements to the cottages. Maurice replied with suggestions of his own for Castle Nugent, but nothing was ever done about them after the trees failed. Mrs. Nugent was never seen. She had retired to bed many years before and some of the neighbors even thought she was dead, if they thought of her at all. The house was swarming with unpaid servants. Celia, who was a year younger than Robert, was the only other member of the strange family.

Celia had soft brown hair with a natural curl, and her eyes were dark brown, very large and with long lashes. Older women said it was a pity that better features didn't come with these advantages. Her nose and her neck were too short, her forehead too high, and she should have been at least four inches taller. Robert had heard them at it in Mount Brien, Fanny and Sarah, and he was astonished at the exactness of their description while they still left out so much—her light step, her joyful laugh, her warm, friendly expression, her gentle, clear voice, her air of confidence and freedom—things that would not have been affected at all by a long neck or a lower forehead or a few more inches in height. Robert had known her all his life, and she was always at ease and calmly sure of herself, even as a child, until the day he had ridden over to tell her that he was going to France to study. She wept and clutched his hands and sobbed that she would die, and implored him not to leave her. He felt that he was with a stranger. It had never occurred to him that he could have this effect on any girl. It was the first time that he touched her. Tentatively he took her in his arms, right there in her father's drawing room, watched beady-eyed by the stuffed foxes and badgers and squirrels that lined the walls in glass boxes. He held her against his breast until she was quiet again. Then he said:

"We'll be married when I come back. Will you wait for me?"

She gave a kind of snort and said:

"Wait? Of course I'll wait. But will you?"

Shocked by the sharp question he said aggrievedly:

"Of course I'll wait too. I'm only going to study. I'm coming back!"

He had said it exactly as he did now to Katta. His father knew that he did not want to leave Ireland forever, that he had no interest in the French army, where a commission would be available to him through Dillon and Brien cousins at any time. If anyone went to the army it should be the younger boys—Robert had always known that. Mount Brien was his and he meant to have it. He would come back when he was ready, and he and his father together would make this clear to Fanny and to everyone else. He went to visit Celia, or she came to Mount Brien, most days since the one on which he had committed himself to her, and of course the visits were noticed and commented on loudly by Aunt Fanny:

"There's someone that would like to get her crooks on the best land in Connaught. What brings that one here so often? It's not fresh air she's after, you can bet your boots."

Aunt Sarah was quieter but her method was just as bad, coming into the drawing room and hissing to the assembled family:

"*She's* here again. Asking for Robert, quite bold. You'd better go out to her."

Maurice would never allow that, and either sent a servant or went himself to escort her into the room and seat her near Robert where they could talk quietly. In any other house she would just have marched in, but Sophie had imposed formality for visitors and no one had the nerve to go against her. Celia laughed at Fanny and Sarah's behavior, saying:

"Give them time. They'll get used to me. Perhaps poor Sarah thinks there will be no place for her when I come in. You'd think they would be glad of a Protestant bride for you."

She appeared not to know that it would be illegal for them to marry. Robert only said:

"But I haven't told them anything! I haven't said a word!"

"They can guess. You don't need words to say things like this.

They understand everything."

When he was riding home with her for the last time she said: "Your grandmother likes me. I know that."

"Has she spoken to you?"

"No, but I can tell by the way she looks at me. Are you surprised?"

Taken off his guard he said:

"Yes."

"Why?"

"She always prefers French people."

"Then she doesn't speak well of me?"

"Not that—she doesn't speak of you at all."

But he knew she would have, if he gave her the chance. Everything about her attitude to Celia was clear to him, though fortunately not to Celia herself. There was the faintest tightening of her lips, the faintest widening of her eyes, and always a very slight pause before she answered anything that Celia said to her directly. Once when Celia asked her a question, she had stood up and walked out of the room without replying, as if she were deaf. She never began a conversation with her. Besides, there was a lifetime of contemptuous comments on the ineptitude of the whole Nugent family, not excepting Celia, and not to be forgotten in a few weeks. Sophie even gave him the impression that she was willing to rescue him if he showed any sign of confiding in her.

The effect of this was to make him feel that he was in a trap, though all Celia had done was to let him see what were her feelings toward him. The rest was his own doing. Perhaps his wish to comfort her now was the strongest proof that he did indeed love her.

At her house there was no one about, not even a groom to take the horses. He helped her down, then held her in his arms for a moment. He knew as surely as if she had said it that she would let him go inside and make love to her in the dark drawing room, that this was the comfort she wanted. Some last remnant of sense made him kiss her quickly, then hold her off, saying gently:

"Celia, I really will come back."

"You'll never come back. I'll never see you again. Why must you go?"

"I can't stop it now. I love you, Celia. We must wait."

"Why? Why should we wait?"

There was no answer that he could make to that. He led her, weeping miserably, into the house, then took her horse around to the stables where he found a sleepy groom to put it away. Galloping home he felt lonely and frightened, longing to rush back to her again, while another part of him coldly said that he had shown his first sign of good sense in weeks. The visit to Creevagh made it impossible to see her again.

Matthias walked the first mile of the road home with them. Katta was so upset that she could not come, and she and Colman and the rest of the family stood in the doorway to watch them as far as the turn of the track that led to the lake. At last Matthias said:

"Keep to the shore as long as you can, until the road turns uphill. Then it will get wider, and it will take you straight into Oughterard. You'll be all right from that on. God speed ye both. Come back safe to us." He gave his strange barking laugh. "Tell the king of France that I was asking for him. Tell him to send over an army quick to fight on our side and we'll fly the green flag from shore to shore and give him a great welcome."

"I'll do that," Robert said.

Darkness was falling and heavy clouds formed and reformed above them, constantly threatening rain. Dim lights showed in the hovels of Oughterard. The street was blown clear of dust by the January winds so that the horses' hooves clattered on the bare stones. Here only a few people came out, enough to tell everyone in the village that it was the young Briens who had passed by. Then they were on the Galway road. In a few miles they began to pass the Mount Brien fields and then they were trotting between the twin gate lodges and up the long avenue. Glancing up at the front of the house they saw, as usual, that Sophie was at her window, watching for them.

4

Father Burke had announced that Mass would be at six o'clock and the whole household was to be there. The chapel was in the attic, since it was forbidden by law to have one at all. It was not the main attic, but one that could only be approached by a back staircase. It ran at right angles to the main block of the house, over the kitchens and the dairy, and had windows at both sides. One side looked into the yard, the other over the huge meadow through which part of the avenue ran. Thick blinds could be drawn to cover the windows at that side, but in recent years this was thought not to be necessary. As Fanny said, everyone for miles around knew that there was a priest and Mass at Mount Brien, so there was no point in taking extra precautions.

Louise was awakened by Biddy, just back from spending her last night with her mother in the back gate lodge. She was eighteen, two years older than Louise, and her excitement was beginning to give way to a new sense of responsibility which showed in her anxious frown as she shook Louise's shoulder, standing over her with a lighted candle in her hand.

"Get up, Miss Louise. It's five o'clock. If you keep going, you'll be ready just in time. Come on, now, wake up, there's a good lady."

Louise stretched her arms as far as possible above her head, then grabbed Biddy around the neck and pulled her down to kiss her. Holding the candle away for safety Biddy said:

"Ah, now, there's no time for that. What's on you at all? You should be crying, like me."

"You're not crying!"

"I was, but I'm not now. The sight of my mother did it to me." She stopped suddenly, remembering that Louise had no mother to cry for. "There's no time for talk. Out of bed now and I'll get something on you. You can't travel the roads of Ireland in your nightgown."

Giggling with excitement, the two girls set about the business of dressing Louise, Biddy holding each garment for her while she stepped into it or got it over her head. Today she had a new dark-brown traveling-dress of fine wool, very wide in the skirt, with a triple collar and trimmings of soft squirrel fur. It had been carefully planned by Sophie to keep her warm in the coach on the way to Kerry, and later on the ship to Le Havre, by which time Sophie said it was unlikely that she would ever be able to wear it again. There was a hooded cloak too, and wrapped in both of these Louise would be well protected from the cold. Another traveling dress, of a lighter brown, with a satin-lined cloak, was in one of the trunks, and she was to put it on when they were a day's journey from Paris so as to arrive in proper condition for a lady. Biddy had to repeat her instructions many times, until Sophie was sure she was capable of making the right impression on Cousin Charlotte. Sophie became so anxious about this that she even considered sending old Amélie along too, but she was persuaded to abandon the idea. Maurice said:

"The ship will be a very small one. Amélie is too old for that hardship."

"She crossed the sea with me, before."

"That was a long time ago. And she has lost so many of the habits she had in France, she might let us all down before the French cousins."

"You think so?"

"Yes, Mama. And times must have changed there as well as here."

So Biddy had to be warned all over again. She was to watch the other maids and see how they managed things, ask as few questions as possible but keep her eyes open and gradually learn what was expected of her. Cousin Charlotte might help but it would be better not to ask too much of her either, lest she might think the Irish were not civilized. Biddy understood what she was to do: give them nothing to laugh at, not talk too much but let them see that nothing surprised her, avoid answering questions and above all stay close to Louise at all times, to make sure that she was safe. Robert would come every week, so they would not be lonely, and he and Louise would write letters which Sophie would read to Biddy's mother. Sophie looked at her doubtfully again, and Biddy said, with tears in her eyes:

"Madame, I think you don't trust me at all. Why wouldn't I look after Miss Louise properly? I'll never leave her, as long as I live."

"All right. I do trust you."

She was satisfied at last and Louise told Biddy later that her grandmother had said Biddy was as good as a French girl.

When the dress was safely hooked up, Biddy turned Louise's long pigtail of blond hair up into a wide flat bun that covered the back of her neck. Then she handed her a black lace veil to wear at Mass and they were ready to go. As they came down the main stairway into the hall, they could hear whispers and the shuffling of feet on the flags of the back entry as the outside workers and their families came in and made their way up to the attic. This would be their last Mass for a long time, perhaps for months, until Father Burke came back. Louise and Biddy waited a moment or two and then followed the crowd.

Perhaps seventy people were assembled by the time they reached the chapel, and more kept coming. Father Burke was already there, in his vestments, sitting to one side, quietly reading in his breviary. The old people were folded right down on the floor, their heads bowed, their hands joined, moaning and crooning old prayers to themselves and swaying gently to and fro. The younger ones were quieter, more self-conscious, kneeling up straight, especially those who worked around the house and who wore uniforms or livery. These had come closer to Sophie's eye and she had trained them to an unnatural stiffness. A few chairs had been placed close to the altar, for the family, and Louise went there to sit with Sophie and Fanny at the women's side. Maurice and Robert and the three sleepy little boys came in a minute later and took the remaining chairs. The candles on the altar each had a halo of brilliant light in the damp, cold air, so that Louise's eyes were dazzled and Father Burke's huge shoulders looked even more massive than they were. He was wearing green vestments and there was a green cloth on the table that served as an altar. Mass began, with Robert answering Father Burke:

"*Introibo ad altare Dei.*"

"*Ad Deum qui laetificat juventutem meam.*"

"*Confiteor Deo omnipotenti. . . .*"

The Latin words were lost in a soft hum as the people took up the prayer in Irish. Of the family, everyone except Sophie joined in. As Mass went on, Louise kept her eyes on her grandmother. Her back was straight and her face almost without expression. She had often told Louise the importance of cultivating this blank look, to deceive the servants or anyone else who should not be allowed to see a chink in a lady's armor. Louise did her best, knowing that everyone was watching her this morning, but the candles cast frightening shadows and all at once she found that she was afraid of the sea journey. It could take weeks if the weather were bad. Often those little ships were never seen again after they left the shores of Ireland. Big ships were safer, and plenty of them came from France into the port of Cork, ships of four or five hundred tons, Maurice said. But he said that it would not do to attract attention to his family in any way, so they had to take this unorthodox route, the route of the smugglers of goods and people in and out of France. Sophie was afraid for them too. Sometimes in the last weeks her cool expression was replaced by one of terror, lasting only an instant, when they talked of the voyage. Louise felt a wave of anger sweep over her, so that she gave a moan as if she were in physical pain. Beside her, Biddy looked at her anxiously, then touched her arm and whispered:

"Are you not well, Miss Louise?"

"I'm all right."

It would be wicked to frighten Biddy too, since she was being sent into exile without her consent. At least Louise had chosen to go, since to stay at Mount Brien without Robert would be intolerable. At that moment Father Burke turned around and intoned a blessing:

"*Pax domini sit semper vobiscum.*"

Everyone answered:

"*Et cum spiritu tuo.*"

Louise could barely see Fanny, beyond Sophie, her chin

triumphantly high, her eyes piously closed, her big rough hands joined and her lips moving as she prayed with a twittering sound. Maurice had tried many times to break her of this habit but it was no use. There was something singularly unpleasant about the sound, which was not in any way related to the soft murmurs of the rest of the people, and a peculiar falseness in the way she beat her breast like the old people when Father Burke said three times:

"*Domine, non sum dignus ut intres sub tectum meum, sed tantum dic verbo et sanabitur anima mea.*"

Mass seemed endless this morning. At last Father Burke turned to glare at the congregation, intoning prayers in Irish for a safe journey to France, and prayers that the people would behave well while their priest was away so that he would not come home to find them gone back to the condition of wild beasts, and his usual prayers for Ireland where some day the natural owners of the country would be treated as if they had at least some right to be alive and breathing their own air. In the meantime, he said, Sir Maurice was in the position of a king and everyone knew that they owed him obedience and that his judgments would be sound, and if he condemned any man, the chances were that that man was a scoundrel and a blackguard and deserved all he got. This statement was on exactly the same note as the rest, so that everyone would know that God was listening.

At last it was over, and the servants and neighbors were crowding up to the altar to get the priest's blessing before he left. He put his hands on their shoulders and bent to speak to them, now and then whispering some words of very private advice or encouragement. Several people wanted to go to Confession since this would be their last chance for a long time, and he waited for them until the rest were gone. While all this was going on, the family moved down through the chapel and went towards the dining room, where very soon breakfast with eggs and coffee began to be served.

Louise tried to eat but the tension in her throat was more than she could bear and tears kept coming into her eyes no matter how she tried to prevent them. She was sitting beside Maurice, and at last he took her left hand in his and held it silently, watched by Fanny with a certain amount of sympathy.

Then Fanny gave a loud, artificial sigh and said:

"That's how it always is with the young. When they grow their wings they must fly the nest, out into the big world to see it for themselves."

No one replied to this, though Sophie raised her eyebrows. A moment later Father Burke came into the room, rolling up his stole and pushing it into his pocket as he came. Fanny raised her voice a tone, giving it a somewhat hysterical note, and repeated her foolish remark:

"I say, when the young grow their wings they always want to fly out into the world. It's nature never to stay in the home where you were reared."

Sophie pushed her chair back violently. Ignoring Fanny as if she were a cat or a dog, she went around to Louise's chair and stood behind it for a moment while she said:

"Try to eat something. There will be food in the carriage but it will not be so pleasant to eat while you're traveling. I'll go and see to it now."

Then she went out of the room. Fanny, very red, said:

"She needn't—I didn't—that's always—"

She stopped, because after all Sophie had said and done nothing at all, to her.

In a few minutes they would be in the carriage. The four best horses were going to take them the first fifty miles and then be left to wait for the return journey. Relays had been ordered at their various stages and two grooms had gone ahead to see to it. Five days had been allowed to reach Cahirdaniel in Kerry, where the O'Connells had promised that the next ship to come would be delayed for them. Maurice repeated these arrangements to Mike Conran, the coachman, as he stood with his team at the foot of the steps. A short distance away the four outriders were holding their horses, all ready to go. From her place just inside the open front door, out of the cold morning wind, Louise saw this in a dream. Biddy was already in the carriage, waiting for her. Robert was talking to Martin Jordan, his own servant, who was to ride beside Mike on the box, and Robert was saying that he would have to move over and leave room for him too, so that he could view the countryside, most of which he had never seen before. He was in hilarious humor this morning, apparently not at all frightened as she was.

Maurice looked anxious and tired, moving quickly around the carriage, examining the packing of the baggage, even helping Biddy to store the hat boxes in the best way to leave room for their feet. In the darkness of the hall, Louise found that Sophie was at her elbow, tugging at her sleeve, saying nervously:

"Into the drawing room for one moment. They can't go without you. Come along. There's just time."

Dawn was beginning to break, outlining the sofas and chairs, coloring the gilt mirrors a faint gray, showing the curled gold legs of the console tables and of the long, marble-topped table where wine was always served in the evenings. She took it all in again, mean and dead in the dim light, and turned to face Sophie saying:

"What is it, Grand-mère?"

She had never seen Sophie like this before. Her mouth was working painfully, her thin hands were still clutching Louise's arm, the fingers clawing so strongly that she could feel them through the thick wool of her cloak. The drawing-room door was open and she could hear people passing through the hall, hurrying feet, voices giving orders, all to get the two of them out of the house and away where they would be no further threat to anyone. Louise suddenly put out her arms and hugged her grandmother as she had never dared to do before, holding her as close as possible, hearing the anguished voice in her ear saying:

"Don't let them marry you to someone you don't love. Don't let them trade with you or give you away. Whatever happens, don't marry to oblige them."

"Who are they?"

"All the cousins, especially Charlotte. They'll try to make you feel inferior. Pay no attention, promise me."

"Yes, yes, of course."

"I know their ways very well. Cousin Charlotte is near my age but we never liked each other."

"Then why must I go to her?"

"She has your property. She is obliged to have you."

"Does Robert know about her?"

"Men don't have to know the things that women do. You are more sensible than Robert. Will you remember what I'm telling you?"

"Yes, I'll remember."

"And you must be sure to see your husband before you agree to marry him. You must not take someone you have never seen."

"Yes."

"And it must be someone you like, not just one you respect. How can I tell you? Men are sometimes very dull creatures. If you get one of those, you must make him respect you, make him let you live in your own way."

"I don't understand. How can I do that?"

"They're waiting for you. It's time to go. Marry for love. Marry a friend."

"I don't want to marry at all," poor Louise said, now at last beginning to understand what Sophie was trying to tell her.

"Of course you will marry. Everyone does. I'll write to you. Now here they come—good-bye, my dearest girl. Be happy."

Sophie pushed her out of the room, toward the front door where it had suddenly got very quiet, though a crowd of people had gathered out there, servants and tenants from the nearby cottages.

The carriage door was standing open. Father Burke was already inside. Louise could see his long legs, in black stockings, stretched across the width of the floor. Then everyone was suddenly hustling her to the carriage, people were waving and cheering, some of them crying, there was one long piercing wail and a voice that called: "The wild geese are flying!" Maurice hugged her, openly weeping now, even Fanny looked sad, the small boys clung to her hands, wanting to know when she was coming back. Biddy was cowering as far as possible into her corner, to avoid a last agonizing look at her mother. As the carriage gave a groan and moved off, Sophie ran a step after it, actually ran, and said:

"Louise! Remember what I said!"

Then they were trotting down the long avenue, leaving the whole world behind.

5

The O'Connells' house in Kerry was a strange gloomy place. It was built partly around a cobbled courtyard, into which most of the rooms looked, so that the whole house was made dark and mysterious. Paneled walls and high, narrow windows sucked up the last of the light. You went into a room, fancying yourself alone, and a voice spoke out of a corner where someone was sitting waiting for you, or so it seemed. They were certainly doing nothing else, Louise thought frantically, after she had been addressed thus by three old people at different times on the first day. She could not even decide whether they were male or female. They all had deep voices and they all wore long skirts, and they glided out of the room, having wished her well in old-fashioned English, leaving her with a feeling that she had displaced them from a valued refuge.

The fourth day of their drive from Galway had brought the Briens late in the evening, after dark, into a house full of whispers, where she was instantly hurried upstairs and into a big cold bedroom. A wild-looking manservant brought a tray with supper, and waited while she ate it, handing her things with grimy hands as he thought she needed them and chatting to Biddy in Irish over his shoulder at the same time. When she had finished, Biddy helped her into the ancient four-poster bed, then ate her own supper and at last got in beside her. They clutched each other in the dense blackness, listening, but very soon they fell asleep.

Coming downstairs that first morning, Louise found only the old people. Later various members of the household came and went in outdoor clothes, horses pranced at the doors and scraped the cobbles in the coachyard, evidently as restless as their owners. She caught sight of Robert but he disappeared almost at once, and there was no sign of Father Burke at all. A bell rang in the middle of the morning, however, and following the sound and the shambling footsteps of the old people, she discovered him saying Mass in the dining room.

Throughout the morning, servants scurried about as busily as if her grandmother's eye was on them, polishing and cleaning, and tending vast turf fires in the main rooms. At noon she walked for a while with Biddy over grassy hillocks and came to the Atlantic ocean, only a few hundred yards from the house. A path along the top of the shore led them to an almost land-locked harbor, with opaque indigo water, sheltered from the fierce January wind by a black wall of natural rock which was topped by sparse grass. Beyond this shelter the sea made a sound like thunder. White-capped waves scuttled along, their tops blown off in misty spray, each wave landing with a heavy crash preceded by a second of sickening silence.

She gazed in horror at the gray-green water of the ocean outside the harbor, twisting restlessly about. A mist hung over the horizon, which merged in various gradations of white and gray into the white sky. Tomorrow, perhaps even today, she would be expected to set out on that terrifying sea and be battered by the four winds for weeks before reaching the shores of France. Without warning, a vision rose before her of Fanny's smirking face, the narrowed sideward glance and the set mouth that expressed fury and contempt There could be no question of going back to her. She could hear Fanny's biting voice saying: "So the big world wasn't too inviting after all, Miss Grandeur." That was the private name she had been using to Louise lately. Maurice never heard her do it, of course, and Louise couldn't bring herself to complain to him. Remembering his dog-like suffering eyes imploring her silently to keep the peace, she felt a wave of irritated affection for him. As they walked back to the path Biddy said:

"You're afraid of the sea, Miss Louise."

"Yes."

"You were never on it, that's why. My uncles have grand boats out in Carraroe, big enough to take you to America. They say Saint Brendan went there in one of them long ago, the very same pattern. When we go to France the boat will be even bigger than them. We'll be snug and warm in it, and sure when all is said and done, there's no other way of going to France."

Later in the day she regained some of her courage. Dinner was at four o'clock and Biddy hurried her so quickly away to rest that all she remembered was a crowd of busy, confident people, jabbering in rapid Irish, dozens of them going in and out, of whom at least forty sat down to table. It was impossible to disentangle the faces and names, and at suppertime she found that she had to be introduced all over again. They were all ages, almost all cousins, and they were nearly all named O'Connell. She was further confused by the fact that the women had not changed their names when they got married, so that she could not connect the husbands and wives correctly. There was a tall, bony tutor and some crafty-looking children, but these kept their eyes fixed on their elders at first and later scuttled out of the room to get on with some secret business of their own.

Several sharp-eyed uncles and aunts, probably those who had lurked about the house earlier, were seated in state at the top of the lighted table in carved oak chairs. From the beginning of the meal they shot sudden questions at her, leaning forward eagerly to watch her as she replied. They spoke to Robert too but it was Louise who seemed to interest them the most. At the end of the hearty meal, as huge dishes of oranges were being placed down the middle of the table, the oldest of the women raised her voice and called out:

"Well, so! When you go to Paris you will be asked about Ireland. What will you say?"

All the eyes were turned first on Robert and then on Louise. As Robert was silent, Louise stammered:

"That it's poor. That the people are starving."

Fierce long fingers bored toward her from all sides and harsh voices shrilled:

"They won't care about that. The people you'll meet are all rich. They'll ask you about politics, representation, development, taxation, the army, the landowners, the roads, the bridges, the horses and cattle, the sheep, the wool trade, the linen, the leather, the laws against Catholics, the laws about land and education. What will you say to that?"

"I'll say the laws are not as bad as they used to be. I'll say you can get around some of them. I'll say they're not all enforced. I'll say the Americans will come to our aid when they get their own independence and we'll soon have free trade. I'll say that better times are coming."

"Nonsense, girl!" This was another old woman. "That's not the sort of thing to say. They'll answer that if this were true your brother wouldn't have to leave the country to get an education. They'll ask how it is in Dublin. They'll say you're only speaking for Connaught and that's a backward place as everyone knows. And they'll say that if the times are so much better there's no need for the king of France to send us an army to set us free from our tyrants, the way he's doing for America." There were growls from some of the men at this and then they all started together:

"You'll have to have better answers than that ready."

"You'll have to know your history."

"You'll have to remember that you're an ambassador for your country."

"You'll have to find all the good Irishmen in Paris and tell them to hurry with their help, to keep on asking the king —"

The voices were like dogs, yapping all around her. She felt tears fill her eyes and her face get hot, while her heart beat quickly with anger and excitement. She looked desperately to Father Burke for help, but he was sending her that look of sad disappointment that she knew so well, which meant she had failed in some lesson that she had had every chance of knowing. Sure enough, he said heavily:

"I'll tell her what she's to say, and until I'm sure she knows it, you may rest assured she will say nothing."

"Very good," they said. "She could do a great deal of harm with her tongue, and by looking so pretty and distinguished, coming straight from Ireland where we're all supposed to be down and out."

This raised a loud cackle of laughter and about twenty-five of them lifted their glasses and drank a toast to Ireland, and the best of good French wine in every glass. It was proposed by a powerful, heavy-faced man named Morgan O'Connell who sat at the head of the table and seemed to be the father of one section of the tribe. Suddenly Louise heard her own voice say loudly:

"By the God over us all, I'll say nothing but the truth, that the O'Connells are living like kings. They're not getting thin anyway!"

There was dead silence. A hammering had started in her head but she forced herself to stare back at them. Robert, at the far end of the table, made no move to come to her rescue though she knew he had heard her clearly. Earlier he had been absorbed in conversation with a tall, solidly built man several years older than himself, who was sitting beside him. This man had arrived a little before dinner and was still in his traveling clothes. Louise had seen his servant take several trunks up the stairs to one of the bedrooms, which meant he was a special guest. Most single men would be put to sleep in the long bare room known as the barracks, on straw beds if they had not brought their own pallets. He was watching her now, and she thought he looked more sympathetic than the rest of them. She could run out of the room. She could get back to Biddy, who would put her to bed, where she could weep to her heart's content. Weep? What nonsense! Grand-mère would be furious. So were the old ladies at the table now, bridling, muttering words she couldn't hear, making indignant sounds like wind-blown hens. Then one old woman said:

"She should be married off quickly, that one. She's fit for it. A taste of that would quieten her in no time."

Raucous laughter grated on her ears. Again she looked wildly along the table towards Robert but still he said nothing. She felt another retort rise up in her, then saw Robert's companion shake his head ever so slightly, to indicate that she should be silent. He was looking sardonically at the company, his full lips pressed into a thin, hard line. They were very red lips: she had already noticed them. And his skin was darker than anyone else's, as if he had come from a sunny climate. She had specially noticed his hands, twirling and twirling his glass restlessly, though he drank very little. They were beautiful hands, and he had a habit of absentmindedly laying them on the table with the fingers spread, as if he himself were admiring them. In spite of his broad shoulders there was something effeminate about him, almost displeasing, something connected with the soft look of his eyes and mouth. She could not make out whether his eyes were dark brown or hazel with a fleck of green. The candlelight was deceptive. There was lace on his fine linen shirt, and though he had been traveling his wig was curled and powdered neatly as if he had just had it dressed. The men of Derrynane wore their hair natural, tied back with black ribbons.

She had stared at him too long. She realized it suddenly and felt embarrassment flood over her. How could she have spoken out so loudly, in such a coarse, hearty way? She never did this at home, and to save her life she couldn't have done it again now. She could heard Grand-mère's voice tinkling in her ear, almost as if she were present:

"A young lady never raises her voice when there are gentlemen present. If she has the misfortune to do so, she should note carefully who is there, because none of that company will ever respect her again. Ever afterwards she will have to avoid them."

She didn't even know this man's name. He was someone they admired, it appeared a moment later, when he said in a low, rather hesitant voice:

"It would be no harm if all the ladies who appear at the court of France were as elegant as Miss Brien."

Then he spoke to her directly: "We'll meet in Paris, Cousin."

Robert said eagerly, suddenly finding his tongue:

"You're coming with us, then?"

"Not yet. I'll come in a few weeks. I still have people to see in Ireland."

The same old woman who had said she should be married off quickly gave a loud snort and said:

"Andrew has an eye for the girls, sure enough, the younger the better."

Morgan slapped the table angrily and his voice resounded through the room:

"Better manners, here, if you please! Our visitors will think we're nothing but wild country boors."

This was exactly what Louise was thinking. They turned to each other at once and began an argument among themselves about whether help from France was what the country needed. She wanted to stop her ears from the thunder of their arrogant, self-assured voices. The women were most in favor of an armed rebellion and were able to shout down the men, who seemed to want a quiet life and no disturbance. Several of the men had held high positions in the Austrian and French armies, and these supported the women, saying that a few battles would prove that the Irish were well able to take care of themselves. Morgan O'Connell said soothingly:

"We'll have our own parliament soon. One thing at a time. There's no need for battles. Never talk politics to an old soldier."

An old woman said fiercely:

"It will be a parliament of Protestants, if we ever get it, like a parliament of cats making laws for the mice. What we need is an army from France and another from America and we'll beat the English out of the country and have it to ourselves for a change."

"We might be a lot worse without them."

"How could we be worse? They have the people beaten into fools."

"Too much of that talk and you'll end up on the gallows."

"That's women's talk. They always stay comfortably at home."

"They have to bury their dead."

While they were hard at this, a servant hurried in and whispered in Morgan's ear. Immediately he started to his feet saying:

"The ship is in. The Captain is in the kitchen at this moment."

"Which ship? Which ship?"

"The *Valiant*."

"Thanks be to God. Good times coming!"

Morgan said to Father Burke:

"There's a party of five to come from Cork tonight. You'll be off tomorrow. You see, you didn't have long to wait after all."

"How many passengers will there be?" Father Burke asked.

"Eleven, so far as I can count, and eight servants. If the wind rests where it is you'll be over in three days or four."

"Will it do that?"

"Who knows what the wind will do?"

It was rattling the old house now, shaking the windows and doors, giving a surprisingly soft, clear whistle as it rounded the corners, sometimes sending a great whoosh of smoke down the chimney to whirl and curl around the room. The bitter smell of that smoke was a symbol of everything she was leaving behind, a civilization as old as the black rocks down by the cove.

The announcement that the ship had arrived caused great excitement among the tribes. The women began to chatter about the cargo, which should contain French brocade and silk and lace and wine, and Spanish brandy and oranges and silver. Everyone left the table quickly to go to the kitchen. Father Burke waited for a moment, looking uneasy, then followed Robert out of the room. As he passed her chair he said to Louise:

"Don't mind them, girl. They're good-hearted. They mean no harm."

He looked at her intently and she knew he was hoping for a sign of friendship but she would not give it to him. He had let her down abominably before these pirates. He gave a noisy sigh and turned away. The man called Andrew waited until he was gone, then said very quietly:

"If we had more families like the O'Connells this would be a different country. They have never been intimidated, probably because no one can get at them in this remote place. If you stayed here longer you would come to like them and enjoy them."

"I can't imagine that day coming."

"You're rather like them in some ways. You speak your mind."

"I hope I'll never have a mind like theirs to speak."

"Your grandmother has set you too high a standard. I'll tell her so when I see her."

"When? When will you see her?"

"Next week."

"Oh, please don't tell her about this evening. I didn't know you knew her. Have you been to Mount Brien before? I've never seen you there."

"I came and went too fast. We have met there, when you were very small."

How could she have forgotten him? She shook her head, trying to remember. He said:

"I won't tell her how angry you were. I'll just say you gave a good account of yourself."

"Yes, that's what she would like to hear." Without thinking, she said suddenly: "We're on the edge of the world, on the edge of a precipice. When we sail away from here we'll never be heard of again. We'll just disappear into nothing. We'll fall off the world into the pit." She laughed hysterically. He said:

"The O'Connells know their business. This coast is so wild, they must have good ships or they would never be able to trade from here at all. I've come and gone with them from France so many times I've lost count. They never go to America so far as I know but they could do it if they wanted. Usually I go to America from France."

"Usually! How many times have you been to America?"

"Four. Soon I must go again. You see, it's not such a terrible thing to go to France."

"What takes you to America?"

"I have been Dr. Franklin's messenger. There are hundreds of American prisoners of war in Kinsale at this moment. I'm trying to get them exchanged for English in America. They would die of starvation if the people of Cork didn't send them food. Then I'm going to several centers around the south with passports for men who want to go to America—they can go with their families and settle there if they like. The Americans would prefer that than to have them join the English army. I'm recruiting for the American army too."

"They're not joining the English army these days. They don't want to be sent off to America to fight the colonists."

"Have you heard that in Galway?"

"Yes. They're joining the Volunteers instead. They said that when they have guns in their hands they can band together and fight for the freedom of Ireland."

"Aren't you afraid of all this talk of fighting? You're afraid to sail across to France."

"I just think it's very exciting."

"What about Robert? Would he join the American army?"

"That's only for poor people. If Robert were to join anything, it would be the Dillon regiment, like my uncles."

"Plenty of French gentlemen have joined the American army. What will Robert do, then?"

"Didn't he tell you? He's to go to the University. Is that why the O'Connells were laughing at us?"

"Not at all. They're rough people but they believe in education. And as Father Burke said, they're good-hearted."

This conversation, desultory as it was, comforted her during the long restless night. Before they embarked, early the next morning, she learned from Biddy that her outburst had had a good effect on the O'Connells, who had been furious at finding that there were two girls in the party. They had only bargained for Robert and Father Burke, and had talked of sending Louise and Biddy back to Mount Brien bag and baggage. Biddy said:

"When you answered them back they couldn't say you'd be too frightened to go to sea, and later on the priest shouted the last of them down. He said they were likely to make an enemy of the king of France, turning away the cousin of Madame Dillon that's the Queen's best friend. Is that true?"

"I don't know. Yes, I have heard it. Grand-mère said it."

"Well, true or false, one old woman stopped in the middle of a screech and snapped her mouth shut so that I thought she'd surely have swallowed her tongue. But you'd best keep very quiet all the same. It would be a disgrace to be sent home now."

"Perhaps they won't sail in this weather."

"They've sailed in worse, they say. They were talking about it in the kitchen with the Captain. It's how they like it, not a coastguard in sight and no one abroad but the like of themselves."

Louise would have liked to see Andrew again but she found that he had left very early.

Everyone in the house went down to the ship. The sky was alive with gray flying clouds and the wind, sharpened by its passage through the bare branches of the oak trees that surrounded the house, stung their faces bitterly. The old people went in front, bundled in shawls and scarves, swaying along the high path that led to the cove, sometimes looking as if they would be blown off onto the shore below. The masts of the little ship were visible long before they turned the last corner. They seemed to leap into the air, then slide sideways until they were almost out of sight, before coming up again with a stabbing motion. A swarm of small boats came and went from the sandy beach with bales and boxes before loading the passengers. Then the dark water was horribly near and the waves struck the boat with an ugly, dead sound. They climbed up and over the swell in long nightmare sweeps, the two oarsmen in their long woollen caps constantly turning to make sure that they were not being blown off their direction. Closely wrapped in her traveling cloak with the hood up, Louise looked around too and saw the little ship tugging spasmodically at its moorings while it pitched and rolled in a crazy rhythm. A wooden ladder was over the side, ready for them. Somehow, like the bales of wool that were being exported, they were heaved aboard.

Throughout the journey to France she scarcely saw the other passengers. Robert and Father Burke were in a cabin in the stern of the ship with the Cork passengers, who were young men on their way to the Irish College at Bordeaux. Once she passed by the open door and heard horrifying groans, and saw several of them lying on their bunks rolling with pain. Biddy too, for all her boasting, was deadly sick, unable to move from the tiny cabin that had been allotted to them as the only women on board. Now their roles were reversed. It was Louise who had to fight her way to the galley amidships, where the cook was wedged in among his pots, and try to carry back a little soup or coffee without losing it on the way.

The sea was slate gray tipped with white, a foaming white desert as far as the eye could see, but there was something exhilarating about it that she loved. The noisy creaking of the timbers and the roar of the wind in the sails became for her happy, agreeable, natural sounds. The ship was frighteningly small, not much bigger than the dining room at home, but the crew and the Captain had an air of certainty that quieted her fears after the first day out. At night she slept heavily, dragging herself awake with difficulty when Biddy's cries became too loud, going to her to offer useless comfort and then sliding back to sleep again.

There were three days of this before they sailed into calmer waters close to Le Havre. They saw land in the late afternoon of the next day, low hills overhung with dark clouds, then a long line of cliffs and at last the port, full of tall swaying ships that had come in to shelter from the storm. The quays were lined with sailors to watch the O'Connells land, amazement and respect on all their faces. There was a short, hideous trip in a battered longboat and at last they were in France. Only when she was sure of this would Biddy lift her head, but she began to improve from the moment she found solid earth under her feet. A carriage had been sent by Cousin Charlotte, with a coachman and six outriders, to take them to an inn for the night and to continue with them to Paris the next day.

PART TWO

6

The rue du Bac was a long, narrow winding street. All of the houses looked massively unwelcoming, their windows barred, their huge double doors blankly shut. The coachman hammered with his fists on Cousin Charlotte's doors and after a shouted conference with someone inside they were swung open and the carriage drove into a long cobbled courtyard with buildings facing each other at either side. When Louise climbed out of the carriage she saw that another courtyard opened off the first, a kind of garden with a few trees, and plants in tubs. A servant came out of the house, conducted a sharp, apparently unfriendly conversation with the coachman, then led them grudgingly into the house.

Inside it was better, a big, square, stone-flagged hall with a stone chimney piece and stairs just visible in a passageway beyond. They were kept waiting in an ice-cold room to the left of the hall, whose windows looked out on the street. Father Burke seemed suddenly to have doubled in size, standing awkwardly in the middle of the room, apparently too excited to sit on one of the stiff little chairs. Biddy and Martin Jordan stood by the door, both with a suspicious air, as if they feared that someone would seize and run off with their masters' personal baggage, which was heaped by their feet. The big trunks were being unloaded by the house servants, as was shown by various thumps and shouts from the hall.

"Smell that air," Father Burke said in a low tremulous voice. "There is nothing like the air of Paris."

"I can believe it," Louise said, wrinkling her nose in disgust.

It was a mixture of river smells and bad drains, still unfamiliar to her, as far removed as possible from the smells of home. Father Burke said anxiously:

"You won't say anything derogatory—French people love Paris—you won't say a word."

"Of course not. Why should I?"

"Be careful, my girl. It's a wicked city. There are people here who will deny and contradict every single thing I've told you. Oh, a wicked, wicked city!"

But he said it in such a tone of admiration and wistful respect that it was hard not to laugh. Though he had lived in the house for two years and had been her teacher every day, it seemed to her now that she scarcely knew him. She would be glad to get away from him. He had often terrified her with sudden bursts of temper, when he had locked her and Robert up for hours with some huge task to keep them busy. Her strongest memories of him would be of such unpleasant things. Robert was barely listening to their conversation, sitting sideways on his chair, his hands twitching with impatience. Now he said:

"What a welcome! Where are those cousins of ours? Can you imagine how it would be if they came to Mount Brien?"

"Now, now, the ladies are probably occupied with some important business. They don't live as we do."

"Evidently."

"Be quiet, the pair of you. We're guests in this house."

"I'd never have known it. This is not how we treat our guests. You may be sure I won't trouble them very often, after this."

But then they were quiet and the priest went to look out of the window, his huge back cutting off half of the light. It was a quarter of an hour more before the same servant came back and conducted them upstairs to meet Cousin Charlotte.

She was sitting at the end of a long salon, beside a tall stove which gave out a welcome glow of heat. While she talked she held a piece of half-worked tapestry on her knee. At first Louise thought she was lame because she made no move to get up but put out her right hand dangling at the end of a long languid arm, to be kissed by Robert and by Father Burke. Louise curtseyed as Grand-mère had taught her to do and for the first time heard Cousin Charlotte's satirical laugh, which was later to become as familiar as the cackling of the hens at home. She said:

"Ah, yes, old-fashioned manners. I can see there is much to be done. Teresa!"

The girl who was sitting a little apart from her mother stood up and advanced a step or two, then made a long, slow curtsey before going back silently to her chair. Again Louise curtseyed, this time so uncertainly that she was in danger of falling over her feet among the whole lot of them. Robert came to her rescue, saying:

"My sister is tired—we are all tired. We had a dreadful voyage. Thank you for the carriages."

"Ah, yes. And how is Cousin Sophie? And your father?"

"Very well. We have brought letters from them."

"I'll read them later. Now someone will take you to your lodgings. Embrace your sister."

"Robert!"

Of course he was leaving her. She felt faint, as she had last year at early Mass. How odd to feel like this at the thought of being left with Cousin Charlotte when she had not once weakened during the voyage.

Robert and Father Burke were gone in a moment. Standing at the door of the salon she watched them pass quickly downstairs and out into the courtyard. She shouldn't have run to the door. She heard the heavy street door, padded with leather, swing shut with a soft, cushiony sound. She waited, impolitely, but could not hear the carriage move away. There was nothing for it but to turn back.

Then servants were leading her and Biddy to a bedroom on the third floor above the reception room in which they had waited first. Here was more of that strange smell, almost a taste now, accentuated by the dusty smell of old brocade and Aubusson carpets like the one in Grand-mère's bedroom.

Biddy waited quietly until the French servants had left the room and then went swiftly across to open one of the tall windows. Fresh air flooded into the room bringing with it the strange sounds of the street, the pattering of wooden shoes and the trampling of horses, the somber clatter of carriage wheels on cobblestones and the calls of the coachmen.

Louise ran to the window to look out. Now she understood

Father Burke's excitement. She whirled around saying:

"Biddy! Undo the trunks and take out everything. We must make ourselves at home immediately."

"At home! What did that lady say?"

"She asked for news of my father and grandmother."

"It didn't sound like that to me."

"Now remember Grand-mère's instructions. We must fall in with the way of life here. She said that, remember?" Biddy nodded doubtfully. "It's a marvelous city. Can't you feel it Aren't we lucky to be here? Look, this door must lead into the anteroom, and here is your bed, and there are lots of cupboards, and your window leads around to my balcony. Now we'll take out things and hang them up. I'll help you and we'll be finished before dark."

Biddy began to look a little less doleful but they had barely lifted out the first of the dresses when there was a tap at the door and Teresa came in, followed by a middle-aged woman servant that Louise had seen already downstairs. Teresa said:

"I've brought my Catherine to help your maid."

Catherine gave a little shriek of horror at the sight of Louise with a dress in her arms. She ran forward and snatched it, then hustled Biddy into the next room with clucks and chirps like an anxious hen, shutting the door sharply. Louise started to follow, fearing that Biddy would be frightened, but Teresa said:

"Leave them. Catherine was shocked at seeing you handling your own clothes, that's all. She'll show your maid everything. What is her name?"

"Biddy—Bridget."

"How funny it sounds. Now sit here and talk to me. I could say nothing to you in the salon, with Mama there."

"Did I look terrified?"

"Yes, but I know how it is to walk up that long room. Mama arranged it like that on purpose, to see how you would do it. How old are you?"

"Sixteen."

"After you had gone Mama said you look older. She said you'll be all the rage in a year's time. Don't look so distressed. I wish she would say things like that about me. It's better to be all the rage than to be left out. Blondes are in fashion now and you won't have to powder your hair. Do they powder their hair in Ireland?"

"If they have been to France."

"Are there many French people in Ireland?"

"Not many."

Teresa smiled so sweetly that she might have been deceived but Louise saw a little devil looking out of her eyes, a mean, cold look that was unmistakable in its hostility. This was her only defense, she thought, to recognize truth from falsehood—her only reliable asset in this house of thieves. Talk of powdered hair, the too-strong embrace as she was leaving, the kittenish turn of Teresa's head, were all transparent lies. Her sour tone when she spoke of her mother was the only thing that had the ring of truth.

At seven o'clock the next morning, when Biddy brought her coffee, she said that Father Burke was waiting for her in the small sitting room beside her bedroom. Dressing hurriedly in a loose gown that Grand-mère had said would be suitable for mornings in Paris, with her hair only half brushed, she ran to him, not knowing what disaster had brought him so early. He was sitting at the table, a range of books and papers before him, quickly turning pages and making notes in a small book which he had in his left hand. He glanced up saying:

"Late as usual. Getting bad habits already. You went to bed early, didn't come down for dinner, I was told."

"I didn't know you were coming—I was so tired—the long journey yesterday, and the excitement—I couldn't sleep—"

"Excuses, excuses. When will you learn not to defend yourself Sit down. Enough time has been lost already. Now here is your geometry. Your giddy head will be full of nonsense. Geometry is the best cure for that. Euclid, all of it. Go back to the beginning. Work out all the proofs and cuts again. You've probably forgotten them all by now. Those silly women will do their best to drive out anything you have the wit to remember. There is your algebra. You needn't go back to the beginning of that. No one could possibly forget the logic of algebra. You can give yourself a course in quadratic equations first and work on from there. Do all the problems. I've brought you a new book to do them in, and mind you keep them in order and keep the book clean. I'll go through every one of them when I come back."

She asked meekly:

"Where are you going?"

"To Bordeaux, of course, and you needn't look so pleased. It's not very far. I could take a notion to come to Paris at any time, to see how you're doing. Now the Latin. You were doing well with Virgil. I've marked the pieces you're to memorize, and remember to keep the rhythm correct. You must say them aloud even though I'm not here, or you won't get them right. And think about what you're saying or it might as well be a donkey braying. It's beautiful stuff, beautiful. Then there are Plinius's letters. You can translate all of his letters to the Emperor Trajan into French. That will be good for your French too."

"How many letters did Plinius write to Trajan?"

"Plenty. Enough to keep you busy. And the Latin is the finest ever written, no matter what anyone may say. Remember that while you're working on them. You can write me a letter every month in Latin, in the style of Plinius, telling me about Paris. Perhaps you should memorize some of the letters too—but I think you would be better employed learning some French sonnets instead. Yes, that would be better. Let's see, here is the book. Here's a beauty: '*Quand vous serez bien vieille, le soir à la chandelle.*'" He glared at her suddenly from under his eyebrows, his head on one side and his face half in shadow. "You think it's too much? You think this is not what you came for? Don't forget, you're still a child. Those fine cousins of yours will ruin you if they can, with their balls and their courts and their operas and their theaters and their goings-on of all kinds. Paris is a wicked city, a wicked, wicked city."

"I thought you said it's a wonderful city."

"So I did, so I did, wicked and wonderful," he said with a heavy sigh.

"What will you do in Bordeaux?"

"I have my parish, and I'll teach Latin to the students at the Irish College."

"Is Bordeaux a wicked city?"

"Wicked enough. Now that's enough of that. Do you understand what you are to do? They'll take you off to one of their fine country houses for the summer, maybe in May, maybe earlier, but you will have your work. You won't have to go gallivanting with them everywhere they go. You can say that you're busy."

"Cousin Charlotte is going to teach me the manners of Paris and take me to Versailles, to the court."

"And where will that get you, miss? You'll have to stand up to temptation, like the rest of us."

"How can I stop it? If they say I am to go, what can I do?"

"Well, well, don't cry. Of course you'll have to do as you're told. But when you know you shouldn't go, you'll always be able to say you have work to do. Follow me?" He closed one eye in a slow, massive wink, the other eye rolling meaningfully at her so that she had to giggle. "That's better. Now be a good girl. God didn't give you that good brain for nothing. You're not to turn into a ninnyhammer on me. Well, well. When I went to your father's house, I knew it was not for long. It was said, many times, I would be going back to my work in Bordeaux, you would be going to Paris and all that. Yes, it was all made as clear as daylight."

He stood up with a lurch and plunged across to look out of the window, pulling a huge handkerchief out of his pocket and blowing his nose vigorously, with a sound like a trumpet. She sat watching him, not knowing what to say. After a minute he turned around and faced her again. "Your brother has said he'll come every day. I think he's taken a fancy to his cousin—he was making sheep's eyes at her yesterday. I've warned him to be careful there. They'll be hoping for better than him for that girl. They have someone in mind for her already. In fact I think it's all fixed up. You can add your word to mine if you see that's how the wind is blowing. You don't know what I'm talking about. How could you? You're only a child."

"I'm not a child. Grand-mère told us that Teresa is engaged."

"For God's sake don't cry, girl! Where did you learn that nasty habit? I'm not insulting you. It's only that I wish I were not leaving you in this nest of vipers—"

"Vipers! How can you say that? Cousin Charlotte seems to want to be kind."

"Well, well, we must not make judgments. But be careful. Don't forget my warnings. I'll say no more. Now get down to your work. I must see you at it before I go."

"When are you going?"

"Now, this moment."

She leaped out of her chair and ran to him, burying her face in the snuff-stained cloth of his coat, and felt him hold her gently in his arms while heavy tears splashed down on her neck. Then he lifted her slowly away from him and turned to go out of the room, shutting the door quietly and not once looking back.

She went to sit at the table, looking blankly at the papers and books that were her tasks, trying with all her might to calm herself and understand the things he had been saying to her. One of them had been that the study of geometry clears the mind, and after a while she began to work on it, slowly at first, then finding real consolation in solving the familiar problems. But a sudden break would come in her concentration and she would sit for a long time, quite still, doing nothing, barely thinking, as if she were trying to find her way by some magic through all the new traps that had been laid for her. Grand-mère had warned her. Father Burke had only confirmed what she knew already. There was no refuge now. Austerity and work were Father Burke's cure for everything. She giggled hysterically and imitated his "Well, well." Her voice sounded ridiculous in the empty room.

Distractedly she stood up and began to walk about, stopping sometimes to look out of the window, or for no reason at all to stand for a few minutes in the middle of the floor. The house was fully of tiny noises, feet passing along the corridor outside, doors opening and closing, but no one came in, not even Biddy. Perhaps Father Burke had told her to keep out, or perhaps they had all forgotten about her, the stupid little Irish cousin who had so much to learn. An intense longing filled her to go back to her own place, to smells and sounds that she understood, to country things, horses and cows and butter making, and silent, black nights where not even a bird hooted.

At last she went to sit in the big chair that Father Burke had left half-turned to the table. It was there that Teresa found her when she came in at noon, laughing and full of plans for the afternoon. She stopped dead on the threshold, then ran forward and lifted Louise up, hugging her closely, holding her off to examine her distressed face, saying:

"That brute! I should have known this would happen. What has he done to you? I'll never again leave you alone so long. Your first day too. He said none of us was to come near you."

"He gave me work to do. I was not idle."

"So I see." Teresa glanced with displeasure at the table loaded with books and pencils and paper. "You must have a rest from all that."

"He has gone off to Bordeaux. He wanted to tell me what to do in his absence."

"Well, you can do it later. You're to be my companion, Mama says, until André comes back."

"André?"

"My fiancé, André de Lacy. He's at the war in America, I think. I never really know where the wars are—anyway they're all mixed up together now. Don't look so surprised. I hardly know him. Now it's time for luncheon," she sent on briskly. "You can come down as you are. No need to dress up until afterwards."

"Are there guests?" Louise demanded in panic.

"Just the usual people, not too many. Now don't worry. You look charming in that dress. Everyone will be wanting to see you. They like to see young girls in *déshabillé.*"

The dining room seemed full of stares and titters but soon the guests turned away and took up their conversations again, only occasionally turning to look at her. Then one of the older women made a low-voiced remark and all of her little circle burst into shrieks of laughter. Louise's face burned with anger but she kept her eyes lowered and stayed close to Teresa, who seemed quite unconcerned at their behavior.

7

Teresa kept her promise and in the following weeks Louise found that she was scarcely ever left alone to study. Every day she made new discoveries about how the world of Paris worked. She learned to laugh even when she had no idea what the joke was nor whom it was against. Most of the jokes were against someone but the stories meant little to her because she knew nothing of the participants. One concerned a lady who dressed in the livery of her own postilion and drove through Paris, arms folded, standing on the back step of her carriage. There was a scandal about a mother who was dreadfully worried because her son refused to take a mistress. She was said to be scouring the city now for a suitable married woman who would undertake the task of stimulating him. She said that chastity was the first sign of decadence and that the whole of France would be endangered by this notion, if it were ever to take hold. Even for Paris, this was a little too much, since what was the fun if there need be no secrecy? Louise listened quietly to this, then studied the other girls to look as much like them as possible, carefully watching and analyzing their expressions, their gestures, their attitudes, trying to think as they did, so as to be a part of them.

Her appearance changed completely. Cousin Charlotte demolished most of her carefully planned dresses, leaving her only two, and set about getting them remade in a newer fashion. Hours and hours were spent with teachers of deportment. Catherine taught Biddy how to do her hair high and smooth, drawing it up and up on a frame and fixing it with long bone pins which were meant to keep it steady but which left Louise afraid to move. Biddy stuck feathers in it, and wound in a pearl necklace so that it showed here and there, coming and going through the hair like a shining snake. She pinned on brooches or ostrich feathers or an artificial flower, building up until the whole edifice was more than twelve inches above Louise's head, waving like a crazy cornfield. She had to turn slowly, her head erect, her hands carefully holding up the voluminous silk of her skirt, which had panniers that stretched out for a foot at either side, her shoulders held steadily back and her breasts thrust forward to keep her back absolutely vertical. The first time this was done, Louise thought that there was to be a very special party but she found that it was usual to keep the hair in this condition every evening of the week.

Now and then she paused to wonder at the strange things that she was doing, and whether she would ever succeed in becoming one of the company around her. There was not much time to consider such things, and gradually she found that she was drawn more and more into the false manner that was her only safeguard. She learned to make puns and innuendos and to gossip glibly about people she had never even seen, and presently found that she did indeed pass for one of the courtiers who came daily to her cousin's house.

Absorbed in the idiocies of her dress and coiffure, one evening in February, when she had been six weeks in Paris, she entered Cousin Charlotte's salon at seven o'clock. As usual, the gentlemen were standing about waiting for the ladies to appear. A few had been there all day, had come in the morning and waited for dinner at three, showing no sign of moving even when the ladies left them to dress for the later part of the day. Louise knew most of them by sight, and immediately one or two of them came forward and made their clockwork complimentary speeches, to which she replied in the same way. The dark old rooms needed many candles. Their shimmering lights were always a sharp pleasure, unexpectedly brilliant, nullifying her first impression of the house and especially of the salon. She knew now that the company had been sent away that first day because she and Robert were expected. Usually there were at least twenty people there. No matter how often she entered the salon, it was always with a feeling of excitement and anticipation. Every day she expected that something astonishing would happen and it always did, because just to be there was an astonishment in itself. The embroidered coats and powdered hair of the gentlemen, the scent and rustle of the ladies' clothes, the delicious snacks handed around by the house servants, the unending stream of compliments for herself, for her hair, her figure, her wit, were all intoxicating.

This evening, as usual, every head turned when she appeared, and a gratifying murmur went up from the company, a mixture of admiration and amusement that their newest toy had arrived. Cousin Charlotte looked pleased. She had told Louise that she had had no idea that the Irish cousins would be fit for company at all. The fact that they were cousins of so many of the English nobility was no guarantee that they would know how to behave. Besides, Lord Falkland, Lord Lichfield, Viscount Dillon, Lord Stafford and the rest of them had not seemed very anxious that special care and prestige should be given to Louise and Robert. Not even Lord Kenmare had written, though he had known very well that they were coming. Only Madame Dillon had shown friendship, and had left a message that they were to be invited to her house. She was away in Brussels with her little daughter, visiting her sister, but she had said that her mother was to take care of them.

Louise had learned to turn her original frightened pause on the threshold into a coquettish entrance that drew every eye to her. Nevertheless, carefully trained by Cousin Charlotte, she held her first glances in check until she had greeted Archbishop Henry Dillon of Narbonne. It was easy to see that he was there, because when he came to supper he always took up a position at the far end of the room beside a small table, with a clear space in front of him. He was usually accompanied by Madame Dillon's mother, Countess de Rothe, who lived in her daughter's house with her uncle. She was about Cousin Charlotte's age, with the same terrifying dignity and assurance.

The Archbishop was there this evening, a very tall, thin, handsome man, always perfectly dressed, leaning tiredly back in his chair. At their first meeting he had spoken to her about Mr. Burke and she had poured out her complaint of the amount of work he had left her to do in his absence. His eyes twinkled with amusement now and he said as he gave her his hand:

"Well, little cousin, how are your studies going?"

"Not very fast, Your Grace. If Father Burke comes soon he will not be pleased. I'm enjoying life too much for study."

"Charming!" the Countess said acidly, indicating by a tiny jerk of her head that Louise should move aside and allow the next person to be presented. She curtseyed in the new way that Cousin Charlotte had taught her and hurried towards a door that led into a smaller salon. Her face was hot with embarrassment and she paused, so as not to seem upset, to listen to Madame d'Ossun who was talking about the Queen as usual:

"So elegant, so sweet, so good," she said in a high, fluting tone, and everyone around said: "Ah!"

People found Madame d'Ossun tiresome and the personnel of her little group was constantly changing as her hearers drifted away and others came to pay her court. Louise knew better than to stay for more than a moment: the very young were barely tolerated by that circle unless they were of such a powerful family that even their dogs had to be respected. Louise was looking for Robert, who now came every day and spent his time with her and with Teresa as if he were a Parisian man about town. Slowly she moved around until she was near the door of the small salon, which she opened, thinking that he might be in there with one or two other young people.

The small salon looked out on a side street, even narrower and darker than the rue de Bac. At first it seemed that the room was empty. A single lamp stood on a low table, its shade so heavy that only a small circle directly underneath was lit up. Disappointed, she began to move out again when a slight sound caught her attention, no more than a second's indrawn breath from the darkest corner. Looking there quickly she saw two pairs of eyes fixed on her and she made out two forms on the sofa, interlocked, almost appearing to be struggling. Then Robert's voice said in a hoarse whisper with a sort of giggle in it:

"It's Louise. It's all right."

She closed the door fully and stood with her back against it, feeling with blind fingers for a key that would lock them all in forever. There was none, and she stood there in terror. They began to stand up, and she saw clearly that the second person was Teresa. For a moment she had hoped that she was mistaken. Tears of fury filled her eyes and she hissed:

"Are you both mad? What are you doing?"

But she knew what they were doing, all right. Teresa stood silently smoothing her skirt, her head bowed, her hands making deliberate, slow movements that went on longer than was necessary. Robert said softly:

"Now, don't be silly, Louise."

"Silly! Do you realize that anyone—*anyone*—could have come through that door?"

Robert came toward her. In the dimness she could barely see his face but an extra swagger in his step suggested that he was uneasy. He said:

"We came in by the other door. No one saw us."

"How do you know? Everyone in this house has a thousand eyes." On the edge of tears she restrained herself forcefully, knowing that the black that Catherine always insisted on putting on her lashes would run and get mixed up with the pink on her cheekbones. She drew a long, slow breath, shuddering with the effort of not letting it become a sob. "Do you want to ruin us both?"

She could not bring herself to speak to Teresa, who had turned her back now as if to leave them to themselves. Louise watched her go to sit in the chair by the lighted table, her face in shadow and the light falling on her tensely crossed feet. If only she could run out of the room and get away from them, upstairs, anywhere—but there was no escape. To disappear from the company now would draw attention to herself and to Robert and might indeed ruin them both. Robert said, sounding angry:

"Don't be provincial." He paused for a moment and went on in a voice that trembled with defiance and excitement. "Anyway, you would soon have heard about it. Teresa and I are in love."

"And how would I have heard about that, if you please? You can't be. Teresa has a fiancé, away at the war. Oh, Robert, please talk sense."

"I am talking sense. She doesn't want to marry André. She will marry me."

"Marry!"

"Not for a while. I must study first, or perhaps go into the army after all."

"Cousin Charlotte will be furious."

"Why should she be? I'll have Mount Brien some day. I wouldn't be the first Brien to marry a French cousin."

"How sure of yourself you are." She glanced towards Teresa, still sitting silently in the shadows. "How did it all begin? Why did I not see what was happening? Or did it come on suddenly?" She stopped, realizing that she was speaking as if of an illness, then went on lamely: "But we've all been together."

"Not all the time. You have been off at your dressmakers and your dancing classes. We've been spending our time better."

"How can you joke about it? Think of Cousin Charlotte—what will she say?"

Robert's voice sharpened as he said:

"How should I know? Come, now, don't be so touchy. Sit here with us. Why shouldn't we fall in love?"

"That's not how it's done."

"Not in our circles," Teresa said coolly. Her voice sounded very low, as if she had suddenly become much older. "You're quite right. And you're right too that Mama will be furious. She was very set on my marrying André. He was her choice."

Her words might have aroused sympathy in Louise but her tone did not. She asked in terror:

"What are you going to do? Are you going to keep it secret? For how long can you keep it secret?"

"We haven't thought it out yet."

Louise tried to adopt Teresa's cool tone though her hands were hot with fear and she could not keep her voice from trembling as she said: "Of course I'm glad—I'm happy for Robert."

Teresa said:

"That's better. There is no need to speak about this for a while. If we go on exactly as before, nothing will be suspected."

"You think you can do that?"

"Yes. We can be more discreet. We must be. It's unfortunate that you came in just now. You needn't have found out for a long time."

She looked at Robert impatiently, as if Louise's appearance had been his fault.

At that moment the door opened and they all had to stand up to allow several people to settle with their trictrac at the table. Then all three went back to join the company in the main salon as if nothing at all had happened to them.

8

Robert was living now in a state of permanent exaltation. He knew that Louise felt nothing of the sort, that the effect of their revelation was to increase her distrust of everyone in their brilliant circle of acquaintances. Hardly seeming to realize that she was condemning Teresa too, she said bitterly:

"There is not one of them that can tell the truth."

Robert said:

"Paris is a different world from the one we were used to."

"They cheat each other, they deceive each other all the time. They think nothing of the truth, so long as they get what they want."

"It's easy enough to see through them," he said confidently. "And remember, one has to play their game to survive. I've learned that from Teresa."

He said her name with reverence. Every minute and hour of the day he longed to say it but Teresa herself had warned him to be careful about this. She said that the giggling and innuendo always began when someone noticed a pair who could not prevent themselves from dragging each other's names into every conversation. Even the most sophisticated and experienced fell into this trap, she said, and he swore to be careful, though sometimes his tongue seemed about to choke him with the effort. "Teresa, Teresa, Teresa!" It was a name from heaven, and it seemed to him that he had always known it would be the name of his beloved.

From the moment he saw her in her mother's drawing room, her luminous eyes had drawn him to her, her elegant, sinuous body had seemed to be created only for him. When he sat alone in his room, he conjured her up so clearly that he could almost have put out a hand and touched her. His father had married at twenty-one. In a year, when Robert would be twenty, there could be no opposition. He would go into the army until then. One of the Irish regiments would give him a commission. There were many possibilities.

The only shadow on his happiness was that Teresa would not allow him to go to Cousin Charlotte and tell her that they loved each other. He could see that she was right. Cousin Charlotte had never really made him welcome. There was always something uneasy in her attitude to him, as if she suspected him of something. He was watching for every opportunity to reassure her but in a few weeks there had not been much time for them to get acquainted. She knew nothing of his fortune, which was independent of his sister's.

All of these things would have to be gone into, but not yet. As time went on, Teresa said, gazing at him with her wonderful, mysterious, gray eyes, her mother would come to love him as Teresa did, and she would not want to oppose their wishes. Teresa would tell him when the time was ripe, she would sound out her mother now and then until she found that Cousin Charlotte was truly captivated by him, and then she would give him leave to approach her with his proposal. Even before that, Robert said, in spite of all their precautions they might have betrayed themselves, or someone might notice and remark what a suitable couple they would make. Teresa gave him a startled look and warned him again that he was not to reveal their secret until she was ready. He never, never would, he said, and she relaxed and was happy again.

He told all this to Louise, when he could find her alone, which was not very often. If he came early in the morning, sometimes she was in her room with her books but this made him feel guilty for his own idleness, and besides he soon found that early visits were looked on with disfavor by the household. Teresa said:

"That is exactly how to make people suspicious. No one will believe you have only come to see your sister."

To please her he agreed not to come so early and soon he found it almost impossible to have a conversation with Louise alone.

The one thing he could never say, even to Louise, was that it was Teresa herself who had made the first advance. He would have been content to adore her from a distance, and he had been astounded when she came close to him, pressing her knee against his in an unmistakable invitation. The first shock was succeeded by pure delight and he turned to her instantly, but she restrained him with a quiet hand on his arm. It was only three weeks after his arrival in Paris. They were on the terrace of Cardinal Rohan's beautiful house, during the most dazzling reception that Robert had ever seen, ladies and gentlemen shining like stars with jewels and gold, and pearls as big as eggs. She alone was dressed quietly, in a soft, dark dress that showed the lines of her body, making her as conspicuous as a blackbird among peacocks.

The Cardinal's house had been opened for the evening only, while he made a flying visit from his great palace in Alsace, but it glittered as confidently as if it were used every day of the year. Servants ran about with trays of glasses, glorious food was laid out in the anteroom where the guests went whenever they felt like it, the Cardinal himself walked about with his chin up, as grand as a king, which was not surprising since he was King Louis's godfather and came of a line at least as ancient and illustrious. Still there was something ridiculous about him, and here in his own house Robert had heard him called "La Belle Eminence," a gibe at his effeminate ways. The ladies all loved him, perhaps because he could never be a serious threat to their establishments.

He had welcomed Robert and Louise this evening with special warmth because of their saintly martyred country, he said. Louise was looking particularly beautiful, her thick, blond hair glowing with life. her natural, fair complexion needing no help from the paint she wore, her innocent eyes still offering trust and friendship. She could not look the Cardinal straight in the face when he made that remark, but she had already learned not to retort that there was not much saintly martyrdom around his salon.

Robert wandered by himself through the rooms, never far from Teresa. He knew that this was a shameful infatuation, since she was already engaged to be married to her cousin, André. He knew that she had come out of a convent in Paris specially for him, and that the papers were all signed and sealed, but he could not rid himself of his obsession. Then, on the terrace, the miracle happened. Other groups stood about but no one was particularly interested in the gauche young man from Ireland. She came gliding out through the tall open windows on to the terrace and edged close to him, and then suddenly he knew she was his. His first word was so stupid that he could not forgive himself for it for days afterwards:

"André—what about André?"

An impatient sigh was her answer, and she repeated the pressure, then said:

"André is not here. We are. I have been watching you." She dropped her gaze modestly. "I know how you feel."

A girl brought up in a convent could scarcely say more but words were not needed to express her feelings. She began to tell him about her former life. She moved a little away from him while she spoke, only now and then coming close to him again and touching his arm or his knee with hers. Around them the bright crowd moved and turned, with no idea of the miracle that was happening in front of their eyes.

Now for the first time he heard the full story of Cousin Charlotte and her family. He found that Grand-mère had either been too reticent about it or had not known it all. Cousin Charlotte was the widow of Count de Laval and she would have been very rich if her husband, Teresa's father, had not left so many debts that she had no hope whatever of paying them off unless she reduced her standard of living to the lowest possible level for several years. With three daughters coming up to marriageable age, she was distraught at the prospect of having to do this. By the time the debts were paid off, the daughters would be too old to marry at all. Teresa was the eldest of the three, and on her own suggestion she retired to the convent of Sainte Marie de Chaillot for four years, until she was eighteen years old. Her two younger sisters went off to live on an estate in Languedoc with their father's mother. They were not enjoying life there, Teresa said, since their grandmother was almost eighty and went to bed, the house locked up and the servants on guard duty, at eight o'clock in summer, seven in winter.

Teresa had not fared much better but at least she was nearer to her mother and could watch the progress of their fortunes. Mama had been clever, she said, and had somehow got hold of enough money to keep the house going and to entertain now and then. This was absolutely necessary, to ensure that she would be entertained in return. For her daughters' sake she could not drop out of the picture. Cardinal Rohan gave her money from time to time, as he helped many people. Teresa used her time in the convent to read the French philosophers of the last century and to learn Italian, which she now spoke perfectly. She loved Italian poetry especially, and it helped her to pass the long days in the convent. She said:

"You have no idea how long a day can be. When I thought it must be at least noon, it was only nine o'clock, and at noon I thought it must be five. The nuns were busy doing household things, praying in the chapel, having visits in the parlor. They never looked bored but I could never bend my mind down so far. I watched how they did it: they had a passion for neatness. and the world is not a neat place. You could spend your whole life in setting it to rights. You could roll up pieces of string and fold away cloths and straighten rugs and polish parquet and arrange flowers and pick weeds and gather fruit in the garden and make preserves and bread—there is no end to the things that people can do to pass the time until they die. Some of the nuns studied but most of them were doing nothing but domestic things."

"But were you the only girl there? Was it not a school?"

"Oh, yes, we had endless classes, all directed towards making us into good nuns. That was what most of the girls were going to be but I never lost hope of getting out."

"You make it sound like a jail. In a moment I expect you'll tell me that you had a pet rat in your cell."

"Not quite that." She spoke brusquely and he shivered with fear that he had offended her. After a moment she gave a quick sigh and went on: "Well, that's how it was, until Mama came in one day last November and said there was an offer of marriage for me through her brother, and it was Cousin André de Lacy. I had met him once or twice at parties four years ago and he looked all right. My younger sister, Emilie, had an offer too. Hers is from a neighbor of my grandmother in Languedoc, quite rich but awfully old. He can't expect a dowry with her,

Mama says, because of his age. When I heard that, I accepted André like a shot."

"Won't André expect a dowry?"

"There will be a collection among the cousins for me." She made a grimace which would have been ugly on any other girl but which he found delightful on her. "André has estates in Ireland and France, and a house in Paris. He'll probably be away at other wars too. That's how it goes."

"You don't sound happy about it. I thought that girls like to be engaged."

"The silly ones do but I was never silly enough for my own good. If I were, I suppose I could have been married long ago. André is all right but I don't find the prospect exciting. You'll see when you meet him, if he comes while you are here. He has a cold eye, a calculating look. They don't like him at court and he does nothing to try to please them. He has no ambition, only a lot of principles that get in the way of all the fun. He's not the kind of husband I want—he was born old. Even if he were younger I don't believe I could like him any better. Are you shocked?"

"Not at all."

But he had never heard a girl talk like this before. Now his whole concern was to keep her with him, to make sure that she didn't give one of her sudden impatient gestures and shake her head and walk away, as he had often seen her do with other people. Afterwards she would say that they were stupid. That was a great word of hers, stupid. He was not quite sure what she meant by it. She liked people to be witty and amusing and able to make sharp comments on the behavior of others. Once he had heard her with her friends at a game of comparing the visitors to her mother's house with various animals—one was a lion, one a stork, one a cat, one a dog and so on. He had listened carefully to find out what he was, but he had not been mentioned at all.

Now, by a miracle, she stayed with him a long time, asking about Ireland and his family there, telling him about her childhood, as if she asked nothing better in this glittering company than himself. At last an elegant young man, Count Philip de Loudun, came bounding out on to the terrace and took her away, talking about some game that she had promised to play in one of the upstairs rooms. She seemed reluctant but she went with de Loudun all the same, giving him one last look over her shoulder before disappearing into the house. He hoped wildly that she would come back and ask him to come and take part in this game too, but she did not.

He stood on the terrace for a long time, going over and over what had happened to him. She had spoken with dislike, almost with contempt, of her fiancé. Surely that amounted to an invitation, especially in the kind of company she kept. He had seen couples retreat into dark corners and thence into bedrooms at several parties just like this one. Perhaps that was what she had been suggesting, yet she hadn't really given him a final, clear invitation. He was quite sure of that.

He rehearsed their conversation until, tantalized unbearably, he glowed with longing for her. He knew how she would look, her long, slender legs, her narrow shoulders, her little, delightful, soft breasts. He whirled around, wanting to find her, to take her away somewhere or other in this huge barrack of a house, to make love to her as he had longed to do almost since the first day he saw her. It was she who had brought all these half-realized passions to the surface. It was what she wanted too.

Walking in a crazy dream he wandered through the rooms looking for her, but it was not until they were about to leave that he saw her again. She was standing in the hall, having her cloak placed on her shoulders by one of the Cardinal's servants. Philip was standing beside her, his eyes lit with adoration, elbowing Catherine out of the way when she went forward to take Teresa out to the carriage.

Robert almost staggered with the shock of it. He leaned against a pillar, making no move towards her. She saw him, however, and sent him a glance full of warm understanding, so that he straightened up like a watered flower and walked a step towards her. But then her mother appeared and they left at once.

The next morning he awoke alertly, like a fox in a covert. It could not be true. She could not possibly love him. How could she? Paris was a different world, common things that had made up her whole life had never been in his. But she had said once, not yesterday but another day, when he had been too stupid to see that she was making an advance to him, that his life so far had been so fresh and clean that it fascinated her. Fresh? Clean? Those were the words she had used. He had never told her about Celia. While he let Martin dress him he went through agonies of doubt and self-distrust. Her time was spent with people whose days were given up to dressing and powdering and watching for fashions in clothes and behavior. Tiny memories of expressions and words came to torment him. He drove like fury in his new yellow cabriolet, with Martin clinging on behind, and arrived trembling at the rue du Bac. He ran up the steps and knocked sharply on the door, not waiting for Martin to go ahead of him and do it, as a gentleman should.

Then, when the door was opened, there was Cousin Charlotte, like a douche of cold water, standing in the hall. She was dressed to go out, the little packet of lists that she always carried ready in her hand. She looked at him with surprise and suspicion. He stopped dead, then walked slowly past the servant into the house. She said raspingly:

"Well, young man. You're early this morning."

"I'm sorry. I've been up for hours. I thought it was much later."

"Clocks were made for people like you."

He kissed her hand, bending low over it so that she would not see his fierce blush, then said:

"I was hoping to see Louise before she goes out. She leads such a busy life, I often miss her."

"You're in plenty of time. What a devoted brother."

She could not possibly suspect anything, since until last night there had been nothing to suspect. But her hard stare frightened him cruelly, before she swept out to her carriage, which had been standing there in the courtyard waiting for her all the time. In his agitation he had not even noticed it.

He slowed his step deliberately and started up the long stairs, as if to go to the little sitting room where Louise might be found.

He was in luck. Teresa had seen him coming. She was waiting for him at the turn of the stairs and drew him into her own sitting room where he had never been before. Its bareness surprised him, not a single feminine touch, not a flowered cushion, painted box, embroidered cloth, not one of the things with which women love to decorate their rooms. A plain desk and chair, a few books, armchairs that looked as if they had been cast out of every other room, gave a look of austerity which verified an aspect of her character that he had already noticed and admired. She could do without things—that was how he had put it to himself. This room was like the room of a nun.

She was watching him, perhaps giving him time to recover, a slightly sardonic look in her lovely eyes. Then she said softly:

"Mama has gone out. I heard her speak to you."

"She said I'm a devoted brother."

"Then that's all right."

"Is it true, then? Is it really true?"

"Yes, it's true. Come here."

Holding his hand in hers, she went to the door and deliberately turned the key in the lock. He gazed at her with rapture. Then some spark of sense flickered for a moment and he said:

"What about the servants?"

"They know better than to come here."

"And Louise?"

"She never comes either."

A door at the far side of the room led into her bedroom. As if in a dream he allowed himself to be led in there, until they were standing beside the small, narrow bed. Then she was in his arms, pressing him down on the bed, clutching at his collar, leading his hands to her breasts. In a wild fever he suddenly realized that he was the stronger of the two, and she gave a satisfied sigh as if her plans had come to fruition. She knew exactly what to do, and for one moment he was shocked. Then he gave himself up completely to the sensation of possessing her.

Later, with her head lying on his bare arm and the sun just beginning to come around the corner of the window, she said:

"Now do you believe that it's true?"

"Yes. Last night I thought I had dreamed it, or imagined it. Now I know." He wriggled uncomfortably, until she stroked his shoulder; then he said: "Tell me about Count de Loudun."

"He's no one. Just Philip. He's the third brother. No one pays any heed to him."

"He seems very fond of you."

"Perhaps. But he's stilly, stupid. He means nothing to me."

"You may mean something to him."

"That's his business. Besides, he has a wife at home. He was married when he was fifteen."

"How long have you known him?"

"Years. He's like a brother. Let's not talk about him."

"We'll live in Ireland. You'll like it there. I'm quite a catch, I believe," he said boastfully, suddenly full of confidence. "I'm a Brien of Mount Brien Court. My grandmother will be pleased to have a new French bride in the house."

Teresa laughed softly.

"Your grandmother? Does she rule the house?"

"She certainly does. She's the most important person there, after my father. Louise and I would have a dog's life without her. I'll tell you all about how we live there—"

"Not now," Teresa said. "Some other time. You must go now, before Mama comes back."

And that was the only time she had let him into her bedroom. He lived on the memory of it, savoring each single moment as a starving man keeps each bite as long as possible in his mouth. To be with Teresa was agony, all the worse when she took him aside into one of the dark rooms at a party and let him touch her and press close to her, always shaking herself free after a short while, as if she sensed that he would soon be out of control and would take her by force. She was very discreet in her choice of the places she took him, until she chose the little room off the salon on the day that Louise had found them. A few days later she said in a bitter tone that he had not heard her use before:

"Louise watches me all the time."

He said lightly:

"What can you expect? She would never injure us."

"I wish she hadn't found out about us. You shouldn't have told her so much."

"It's too late to wish for that now."

But instantly he felt himself seized with a new sensation which had been fighting its way to the surface ever since that fatal evening. To his astonishment Louise had become his enemy. Her very existence seemed to threaten him. She could be the cause of his losing Teresa.

He wished he had never asked to have her sent to Paris with him. He had been a child then. She was still a child. An indiscretion of hers could snatch Teresa away from him at any moment. And she spoiled his joy with guilt. She never reproached him but that made little difference. She looked at him, and at Teresa too, and Louise's looks contained a hundred reproaches that she would not have dreamed of expressing.

"We could run away," he said suddenly. "Then they would have to let us marry. André would not want to stick to his bargain then." A shaft of murderous jealousy pierced him through and through, so that he couldn't stop himself from asking the question that had pounded in his brain ever since that marvelous morning when she had led him to her bed: "Have you slept with André? Have you? Have you?"

Unconsciously his hand had gone to his sword, as if he would have run André through with it. Teresa put down her hand and quietly lifted his fingers away from the hilt saying:

"No, of course not. I told you, I met him at parties when I was only a child. I had no idea then that he would ever be interested in me. It was a great surprise when his offer came. I don't really know him at all."

"Then how did you—how did you—"

To go on with his question would have been coarse and offensive. He couldn't do it. Again she was the calm, reasonable one. She said in a low voice:

"Women talk a lot among themselves. When one is in love, everything comes naturally."

Then she lowered her eyes while he watched her with adoration. At last she said:

"It would be foolish to run away. We would be arrested and brought back. You would be ruined. Much better to wait awhile. It won't be long, I promise."

"Teresa, does it seem strange to you that I see all of our life together already, like a long, smooth, silver line stretching across a dark, calm sea?"

"You sound like a fortune-teller."

"Perhaps I am one. We're walking along the line, hand in hand, every step making us happier and more at peace. Do you think that's a silly idea?"

"I think it's beautiful and romantic, and it's why I love you so much. Now we must be extra careful not to give any cause for suspicion. I need time, more time, before I can speak to Mama."

"Isn't it my business to do that?"

"No, no. You must not. I'll do it, soon. After that, everything will be perfect."

9

For days Louise had been avoiding Cousin Charlotte. On the surface nothing had changed, the bland, smooth voice with its perfect articulation was as impersonal as ever, the advice for a young lady anxious to improve herself came as regularly and the cold congratulations on each success were accompanied by the same tinkling, satirical laugh. The change was in Cousin Charlotte's eyes, now like chips of gray marble, flat with hatred and with something else that Louise could not recognize. It reminded her of the look that Patty gave a chicken in the yard at home before she decided that it was ready for the pot.

Louise first noticed that look a few days before she went to Countess de Rothe's house, in the same street as Cousin Charlotte's, for the promised visit. She had never had any difficulty in seeing how the Countess disliked her, though she couldn't imagine why. Biddy, who seemed able to pick up all the gossip, said that the Countess was jealous of every pretty young girl in the family and made a point of treating them rudely. She made no exception for her own daughter, Lucy Dillon, nor for her ten-year-old granddaughter, another Lucy, who was said to be very like Louise.

"The life she gives those two!" Biddy said. "Her father was an English lord and her father-in-law was related to dukes though he wasn't one himself, but they say she screams like a fishwife when her temper is roused. Poor Madame Dillon is nearly finished, Catherine says, spitting blood and all, but that doesn't stop the mother. You'll be seeing them soon, when we go to the country."

"How do you know we're going to the country?"

"Catherine told me. We're all invited to Madame Dillon's house in Hautefontaine when she comes home from Brussels. Now you be a good girl at the party, Miss Louise, or maybe they won't let us go to the country at all. I'm dying for it, to get a sight of a green field again instead of all this dust and dirt."

"I'm not sure that I want to go."

"Of course you do. Look at that, now, my long tongue will be the end of me yet. Why did I tell you anything?"

"Between the two of them, the Countess and Cousin Charlotte, I'll go mad. If it were only the Countess—at least we don't live with her. But now Cousin Charlotte has the same look— what can have happened to her? What does she think I've done? I spend my nights and days trying to please her and do everything she wants and still she glares at me."

"I'm sorry I said a word to you. You're beginning to imagine things."

"I'm not imagining anything. I'm quite sure of it. Please, Biddy, don't sulk. How can I take care of myself if you don't tell me these things?"

"I don't know what has happened to her and that's the truth," Biddy said. "Maybe you're not being a good girl, maybe you're answering her back when she tells you what to do—"

"Answering her back! I'd be afraid of my life to do that!"

"Sure I know you would, God help you. I'll try to find out. Now just be nice to everyone the way you always are, and it will be all right. Do every single thing she says and don't talk too much. Maybe she thinks you get too much attention over her own daughter. It wouldn't be hard for you to look nicer than that one—she's like death warmed up, if you ask me."

Louise was too worried to reprimand her for this. She said:

"I'm afraid to speak at all now, when she is there."

Louise had lost the last of her confidence in Teresa too, though she didn't say so to Biddy. From being the loving friend of the first days she had taken to joining her mother in ridiculing Louise's remaining patches of ignorance of the ways of Paris. Louise pretended not to notice, suspecting that it was the burden of the secret they shared with Robert that was wearing Teresa down.

With all her might Louise wished herself away from the whole lot of them and as the days went on she became more and more angry with Robert's foolishness. The house had an oppressive feel, as if she were caught in a family web of spiders, all closing in on her, all fully in power over her, all in collusion together. Grand-mère hadn't written, though by now she must long have had news of their safe arrival. There was not even a sign of life from Father Burke, a doubtful champion if ever there was one, and yet Louise found herself wishing he would make a visit to Paris as he had said he would, so that she could ask his advice. He might have some clue as to what they were at, or whether there was anything to fear at all. Perhaps Biddy was right and she was imagining it.

But on the evening of the party at Countess de Rothe's house, seeing her with Cousin Charlotte, she felt a blast of animosity from the two of them which was quite unmistakable. She sought out Robert after she had presented herself and found him in an alcove off the drawing room, mooning on a sofa by himself. She said at once:

"Robert, do you really think we should have come to this house? Are we welcome? Have you seen the way they look at us?"

"Who?"

"Countess de Rothe and Cousin Charlotte."

"It's nothing to do with Cousin Charlotte. Countess de Rothe wouldn't have invited us if she didn't want us here," he said idly. "We fill up the parquet. I've heard the Countess say she likes a variety of ages."

"It does concern Cousin Charlotte. Do you think she has found out about you and Teresa? I've thought about it for days and now I'm sure that's the only possible explanation of why she has changed so much. She wasn't like this in the beginning of our stay."

She had his attention now. He asked quickly:

"Where is Teresa? Didn't she come with you?"

"She's coming later. She had a visitor, just as we left, Biddy and I. Cousin Charlotte came earlier. Catherine is waiting for Teresa. It's only a few yards—they'll walk here in a few minutes."

Why was she chattering like this? There was something ugly and frightening in Robert's looks, something she had never seen there before. Always it was he who was confident, optimistic, curbing her impatience with good-humored advice. Now his cheerful, boyish expression was struck with a flash of wildness. Anger against Teresa blazed up in her but she knew better than to reveal it to Robert. He asked:

"Who is the visitor?"

"Count de Loudun, that lively man whose wife is crippled so badly. I met her for the first time only the other day—she's charming, and so learned. She told me she reads all the time, since she can't go about much. Robert, what is the matter? Please, Robert! Don't make a scene. People are beginning to look at us."

Their behavior was certainly beginning to attract attention. One couple had paused and was staring curiously at the young brother and sister, sitting with their heads together, obviously both in a considerable state of agitation. Louise showed hers by glancing over her shoulder uneasily now, and she saw how the eyebrows were raised and the man gave a little contemptuous sneer as he guided his partner on. She said in a low voice:

"I must leave you. Cousin Charlotte will be furious. She has told me over and over again not to get into serious conversations at parties. An insult to the hostess, she said. Oh, Robert, for God's sake don't take it so hard! Remember Ireland, remember that time we rode to Creevagh to see Katta. This is not real at all. It will work out all right—"

She stood up, not knowing what to say to him, her hands making an unconscious impatient gesture as if she would like to shake sense into him. He gave her a long, blind look, as one might look at an animal, without feeling. Then he stood up too, took her hand and kissed it ceremoniously in the French manner, as he had lately begun to do, and walked out of the room without a word. She stood watching him, alarmed at a certain looseness in his way of walking, almost as if he were drunk. With a quick movement she followed him, then paused to watch him mount the two steps that led out of the main drawing room, bowing to Countess de Rothe who was too far away for him to speak to her. A footman opened the double doors for him and he passed through.

Common sense told her to protect herself with a social smile. She lifted her chin and looked around the room at the company. There was no sign of Cousin Charlotte. Madame Nagle, a cousin she had always liked, was with Countess de Rothe and some others, and seemed to be telling them a story. They were all shrieking with laughter, the kind of laughter that sent a shiver up the spine if one guessed at its cause. Louise moved towards the door, as if she were joining someone at the far end of the room. She had almost made her escape when there was a little flurry among the footmen, the doors were opened and Archbishop Dillon came in. His eye lit on Louise at once and he took her hand, speaking to the rest of the company while he held it firmly in his dry old grasp:

"No ceremony, if you please. Just go on enjoying yourselves. We can have ceremony when I go to your houses but we'll have none in mine. Now, little cousin, come and sit with me and tell me what you have been doing with yourself."

He led her to what was clearly his special armchair, a servant placed a chair for her beside him, and there she had to stay, the center of attention, for more than half an hour. In spite of his injunction against ceremony, a line of guests formed and greeted him one by one, and to each of them he introduced Louise as his dear cousin. Only once he asked her:

"And your brother? Is he with us this evening?"

"Yes, he was here but he had to leave. He hopes to come back before the evening is over."

"Young men are always busy at something. Only ladies have leisure."

She knew he could not possibly be delaying her deliberately. He was the most worldly priest she had ever known—she didn't count Cardinal Rohan as a priest at all though she knew he was one—but Archbishop Dillon was a great gentleman, never known to hurt anyone or to fail in his public duty. Short of pretending to feel faint, she could do nothing to escape, and with her healthy appearance no one would believe for a single moment that she was ill. As often as she could she glanced at the door but neither Teresa nor Robert came in.

She was rescued at last by Cousin Charlotte, who came close to her and said smoothly:

"Now, my dear, you should remember not to monopolize the most important person in the room. One would think I had never told you anything."

This came with a light laugh but her eyes were venomous. The Archbishop said:

"Don't scold her. It was I who monopolized her."

But he let go of her hand and stood up, and began to walk tiredly through the rooms, greeting the other guests. It took Louise less than a minute to edge to the door, then she was free, taking her mantle from one of the maids in the foyer, running out into the clear night air, aware that Biddy was following her and calling to her to stop. At the door of Cousin Charlotte's house she waited, saying as Biddy came up:

"I had to come back. Something is happening to Robert. I know it. I can feel it. Where is Martin Jordan? Have you seen him?"

"He was looking for Master Robert at the Archbishop's. He couldn't find him anywhere."

They hammered on the door until it was opened by Michel, the old porter who always stayed at home for this purpose. They ran upstairs, pausing on the first landing to listen while he trotted back towards the kitchens. Very few lamps were lit, since everyone had gone out for the evening. They looked into the salons, then one by one opened the doors of the rooms along the first corridor of bedrooms. Louise felt a choking sensation in her throat and stopped to draw breath. At that moment the door of Teresa's sitting room opened and she stood there, against a dim light from inside the room, staring at them. Her face was dead white, making her loose dark hair seem coal black. Louise shrank away from the look that was hurled at her. Teresa's mouth was opened to show the teeth, like a snarling dog, the upper lip lifted in an odd way, rigid and ugly. Her voice was so low that it was a moment before Louise realized that she was almost hysterical with rage:

"He'll kill him, he'll kill him! Upstart! Infant!"

"Who? Who will kill him? Where is my brother?"

"Bursting in, shouting—the impertinence of it." She clamped her mouth shut and stared again, as if she had lost the power of speech in her anger. Then she forced out more words: "Philip was here. Robert behaved like a madman."

"Where is he? Where?"

"They left together."

"To fight?"

94

"How should I know?"

"Philip was to protect your honor—is that your story?"

Louise took a threatening step forward and saw Teresa put up her hands in fists as if to defend herself. Suddenly she shrieked:

"Get out of the house, you little slut! Get out! No, wait! I didn't do it—it was my mother. Oh, God, I didn't know it would be like this!"

"What? What would be like this?"

But Teresa was now in a fit of hysterics and there was no sense to be had out of her. Louise left Biddy in charge, since there was no sign of Catherine, and ran downstairs again. The hall was empty and she let herself out into the courtyard and then into the street, tears of excitement and fear beginning to blind her eyes. She knew that she should not be alone, that it was all wrong to run through the street in Paris like this. A fool, or was it an infant Teresa had called Robert? She had implied that he and Philip were about to fight a duel, but where? Louise had heard whispers of the Bois de Boulogne but that was miles and miles away. In the dark street the flares lit up the fronts of the houses. She couldn't save him, she could do nothing for him, even if she were to find him. But she couldn't go back into the house either. It was impossible to abandon him without a search. Where would he have gone? If they were to fight, surely it couldn't be before tomorrow morning. Standing by the huge outer doors of the house she turned first this way, then that, not knowing what to do.

A carriage had pulled up a few yards away and some people were getting out. She glanced towards it in fear that Cousin Charlotte had come home but saw at once that there was a bustle of strange servants and a tall man was springing down into the street and coming towards her. She felt ashamed, looking as she did like a cat thrust out of the house for the night. At least the darkness would go some way to cover her embarrassment but her ridiculous headdress would reveal instantly that she had no business to be there alone. He was smiling, though with a strained and puzzled expression. As he spoke, she realized that they had met before.

"What is this? Why are you here alone? You look lost. What's happening?"

"It's Andrew!" She felt hot all over and put up her hands to cover her face, then removed them to ask suspiciously: "What are you doing here?"

"I've just asked that same question," he said in an amused tone.

"I hardly know myself. I never heard your other name, monsieur. We met in Ireland. You remember my brother."

"Of course."

"I think he has gone to fight a duel. I came out to look for him."

"Have you any idea where he went?"

"None—I wish I knew."

"Get into the carriage. Tell me what happened. Or can we go into the house?"

"No, no!" She climbed into the carriage as she spoke, aware that Cousin Charlotte wouldn't have approved of this. "Why are you here? Where have you come from?"

"I told you we would meet in Paris. Now tell me exactly what has happened."

Overwhelmed with relief, she poured out the whole story of Robert's infatuation with Teresa, who it now seemed had been deceiving him all the time with Count Philip de Loudun, a man-about-town who was married already. His wife was hopelessly crippled. To her surprise he asked:

"In what way is she crippled?"

"Her back is curved right over. It happened after they were married, when she was fiftten. He went away to the wars for two years and by the time he came back she was like this. It distresses her terribly but she doesn't complain about it. Teresa told me."

"And Robert thought that he and Teresa would be married?"

"Yes, of course. He should have known—they're all false here, every one of them. But he believed in her. He told me that she said her mother was not to hear of it for a while, because she was engaged to someone else—"

All at once she found that she couldn't utter another word, as complete understanding flooded her mind. She closed her eyes and leaned against the hard cushions of the carriage, her body gone slack and almost motionless. Beside her she heard him say:

"Louise, Louise! Don't faint now, whatever you do. Put your

head down, right down, take my hand. I won't let you fall. Now draw a very deep breath. Sit up again, child. Now, are you feeling better. You must go back into the house."

"I can't, I can't! She told me to get out—I can't go back—"

"Teresa is in there now?"

He said her name in a quiet, flat way that terrified her. She said:

"I left my maid with her. She was hysterical. I couldn't stay with her but I left my Biddy."

"If you can't go back, where do you think you can go?"

"To my cousin, the Archbishop of Narbonne, where the reception is this evening, where I was until a little while ago. I don't know any other place. But Cousin Charlotte is there now. I could go to Madame Nagle, if she will let me in."

"Our cousin, Madame Nagle?"

"Yes. She's always nice to me but perhaps she'll throw me out now too. Oh, Monsieur de Lacy, I wish I could go home to Ireland!"

"Now don't lose your courage. You had plenty a moment ago. First you must go back to that party, then I must find Robert. I have one or two ideas of where they may have gone."

"Where?"

"I know Paris. There are very few places where one can fight at this hour of the night. I'll find him. Now I'll take you back to Madame Dillon's house."

"It's the Archbishop's house."

"No, it's Madame Dillon's but it doesn't matter."

"Do I look a fright?"

"I can't see properly. You look all right." At the door he helped her down and examined her face in the light of the flare by the door. "Now cheer up. I'll come back when I have news. I'll come in the morning."

"Not until the morning! What will I do when the party is over? She said I was to leave the house."

"You are to sleep in your own bed as usual. You can't be turned out like that. I'll see to it. Now go in and try to behave as if nothing has happened."

For one last moment she breathed the outer air of Paris, full of river smells and the smells of decaying vegetables and horse dung and the thousand other things that gave it its flavor, and

97

it seemed to her quite sweet compared with what she must face inside. Cousin Charlotte was the first person she encountered in the salon, saying:

"I missed you, Louise. Where have you been?"

"I went out with Biddy for a little while. It's so hot in here."

After a long stare Cousin Charlotte said:

"Have you been home? Have you seen Teresa?"

"Yes."

They measured each other, and then Cousin Charlotte looked down. There was a new nervousness in her manner, and later Countess de Rothe spoke to her politely too, perhaps because of the favor the Archbishop had shown her so publicly. It was a pleasant change, whatever the reason. Louise spent the last hour at the party trying to put her fears for Robert at rest. With all her might she clung to the memory of Andrew, so calm and assured and experienced, and so sure that he would be able to find Robert and solve everything. She squirmed with embarrassment for the mistake she had made—never for a moment had she connected him with Teresa's Count André de Lacy. She had never asked the O'Connells what his other name was, knowing how they would joke about him if she showed interest. She had been too busy to think of him ever since.

If only Grand-mère would write, even one letter, in answer to all those that Louise had written to her. Perhaps she was ill— but she was never ill. Gliding from group to group, lingering at the fringes of each without taking part in their conversation, Louise moved through the rooms and at last went out on to the little terrace that was built overlooking the courtyard. There was room there only for a few tubs with plants, and no one thought of sitting there. It was a relief to get away from them all even for a few minutes.

From this place presently she saw that the party was breaking up and everyone was drifting towards the door. She joined them quietly, wished Countess de Rothe good-night and followed Cousin Charlotte out of the house.

10

Sitting on a hard bed in an upper room in the Collège des Irlandais in the rue du Cheval Vert, Robert felt his despair and disgrace in every part of him. But for André he would be dead now, spitted on Philip's sword amid shouts of laughter from his friends. Robert had offered pistols but Philip said mockingly that swords were the weapons of gentlemen, pistols were for buffoons. Then he walked around him, examining him from all sides as if he were an animal at a fair, picking out his good points, commenting on his defects, while his friends threw back their heads and roared with laughter. The place they were in seemed to be some sort of club, and it was full of young men like Philip. Open necks and waistbands, ruffled hair, wine-stained shirtfronts indicated that they had been drinking for a long time. They stood up and waved their glasses and cheered when Philip came in, pushing Robert before him, making it clear that he was a captive rather than an adversary. They joined in the game then, aping his truculent looks, mincing back and forth in front of him, threatening him with mock sword thrusts, their hands empty but their imaginary weapons so real that he sweated with fear. When they saw this they were amused, and then they began to sound uglier.

Impertinence was the word he heard most often, the word that Philip had used when Robert burst into Teresa's room and found the two of them locked in a naked embrace on the narrow bed. While he staggered back against the door panel with a cry of pain, Philip leaped for him like a wild animal, like some savage, hairy monkey, only stopped by Teresa's warning shout. Then he turned aside and pulled on some clothes while Robert stood stupidly, gazing at them. De Loudun advanced on him again, now fully in charge of himself saying:

"Well, little man, what have you come for?" He turned to Teresa. "Shall I throw him out of the widow?"

She covered her head with the bedclothes and made no answer.

And then de Loudun was marching Robert down the stairs, out of the house and through the streets, a hard grip on his elbow, walking fast and steadily, the only sign of his agitation being that continually repeated word: "Impertinence." It seemed a thin, inadequate word but each repetition seemed to enrage Philip further. At a tall corner house Robert was hustled upstairs to a room whose windows overlooked the street on one side and the river on the other. Mosquitoes hung in clouds around the lamps. There were only men in the room, though a smell of stale scent was mixed with the wild river smell that came through the window, and with the smell of overheated men and of wine. After they had teased him for a while with their mock swords, one of them said:

"Let's hang this boy out of the window for a while."

The whole lot of them took it up and some ran to look out and see if the police were about. Robert was trying to gauge the distance to the door, wondering if he would be able to make a dash for it, when it was opened with a crash by André, who waited without moving while he took in the scene, then came quickly across the room saying:

"What are you doing? What's going on here? I could hear shouts even in the street."

The authoritative voice was enough to create a pause, the faces of his tormentors suddenly looked frightened, their eyes darting back and forth from André to de Loudun like the eyes of young foxes. One by one they dropped their hands and moved back; their movements were so slow that they seemed almost to flow aside, until a clear space remained around de Loudun and Robert.

Philip stared at André with surprise, which quickly became arrogance as he recovered from his first shock. He took a step forward aggressively and said loudly:

"I'm not accustomed to being questioned in such a tone."

He advanced on André, his right hand raised to strike. In a daze, Robert saw André's face take on a look of amazement. Then his hand shot out and he gripped de Loudun's arm and held it high, so tightly that the fingers began to dangle with pain and to turn white. After a moment André said:

"You will not strike me, Count. There will be no duel. The laws of this country are very strict on that."

"I'll fight—I'll fight—"

"It wouldn't be the kind of fight you imagine. If there is any question of a fight it will be here and now, in this room, and I will kill you. The law will protect me, since you outraged my betrothed bride. And if we fight, it won't be a fair fight, not the kind of fight you expect. I shall simply shoot you dead."

André said the words slowly, through clenched teeth, with an expression of extraordinary, almost mad, ferocity. Slowly he lowered his arm, then released his hold and let de Loudun's arm fall limply to his side. Still with his eye on him, he said to Robert:

"You can come with me."

Robert darted like a rabbit for the door and stood panting outside. André followed more slowly and then the two of them went clattering down the stairs, aware that an uproar had begun in the room behind them the instant they were gone. André said as they hurried along:

"Those were fine words of mine. The Count will be out for our blood as soon as he gets his wits back. You'll have to keep out of sight for a while."

They turned two or three corners and found André's coachman waiting with his carriage, and were quickly driven through the dark streets. Robert felt his whole body numb, his lungs empty of air, the pace of the carriage seeming impossibly fast, André's voice as unreal as a dream. He was saying:

"I'm taking you to the Irish College first. You can't stay in Paris now."

Robert was silent. The events of the last hour kept flashing through his mind in a series of pictures, a confusion of shock and pain pounding in his brain so that no consecutive thought or plan was possible. The humiliating way in which he had been rescued was the least of his troubles. How could he possibly have imagined that a girl who looked and moved like

Teresa could be an innocent virgin, in love with him? His first doubts had been correct but he had let them be quieted easily. He wanted them to be quieted, she had seen right through him and had been well able to handle him.

"But why? Why did she do this to me?" he burst out suddenly. Then he stopped, ashamed, adding after a moment: "You said she was betrothed to you. She told me there was someone— I didn't know it was you."

André said almost casually:

"There was a church ceremony but I wasn't there. I hardly know her. That makes it easier for me. She has made fools of both of us."

Robert felt a burst of anger against André. In spite of what he had seen, in spite of what he knew of Teresa's contemptible character, still he wanted with all his being to have her again. During the next few hours this longing obsessed him, so that he scarcely heard the conversations that went on over his head about his future. They were let into the Irish College by the Rector himself, who was entertaining his colleague from the Collège des Lombards where the senior Irish students lived. Both of them seemed to know André well. They were hurried upstairs. In the Rector's study most of Robert's story was told, and then he sat in a corner while they went on and on about whether he should be got out of Paris at once, this very night, or whether it was safe to wait a few days, whether he should then be sent to America or only to another Irish College in France. From time to time the two clerics threw him glances of mixed pity and curiosity, as if he were suffering from some strange disease.

Robert was thinking, if she were to come back to him, he would take her again and ask no questions, if she were to repent he would receive her without a word. He would never reproach her. She would say it was all a mistake, that she had lost her head but that her heart was still his. She would tell him to make arrangements with her mother at once so that they could be married without delay. He would take her back to Ireland where there would be no temptations and where she would be his, his, his forever and ever. He gave a long moan, causing all the heads to turn and all the eyes to stare. One of the priests said:

"What's the matter with him? Was he wounded?"

André dropped his voice to a whisper and there were more curious looks, but at least none of them were laughing at him. Then they stopped talking and he was led up to a room at the top of the house, a small, bare room with a narrow metal bed. The building was rather new and the spiral stairs seemed endless. A commode in one corner of the room showed that the occupant need never leave it. The single lamp left shadowy corners. Though the key was on his side of the door and they had warned him to keep it locked, still when they went away he felt that he was a prisoner.

He climbed onto a chair and looked out over Paris, lit by a full moon, a jumble of roofs of every height and shape and size, with clear patches here and there where the parks and palaces were. What a marvelous city it was—and he scarcely knew it. Mr. Burke would be horribly disappointed in him. Just before leaving he had come to Robert's rooms and delivered a sermon on the duties of students and the delights of Paris, the two subjects so intertwined in the priest's mind that it was impossible to tell which he was most concerned with.

Robert had promised to attend to both. In Ireland he had been quite sure that he was safe from the wiles of women. He remembered his relief at getting away from Celia. He was not to lose his freedom for years and years, not until he had had time to enjoy all the things that are lying ready for a young man of means. Then in one week, his very first week, he had fallen stupidly in love and had ruined himself forever. His studies had barely begun, he had attended only three classes at the university, when his wits had deserted him. No one would ever respect him again, even if he got out of this scrape alive. He would be labeled a silly man, a libertine. His father would hear of it, of course, and his grandmother, and stinking Fanny. That was one person who would be glad.

He climbed down from the chair, where he had stood for a long time, and went to sit on the bed, his head resting in his hands. All these questions of respect, the pleasure of others in his misfortune, even the pain of his friends, were all external and irrelevant. What mattered was his disgust with himself. He knew now that his judgments in everything must be worthless. Nothing he could ever do in the future would remove this conviction. He would have to carry it with him wherever he went, to bear with the disgrace of it and to know that everyone was aware, as he was himself, that he was a certified fool. His ears pounded with excitement and pain, and he groaned in agony. He could no longer reason. Nothing was clear. It would have been better to have died in that club among all those young men. That might at least have looked like an honorable end. André, the man he had injured so fearfully, was the person who had helped him. That was the last and the worst humiliation.

At the thought of André, Robert sprang to his feet and began to run about the room, as if he were looking for a way out. After a while he realized what he was doing and came to a halt, then began again to walk a few steps towards the window, then back to the bed, then to the door, until he came to rest at last gripping the footrail of the bed and shaking it to and fro in a frenzy, as if he were trying to break it in pieces. A minute of this brought a sense of reality and he let his arms drop to his sides, then went to sit on the bed again in the same attitude as before, his head in his hands. Sheer exhaustion overcame him at last and he tumbled on to the bed fully clothed, and fell into a twitching sleep which gradually quieted down until he was snoring gently and peacefully.

A loud battering on the door awoke him in the morning, a servant with breakfast on a tray. He crawled off the bed and stretched himself, calling out:

"Wait a moment! I'm coming!"

The servant looked at him curiously, as the priests had done last night. Did the whole house know his miserable story? Then the man said in French:

"The Rector will come to see you after breakfast. He said you are not to come downstairs."

"Why not?"

The question was foolish and of course he got no answer but a shrug. Then he was alone again. Perhaps there was a hunt out for him. Count de Loudun could get almost anything he wanted done, including putting Robert in jail forever with a *lettre de cachet*. Last night he had looked furious enough for anything. Suddenly hungry, Robert devoured the bread and coffee, then tried to make himself look a little more trim in preparation for the Rector's visit.

When he came it was almost noon and André was with him. Robert opened the door to their knock and stood aside to let them in. Refreshed after his sleep, he found that yesterday's adventure no longer seemed the disaster that it had the night before. Though the memory of Teresa still stung him bitterly, he had begun to see that it was not the tragedy to others that it was to him. André said anxiously:

"I hope you were able to sleep. I meant to come sooner. I've been with Charlotte and Teresa. It's a sorry tale, if ever there was one. I've found out what it was all about."

He sat on the edge of the bed while the Rector took the chair and carried it over to the window. André looked haggard and worn, though he was as sprucely dressed as usual. His tone was detached but it was easy to see that he had had an unpleasant morning.

"They're frightened, both of them," he said, "and they're not inclined to make trouble. Charlotte will do what she can to quiet Count de Loudun—he's your main problem."

"Cousin Charlotte! What has she got to do with it?"

"It was her idea. She more or less forced Teresa into cooperating. I'm sorry for Teresa. Charlotte thought she was being very clever but she was desperate. It was a complicated plot, too complicated to work, as it happened."

"A plot?"

"A silly plot, to get your sister out of the house, though I don't see what difference this would have made. Charlotte's brother was in the army with me in America. He warned me that she thought herself clever with money. He said he thought she'd ruin herself and her family before she was finished. When he was dying he asked me to take care of them, to marry Teresa and take the whole family under my wing. I wrote my offer to Charlotte when I gave her news of his death. I was able to tell her that he died contented." He shook his shoulders impatiently, as if he were embarrassed at having been so simple, then went on: "That's what comes of being quixotic, and it's the beginning of the present story. You see, Charlotte has spent Louise's inheritance—well, you must have guessed that by now."

Robert had not guessed it.

"She accepted my offer for Teresa, but then I didn't come at once and she could no longer put off your arrival from Ireland.

Your father was pressing her. Her plan was to say that Louise was too *farouche* for Paris and to send her off to stay with her mother-in-law in the country. They would have arranged a dowerless marriage for her there. But your sister charmed everyone with her good manners and couldn't be disposed of so easily."

"Did she tell you all that this morning? She admitted it?"

"Yes. She needed some persuasion but then she told me all about it. She said the Archbishop ruined her plans by telling everyone about his delightful cousin from Ireland. She said some very ugly things about His Grace. And she admitted that she concealed your grandmother's letters. She stopped Louise's on the way out and kept those that came in."

Robert forced himself to ask:

"Did she know about Teresa and me, then?"

"Yes. That was her last desperate effort. You were to be exposed at the right moment and turned out of the house, disgraced."

"Teresa told me that Cardinal Rohan gave them money."

"Yes, he likes to do that, but it's never much, enough to pay the baker. He does it for lots of people."

"Was de Loudun in the plot?"

André gave him a sharp, appreciative glance, as if to say that he was beginning to learn how the game was played.

"Hardly. He didn't look it last night. His function was more probably to get Teresa to court. She's very ambitious. You know these Parisian aristocrats would sell their mothers to get near the Queen."

"Can't her mother take her? She promised to take Louise."

"She did? No, she's not in that circle at all. Madame Dillon is."

Throughout this conversation the Rector sat silently by the window, as detached as if he were listening to a foreign language that he didn't understand. These two men have been fooled by a woman, he seemed to be saying to himself, their lives have been disturbed by this strange experience. How odd it all is, and how free I am. They will recover, and when they have analyzed the whole affair and have laid bare the truth of what has happened to them, they will find me useful. Sure enough, after a while they turned to the Rector and André said:

"Well, then, Father, what do you think we should do next?"

The Rector had his thoughts in perfect order. Robert had a choice among three courses. He could return to Ireland; he could go to Bordeaux and study law or medicine at the Irish College, where he would have the benefit of Father Burke's supervision; or he could join the French army, preferably the Dillon regiment, and go to the war in America.

Robert paused for no more than ten seconds before deciding in favor of the last.

11

Before he sailed, while he still lived in the upper room at the Irish College, Robert visited Louise several times. André's coachman drove him in a closed carriage, for fear of de Loudun, while Martin kept a lookout, but there seemed to be no danger from him. André had heard nothing from Philip since the night he had threatened to kill him. Louise was in Madame Dillon's house now with the Archbishop and Countess de Rothe. André had arranged everything. Madame Dillon and her daughter were still absent in Brussels. Louise had two rooms on the third floor.

"It's so peaceful," she said to Robert on his first visit. "Everyone in the house is old but I like it much better that way. So does Biddy, though she says the Countess is very bad tempered. The other servants have told her. But we can keep out of her way."

She was glancing at him uneasily all the time, as if to see how much he had changed. He was watching her too, and he saw that she was no longer the simple young girl who had left Ireland. She was quieter and more sure of herself, but the main loss what that she no longer made the cheerful, inconsequential remarks that had always lit up every conversation with her. He had expected nothing else, but though he knew he was responsible he could not bring himself to apologize for what he had done.

The first visit was the worst. After that, his own excitement kept mounting at the prospect of the great adventure before him, whirling him along so fast that the pain of his loss only stabbed intermittently. His manner became unnaturally exuberant, exaggerating all his actions. On his last day he came early and ran up to Louise's room, taking the stairs three at a time and bursting in without ceremony. She lifted her head from the books laid out neatly on the table before her.

"We're off to Brest at once. We're going with General Rochambeau. André is a marvel. Everyone at the college envies me. The fleet is on its way up from Bordeaux. I'm going to see the world!"

He was wearing his uniform, a white coat with sky-blue lapels and a long waistcoat, and a hat with a white plume. He pirouetted so that his coattails flew out. "I'm to be in the hussars. I'll get my new uniform when we land. I saw General Rochambeau today. He had just come back from seeing the King."

"What does he look like?"

"Rather short and light. His mouth is terrifying. He's quite old. Everyone says he's a genius. His knees give him trouble, he has been in so many campaigns. Thirty-eight years a soldier! You should see him."

"Thank God!"

"Thank God for what?"

"That one can be thirty-eight years a soldier and live to tell the tale. Robert, have you written a letter to Papa?"

"Yes, yes, here it is." He took the letter out of his pocket and showed it to her but then he withdrew it again without letting her read it. "I haven't told him about Teresa. That is, I've told him some of it but not all. How could I write that down?"

"What have you said, then?"

"Just that we discovered Cousin Charlotte has stolen the money that was to be yours and that you have moved to Madame Dillon's house."

"And about yourself?"

"That Teresa deceived me and that I can't bear Paris now and am joining the Dillon regiment." They looked at each other sadly. "I couldn't bring myself to tell him any more. You may be able to do it. I have explained that your letters were stopped by Cousin Charlotte."

"Robert, I'm sorry about Teresa."

With false casualness he said:

"Who knows if she's to blame? She's a Parisian. She only does what everyone else does. I should have seen that." He picked up one of Louise's books and fluttered the pages. "Now it's you who are the student and I'm the gadabout. André says that several people have commented on your move here. They had guessed what Cousin Charlotte was up to and wondered how long it would take us to find out. André says that someone should have told us."

"That wouldn't be so much fun for them. They love gossip."

"But not in this house?"

"Things are better here. I'm not quite sure yet how I'll fit in but I'll learn. It's not like Cousin Charlotte's."

"André has told Countess de Rothe enough to make sure she doesn't invite Cousin Charlotte again."

"I had been wondering what I could say if we met. She didn't come out of her room nor speak to me again after that night— the night of the party here."

"And André said he will come to see you before he leaves Paris."

"You'll write to me?"

"By every post. No one knows yet exactly where we're going. You won't hear anything until we land somewhere but then the letters will begin to come. Now I must go."

She gazed at him, stunned with grief. Then she sprang up and came running around the table to him, saying as she threw her arms around his neck:

"Dear Robert, I envy you! What a good time you're going to have! I'll write at once to Father and to Grand-mère saying how fine you look in your uniform and how you're going to be with the General and all the best soldiers, and that you'll come back covered in glory."

But she was not able to keep it up, and when he prepared to leave her at last she was sitting shakily at the table again, saying: "Now I'll be all right. The sooner you go, the better. Don't think about me. I'll do some geometry. Mr. Burke says geometry calms the mind. I'll write to him too, of course, and explain everything. I won't tell him too much. Now go quickly."

He kissed her hand and went softly out of the room, then had to stand on the landing for a full minute before he was fit to go to the salon and speak to Countess de Rothe.

She was waiting for him, her hands laid as flat as two little fishes on the arms of her chair, her voice grating coldly.

"Well, young man, you're off, I see. Very fine. Don't waste time. Louise will be all right with me. I'll take proper care of her. It won't be the first time I've rescued one of the family. We'll try to find her a husband. You understand that it won't be easy now that she has no money."

"Yes."

"But there's always someone who can do with a beautiful, healthy young wife. I'll see to it."

"Will she have nothing at all, then?" Robert asked in terror of this prospect.

"Her father says he can give her nothing. Why should he? She has her own inheritance. I may be able to persuade Charlotte to go into debt and pay back something. Now don't think about it. I've told you I'll take care of it."

"You are very good."

"Not everyone would agree with you. But I'm not like Cousin Charlotte. Now you had better go."

She had not reproached him about Teresa. He was very grateful for this, though he couldn't understand her restraint. Perhaps it fitted the rest of what he knew of these people. They were absolutely practical in everything.

He traveled to Brest with the General's party, trying at every stop to get a glimpse of him but he was always surrounded by such a hedge of aides that this was almost impossible. Then, at Rennes, Robert was put in charge of the General's two war-horses. Their grooms were soldiers who were too old for foreign service. They had gotten instructions to bring the animals from the General's estate in Vendôme. Robert found the soldiers in the stable of the inn, their uniforms and hats thick with wisps of hay, their heavy sabots clattering on the cobbles. It was hard to imagine anything less soldierly. They looked like two countrymen who had stolen old uniforms.

The horses were in splendid condition, however, their skins shining with health and their sharp ears twitching with intelligence. Robert despaired of ever bringing the men's appearance up to the same standard but the older one said indignantly:

"Do you think we were going to let the General see us like this? Of course we have clean uniforms."

The next time he saw them he barely recognized them, they were so smart, in perfect cavalry uniforms with boots and spurs shining like glass. They stood holding the horses' bits, even the angle of their gloved hands symmetrical, their backs straight, not a speck of hayseed to be seen. The General came out of the front door of the inn and inspected them with great satisfaction, then said to Robert:

"Well done, boy. So long as the horses are in good hands, everything goes well."

A day and a half later they reached Brest. It was a miserable place, mud flats as far as the eye could see, the tide gone so far out that it was visible only as a darker line on the distant horizon. Robert went to a nearby farm to see that the precious horses were well quartered and then came back to the town. Soldiers were billeted in every house in the villages around, cursing and grumbling at the endless delay in the arrival of the transports from Bordeaux. Those that had come were little better than fishing boats, some only capable of carrying fifty men even with the most expert loading. His aides reported that Rochambeau sat gloomily all day going over a mountain of papers, which he said would conquer the world if one-tenth of their promises were fulfilled. Admiral de Ternay said over and over that he had been given an impossible task, but neither he nor Rochambeau showed any sign of their uneasiness once they appeared in public. Daily messages came from Paris, the mud-spattered horsemen being cheered derisively as they galloped into the town, while voices called out:

"Hurry along, there, or we'll be gone without you!"

A week later, there were still not enough ships, and more and more men kept coming in. Rumors multiplied. In every inn as night fell, parties gathered to speculate on where this great army was going.

No one knew, except the General and the Admiral, whose aides were questioned with varying degrees of guile and subtlety. They would tell nothing, indeed they knew nothing, but they obviously enjoyed their privilege of being surrounded by inquirers, all looking at them as if they were the commanders of the expedition. Some know-alls said they were going to Jamaica, some said the American continent, and this was where everyone was hoping to go. No one had been there, but the stories of friends and the friends of friends were quoted everywhere. There were rivers as wide as the ocean, trees that touched the moon. Indians that knew the trackless forest like a village street, mountains, gorges and wild animals that had never been matched in any other part of the world. In addition, everyone wanted to be in the army that would strike a blow against England's German king, whose colonies were growing bigger with every year. That was not merely officer's talk: the men said the same, though they talked most of their hopes of good prizes and good pay.

Robert was bored and disappointed. He couldn't understand half of what the other men were saying, since even the officers lapsed into the dialect of their own districts when they got excited. He spent as much time as possible with his horses, the two splendid chargers that now lived like lords in the stables of the General's inn, watching the men rub them down, talking to them, loving the way they turned their heads to greet him when he came into the stable. Often he sent the two old soldiers away and led the animals out to the stable yard himself, feeling an almost unbearable longing for Ireland and the horses he had left behind.

He was leading one of the horses around and around the yard late one afternoon, watching a hind hoof that he suspected was sore, when the gate opened quietly and the General came in. He stopped in surprise and then walked quickly over to the stable and peered inside. Coming back he said to Robert:

"All alone? Where are the grooms?"

"I sent them away. I like to be alone sometimes, with the horses."

Rochambeau stroked the horse's neck and it nuzzled his hand, turning its head with a beautifully elegant movement, like a woman. He covered its muzzle with his hand and it licked his palm. Then he looked sharply at Robert saying:

"They like you, the horses?"

"Yes, I think so. I know how to manage horses, from home."

"Home? Where is that?"

"Ireland."

"A Dillon?"

"A cousin only."

"All you Irish are cousins. Looking for adventure, are you?"

"Yes."

"You're going to get it. Have you gone soldiering before? You look too young to have gone far."

"Never before."

The old man gave a heavy sigh, then said:

"The horses are not coming with us. The Admiral says there is no room for them."

"There must be room—they must come—your horses—" Robert stuttered foolishly, then stopped, very embarrassed, while Rochambeau looked at him quizzically.

"I've pressed the Admiral hard but he replies always that there is no room unless I keep them in my cabin. Even two horses take up a lot of space. I've had to obey—remember that, boy. A soldier's first duty is to obey."

"Yes, sir."

The man stroked the horse's neck in a long, gentle movement, then said:

"I could send you back to Vendôme with them. How would you like to serve your King on my estate in Vendôme? Don't look so frightened. I'm not going to do it. But you know my horses and it would be good to think of your being with them when I'm out in that savage country. No, we'll send them back with their old grooms, all the way back, and hope I'll survive to see them again." He slapped the horse's flank so that it danced away from him. "I don't want to see them again here. It distresses me too much. How can I be such a fool about a couple of animals at this time of my life? The Admiral says there are hundreds of better horses to be found where we're going. Well, he knows best, and the ships are his. You'll come in my staff, boy. What is your name?"

"Robert Brien."

"Count?"

"No. My father is Sir Maurice."

"Was he ever a soldier?"

"Never. His brothers are."

"Of course. I know them. They're in Sainte Lucie and Saint Dominique."

"Yes. I haven't seen them since I came to France."

"Perhaps you will, perhaps you will."

He stroked the horse's neck again gently and left the stable yard, pausing for a last brief look from the gate.

The evening before they sailed, or rather before the General decided to go aboard the *Duc de Bourgogne* and stay there until the weather made it possible to sail, Robert wrote a letter to Louise:

"So we are leaving at last, or making a move towards leaving. Almost half of April is gone and we should by now be in the middle of the ocean. Idleness has been bad for everyone. I know now that when all this is over I'll go back to Ireland as we said we would.

"Our cousin Arthur Dillon is good to me. He seems a fine man but he went absent without leave last week and came back with two sword wounds. The General had him arrested. He had gone off to Nantes to fight a duel, if you please. Now he's confined to his inn, lying in bed recovering. No need to tell this to Countess de Rothe. No one knows who he fought with nor why but they think it was about a woman. He is to come with us, though a great many will have to be left behind under the command of Count Wittgenstein, because there are not enough ships. I would have been one of those only for our General. He said I was to come with him because he liked the way I took care of his horses. I think he is the greatest general in the world. We hope to sail early tomorrow when the tide is right. André de Lacy has just arrived and is coming with us, so you see I'm in good company."

He finished off the letter quickly then, overcome with a dreadful sense of the reality of what he was doing. It was as if the whole world stopped spinning for half a minute and everything held its position, every object clearly seen, every pain piercingly felt. Mount Brien with its gardens and lawns, and its boats on the river, the call of jackdaws in the high, singing pines, the evening call of the corncrake that had seemed so mysteriously to move from place to place through the wide meadows, the gentle country people that he had known all his life—was he ever to see all these again? He laid his head on his arms and wept, something he had not done at all when he was leaving Ireland.

PART
THREE

12

At the last moment Count André de Lacy went to Brest where he joined the naval escort that accompanied the transports. Far from being indifferent to Teresa's behavior, he felt insulted and humiliated. At Brest he asked the first soldiers he met to direct him to the inn where his cousin Colonel Arthur Dillon was staying, and was shown up to his room. Arthur was still confined to the hotel, technically under arrest. He was lying on his back in an armchair, his feet on a stool, and he was wearing several bandages. His handsome face looked bored and sulky. André stopped on the threshold saying:

"What on earth has happened to you? Has the war started already?"

Arthur lifted his long legs off the stool, clearly pleased to have a visitor.

"Haven't you heard? I was winged in a duel—nothing important. I hear that things have been happening to you too. I've got young Robert Brien here. He said you sent him."

"Did he give you any details?"

"Not too many but my wife filled in some more. She came with Lucy to see me at Amiens. She's gone back to Brussels to her sister but soon she'll be in Paris. Lucy is very pleased at the idea of having Louise Brien for company."

"How is your wife?"

"She's never in good health, not since the last child died. I hope her mother will take care of her. I wish I were not leaving them but there's nothing else I can do. Are you coming with me? Just say the word, if you want to."

"I'd like to come. You'll need people who speak English. And I've been to America before."

"It's not certain that we're going to America. Some say it's the colonies. I'll see that you come, though half of France seems to want to be with us. De Lauzun will do it for me."

He hesitated for a moment, as if he were changing his mind about what he was about to say, then said: "You've only just come back."

"I had meant to stay," André said, "but now I want to get out as soon as possible."

"These things happen every day."

"Yes. I had looked forward to settling down. I had all sorts of plans for the estate near Bordeaux. Perhaps it's the hand of God. I'll be better employed in America, if that's where we're going. Cousin Charles Lally is farming in Connecticut now. He's supposed to be organizing for us but I haven't heard lately how he's doing. You know what I'm talking about?"

"Ireland? Poor old Ireland!"

"Would you help us?"

Arthur laughed uneasily.

"Soldiering and politics don't mix."

"La Fayette is mixing them."

"It nearly lost him his head, haring off to America, joining a foreign army without leave. You think the Americans will help Ireland? It seems to me they have enough trouble at home."

"They've promised to help when they've settled their own affairs. I've just been recruiting in Ireland for Washington's army, on that promise."

"It sounds a long way off."

"It is, but it will come." André walked over to the window and looked down on the town square. "What a time of year to bring thousands of men into a village this size! The streets are a solid mass of mud. I thought my horse would stick."

"I ought to be glad not to be out there, I suppose, but Papa Rochambeau is furious."

Dillon grinned cheerfully and André felt his own spirits rise. Arthur and he were almost the same age and had known each other since childhood. They had always been friends, though they differed so much in temperament. Arthur could never be gloomy for long. He loved fine clothes and good company. Even his gambling debts, which would have driven anyone else to suicide, seemed not to trouble him much. They kept him on the move, however. Having run through his patrimony and with no income but the regiment he had inherited from his grandfather, he was always setting off to some war or other, as he was doing now. In spite of his affection for him, André felt no inclination to confide his real feelings about Teresa to him.

The truth was rather different from the impression he had deliberately given to Robert. André had fallen in love with her when she was fourteen, and had immediately proposed for her to her mother, and been rejected. Charlotte had made no secret of the fact that she was hoping for something better, and had listened impatiently to his account of his property, the estate near Bordeaux, the small house in Paris, the estate in Ireland which was in the hands of a cousin who had officially turned Protestant but who would be obliged in conscience to return it when the laws against Catholics were repealed. He had hoped that Charlotte would change her mind in time, and he had been overjoyed when her brother had spontaneously suggested that he should try again. Then, even after he was accepted he delayed coming home. Charlotte's slighting remarks about the condition of his property kept coming back to his mind, and he began to suspect that she had only agreed to the marriage because no one else had offered, and that she might change her mind later.

During that interval he had often wondered what were Teresa's feelings towards him, whether she felt the magnetism that drew him so strongly to her, or whether she had been consulted at all. He thought it unlikely that Charlotte would have arranged it without her leave.

He had kissed her once, idly, during one of those long, tedious games that were played at parties, and had been startled to find that her lips clung expertly to his. His whole body responded, and it was the beginning of his love for her. Surely she remembered that occasion. At first he had been shocked, but then he reflected that she was a child, just turning into a woman, and her triumphant little smile suggested that she had discovered her own possibilities.

It was clear now that she had learned the game all too well. She had been able to satisfy both Robert who was as innocent as a kitten and Philip de Loudun who was a certified roué. André wanted desperately to believe that her dreadful mother was the only villain but he knew that Teresa's cooperation must have been willing. She could easily have fled back to her convent when the plan was suggested, but she had done nothing of the sort. He had to conclude that she had a liking for a certain kind of excitement. He couldn't bear to think of what were her plans for herself.

Finding himself on the same ship with Robert was an unpleasant surprise. He asked, and was told at once, that the General had taken a fancy to the boy. André feared that there would be all kinds of unwelcome confidences but he soon found that Robert had no inclination towards anything of the kind. In fact he seemed to have put the whole incident behind him and deliberately to speak of anything but what had brought them together. Just before the ships sailed André asked him:

"Now that you're in the French army, do you mean to spend the rest of your life in France?"

"It looks as if I may never get back at all."

"Of course you will. This will blow over. De Loudun is a well-known brawler. He'll land in the Bastille one of these days, if he's not careful."

"I can't afford to look too far ahead."

"Do you want to go back to Ireland?"

"That's what I would do if I had a choice."

"Soon there will be an independent Parliament, like the American Congress."

"A revolution?"

"It may not be violent at all. But if it doesn't come peacefully there will be a rising."

"A new Parliament won't change anything for the Catholics It will be a Protestant Parliament, you may be sure."

"No thinking Protestant wants to perpetuate those old laws."

"Show me a thinking Protestant. When we were in Derrynane, there was a young widow, Eileen O'Connell, whose husband was Arthur O'Leary. He had been shot by the soldiers on the orders of a man who coveted his horse. That old law is still in force. That's only seven years ago, they told us. The horse beat every animal on the course in some race or other, and this man was able to get the army out after the owner because he was a Catholic."

"But O'Leary did race the horse."

"Only because he had forgotten the laws. He was a Colonel in the Austrian army, come back only a few years. That's Ireland. The widow made a lament for him, and everyone in Derrynane seemed to know it by heart. Even in Mount Brien we take care to keep our best horses out of sight. The very day before I left home, I heard the country people talking about fighting."

"Well, perhaps it will come to that. But if it does, there will be Protestants and Catholics side by side. You'll meet plenty of thinking Irish Protestants in Paris when you get back."

"You think I'll get back?"

"Of course."

Suddenly he had a look of Louise, the same intelligent, friendly look with a certain sharpness in it, that André had begun to think of as typical of her. Abruptly he asked:

"Are you and your sister twins?"

"Heavens, no! She's three years younger than me. She's only sixteen."

Then André regretted that he had mentioned her because Robert was instantly plunged into gloom.

Those who were on the flagship with the General knew their luck. It was a splendid line-of-battle ship, of eighty guns, not at all overcrowded. The General's son, the Vicomte de Rochambeau, Mr. Blanchard, the commissary, Mr. Robin, the chaplain, and Admiral de Ternay made excellent company. Moreover they were all gourmets which meant that the food was superb. Rochambeau's affection for his old friend de Ternay reduced the grumbles at their extravagance which would otherwise have spoiled many a delightful meal. The officers took turns in sitting at the Admiral's table, waited on by their own servants. Long before they sailed, a pleasant routine had been set up and even Beau Dillon was back in favor, though Rochambeau growled at him wordlessly from time to time. He never revealed the cause of his duel, and he had made sure to use a second who was not on the expedition.

The thirty-six transports were the first to leave, the men delighted that something was happening at last, though they had had a miserable time of it boarding. Their wooden sabots sank like stones, and the mud seized them by the ankles and threatened to pull them under. As they sailed out of the harbor their cheers were carried back to the town on the light breeze. Early next morning the twelve ships of the naval escort followed them, but at the mouth of the harbor the wind changed. A black coldness settled around them and there was a sharp edge on the wind that had been so sweet the day before. To everyone's disgust, the Admiral signaled that they were to turn back and anchor in the roadstead. Late in the afternoon, there came the transports back again, running before the storm.

For nineteen days they lay, the men never allowed to go ashore, all the ships straining at their anchor chains. They were too far out to be able to see the town clearly but it was easy to imagine the English spies with their telescopes, counting sails and making notes at their ease. The only comfort was the knowledge that they also were hampered by the weather and had no hope of sending messages to England until the storm died down.

At last, on the second of May, they were able to leave the harbor but choppy seas and head winds made their progress painfully slow. When they were a week out, another storm blew up, and now there was no harbor near enough to be a refuge. André was amused at Robert's remark, that this was much better than the journey from Ireland in January, when the O'Connells' little ship was the only one that had the courage to go to sea at all. He asked:

"What did you think of the O'Connells?"

"Exactly what Louise did. They're too comfortable to be any use. They'll never change anything."

"If they want to change things, they'll do it in their own way. They're great talkers, and they're not afraid of anyone. We need a few good talkers in Ireland, the kind they have in Paris. How much did you see of Paris?"

"Mighty little. I never even got to Versailles."

Hove-to in mid-ocean they rode out the storm and saw that many of the small ships were in danger of being blown to pieces. Whenever the thick mist of spray cleared a little, shattered spars could be seen floating on the wild water but every reckoning from the *Duc de Bourgogne* showed every ship still there. They could see the sailors hanging like spiders from the ships, repairing the damage as well as they could. After ten days the storm eased and a good wind blew them southward before it. The small ships battled along surprisingly well, considering that they were only coasters, and the navy ships accommodated their pace to them so that the whole fleet stayed together. But gradually the wind died down, until in the first days of June they found themselves washing helplessly to and fro, somewhere near the Azores, on a sea as smooth as a pan of milk.

It was a beautiful scene, pale-blue satin water reflecting a pale-blue sky, with here and there the tiniest ripple or flaw to show that the ocean was not entirely asleep. Every evening the colors changed to pale green and yellow, then to a short, highly colored sunset, and at last to a sky alive with stars and a crescent moon.

Admiral de Ternay and General Rochambeau walked the deck together for exercise as usual, back and forth, back and forth, as isolated as wild beasts in a zoo. As the days went on the tension rose unbearably. André saw how his fellow officers watched their two superiors first with awe, then with fear and finally with hostility. On the morning of the third of June, the General sent for André and said casually:

"Count, you may summon a conference of officers, one from each ship—no, all the Commanders, and two senior officers from each."

"Now?"

"You think we should wait longer?"

Rochambeau's mouth was pressed into a beak and he cocked his head alertly on one side, rolling his eyes anxiously, as if he were uncertain what to do. Then he drew a deep breath through his nose and his eyes opened wide with amusement—his favorite amusement of teasing his officers. André said:

"I'll go to some of the ships myself."

"Yes, that looks well. You do that."

André had himself rowed first to the *Comtesse de Noailles*, which was the nearest. He was hailed on board as if he brought water to men dying of thirst.

"What's going on? What in hell are they doing over there?"

The officers were overjoyed at the news that there was going to be a conference at last. Baron Von Closen was so excited that he implored André to take him along to the other ships, saying when they were settled in the stern of the longboat:

"I'll go out of my mind if something doesn't happen soon. We should have been somewhere long before now. I had no idea the world was so big. Where are we going? Does anyone know?"

"I think we'll hear it at the conference."

"Thank God! You're lucky to be on the *Bourgogne*. We're bored to death on ours. And speaking of God, you should hear our Captain praying night and morning. That's a circus. He has one hymn that he loves:" And the Baron burst into song, to the delight of the men at the oars:

" '*Je mets mon confiance,*
Vierge, en votre secours,
Et quand ma dernière heure
Viendra, guidez mon sort.'

He beats it out like a dirge, and the men are supposed to be perfectly respectful. If he happens to see some sailor who's not attending properly, he lets out a string of oaths that would raise your hair. The sailors seem full of life but our men are in a bad state already. They won't make much of an army if this goes on. That sabot we're on is awful. One moment we're swallowed up by the sea, the next climbing to the tip of a wave, then down again. And the noise! My God, the noise! That's something I never expected—sails cracking like whips, timbers creaking as if the whole bucket were falling apart—dry land for me from now on, I can tell you."

André was helpless with laughter.

"Are you going to stay in America, then?"

Instantly Von Closen said:

"So it is America?"

"I think it must be. No harm in saying so now."

"What's all the secrecy about? Does the General think someone will get back to Europe with the news from here? If he did, he'd deserve his luck."

"If it's America," André said, "we'll get a royal welcome. When I was there last Washington had his back to the wall."

Von Closen said:

"Our men won't be much use in their present condition. We have six hundred, and forty-six officers. No wonder the men are dying like flies. They feed like horses, from mangers, biscuit and wine for breakfast, salt meat at noon, soup and sauerkraut in the evening. You never saw such a revolting mess. We brought lemons and sugar but that's officers' rations. I'm sorry for the men. Half of them have the scurvy. The smell is so awful, I can't bear to go down into the hold any more. There should be fresh vegetables but how can you feed five thousand in the wilderness? The sailors do better—they seem to have a gift for survival. They fish, and they catch flying fish these days and cook them in braziers on the deck. That's allowed, I believe, but only for the sailors, not for our men. They eat seaweed too, they say it's as good as cabbage for warding off the scurvy. Only for that they would all die, I swear. You're well fixed on the *Bourgogne*. You should try twenty-four hours on our bucket."

He chattered on while they went to the *Conquerant* and the *Surveillante* and finally to the *Provence*, where de Lauzun was in command. He had the regimental band on board and as he left in the ship's longboat with his own men, he gave orders for a concert to start. As all the longboats approached the *Duc de Bourgogne*, marches and polkas and mazurkas crackled through the warm air and cheers went up from all the ships.

The conference was in Rochambeau's cabin, all the men somehow squeezing inside and pressing themselves in the doorway so as not to miss a word. The heat was intense. Arthur Dillon was already sitting with the General and he made room for André on the bench so that the three of them were facing the other officers. There was barely room on the little table for André's notebook. Rochambeau had a pile of papers in front of him, neatly arranged, which he kept patting closer into place until there was complete silence. Then he looked around at the officers with his slow, opaque gaze and said softly:

"Gentlemen, thank you for coming."

No one even smiled.

"I have here before me the instructions of the King on the conduct of our expedition, and exact instructions too on where we are to proceed. This is not news to me though I have only this morning opened the box containing the documents. Long before we left France I had many meetings with the King. We are on our way to America to help her in her great struggle for independence."

Near the door a high boyish voice shouted:

"Bravo!"

One or two others echoed him feebly and then went silent. The old man peered towards the door and said:

"Bravo, indeed. It is a privilege, and this time there must be no mistakes. The whole outcome, success or failure, will depend on our officers. This magnificent destiny is yours. I envy you your youth." A rasping note came into his voice. "But I do not envy you your inexperience. Any one of you, in the next few months, could be responsible for destroying the efforts of years and delaying, perhaps even making it quite impossible for this great nation ever to achieve its freedom. I should not like to be that man."

He paused for a full minute, gazing blankly around, his expressionless eyes falling on one face after another. After what seemed an aeon, he went on again in that soft voice towards which everyone had to strain:

"General de Washington is our General, mine and yours."

This set up a murmur which lasted barely five seconds. "You are right, gentlemen. This is the most important part of my instructions. The Marquis de La Fayette is our source of information, not only from the military point of view but also from the point of view of our relations with our allies. We must never lose sight of the purpose of this expedition. We are not coming to conquer, but to aid. We are not coming to free a nation which has done nothing to free itself. We are coming to help strike the last blow for freedom for a nation which has almost achieved that freedom by its own efforts. We must realize that the Americans are a dour, backward people. Their way of life is hard and cold. They have none of the ordinary comforts of life as we know them. When we reach America, all of our men will have to be encamped. You will be billeted in the towns, and you must exercise the greatest care not to anger the natives with excessive cheerfulness. This is the advice of the Marquis de La Fayette who knows that country well."

He lowered his voice still further and seemed to be talking to himself. "You think this is no subject for the general of a great army. You may learn something, gentlemen: it's far easier to fight in an enemy country than in a so-called friendly one. To the Americans we will be a great foreign army wandering about, eating up food that they need, requisitioning horses and fodder, above all lording it over them as if it were a disgraceful thing that they had to call in outside help. If it were an enemy country, we could take what we need. Here we must make sure to pay for everything and to ask only fair prices for the things we have brought for sale. All of this will be your responsibility, as important as directing your men in the field.

"There is one other thing. Never forget that General de Washington is a great man and a great general. The Marquis de La Fayette told the King that he has seen the Americans fight professional soldiers from Hesse and from England as bravely and as honorably as if they were the army of France. Remember, we are auxiliaries to that American army and happy to be so. By the time we reach America the Marquis will already have brought news of our coming to Boston, and also of the naval squadron from the West Indies which is on its way, commanded by Count de Grasse."

Again he paused, gazing gloomily from face to face, his expression changing gradually to one of irritation and then to contempt. Suddenly he burst out into a low roar that sent a shudder of terror through the room: "Courtiers, fops, schoolboys—that's what half of you are! Our skins, yours and mine, will depend on the other half. I don't intend to lose my skin if I can help it."

He dropped the papers that he had been clutching and put his head in his hands, and André could have sworn he heard the sound of grinding teeth. Colonel Dillon stood up saying:

"That's all, gentlemen, I think. You may go back to your ships."

Still the General did not raise his head, and it was only when the cabin was almost emptied that he looked up suddenly and alertly, then fixed his mouth in a tight line and watched while the last officer squeezed quickly through the narrow doorway.

The inspiration generated by the so-called conference had begun to seep away when two days later the lookout on the *Duc de Bourgogne* yelled that he saw a squadron of six ships coming from the east. Instantly flags began to wave, signals flew from ship to ship and the *Duc de Bourgogne* began to hum with life like a beehive when a mouse comes near. André was astonished and delighted at the change that came over all the bored young faces. It would be a battle, a real sea battle at last, the very thing they had hoped for—they were not to sail tamely to America without firing a shot after all.

For a while it looked as if they were going to have their wish. The Admiral rallied his seven ships of the line and then brought them boldly out to face the enemy. The squadron moved fast before the wind, while the English ships veered in a great arc to come around, their giant wings dipping and rising as they tacked into position. The first shots came from them and were answered smartly by the French. Suddenly the air was darkened and sour with the smell of burnt powder. Then one of the English ships moved away from the others and came within reach of the French line. The gunners jumped up and down with excitement like leashed dogs that have spotted a rabbit. Flags waved wildly and the chase began, all seven French ships pursuing the single English one which now tried desperately to make her escape. Cheering broke out from all the French ships when it seemed certain that they would capture the enemy. They could see the desperate faces of the sailors, full of mixed terror and determination, as they drew closer and closer.

But more signaling from the Admiral's bridge forced all the French ships to lessen sail and drop back to accompany the *Provence*, which was not able to keep up with the rest. The English were now bearing up before the wind and had obviously seen their advantage. They began to try a wide maneuver to cut off the *Provence* but de Ternay retaliated by threatening their separated ship. It was like a vast game of chess, André thought, not in the least like a battle on land, when it was almost impossible to know what was happening anywhere other than in one's immediate vicinity.

The single English ship was now on her way back to her own squadron, while the French poured useless broadsides after her. The fever of excitement on the *Duc de Bourgogne* was at its hottest. The two squadrons were firing away at each other. Belowdecks, where the guns were, the smoke was so thick that the gunners could not be distinguished at all. All the shots were falling short. The seven French battleships were far ahead of the little merchantmen, which were hove-to in a pathetic huddle like a herd of frightened cows, as they waited for the battle to finish. A splendid orange-colored sunset had begun to shade into red. Then, suddenly, there came de Ternay charging down from the bridge, stumping into the cabin, leaving his first officer to see that his instructions were carried out. They were to abandon the battle, the glorious battle, and continue on their way. No one groaned, no one made a single gesture of rebellion, but all the furious young faces showed clearly what was in their minds. General Rochambeau, who had stood with de Ternay throughout the battle, watched them now, almost seeming to hope that one of them would express his indignation. No one did, and at last he said quietly:

"God has sent us a wind, gentlemen. Let us use it to do what we set out to do, not to play games."

Even after he disappeared into his cabin no one dared to say what was in the minds of all of them, but later that evening there were low-voiced grumbles all over the ship, barely above a whisper:

"No one will get rich on this voyage, that's certain. The General is too old to fight—he has seen it all and he doesn't care a hang for us. He doesn't care for the honor of France either. Even when six ships fall into our hands he does nothing. This is a dreary expedition and no mistake."

On June 18 they became more cheerful, when a single English corsair rambled out of the early morning mist and sailed into the arms of the *Surveillante*. She was captured before there was time to ask leave of the Admiral and everyone who had been disappointed gloated over the restoration of a tiny scrap of French honor. While his ship was being unloaded of its stores, the English Captain was rowed over to the *Duc de Bourgogne* and entertained at dinner in Chevalier de Ternay's cabin with Rochambeau and several other officers. The Captain had bad news, confirmed by newspapers which he brought from his ship. Charleston had surrendered and the English were back in possession there with a garrison of five thousand men under Lord Cornwallis. The rest of the English troops that had taken part in the siege had been brought back to New York, with General Clinton who had commanded them at Charleston. This increased the New York garrison to fourteen thousand. The Captain said that he was one of a squadron commanded by Admiral Graves, that he had lost his way several days before and that by this time the Admiral would almost certainly have joined Admiral Arbuthnot at New York. He thought that the English squadron with which the French had almost done battle was returning to Jamaica, having conducted a convoy to Bermuda.

From that day onward, a more realistic anxiety replaced the former mood of optimism. As they approached the American coast, fogs slowed the ships down to three knots and the melancholy sound of drums and rockets echoed against the wall of damp air. Conferences were constantly summoned in the Admiral's cabin, four or five officers at most, while the instructions for landing were repeatedly discussed and considered. The uncertainty of what awaited them meant that a hundred speculations had to be made and a hundred plans devised to meet every possible contingency. The most urgent and most obvious requirement was to avoid sailing into a port which the English had reoccupied since the last news had come. The English fleet was in complete control of the coast, but not of all the ports. Only a little bad luck would force them into a full-scale sea battle. Over and over again Rochambeau said:

"We must be the superior at sea—otherwise we may as well turn now and go home."

Exasperated, de Ternay said at last:

"Very well, sir, you may do so at once. We are not superior. A child can see that. Do you call this a navy? We'll fight—we'll fight for our lives if we have to, but I was told to transport an army to America and that's exactly what I'm doing."

He was soothed with difficulty and the conference continued. The army was to be landed in Rhode Island, which the English had evacuated when they decided to concentrate on the defense of New York. Several French officers who were serving with General Washington were to come to Block Island, off Narragansett Bay and wait for them, signaling to tell if it was safe to bring in the ships. If the American flag went up, it would mean that the English were back and that the ships were to sheer off. If it was the French flag, it would be safe to enter. If no flag was seen the whole squadron with its convoy was to sail for Boston Harbor and await instructions. The words of reconnaissance at Rhode Island were to be "Saint Louis and Philadelphia." If the convoy were driven south by contrary winds it was to go to the capes of Virginia. A French officer was supposed to be stationed at Cape Henry to wait for them. Here the password was "Marie and

Boston," and the same flags were to be shown, but General Washington might then decide to keep the squadron there instead of sending them north again to Rhode Island.

In the event, little of this elaborate planning proved useful. On the evening of July 9, when they had been sixty-nine days at sea, a small, squat coaster was sighted and soon came close enough to be hailed. When it was alongside the *Duc de Bourgogne*, the Admiral himself came to speak to the Captain, who looked up curiously from the bridge of his vessel at the strangers. André was called to interpret.

"Where are we?"

"No Man's Island." The man laughed, as if he had appreciated the oddity of the name for the first time. "Martha's Vineyard is over there, if the mist would let you see it."

"Where are you going now?"

"Home to the Island—Rhode Island, that is."

"Are the English back?"

"No, sir, neither sight nor light of them, and no loss."

"Can you send us a pilot?"

"Surely. Where will you be?"

"Here."

"Very well."

On his own account André asked:

"What is your name?"

"John Sullivan, sir, a good Irishman, and I'm glad to give you a hearty welcome to these parts, if I'm guessing rightly why you're here."

"I'm Irish myself."

"French—Irish?"

"Yes."

"You're welcome anyway."

When they had gone, the whole squadron hove to and anchored for the night. Two pilots came at noon the next day but it was evening before they saw the mainland clearly and then, as if to play a final trick on them, a heavy fog rose from the sea and enclosed them completely. After several hours it lifted, and at last they were able to make out the flag of France, flapping heavily in a light wind, on a flagpole at the point. This time the ships of war led the way, nosing into Newport Bay on a calm sea.

No one had the heart to speak. It was like a fleet of dead men, a ghost fleet, André thought, perhaps haunted by the hundreds who had died on the voyage, their bodies slipped out through the portholes in the darkness of the night so as not to discourage those who were left. Ghostly figures came up from the depths of the ships all around them, haggard, skinny faces looked without belief or interest at the country for which they had suffered so long and so much, and scarcely anyone was able to raise his eyes to look at the flag that had brought them there. Then, once more, a heavy, dripping fog covered land and sea.

13

Rochambeau included André in the party that went ashore. The Vicomte de Rochambeau and the Marquis de Laval, who had both been deadly seasick throughout most of the long journey, were the first into the longboat. Next came several aides and then Arthur Dillon, looking splendid in his uniform with a red plume that matched the red lapels of his coat. His ruffled white shirt gleamed with starch, a miracle after such a voyage, and his servant stood by watching him, stiff with pride, like a groom watching a favorite horse.

André handed the General down the ladder. His uniform looked as if he had been wearing it for a week. His small size was exaggerated by his limp, which had worsened during the voyage. Four sailors rowed, taking one of the long oars each. The fog that hung above the water filled their lungs unpleasantly. Close to the harbor they could see several deserted fishing boats, quite motionless on the still water, and beyond that the roofs of the town. There was no sound except the soft dip of the oars and the occasional breaking of the sea on the shore. When he looked back, André saw that the warships had become wraiths, barely visible through the fog. Rochambeau kept his eyes fixed on the mainland, his body hunched forward as if to urge the boat on.

At the landing, their voices echoed oddly against the stone steps. Arthur was the first ashore, offering a hand to Rochambeau, who looked around him, swaying slightly for balance after the long weeks at sea. Not a soul was to be seen. The General said quietly:

"Saint Louis and Philadelphia! I wonder if this is the new

world at all. Where are all the people? The Captain of that little ship yesterday must have told them we have arrived."

André said:

"Perhaps he was afraid, sir. We gave him no instructions."

"Well, there must be someone here. Let's go and find them."

He marched forward, while the rest of the boatload was still scrambling ashore. André hurried to catch up with him and Rochambeau said in a low voice:

"It will be very important to keep up the men's spirits, Count. This is a strange reception. There must be no criticism of anyone. Criticism only destroys, it never builds. Your English is good?"

"As good as my French."

"Stay close to me, then. I've never bothered with languages. I should have learned German and English, very useful languages, but there never was time. Latin, yes, I know Latin, but who in this benighted country is going to speak to me in Latin?"

"I have met some well-educated people."

"I remember now that you have been here before. Count Dillon told me about you. Splendid. You will be useful. Anyone who knows English and who knows the country, these must stay with me."

As they came into the town, one or two people could be seen here and there in the dim, smoky light. Several times they saw curtains lifted aside and were aware of timorous faces gazing at them for a moment before the lace was dropped again. But the French flag had been flown. Someone had seen to it. Where was the town council, the Governor, where were the chief citizens of this dismal village?

In what seemed to be the main square Rochambeau stopped and said to those who had been able to keep up with him:

"Gentlemen, this welcome is a soldier's dream. The other way is to be welcomed with cannon fire. That looks like an hotel. See if they have rooms."

The hotel was empty because of the war, the landlord said, and he asked suspiciously whether they had money to pay. Rochambeau gestured to one of his aides, who came forward with a genial smile and spread a fistful of gold coins on the counter. The landlord quickly offered some plain, clean rooms and André asked if they could have dinner for the whole party, first taking him aside and explaining who his guests were.

"I might have known by your fancy clothes," the man said. "You'll get a welcome, all right. Can I send the boy for a few people who'll be mighty glad to see you?"

"Please do."

A boy of ten or twelve had been darting around in the shadows of the hall since their arrival. He skipped out like a bird, his whole body twitching with excitement.

Long before dinner could be served, five grim-faced, middle-aged men filed into the dining room where the French party was waiting and stood gazing silently from one officer to another as if they distrusted the whole French nation. Rochambeau watched them first with irritation, then with pity, and at last said to André:

"For God's sake get them to say something. Ask them where Governor Greene is. Tell them we must see him at once."

"He's in Providence, sir," one of the men said in answer to this, addressing Rochambeau directly.

"Ask him if they can send a message."

The same man said:

"Surely. I think I know where to find him."

Another said:

"I'll go myself. What should I tell him?"

"That the French have landed with five thousand soldiers and at least double that number is on the way. You can say we have orders to succor the American army in every possible way, with troops and money and especially with professional soldiers. This is what we have come for. There is nothing to fear. The King of France is the friend of General de Washington and his army. We know what you have suffered. That is over now. Failure must teach us all how to succeed. Tomorrow we'll begin to land our army and take care of the sick, and make arrangements for barracking our men. All of these things will be attended to. Soon everyone will be able to sleep in peace."

As André translated this, the dour faces began to look more welcoming and one or two of the tight mouths actually relaxed into smiles. Then the first man said:

"It's true, things have been cruel here. We've had four years of war, you might say, and our city and the whole countryside

around is ruined by it. The English forage parties seized everything and stole a lot for themselves beside. We're a little afraid
that the French may do the same, and that's the truth."

"Nothing of the sort will happen," Rochambeau said energet-
ically, when this was translated for him. "We're here to give,
not to steal."

"Very well, very well. It was a disappointment to us when the
last Admiral that came from France turned out not to be able
for the English. But I'll make a personal remark, sir." He still
spoke directly to Rochambeau, quite unconcerned that he
would not be understood. "You're a very different proposition
from the last one. He seemed to think that if you make a good
show you'll win the battle. We didn't go for him, sir. It will be
different with you."

André translated:

"He says that you inspire more confidence than Admiral
d'Estaing."

Rochambeau bowed politely. When the men had gone away
he said gloomily:

"Tomorrow, then, we disembark the army and see how many
of them are fit for work."

While he was speaking they heard the landlord's voice in the
hall shouting:

"Yes, yes, of course they're here. Didn't I send you a message?
Why do you think I'm lit up?"

The door was flung open and several officers in worn, drab
uniforms came quickly into the room. They stopped and gazed
in astonishment at the French, glittering like peacocks, then the
senior officer came forward and said to Rochambeau:

"Colonel de Corny, sir. We met in Paris two years ago."

"Yes, of course. Tell him I'm glad to see him. Tell him I
thought we had come to the wrong country. Tell him it's good
to see an army uniform."

"We should have been here to meet you. We've waited so
long. I've just gotten back from Providence, only an hour ago,
these men too. We were arranging about billets and about the
hospital for your men. Right on the doorstep here we met Mr.
Varney and Mr. Willetts and a few others."

"Come and sit with us," Rochambeau said. "You're in good
time."

Dinner appeared just then, a watery soup and some old, boiled chickens. De Corny and his aides sat at the table while they were eating and gave an account of their preparations in Providence. Everything was going smoothly, they said. Rochambeau asked instantly:

"Is the hospital ready, then? That's the most important. Two thirds of my men are down with scurvy."

"Yes, yes, all ready. We had great trouble with that. It's the college building and it had just been given back. We used the college for our soldiers while the English were in Newport. They didn't want to see it go again without a struggle but General Greene and Dr. Craick worked it in the end. For the present the rest of the men will be housed in tents."

"There will be no complaints about that," Rochambeau said. "Dry land of any kind will please them very well."

"And I have a message from General Heath. He's been waiting in Narragansett Bay for you for several days but his ship is becalmed. He'll be here in a day or two. This has been filthy weather, nothing but fog and mist. That's how you managed to slip ashore without being seen."

"I hope we'll be the last to manage that. What are the billets like?"

Every possible building would be made available for the troops before winter began, de Corny said, but they would have to be put in order gradually.

At three o'clock the next morning the work of disembarking the men and stores began, and continued during daylight hours unremittingly, for twelve days. When Major-General Heath arrived, he was able to send in five thousand militiamen from Massachusetts and Rhode Island to speed up the work. The Americans were astonished at the cheerfulness of the French, who sang and whistled about their work as if they were enjoying it. Mr. Blanchard, the Commissary, bought apples and fresh vegetables for the French at once and within a few days they had changed completely from the miserable wretches who had crawled ashore.

First to be unloaded were the brass cannon of all sizes, from four- to forty-eight pounders. Rochambeau had batteries erected for these, flanked by outworks and protected by trenches at every point where the enemy was likely to land. He had the lines that the British army had left behind repaired and put into use. The sick soldiers were sent off to the hospital in Providence, loaded on oxcarts, a melancholy procession, but the remainder worked well, thankful as the General had said to be on dry land and alive. Their tents were in beautiful farmland on a rise overlooking the town. Every day Mr. Blanchard sent off some officers to make contracts for food, and they reported the astonishment of the farmers at being told they would be paid for it. Firewood was very had to find, as the English had cut down every piece of suitable timber on the whole island. Forage parties went far afield for that, and in a few days it began to roll in on oxcarts. Workshops were set up, a saddlery and harness shop, a shoemaker's, a tailor's, a foundry, a farrier's, and their tools and materials were installed. A ruined building in the town became the bakery.

For the first two days the people of Newport watched the busy Frenchmen suspiciously but on the evening of the second day a hurried meeting of the town council decided that there should be a celebration. Every householder was instructed to put candles in the windows to show a welcome to the liberators. Anyone who couldn't afford candles was to get them at the expense of the town. Governor Greene came over from Providence that day and went about everywhere with Rochambeau, requisitioning billets for the officers and making arrangements with the owners of houses to take them in. In the evening the church bells rang and a few fireworks were let off but there was not much heart in it. The day after that, the Marquis de La Fayette arrived.

He came galloping into the square with a troop of servants and soldiers, bringing with him an air of festivity and confidence. He was dressed in the blue, white and gold uniform of an American major-general, with a black and white cockade, the new symbol of the alliance between France and America. A little crowd of officers came out of the hotel at the sound of hooves and the Marquis called out cheerfully:

"The General! Tell him I'm here!"

"So I see, my boy, so I see."

La Fayette leaped to the ground and came running forward to take Rochambeau's hands, saying:

"Forgive me—I didn't see you among the others."

"I was at the back. I'm often at the back. You look very splendid. Where is General de Washington? Is he coming?"

"He sends his greetings and a hearty welcome. It's too far for him to come."

"Too far? I've come rather a long way myself."

"General Washington appreciates that. He said I'm to give you a full account of how the war is going and to make plans for the next part of it."

"So you're the Commander-in-Chief, then?"

"No, no. I just speak for the General."

"Well, well, I do my own speaking, but I'm old-fashioned. Come inside. We'll all go in."

They had hardly seated themselves at the long table in the dining room which was their temporary office when La Fayette began:

"The best, the most urgent thing now is to attack New York. General Washington wants this above all things. It's absolutely necessary now. Nothing else will do."

Rochambeau sat back in his chair as if he were being physically attacked.

"But we haven't got the numbers. We had to leave half of our troops behind. We have no support from the sea. If we had thirty-five fighting ships it could be done, but with what we have now it's quite impossible."

"It's not impossible. It can't be impossible. Now is the time to attack. I know this country. General Washington agrees." He gazed in a frenzy of impatience at Rochambeau, who gazed back calmly, a look of secret amusement in his eyes that his regular officers recognized very well. "Now is the time to attack," La Fayette repeated. "New York is the last English stronghold. If we can drive them out of there the whole continent is ours. We don't need the navy. It's not worth while waiting for it. Those ships may never come."

Rochambeau said:

"We must wait, we must wait. They will come. I've been promised a second detachment, ten thousand men and twenty ships, with guns enough to drive off the English navy while we go to work on land. The infantry can't do it alone."

"The French infantry is invincible! The French army is the best in the world!"

"No doubt, my boy, no doubt, but the French army is not all here."

"General Washington agrees with me, the time has come to strike hard, in the right place."

"Monsieur de Washington would agree with me if he were here, that the right place is the weakest place, not the strongest. We will strike New York eventually, but not yet."

"The effect would be tremendous. The people are dispirited. They're tired of the war. They need something spectacular to raise their spirits."

"Your beautiful uniform will do that, and so will ours. We've heard conflicting reports on the morale of the people. Our consul in Boston says they're ready to make peace at any price. Our Minister-Plenipotentiary in Philadelphia says the opposite, that they're ready to fight on till victory. Which are we to believe?"

"The Minister," La Fayette said quickly. "It's true that people are troubled by rumors that there's a stalemate but they'll fight at the first sign of good leadership. American money is worth nothing now, and prices have gone up as well, even if they had gold to pay. Food is scarce, clothes too. Shoes that used to cost half a dollar cost six now—that kind of thing one hears. And the *Royal Gazette* published a story that the French will entrench themselves here and never go home, and force Catholicism on the good Protestants of America. But you'll see, the people have plenty of courage still and they don't believe everything they hear. They need a victory, General. That's what they need more than anything."

"One must plan carefully for a victory. A defeat would do no good to the people's morale. I must meet General de Washington as soon as possible. You tell him that."

"He speaks no French. He has given me his thoughts and I'm instructed to pass them on to you."

At your age, my boy, you couldn't possibly have the thoughts of a general. Don't be offended. I must meet him as soon as possible. Now tell me the condition of the American army."

"They're short of everything, clothes, guns, food—they always have enough cattle but never enough bread. They haven't been paid for months. But they have courage, as I told you, and they're fighting for their homes." La Fayette seemed not to notice that Rochambeau was teasing him, or he was too excited to care. "The numbers go up and down. It's hardly an army at all, in our sense. The militiamen leave their farms and fight well, when they know they're needed. Then they go home again and get on with their work. They won't travel far from home, so you have to keep on raising new armies everywhere you go. It's not such a bad system in some ways—it saves a lot on transport. General Washington was hoping to have twenty thousand Frenchmen."

"So was I," Rochambeau said dryly. "I fought hard to get them, I can tell you. In the end I had to take what I could get. We must make do with them as well as we can. Good news for the General is that we've brought plenty of French money and there's more to come. We need a bigger army at once—eight hundred of our land forces are sick, about fifteen hundred in the fleet. It's always like this when we transport them overseas. By now Admiral Clinton must surely know we're here."

La Fayette gazed sadly, accusingly at Rochambeau.

"It's always the same, never enough men, never in time."

"It's the way of the world. Clinton may strike at any time. Can you support us?"

"I wish we could strike him first."

When La Fayette had gone Rochambeau said patiently:

"Such enthusiasm. Well, one is only young once."

The threatened attack seemed imminent a few days later. The General, with Admiral de Ternay and Governor Greene, was inspecting the fortifications when a courier came in to say that twelve English line-of-battle ships were harassing the French squadron anchored in the bay. De Ternay had himself rowed back at once to his ship, while de Lauzun and André accompanied the General and the Governor to the slight rise above the main camp, from which they could see the whole bay.

Though the sky was clear, a strong northeast wind kept the surface of the sea ruffled to an opaque indigo, blurred into gray by the spray that flew continually over it. Farther out, this spray became a sea mist which gave a ghostly, unreal look to the line of English ships, hove-to a mile away. The French battleships had formed a solid line as close to shore as they dared to come, and in their shelter the transports were anchored, their longboats still plying endlessly to and fro with supplies. They were being unloaded and the contents packed on handcarts by soldiers waiting on the shore, and then wheeled up to the stores that had been requisitioned in the town. Rochambeau said:

"What a pretty sight it is!" He gazed around at the whole panorama as if they had come up here for a pleasant stroll, then he gestured towards the ships with his elbow. "We can wait. Set watches here and keep an eye on them. What's happening in New York is more important. I want to see every messenger the moment he arrives."

One came before nightfall. Admiral Graves had been delayed by bad weather and then by stopping a ship full of cargo for the French East India Company. He couldn't resist her and actually towed her back to New York. Like the French, his men were sick when they landed and had to be given a week to recover. Best of all was that Sir Henry Clinton and Admiral Arbuthnot were quarreling between themselves. The English ships that were off the coast of Rhode Island now were helpless without their land troops, and in spite of Clinton's appeals, Arbuthnot refused to send them.

At dawn next morning another courier arrived, his clothes thick with dust from his ride and his face barely visible through a coating of sweat-streaked grime. Clinton had got his way, and had actually embarked six thousand men at Throgs Neck when he was told that an army of fifteen thousand was on the march for New York. It was only La Fayette's dream army but word of it had reached New York in quick time. Instantly Clinton abandoned his operation and turned back, to land his troops on Long Island. By now they were probably all ashore.

The English ships waited only a day longer before they sailed away and then it seemed that the French were going to be left forever in peaceful possession of most of the eastern coast of America. The General sent the militiamen home to bring in the harvest.

André moved to a room on the second floor of a plain white wooden house on a street corner, which had been given to Rochambeau as his headquarters. As the weeks went on the General became more and more irascible, and more impatient for the arrival of the new transports from France. Still he was never idle for a moment. He supervised the housing and the discipline of his troops, attending parades and reviews as if he were at home in France. He read and answered dispatches and devised new codes. He received visitors and gave dinner parties, wearing his best uniform, and went to dinners given by his officers and by the people of Newport. Always he had the air of someone listening for a distant voice, and sometimes he seemed not to remember in whose house he was or why he was there. He had an assembly hall built in the garden of the house where he was billeted, so that the officers would have a place for their balls and card games, and he encouraged them to go on long rides through the countryside and to make friends with people who would invite them to their houses. If they were not fighting, he said, they had better have some other exercise.

Still the one man he wanted to meet, General Washington, never came, only sending that boy, La Fayette, as Rochambeau called him, with messages repeating his wish for an attack on New York. Rochambeau replied with one patient letter after another, saying that he was not strong enough. Slowly he dictated:

"General Clinton expects us to attack New York because we lost in Savannah. We are not concerned with revenge, only with victory. I believe that one should never oblige the enemy by doing what is expected. By doing the unexpected we double our strength. At this moment the time is not ripe for victory but it will come."

Every letter finished in the same way:

"Above all, my dear General, I wish for us to have a meeting as soon as possible. In fifteen minutes of conversation we should reach an understanding that could not be achieved in a hundred letters."

It was the second week of September before he got his wish. Washington was free at last and they were to meet at Hartford. He would ride from Preakness in New Jersey in two days, and Rochambeau might do the same from Rhode Island. The meeting place was the house of Colonel Jeremiah Wadsworth, the day, September twentieth.

"Wadsworth, Wadsworth—what a name!" Rochambeau said. "Now thanks be to the good God, we can begin to make plans."

14

An advance party left Newport two days before Rochambeau and Admiral de Ternay set out, to arrange for their lodgings on the way and to see to their quarters in Hartford. André left a few days early so as to stop and visit his cousin Charles Lally, whose farm was twenty miles east of Hartford. The afternoon before he left, he was invited at the last moment to dine with the Duc de Lauzun at Mrs. Hunter's house, where he was billeted. There were to be twenty guests including Mrs. Hunter and her three daughters and de Lauzun seemed quite unconcerned that this number was about double what the little drawing room could hold. When André arrived he found that most of the guests were already there. De Lauzun came over at once to greet him.

"My dear fellow, I'm glad you were able to come." In a low voice he went on quickly: "For God's sake go and talk to that old man in the corner. He's boring everyone to death. Most of us only understand half of what he's saying, a lot of nasty things about our army and our country, and none of us except de Ségur knows enough English to answer him. He won't be bothered. He just laughs."

He pushed André towards the far corner of the room where in spite of the crowd a space had cleared around a small man in black, who was discoursing in a high, querulous tone to no one in particular. He had evidently noticed that his audience was disappearing, for he immediately addressed himself to André, fixing his pale-blue eyes on him as if this conversation were of the greatest importance to the two of them. With his neat black suit and white hair tied back with a black ribbon, he reminded André of a black-backed gull. He had the same sharp, round eye too, and a tight, beak-like mouth which gave him an entirely gratuitous air of wisdom. Seeing that André was prepared to take on the task of listening to him, the nearest officers moved even farther away.

"So you see, my dear sir, the mistake was in not having full information before the attack on Spring Hill. Simeon Dean, your servant, sir." He gave a little dipping bow. "Now, why did Admiral d'Estaing not have that information? Do not answer, sir. I know the answer. I speak in this way to make my point more strongly. He didn't have that information because he didn't take time to get it. Why didn't he take time? Because the French are always in a hurry. They come here and stay a little while, then they hurry home again. They spend as little time here as they possibly can and lose hundreds of men in every campaign. I've told them many a time that all of that could be saved by just taking a little longer."

"It's not easy to get an army here at all," André said mildly.

"Aha! You admit it! You admit it! And when they come, they are never enough. I know that d'Estaing was wounded at that battle but what use is that when he didn't win? Those are not honorable wounds."

"What do you suppose are honorable wounds, sir?"

"Wounds received during a victory, of course." Dean seemed surprised at the question. "Wounds received during a defeat only add to the disgrace. But I must admit, sir, that France is the only country that has come to our aid at all, and she is the only country that can save us now. You may tell that to your General. You have my leave. And you may tell him too that this inactivity is a disaster, a disaster. Something must be done at once, at once."

"I think our General would agree with you."

He became aware that he was about to be rescued by a young woman who was hovering near them. He turned quickly saying:

"Miss Lawton, Mr. Dean is telling me about honorable wounds."

She said seriously:

"There are no honorable wounds and thee knows it, Mr. Dean. All war is wrong."

He flared at her:

"How can a war against injustice be wrong? Do you think this country should stay forever enslaved to England, just because the first settlers were English? Should we pay taxes to a country and a King that does nothing for us?"

"Our duty is to the King, sir, whether or not he knows his duty to us."

"Which king? Which king? Why not the King of Timbuctu? Answer me that if you can!"

She answered quite calmly:

"We should never interfere in other people's business except to reconcile them and prevent bloodshed."

"This is our own business, miss. We are not interfering, we are protecting ourselves from oppression."

"Then the French are interfering."

"By your reckoning they are, and we all bless them for it. If no one interferes in our business, we'll be slaves forever. Would you think that a good thing?"

"Certainly, if it's what God has ordained. Then we must submit."

"Do you approve of slavery?" André asked curiously.

"No, sir, I do not. But I can see that to answer a heavy blow with a heavier one does no good at all. The enemy answers with a still heavier one and so it goes on."

"The people of Newport buy and sell slaves on the Guinea trade."

"It's a disgusting trade. One can't sell a man."

Now that she had joined them, the escaping audience began to come back. She seemed quite unaware of their admiration. Like all the Quaker girls she had taken trouble to make herself as unattractive as possible, with a plain white muslin dress and a white linen cap that covered all of her hair, except for a wisp of fair curl at the ears. Her pale, fair face was exactly as nature made it. Remembering Versailles and the gaudy company there, André had a momentary vision of how it would be to introduce her to them. Count de Ségur edged closer, his round, alert, dog-like eyes fixed on her face as he said:

"Miss Polly, my King has ordained that I come here and fight your enemies for you. Do you think I should have refused?"

"I have no enemies, sir," Miss Lawton said in her soft voice, while all the young men listened with half-closed eyes as if they were listening to music. "The King has ordered thee to do something unjust, inhuman, against the law of God. Thee should obey thy God and disobey thy King. God preserves, the King destroys."

"Delightful!"

She looked de Ségur over calmly, no sign of disapproval in her large gray eyes.

The room had filled up intolerably and now the major-domo called from the doorway that dinner was ready. The Duc de Lauzun offered his arm to Miss Lawton and led her to the dining room, where two long tables were laid. The officers' personal servants were already standing behind their masters' chairs and others were waiting at the sideboard where there were huge silver dishes with roast meat and vegetables. On another table there was wine in silver buckets, each with de Lauzun's crest, and a rack of glasses. When everyone was seated, Simeon Dean intoned a long grace and the meal began. As the daylight faded, the soft light of the candles grew brighter and shone in calm pools on the white cloths, glowing warmly on the polished silver and glass. De Lauzun became hilarious, urging everyone to fill their glasses and drink toasts to General Washington and General Heath, then to freedom for all nations under the sun.

"To Ireland!" he said, lifting his glass towards André.

Simeon Dean proposed a toast to the health of the King of France and afterwards to General Rochambeau and Admiral de Ternay, apparently undeterred by his disapproval of the French conduct of the war.

Soon afterwards De Lauzun announced that there would be dancing at the assembly hall in an hour, to the music of the regimental band. André walked home through the darkening streets in a strange mood of excitement. That girl who spoke out against war and slavery, in such company as he had just left, had brought back the scene in Derrynane when Louise had denounced the whole tribe of the O'Connells. A slightly acid breath of autumn flowers came to him from some garden and he stopped to sniff it. What if Countess de Rothe arranged a marriage for her while he was away? As if he were addressing someone else, he said to himself: "So that's how it is! She has been in your mind all along. You could have her yourself." The idea was delightfully simple. The behavior of Polly Lawton had cleared his head, though he would no more have wished to marry her than to sleep with a marble statue.

Why should he wait? His engagement to Teresa, long broken off, now seemed never to have been real at all. In his room at the Vernon house, André sat at the table, chose a new quill pen and wrote a letter to Countess de Rothe offering his hand to Louise and describing his financial condition in the most business-like terms. Then he went to look for Robert.

He found him in the card room at the assembly hall, next to the dance hall. The music and the rhythmic pounding of feet quickened his pulse so that he felt a strong wish to join the dancers. Robert was playing cards with three other young Irish officers, Charlie Kilmaine, Séamus O'Moran and Tommy Morgan. They were all tapping their feet in time to the music and looked rather warm, as if they had recently come in there to rest. André had not seen Robert for several days, since he had been put in charge of the section of the camp that was farthest from the town.

Robert was so completely at ease and so concentrated on his cards that he didn't notice André's entrance for a moment or two. Then he turned suddenly and said cheerfully:

"André! How delightful! Are you going to join us?"

"No, thank you," André said, smiling. "I'm off to the country in the morning. I brought a letter that I want sent to France."

The others had politely stopped their play and were holding their cards loosely in their hands. Kilmaine groaned in mock agony, saying:

"I've sent a dozen letters to France and haven't had a single answer. My father promised to write every week. Perhaps France has sunk into the sea."

Robert said:

"If it has, we'll be able to stay here. We'll marry Indian girls and farm the land out in the middle of nowhere."

"You'll probably get a wagon-load of letters all together," Morgan said.

André stood holding the letter, hesitating whether or not to tell Robert what was in it. After a moment he said:

"Can we have a word together?"

"Of course."

Robert stood up at once and they walked through the assembly hall behind the dancers, then out into the garden. Night had fallen and the air was full of the endless choruses of tree crickets and frogs. The sky was blazing with stars. Robert drew a long breath and said in ecstasy:

"What a beautiful night—what a beautiful country!" He laughed uneasily. "I'd never have believed I could enjoy life again so soon. There's something magic in the air here. I've almost forgotten France."

"You have very good company."

"You like them? I think they're the finest people in the world. Charlie's father is a doctor in Charente but Séamus and Tommy came out from Ireland, like me. They both went to the Irish College. Funny how Father Burke insisted on my going to the Sorbonne. He said I'd make a great scholar and I believed him. I think now that I've had a narrow escape. I love army life. I've learned more in the last three months than in my whole life until now. Colonel Dillon is very good to me—he treats me like a young brother. He talked to me several times about home, and about Louise, so that I don't feel so bad now about leaving her."

"Would you trust her to me?"

"Is that what's in your letter?" There was no mistaking the spontaneous delight in his voice. "You want to marry Louise?"

"Yes. I've written to Countess de Rothe. I'll write to your father too. He knows all about me."

"He will be pleased. Before we left he told me he was worried about her marriage, but he trusted Cousin Charlotte to arrange something. This is the best possible news."

"Do you think she will accept me?"

"I'll write to her at once and tell her she must."

Alarmed, André said:

"Is that a good idea? Will she listen to you?"

"Of course she will. Louise and I have always had to stand up for each other. You'll see when you come to Mount Brien. André, you'll be my brother. Let's celebrate!"

"Wait, wait! She hasn't accepted me yet. She may not like the idea at all."

"Of course she will."

"I wouldn't want her to accept me out of duty. Be sure to say that in your letter."

"Oh, all right," Robert said. "I'll tell her she's free to refuse you but that it would be very foolish. Look, you're grinning from ear to ear. You know she won't refuse. How could she?"

"Very well," André said laughing, "but there will be no celebration until her answer comes."

As they walked back to the assembly hall together, the band was beginning to play a quadrille. Robert said:

"Do you think we'll be here for a long time? We have just got orders to move the troops into winter quarters in a month. My men are working on the houses already. How long do you think it will be before we go into action?"

"We must wait for the second division and some kind of support from the navy. Otherwise we can't move. Just enjoy the rest while you can. There won't be much of it when we get going."

"I envy you—you were with d'Estaing, weren't you?"

"Not all the time."

"I wish I had been but I wouldn't have been old enough. Well, so long as we can stay in Newport we won't complain. You know my servant, Martin Jordan? He has got a new fancy since we came here, running with the officers when we go riding. The French servants grumble furiously about it but Martin was a footman at home and he's well in practice. He asks nothing better than to go racing after us when we range the country. He says he's seeing the world. He doesn't mind at all when the Americans laugh at the sight of a half-dressed man trotting along behind the horses." At the door, he stopped André with a hesitant hand on his arm. "I really am very pleased about Louise. I wish there could be something like that for me."

"Give it time," André said uneasily. "You're young enough."

"That's what people always say—you're young, you'll get over it. I don't believe I'll ever get over Teresa."

All his recent gaiety had vanished and his voice had become monotonous with pain. André said gently:

"I didn't mean to be callous. There are other girls. I know you'll fall in love again."

"I'll never find another girl like Teresa. She's one in a million. I'm sure you think I'm a fool but I know that's the truth."

"You can't spend the rest of your life regretting her."

"One doesn't have a choice. You're extra lucky, that's all."

15

The ride to Hartford should have taken two full days but by not resting at all André and his servant were able to reach the Lally farm on the late afternoon of the second day. They followed the stagecoach road through forests and farmland. André knew the way, having been there two years before. It was an old Dutch house with white-painted shingles. A wide, deep porch had been added along the whole length of the front. A green lawn sloped down to a small river, where two canoes were moored. André loved the air of prosperity and peaceful order that enveloped the whole farm. Now in the autumn the apple trees in the orchard beside the house were loaded with fruit whose color was beginning to be matched by the changing leaves of the trees that bordered the property. Red clover had been sown under the trees and was almost ready for cutting. Lally's cattle grazed on the broad pastures behind the house, tended by a small black boy. As they rode up they noticed that delicious smells were coming from the cookhouse, where other black children clustered hopefully around the door.

Hearing the horses' hooves, one of the house slaves came to the door. André knew her from his last visit and called out in English:

"Hello, there, Agnes! Is the master at home?"

"Mr. Andrew, sir, you're welcome! He's gone across to the inn for news but he'll be right back. Mistress is here—come in, come in!"

He found Pauline in the long drawing room that looked out on the lawn and the river. She was a pretty, kitten-faced woman who should always have looked contented but instead she had an expression of perpetual anxiety. Two children were with her, a boy and a girl of about seven and eight years. She was sitting at a table by the window with them while she supervised their lessons. She jumped up at once when she heard André at the door and came forward, and he saw that she was once more pregnant. He took her hands, asking after the health of the family.

"The baby died," she said instantly, "the boy that was just born when you were here last."

"I'm sorry."

"He lived two months only. He was never well. They say the babies should be born in the spring, like lambs, but how can one arrange that?"

Her sour tone was unpleasant. Wanting to change it he said:

"The place looks more beautiful than ever."

"It's not a healthy place."

Even while she led him to a chair she kept glancing anxiously at her children. They went on peacefully with their work, writing in little books, probably copying something she had set them.

"Charles went across the river to get some news," she said. "The stage must be in by now. Did you meet it?"

"We passed it two or three miles back. May I stay with you a day or two? I have only one man with me."

"Of course. We have so few visitors, it's a pleasure to have someone come." The kitten face took on an almost vicious look and she leaned forward to say in a half whisper: "Before he comes back, I want to tell you, I'm trying to get him to move back to France." She was squeezing her hands painfully around and around, the knuckles going white with the strength of it. "We can't stay here. I won't die here. The children never see anyone. They learn that awful language the nigras speak, a drawl—aaw, aaw, aaw—I can't even make the sound. American women are used to it. They don't expect anything better. They think that if you bring up two children out of six you're doing well. They say it's the will of God and they submit. If I hear 'I submit' once more I'll go out of my mind. I will not submit, I will not. Charles doesn't seem to care. He has his farming and his horses and they keep him busy and happy. You'd think he had never been in a civilized drawing room. I want to go home."

She looked down at her hands and stopped twisting them, as if it had to be done with a deliberate effort of will, then lifted her head to send him a look of appeal as she went on: "Please take my side. Charles will listen to you."

"Don't you feel any attachment to this place? Have you put down no roots? When you came first, you were full of courage."

"I believed in Charles. I just followed him. So you're going to take his side."

"Pauline, for God's sake, there will be no sides. Of course I'll help you to put your point of view. I just want to be clear about what it is."

She accepted this and gave him an appraising look, as if she were judging his capacity as a defender. He asked:

"How long have you been here? Five years?"

"Six. Emilie was just born. Of course I wanted to come. It was new and exciting and I wanted to see the world. I suppose I had courage then, for a while. I thought that things would improve but they haven't. The house is nice, not like a French house but it's all right." She looked around the pretty room vaguely, as if she scarcely saw it. "But if all my children die here—" She stopped, as if she were herself shocked at what she was saying, as if by expressing her misfortune she had made it more true. Then she looked at him suddenly. "That's what is wrong, and it will never be better. This child I'm carrying now, it will be born, I'll see it for a few weeks or a few months, perhaps even a year or two. Then it will die. That's how it always is."

Appalled, André asked:

"How many babies have died, Pauline?"

"Four. They always have a name for the sickness, usually a malignant fever. That's what they call it. It comes from the river. That's what they say but I think it's in the air. I can't bear it any longer. We were seven children in our family and only one died. I know how to keep children healthy in a good country but I can't do anything here. Why should we suffer all this? What is the use of being alive and giving life, when we only bring them into the world to die? It's like murder. And I'll tell you something I know, André, that I can't tell Charles. They know it. The babies know they're going to die, and they're frightened, and angry because I can't help them, and they look at me so sadly in their last moments—"

She bent her head to hide her tears, wiping her eyes absent-mindedly with the piece of embroidery that lay beside her on the sofa, then realizing what she was doing and pushing it away from her violently. "I'm losing my senses. It's like walking through a big swamp where you know there are venomous snakes, or where you could be sucked down at any moment, and though you could save yourself by going back, you just keep stupidly going on as if there were no danger. I've argued with Charles until there is no more to be said. Please, André, please talk to him."

"Of course. I'll try. You still have the estate in Languedoc?"

"No. That was sold, and the château too, to buy this place and to bring us here. We had to buy slaves and farm animals when we came. Charles says that if we can stay on even a few years longer, things will improve, but in a few years I'll be too old to have children and these will all be dead—"

She had raised her voice to an almost hysterical pitch and the children were watching and listening from the end of the room. André said:

"Hush, Pauline. Don't let them hear you say such things."

She said bitterly:

"What does it matter? They have probably got used to it. Now they hardly look at the new babies at all. They know it's not worth while getting fond of them. They prefer their dolls."

When Charles came in a few minutes later she had recovered herself and gave no sign of her recent distress. Neither did the children reveal that they had been upset but André had seen their heads together as if they were whispering comfort to each other.

Though they were not very closely related, Charles and André had a family resemblance in their coloring and in a characteristic droop of the eyelids, which, as well as their great height, made them look like brothers. After they had embraced Charles said:

"I went across to the inn for any news that might come with the stage, and here was the best news bringer of all, right in my house. How are things in Providence?"

"I've come from Newport."

"Still in Newport! We had your letter a few weeks ago. We thought that by now you would be marching on New York."

"We're still waiting for reinforcements."

While they talked about the war, Pauline sat silently watching them, turning from one to the other as if she didn't understand their language. Absorbed in their conversation, Charles seemed not to notice this but later, when they were alone after dinner and she had gone away with the children, it was he who began to speak of her, saying:

"Did Pauline tell you she wants to go back to France?"

"Yes, because of the children. Would you not think of doing that, for her? I can see how much work you have done here and how much care and thought you have put into it, but what use is that if you have no children at the end of it?"

"I have two. You saw them. They're quite healthy."

"Don't be offended. It's too serious for that. Do you think I should say nothing of what's on my mind?"

"Of course not. Pauline talks to me endlessly about going back. What can I say to her? She knows my reasons but she doesn't think they balance hers. I know, I feel sure, I can almost smell the terrible things that are going to happen in France. The people get more and more discontented. There will be a huge uprising of some kind and when it happens it will be on a scale we never dreamed of. I don't trust anyone, not even the King and Queen. When I saw what became of our cousin Thomas Lally, after all his life spent in the service of France, to be hauled out to public execution, with that crowd of beasts watching as if it were some sort of show, I knew I could never serve a king who would allow such things to happen."

"It was a different king."

"The people are the same. The intellectuals talk and talk about the age of reason, while behaving like prize fools at the same time. In the end they'll drive some terrible logical force out into the open."

"It could be a good thing for Ireland."

"You never stop thinking about Ireland."

"It's my whole life," André said, surprised. "You know that. In a way I feel as you do, that we should have a place of our own. You promised to find us some more recruits—have you succeeded?"

"One or two. The war here is filling everyone's mind now. If it ever finishes, there will be plenty of recruits for Ireland. If I had married an Irishwoman I suppose my ideas would be the same as yours. It was madness to bring Pauline here. I had no idea she would transplant so badly. She was full of enthusiasm in the beginning." He shifted restlessly, then burst out angrily: "It amazes me that she worries so much about her children. She could drive past an execution in Paris and hear the screams of the victim without turning a hair."

"It's part of life there."

"It will not be part of mine. The people of Paris are barbarians. Ever since the day of Cousin Thomas's execution, fourteen years ago, when you and I were only boys, I have wanted to get out of France. Even if I had had nothing to sell, I would have come here. I might even have gone back to Ireland."

"Would you consider going back there now?"

"That would be another kind of madness, though the climate is healthier. If I were Protestant—are you suggesting I should turn?"

Some do, but now I don't think it would be necessary. You couldn't be elected to Parliament but you probably wouldn't want to be, anyway. Things will change there soon. The King is quite interested now, and Prince de Montbarey too, I knew he would be a good appointment from our point of view. When this war is over they'll send us an army to Ireland."

"More wars, more fighting. You're sure the Americans will win here?"

"If they can hold out long enough. When we came first we were told they were finished, spun out, that they had lost all their spirit but we know now that it's not true. If they had guns they would have men, and the guns are coming."

"Do you trust the King to keep his promise about Ireland?"

"He hasn't promised yet but when he does, I believe he will keep it. After all he is the King."

Charles said with certainty:

"Neither of us will ever have a country, André. I want that to stop in my generation. I don't want any more of those songs about the ghosts of the Irish in France sailing home to Ireland to find a peaceful grave. I have a chance now to settle and have a reasonable life, and my children after me, in a place that we need never feel is not our own."

"Your children?"

"Would they live longer anywhere else?"

"Pauline thinks so. If you want to go back, there is my estate in Saint André. It has its own income from the toll bridge and a few other things. You could live there until you get a place of your own. I'll write to the steward about it. No harm done, even if you never go. The house is old but it's in good repair. Charles! Does it mean so much to you to stay here?"

"I told you, I never want to leave this country. I never want to live in France again. Perhaps things will improve there, as you said, but I don't believe it."

André asked after a moment:

"Do you belong to the Connecticut militia, then?"

"No. Why should I? I don't believe in war. The world will never be habitable until there's an end of all wars."

"A likely possibility!"

"Why not? Once people realize the poverty, the misery, the suffering they cause, they'll give them up. Now they spend more to conquer than the prize is worth. In the end they must realize that victory is as expensive as defeat."

"I don't believe that day will ever come. There would have to be agreement, otherwise the strongest countries would simply ride rough-shod over the others, as Russia can do now, or as England used to do."

"You think England is finished?"

"Not yet, and I'll be sorry when she is. The English are a great nation, very like the French. They like each other. You should see, when I was leaving Paris, everything English was the fashion, horses, dogs, servants, clothes. I was astonished."

"In spite of the war?"

"Perhaps because of it. Charles, I wish you would come back. It's impossible to understand what's going on in France unless you live there. It's very stimulating."

"I don't want to be stimulated in that way. This is my country now," Charles said firmly.

But later he talked about the difficulties of farming in America. The climate was an unrelenting enemy. The ground was covered with snow for months at a time so that all the animals had to be kept in stables. This meant that big flocks of sheep were impossible to keep and wool for clothes was in short supply. There was plenty of linen but for warm clothes one had to depend a great deal on fur. Slaves were getting more and more expensive as the war went on and some even said that when it was over all the slaves would have to be freed, but Charles had several families of children around the place so that he would not be in any difficulty for a while. Each year he learned more and more, and so did Pauline. If her children were healthier, she would be perfectly happy. Then he said:

"Of course I wish I could live in France. In my dreams the scenes are always there, little hills with castles on top and absurd roads leading to them, great, slow rivers that never flood, little towns that have been there for a thousand years, old forests—but I know I'll find it all changed if I have to go back. You said it might be possible to live in Ireland?"

"Yes. When I marry, that's what I'd like to do."

"You marrying! I can't imagine that."

André felt a flash of anger race through him as he said:

"Why not?"

"You're so wrapped up in other things. When we were all fainting over the lovely girls, you were standing by looking amused, as if you thought we were a pack of fools, as indeed we were. But we were young, and so were you, and still you didn't take part. You were so sensible. That's all, really. Of course you will be married. Have you made a choice?"

"Yes, if she will have me. I've just written to Arthur's mother-in-law about her."

"The Countess de Rothe? Surely it's not Arthur's daughter—she's only a child. Or has time passed more quickly than I think?"

"No, no. You're quite right. Lucy is only a child but our cousin Louise Brien is living in that house now. She came out from Ireland in January. She's a beauty, quite unspoiled."

"Fair or dark?"

"Fair, like all the Dillons."

"Why didn't you arrange this before leaving France? It will take a long time for her answer to come."

"There were reasons," André said, not wanting to give details of the unsavory business of Teresa since Charles had never known of his betrothal to her. "This was the only way it could be managed. I'm sure she will accept me. My whole life will be different then. Perhaps I'll take a holiday from politics and be as domesticated as you."

"I'd never have thought to hear you say that. She must be a jewel."

"She is."

Even with Charles, something prevented André from speaking as freely as he wished to do. Charles was looking at him so benevolently, with so much affectionate understanding, that in any case there was no need to say more. Before they went to bed he said:

"André, in spite of what I said, if this child dies I can't keep Pauline here any longer. I know this. Perhaps you had better write to the steward at Saint André, just in case we need a home. Bordeaux should be safer than Paris."

"Safer!"

"I'm probably talking nonsense. You're the one who has the political nose. Yes, I'm sure it's nonsense."

"It is nonsense. Things have changed since you left France. There was never so much good sense as there is at present. Why do you think we're here? Everyone is in sympathy with American ideas, there will be a new approach to everything."

"To the poor people in Paris, and in the villages in the country?"

"Inevitably. Everyone has begun to think in terms of the people. Aristocracy is beginning to look old-fashioned. Soon merit will be the only test of whether a man should get a public office."

"Well, I'll believe it when I see it. Let's not argue so late. As I said, I have no political sense. I don't like kings but I believe in monarchy. I always will. Here in America it's perfect—the King is three thousand miles away."

Charles had arranged with some of the neighboring farmers to have a squirrel hunt the next day and André accompanied them. Throughout the day, while they galloped across the huge countryside after their ridiculous quarry, he found that he couldn't forget last night's conversation. Though he thought Charles's fears were unreal, they left him with a feeling of intense uneasiness. It had never occurred to him before that the fashion for philosophy in Paris could be dangerous. Reform would come slowly but it was inevitable now. It certainly was odd that the King was so anxious to help the republicans of America, apparently not seeing that there was a danger to the monarchy in it, and to himself.

France was unshakable. That was the answer. Pauline said this to him just before he went away, when she found him waiting alone in the hall while Charles sent around the horses. She said in a half-whisper:

"Charles has told me that you offered us the house near Bordeaux. I'm so grateful for it. Once we're back there, everything will be all right again. We need never go to Paris—I'll be happy to stay in the country. It will be enough to be back in France."

"Has he promised to go back, then?"

"Yes, yes, as soon as the baby is born. Oh, André, thank you, thank you for doing this for us!"

It was a complete transformation. Her children came running then and she stood holding them one by either hand as if she were a child herself, the picture of contentment, swinging their hands gently to and fro. Then Charles came in from the stables and a moment later the horses came around to the door, led by André's servant and one of the grooms. As he rode off André looked back and waved to the family, grouped together on the doorstep, an intimate and charming picture of what family life should be.

16

For several months after André came back from Hartford he was completely content. His work went well and the General constantly prasied him for the expert way in which he kept his records in French and English. It was all done automatically, since the whole army was living in a state of unreality. Their fearful passage across the Atlantic seemed not to have been in their own past at all, and their future was so vague that no one could speculate on it. For André, his mind full of thoughts of Louise and his own future domestic happiness, the suspense was pleasant. He was perfectly confident. There was nothing to fear. Putting off the day when he would receive her answer seemed to him a blessing to be enjoyed rather than a painful necessity, almost as if he had engineered that delay himself to enhance his pleasurable anticipation. He knew this was foolish but he could only smile at himself and his fantasy. He spoke to no one of it; it was too childish to be discussed, too private and mysterious to be understood even by himself. He threw himself into the endless work of his position as liaison officer to the General, falling into bed dog tired every night.

Even on easier days he danced until he was exhausted, keeping pace with the young men who seemed indestructible, and who were never done paying formal court to the American girls, the Hunters, the Robinsons, the Lawtons, the Steeles, all of whom seemed to feel it a duty to keep the French officers entertained and busy during their long period of waiting.

One of André's tasks was to deal with the townspeople in connection with the billeting of the officers and of the men whose wives and children had come to join them. Schooled in the army tradition, he had never given much thought to the regular soldiers' comfort, but had considered them almost as valuable and likable animals. Now he found that he was looking at them with a new kind of fellow feeling. The men whose wives had been able to come were the best workmen, and they had a specially contented air, walking home to their lodgings in the evening as if they were in their own villages. These were mostly tradesmen, carpenters, saddlers, blacksmiths, millers, bakers. Special concessions had been made for the transport of their families. André made sure that their stark quarters were made as comfortable and as warm as possible, and he was astonished and pleased at the way the women quickly added little touches to make them look like home—a glass with a few wild flowers, a dish of apples, an embroidered cloth or cushion, all of these apparently conjured out of the air in no time.

The whole camp developed a happy, settled air. Papa Rochambeau was satisfied. He and General Washington had understood each other at once and had concerted their plans, and were to meet again soon. Vicomte de Rochambeau, the General's son, was sent off on a fast frigate to France, with messages urging the need for reinforcements to be sent at once. Complaining loudly, de Lauzun was ordered to winter quarters in Lebanon with his cavalry, including the Dillon regiment, since there would not be enough forage for all the horses in Rhode Island. Robert had to go with them.

When he had gone, André found that he missed him horribly. He had formed a habit of seeking him out every day for a few minutes' conversation. By unspoken consent they avoided talking of Louise. The only packet of letters that came was brought by a merchantman and the letters were dated the day before they sailed from Brest.

Winter set in, with heavy snow, and ice that lay like snow on the ground. Harsh winds, laden with salt, tore and bit at the face. It was a completely new experience for the French. Somehow the oxcarts got through with firewood from the mainland and the soldiers were sent out in relays to cut and stack it. The people of Newport went about as usual, seeming to take no notice of the weather, but André noticed that there seemed to be fewer children now. Then, two weeks before Christmas, Admiral de Ternay died, the General's friend, the one man with whom he was always perfectly at ease. Sure enough, the local doctors called his illness a malignant fever and were quite unable to do anything about it. The General called in the French army doctors, who said they had never seen anything like it in their lives. André remembered poor Pauline and all her dead babies.

That day saw the end of his peace. He knew exactly when the torment began, while he was supervising the arrangements in the Manton house where the Admiral's coffin was to lie in state. It was covered first with black crêpe, then with the flag of the United States. The hat, the sword, the epaulettes and all the other signs of the Chevalier's distinction were laid on top. The guard of honor of sailors from the *Duc de Bourgogne* was lined up at either side, motionless, every uniform correct, every face composed and solemn. André stood to survey them and in one instant had a vision of the body that lay within the coffin. It was the body of Louise. She lay calmly, her lovely face full of peace, her long, slender arms by her sides and her white dress carefully arranged in neat folds. He had seen a girl arranged in her coffin once and he knew how they would do it. But her hands should have been joined. He took a step forward, almost uttering a cry of distress. He saw two of the sailors look at him quickly out of the corners of their eyes, then hold themselves more stiffly than ever. He whispered:

"It's all right. Everything is perfect."

He could not rid himself of the mischievous image. Black curtains completely covered the windows and swallowed up the light of many candles. There was no sound except the shuffle of feet as the people of the town came in to pay their respects. Later in the evening, just before dark, the procession set out for the churchyard, twelve priests walking before the coffin, each carrying a lighted candle.

Panic seized him. They were taking her away. This was lunacy. Sometimes the men went mad, from loneliness for their families, according to the doctors. Was this happening to him? At his age, and for a girl of sixteen? If only Arthur Dillon were here. He had often left his lovely wife behind, and he must have learned by now how to live without her. But Arthur was gone to Lebanon with de Lauzun and there was no one else to whom he could tell his thoughts. He had never experienced anything like this before. He began to pray with the priests: *"De profundis clamavi ad te, Domine. Domine, exaudi vocem meam."* "Out of the depths have I cried to thee, O Lord. Lord hear my prayer. Let thine ears be attentive to the voice of my supplication. If thou, O Lord, shalt mark iniquities, Lord, who shall stand it?" He found that he became calmer but the vision was still there.

Rochambeau wept openly when his old friend was lowered into the grave, to the melancholy sound of trumpets. After the burial, when the bands struck up the traditional lively tunes and the men marched back to their quarters, André felt horror at leaving Louise. The morbidity of this fancy shocked him, and brought him to his senses sufficiently to send him hurrying back to his lodgings.

In this climate, instead of signs of spring February brought worse weather. The Americans were quite dispirited, according to the reports that came in from the French intelligence officers. If help did not come soon, the southern states would capitulate and make a separate peace. Still Rochambeau stumped about overseeing everything, urging the officers and men to keep fit, talking to the common soldiers, addressing them by name, promising that the day of battle was not far off, inventing excuses to keep them busy and cheerful. One of these was the celebration of Washington's birthday with a huge parade, though no one could make out how he had discovered which was the right day. It would not have occurred to anyone but Rochambeau to do such a thing.

"And you can write him a full description of the ceremony," he said to André. "Tell him we wished he had been here for it and that we hope he will come soon. God in heaven, how the hell can we fix anything if he doesn't come? Don't put that in. We'll see if this will fetch him here."

A few weeks later, Washington came. There were more conferences and parades and balls. Then the weather improved, and some of the soldiers could be heard speculating as to whether it would be worth while growing vegetables for the next winter, since it seemed that they were never going to leave Rhode Island at all.

It was the second week of May before news came that the frigate *Concorde* and several others had arrived from France with

Vicomte de Rochambeau, and were in Boston harbor. Alternate agony and joyful anticipation tormented André. He invented a reason to go to the other end of the old camp, to inspect the tent sites in case they might have to be put into use again.

The apple trees were in full flower there, reminding him of the huge orchards at his uncle's house near Rouen, where he used to visit as a boy. Their scent enclosed him when he walked under the trees. The air was heavy with the humming of bees. Pauline was right, after all. There was no country in the world with the essence of France. He would go back there, when all this was over, and he and Louise would live on his other estate at Saintes, where he had scarcely been since his father died. As for Ireland, perhaps it was true that things would improve there now. Nothing could be the same, once the American colonies broke free. The English were tired of this war. The King's brother was publicly urging him to stop it and give the traditional British justice to the American colonists so that they could be friends and allies forever.

In Ireland there need only be a few threats and the rest would follow. If the Americans promised help, and if there were a national parliament instead of that nonsensical sectarian committee, a new age would dawn. Irishmen who had lived in America would come home and lay the foundations for a new way of living. There would be no need for the armed rebellion that was being secretly planned. There would be peace. He had done enough. It was time for other people to take over now. After all, he was a Frenchman.

Charles had no difficulty in deciding this, but Charles did not have the bitter words of a dying father ringing in his ears, as André had: "You'll go back to Ireland. The de Lacys will come into their own again in your time." No one should make a weeping boy of fourteen swear to bring about a revolution. Even now, the whole horror of that scene came back to him, the bitter smell of death, the candle held by his father's sister, as if she wanted to make sure that all the pain was fully lit, his father's sudden vigor, then his gradual falling back on the pillows and his surprisingly tranquil death. These were memories that could not be forced out of his mind, at least not until he was married to Louise. Then they might leave him in peace.

There was not a soul to be seen as he walked back to the town but when he reached the little square it was churning with people. The first dispatches had already arrived and everyone had come out hoping for news. He realized that he should have been on hand in case the General needed him and he pushed his way through the crowd until he reached the door of the Vernon house. They didn't want to let him pass. Elbows were jerked deliberately into his ribs and angry voices said:

"We got here before you. First come, first served. Less of that pushing."

Then a man said:

"It's an officer. Let him in."

They handed him through and he waited to draw his breath in the cool hallway. He could hear voices in the room to the left, where the General had his desk. The room was full when he edged his way in. The General was sitting in his usual chair, looking flushed, as if he were smothering for lack of air in the press of hot bodies. He was saying:

"It's all good, it's all good. We must continue to say this to everyone. Get their courage up again. All the interpreters must get back to work at once. No delays. When Governor Greene comes, tell him we'll need every oxcart on this damned island to bring our stuff to Bristol Ferry. We'll need every small boat too, to get the troops and goods across. Get your men in trim. We have four hundred in Boston, half of them sick, of course. Four hundred! And I've been talking about four thousand. Jesus and Mary, what an army! Money, though, plenty of that. That might bring some of the Americans out of the woods. Someone had better go and tell that mob outside that the news is all good, plenty of good French money, thirty-eight ships on their way—you, de Lacy! Excuse me, Count! They understand your brand of English. Off with you and tell them."

Suddenly André found he was being lifted by a shuffling, laughing gang of officers and carried outside, sitting high on their shoulders, facing the crowd which now went suddenly silent. Waves of excitement rose from them in little groans and cries. All the faces were eagerly watching him. He felt helpless, and that no matter what he managed to say it would be inadequate. He was very uncomfortable, half-hanging, half-sprawling on the shoulders of the others. The man on his right peered up at him, his eyes looking unnaturally large at that strange angle. He said hoarsely:

"The General says to tell them the French army is determined to win the day—"

The man looked agonized. What was he saying? André suddenly yelled at the top of his voice:

"Good news! All good! Help has come! We're off at once! *Vive l'Amérique! Vive la France!*"

It worked. Now they were all cheering and shouting together. That was all they needed—noises. He yelled again:

"Victory! Victory!"

The French troops who were scattered here and there throughout the crowd recognized that word, having its counterpart in their own language, and they began to chant it in unison. André said to the men who were holding him:

"Let me down, for the love of God, before you break my back."

They did, and they all reentered the house, leaving a delighted crowd outside singing and chanting happily as if he had made a long and rousing speech.

In the hallway he found that the other officers were now asking each other when the private letters would be handed out. They had come, they were somewhere in the house already, some thought even lying in the great box that stood by Rochambeau's feet. No one dared to ask for them. Almost everyone had left the room now, except the senior officers. André stayed in the hall with the others.

An hour passed. No one wished to go away. Several times they heard a shrill voice raised, always followed by the bear-like rumble of the General's growling reply. The young officers in the hall were cheerful, quite certain now that there would be some action soon and in the meantime that it was all great fun. André felt old, and he could tell by the way they spoke to him that they felt it too. The crowd in the street was long gone home. Someone opened the door and the damp night air drifted in, heavy with the scent of locust flowers. At that moment Baron de Vioménil came out of the office. He stopped to look at the expectant group, surprised, then said: "Ah, yes, letters. There are some here, not many. More to come, I think. Count, would you like to take them? They're on the desk."

The General was leaning back in his chair, talking very fast and cheerfully with de Ségur and Von Closen.

"Blanchard must come at once. He doesn't like long marches. You can go with him, Count," he said to André as if he had been in the room throughout the conference. "He'll need you at every step. Mills, bakeries, fodder—all the things that keep him awake at nights. Find him, find him now. Bring him back here, yes, the sooner the better."

"Sir, the young men are waiting for their letters."

"Take them, take them. Then find Blanchard at once. I know he's somewhere in the house. Give those to someone else to hand out."

His own letter was on top of the bundle. He didn't recognize the thin curly writing. It could only be Countess de Rothe's. He took the bundle and went outside, slipped his own letter off the top and put it in his pocket, then went to look for Blanchard.

He was not easy to find but at last André discovered that he had gone back to the lodgings that he always used when he stayed in Newport. While the servant went to fetch him, André wrenched open the letter. The heavy seals seemed to cling deliberately. Why had she used so much wax? He pulled out the sheet of thin paper, wrinkling it in the process, so that he had to spend precious time in smoothing it out. Then he went to hold it close to the lamp. As he read, he heard himself give a tiny whimper of pain, like a mouse in the grip of the cat.

"Dear Count de Lacy," wrote Countess de Rothe, "I am sorry that your offer did not come sooner as I believe you would have been a very suitable match for Miss Louise Brien. Unfortunately for you, she was married on December 15. He husband is Count Armand de La Touche, our cousin, not the Count de La Touche who lives near Rouen but one of the older generation who rarely comes to Paris. His first wife was Helen Sheldon. His son was killed in Grenada and he has no male heir. His daughter Helen is married to Count de Blezelle of Montpellier, our cousin, and Count de La Touche has an estate there too. He lives mostly at Angers. It is a good match for a girl with no fortune. I wish you may find another young lady of equal charms without too much delay. Please let me know if I may be useful in this. We hear that the war will soon be over in America. The King and Queen are both in good health and we prosper in France as never before. When you see Arthur Dillon you may tell him that his wife has spasms of grave illness and cannot live long."

This was how she spoke of her own daughter—in the first shock of her news this was what struck him most clearly. The King and Queen are in good health—the war will go well in America. Then full realization came to him. He had lost her. He would never have her now. She was Countess de La Touche. Armand—he had seen that old booby once. How could they do this? How could they bring themselves to do it? It was his own fault. He should have asked for her before leaving France, in spite of Teresa, in spite of everything. He had been too stupid. His vision of her—December 15—that was the day of Admiral de Ternay's funeral. Sickened, he let the letter hang from his hand. Blanchard was bustling into the room.

"So we're to move, are we? I hate long marches. This one will take weeks if I'm any judge. I'm to pull supplies out of the air —Count, what is the matter with you? Are you ill?" His eye went to the drooping letter. "Bad news from home?"

"Yes."

There was no more to be said. Silently they walked back to the Vernon house, where they found the General and the French Colonels poring over maps with the Americans, planning the marches. More Americans came in, decisions were taken about when and where to begin, Blanchard agreed to go with fifty hussars to join de Lauzun in Lebanon, André would go with him. De Custine, Baron de Vioménil and his brother, Rochambeau himself, everyone would have his own cares and responsibilities on which the fate of America depended. There would be no time to think. Sometimes he almost forgot her for a few minutes at a time, while he concentrated on accurately translating the ideas and plans of the French. It was past midnight when one of the Americans gave a deep sigh, laid his head on his arms on the table before him and fell asleep. Rochambeau looked at him dispassionately, then said:

"Tomorrow, then, at six o'clock."

When the General had gone, André was able at last to retreat to his room. He took out the letter and looked at it with loathing, then burned it deliberately in the flame of his candle. While his servant undressed him he stood like a stone, and the man kept glancing at him uneasily as if he thought that at any moment he might have to dodge a blow. When André noticed this he said quietly:

"Go to bed, Pierre. I'll finish myself."

The man scuttled out of the room. He may have been right. What filled André's heart then was pure hatred, hatred of all mankind, which might indeed have led him to some act of violence.

PART
FOUR

17

Louise's first weeks at Countess de Rothe's house were peaceful enough. Though Cousin Charlotte lived only a few doors away, Louise never saw her and she soon realized that the family had been glad of an excuse to drop her. Charlotte had never been sensible, and now that she was widowed her silliness about her financial affairs was a constant irritation and threat to the rest of the cousins. No one wanted to be suddenly asked for a large loan, or to negotiate a dowerless marriage, or to bring an ill-dressed girl into society. Of Charlotte's three daughters Teresa was the only one who was at all presentable, and even she was known to wear the same dress too often and to avoid the fashionable colors, not because of her poverty but to attract attention. Biddy was the source of some of this information, which Louise lapped up as fast as she could get it. She knew she should not listen to gossip from a servant but she could never think of Biddy as anything but a friend and ally, and besides she needed all the help she could get.

Countess de Rothe's rages were a subject for awestruck whispers among the servants, Biddy said. They occurred almost daily when Madame Dillon was at home, and by the time she saw the first one Louise was well prepared for it by the tales she had heard of former scenes. She stored away the information though she scarcely believed in it, the Countess treated her so formally and politely. There were many guests every day at luncheon and at supper, and the Archbishop was always present, introducing her with obvious affection. Unless they went to the opera Louise went to bed early, kissing the Countess and wishing her good night before leaving the room to a gratifying chorus:

"Charming!"

"A little beauty!"

"Delightful manners!"

"One would never take her for a foreigner."

"Like an English girl—a true aristocrat."

The wounds she had suffered at Cousin Charlotte's were gradually healing and she began to be confident of the Countess's love and trust. She had shown the beginnings of it by taking Louise into her house and surely the rest of it would follow naturally.

After the first days the Countess decided that she was to accompany her on her drives and Louise made sure always to be ready on time, perfectly dressed and with her hair arranged by the new manservant who had been given to her. She loved these outings. Spring had come and crowds of people filled the narrow streets as they drove towards the Bois de Boulogne, where the carriage was stopped so that they could get out and walk a little and meet other families who were taking the air. A strong pulse of life and energy flowed through this country, all the colors and scents were stronger, the sun shone brighter, and especially she noticed that the people of all classes seemed more lively and cheerful than the depressed men and women one saw in the streets in Ireland.

Apart from the ridiculousness of comparing Galway with Paris, she knew better than to speak of the horrors of life in Ireland in this company. Everyone was talking philosophy and the rights of man, but she had noticed that as soon as one applied these ideas to real people one met with a blank stare, as if some gross vulgarity had been committed.

Preparations went ahead for the move to the country. A room downstairs was given over to trunks and great armfuls of dresses were packed there. Bedclothes were folded into wicker baskets, and there was a special one to contain boots of all kinds. The date was fixed for the second Tuesday in May, and still there was no sign of Madame Dillon. Then, early in the afternoon of the day before they were to leave, she and her daughter came home.

Louise heard the commotion of their arrival from her room on the third floor. It looked down into the courtyard and the windows were wide open to let in the warm air. From up here she could see the tops of the chestnut trees by the Seine, their new leaves a brilliant green. She heard the big double gates being opened and leaned out of the window to see a strange carriage drive in.

First to climb out was a little fair-haired girl of about ten, followed by a stout woman in an apron who was obviously her nurse. Then came another maid and finally, very slowly and painfully, the last passenger. As her feet touched the ground she leaned against the carriage for support and the horses moved in fright, so that her maid had to catch at her to prevent her from falling. Then she straightened, leaning on the maid's arm, and went towards the steps, the little girl walking close beside her.

Without stopping to think, Louise hurried downstairs. When she reached the first floor, the party was in the hall. Sunshine poured through the open door in a broad stream filled with fine dust from outside, as the servants carried in the trunks. The maids were fussing around Madame Dillon, taking her cloak, leading her to the long bench that stood under the curve of the stairs, making her sit and rest before undertaking the climb to her room. A small whirlwind whizzed past Louise, the Countess flying down to the hall, hissing viciously before she reached the last step:

"So you have come back. At least you're in time, just in time. You could have sent a message. I've been frantic to know what to do. In the end I just went ahead with all the arrangements. Why didn't you write? A letter doesn't take so long."

"I did write, Mama. Didn't you get my letter? I sent it more than a week ago."

"How? How did you send it? By some fool as usual, of course. You can never do the smallest thing properly. Not that it makes much difference. I never depend on you. Why are you sitting there? Do you think a lady should sit in the hall?"

"I'm ill."

The answers were so mild and gentle that they should have softened a heart of stone, but the Countess gave a snort of contempt:

"Ill! You're always ill, yet you can do everything you want to do, everything that pleases you. You can hunt and dance and sing when you want to but you're always too ill to consider what I want."

The women servants had moved aside and were standing quietly at a distance, pretending to be deaf to all this. The men had gone away, closing the door almost completely, so that only a tiny shaving of light came in. Still Louise stood on the stairs, knowing that the Countess had seen her, unwilling to flee and perhaps with some idea that this would be resented, or that she should remain there to do something useful, she knew not what. Lucy, the little girl, was standing beside her mother, looking with intensity at her grandmother, but like the servants with a blank expression. Countess de Rothe raised her voice hysterically, her hands opening and closing with temper:

"Get up. Stand up. Walk upstairs. This is disgraceful. I know your game. You don't want to go to Hautefontaine. You want to stay in Paris and enjoy yourself. Nothing is too devious for you. Get up this instant."

She made a threatening move towards her daughter and Madame Dillon stood up at once and faced her quietly. The Countess said with heavy contempt:

"So you can stand. Now walk."

Still the little girl stayed by her mother, pressed against her skirt, perhaps holding her hand in the shelter of the folds, while they walked together up the stairs. The Countess followed. Louise shrank into the corner of the landing, not knowing what to do or where to look, but Madame Dillon gave her a wry smile, full of kindness, as she passed her by, as if to say: "You'll see plenty of this if you live here." The Countess was silent until they reached the first floor, then said:

"You needn't think you can stay in your room. Dinner is about to be served. Your things are ready. You can wear the same traveling clothes tomorrow."

"Tomorrow?"

Madame Dillon sounded as if she would faint.

"Tomorrow at eight o'clock we go to Hautefontaine."

"Mama, I can't. I'm ill. I told you, I could barely manage to get here. I'm longing to rest and get well. Please let me stay here for a few days. Then I'll follow you, I promise."

It was like a child asking for something it desperately wanted, very strange from a grown woman who was herself the mother of a ten-year-old child. For the first time a piteous note crept into her voice but this seemed only to enrage the Countess more. She said:

"Follow! Do you think I believe that? If you had wanted to rest you should have come a week ago, but you were enjoying yourself too much, you were glad to be away from control. Make up your mind to it. I'll never trust you here. You would have ten gallants in here as soon as my back was turned, disgracing this house, the house of an Archbishop—"

"The house is mine, Mama."

"So you're threatening me! You would think of putting me out on the street! Is that in your mind now? And the Archbishop too, perhaps?"

It was the beginning of a long tirade in which the Countess worked herself into screaming rage, while her daughter cowered against the wall, clutching her child's shoulder, answering not a word. Louise crept down to the hall, driven by an animal instinct to protect herself, but she stayed there, fascinated, until the point where the Countess was pummeling Madame Dillon with her fists, shrieking abuse and accusations at her between sobs of rage. Then Louise could bear it no longer. She fled into the kitchen quarters and up by the back stairs to her own room where she found Biddy sitting, white-faced, in her usual place, pretending to sew at the hem of a dress. Biddy said instantly:

"Lord God, Miss Louise, the devil is on that one. I heard the others talking but I had no idea it could be like this. I wish I was at home, so I do." She gave a stab with her needle and howled with pain as it entered her finger, then said as she sucked it, "It's not that I never saw two women having a set-to before but there's something awful about that lady. It's not right, it's not decent."

"We'll have to put up with it," Louise said flatly. "We have no place to go."

After a while she sent Biddy down to find out what was happening, and waited in a state of horrible suspense until she came back with the news that everything was quite calm and peaceful. Dinner was being served, a little later than usual because of Madame Dillon's arrival, but it was still only three o'clock. Already the Archbishop was waiting and the guests had arrived.

Louise hurriedly finished her dressing and went downstairs.

To her astonishment, there was Madame Dillon, serenely smiling, looking perfectly beautiful and contented, wearing a white embroidered dress with a low-cut bodice and with pearls and ribbons in her hair. How this had been achieved in the short time since her arrival was a miracle. No doubt it was the result of long practice. Throughout the meal and during the long afternoon, while guests came and went, she stood near her mother or moved around the salon speaking to different people as if she were quite at ease. Her ash-blond hair, pale skin and slender figure made her the most elegant woman there, but Louise felt nothing but horror at her condition, as if she were already a skeleton or a ghost. Surely her mother could see how ill she was. But the Countess was absorbed as usual in drawing as much attention as possible to herself. She was the Archbishop's hostess, continually bringing people to speak to him where he sat in his special chair, receiving them with a gracious, detached smile.

Louise could not forget the words that Madame Dillon had used, which had sparked off the final scene: she had said that the house was hers. That remark had been enough to drive her mother into a frenzy. Louise felt surrounded by mysteries and deception. There was no one she could trust, no one to answer her questions. Indeed she hardly knew what it was she wanted to know, and the things that occurred to her seemed indelicate to ask. Two of them predominated. Had Cousin Charlotte really made away with all of her inheritance? To ask this would suggest that she didn't trust the Dillons either. The second question was about her immediate future, whether she could stay at the Hôtel Dillon or whether they were planning to move her somewhere else. If no one brought up either of these subjects, there was nothing for it but to keep silent and wait for the answers to reveal themselves in time.

The diversions of the next morning drove these concerns to the back of her mind. The whole household was up soon after five. By seven, five or six carriages of guests had arrived and were waiting in the street outside the house while their owners came in and drank coffee in the salon. The morning was cool and clear, with no wind, and the birds in the courtyard trees were singing a summer chorus. Madame Dillon did not appear until a few minutes before eight. She looked a little better, though still dreadfully pale, and she kissed her mother good morning as if they had never been anything but the best of friends. Punctually at eight o'clock the house carriages moved out through the gateway, as the Countess had said. Louise was sent to the same carriage which took Lucy and her mother and the Countess, while Biddy went with Lucy's nurse Marguerite and three other maids.

In any other company the journey would have been a pleasure but in this it was pure torture. When they were in the suburbs, Louise leaned back against the cushions. She shot up again as the Countess barked:

"Keep your back straight, miss! A lady doesn't lounge."

Sure enough, all three of the others were as straight as if they were braced with iron bars. Louise had imagined that the rules would be relaxed for so long a journey but she knew better than to make any defense. Lucy sent her a timid smile which gave hopes of friendship and sympathy, and from that moment on Louise determined to spend as much time as possible with this worldly-wise little girl.

Seven hours of travel, with a short stop for luncheon at an inn, brought them in the afternoon to Hautefontaine. The château was an old-fashioned, gray stone house, quite plain, looking down over a long green valley that ended in a gorge and the beginning of the forest of Compiègne. To reach it, the carriages drove through woods and meadows, around the rim of a lake, where they crossed a bridge, then drew up at the foot of a long flight of steps down which servants were already scurrying to help them. Before she could prevent herself, Louise said:

"It's like arriving at Mount Brien!"

Friends of Madame Dillon who had come that morning were waiting to greet her. The Countess was busy with her footman, who was to instruct the coachman to take away her carriage immediately so that the others could come to the steps. Blushing, Louise found that no one had heard her except Lucy, and she seemed to have a policy of not speaking at all in the presence of her elders.

Hautefontaine turned out to be much grander than Mount Brien. There were twenty-five bedrooms for guests and they seemed to be all full, mostly with married women whose husbands were away with the army. There were some older men too, some of them relations by marriage or cousins whom she had already met in Paris. Quickly Louise realized that this was simply Paris in another place. There were the same balls and suppers but now no one went home, so that even in the early morning they lived in an unending whirl of entertainment. Everywhere, at all hours, there were games of cards. When the weather was good there were fishing parties and boating parties and walks or rides to the little summerhouses that were dotted here and there throughout the forest.

The middle of the day was given over to music lessons and rehearsals in an upstairs salon, for an opera that some of the party meant to perform later in the season. Madame Dillon had the principal part and sang her arias over and over in a strong, clear soprano, which made Piccini, the Italian music master, almost faint with joy. Seeing Louise hovering in the background one morning, he made her sing a few notes and then dismissed her with contempt, saying:

"Go and play the harpsichord, little girl. It will match your voice."

This was greeted with a sycophantic giggle by some of the ladies and even by one or two men. Louise was constantly amazed at how these arrogant people longed for a word of commendation from Piccini. From association with them she had picked up some of their reverence for him, and she found now that she was mortified at his condemnation of her voice. She knew she had no talent for music and she had simply obliged him by doing what he asked. He turned to Madame Dillon, his hands joined in a typical gesture of admiration, and said:

"How can a blackbird have a cousin who is a crow?"

This raised another laugh but there were one or two exclamations of pity as Louise ran out of the room in tears. She couldn't bear to be with them another moment. Why had she ever come to this dreadful country, to these human peacocks, these music boxes, these puppets? Could her father have known what he was doing to her in throwing her on their mercy? She ran along the corridor and threw herself on a sofa under a window, full length, shaking with childish sobs, aware that she was in danger of being discovered by the Countess on one of her frequent prowlings about the house but no longer caring what became of her. Dimly she knew that Piccini's offhand rudeness was not the real cause of her tears; it was an accumulation of sorrows that overwhelmed her, and most of all her complete despair of ever being able to escape. Even the memory of André's kind face, which was her daily comfort, now seemed to have faded and gone. Robert's desertion, Cousin Charlotte's betrayal, the constant pinpricks of disapproval, added to the ordinary pain and uncertainty of being young, all now seemed more than she could possibly endure.

She stopped wailing when she heard footsteps hurrying along the corridor from the direction of the stairs. She dragged herself upright, mortified now at the prospect of having to explain herself. Half blinded by tears, she saw with relief that it was old Armand de La Touche. He reminded her a little of her father, though he was older, but in any case she liked him because he was the only one of the old men who hadn't seized and fondled her since she arrived in Hautefontaine. The others were a menace. They seemed quite unaware of their age, their displeasing odor, their spiky hands, their silly popeyes, as they clutched her and squeezed her greedily at every opportunity. With anyone else but Count de La Touche she would have thrown politeness to the winds and fled down the corridor to get away from him. Nothing the old boys liked better than to find a girl in distress. You could almost see their eyes snap with the expression of a weasel the second before it springs on the rabbit. The first time it had happened to Louise she was in a carriage driving by the Luxembourg Gardens, the horses struggling through a huge crowd that was coming away from a public hanging. Louise had caught sight of the victims, a man and a woman, and had given a cry of horror. Instantly, old Count Pasquier, in whose carriage they were traveling to the Opéra, grabbed her around the waist and would not let her go, though Biddy was sitting goggle-eyed on the seat opposite them. He paid no more attention to her than if she were a dog, until Biddy said in her new, peculiar French:

"Sir, if you don't let the young lady go I'll tell the Countess what I saw."

That stopped him, all right, though he was very huffy about it, as if it were he who had the grievance. Remembering this incident, Louise's humor lightened somewhat, and through her wet eyelashes she saw that the old man was standing before her holding a large, rather clean, white handkerchief. She accepted it and dried her eyes, then said:

"I'm sorry. I should have gone to my room." Then, with a sudden lust to tell the truth: "They're such pigs!"

He asked anxiously, "Who?"

"Those—those—*opera singers.*" The tone of her voice made the word sound like an insult. She saw that he knew what she meant. His eyes lit up with a flash of sympathetic understanding, nothing to do with her person so far as she could see. He said:

"Ah, yes. One must learn to know them and then to be one of them. That's what all the ladies have to do. Make no mistake about it, they're very intelligent. One can learn a great deal from them, very necessary things."

"I don't want to be one of them. I hate them, their airs, their philosophy, their ideas on all kinds of things they know nothing about." She clenched her fists with fury, squeezing the damp handkerchief tightly. "Have you heard them talking about discipline in the army? Have you heard those long discussions about whether it would be good for the solders to be beaten with the flat of a sword? Not with a stick—that would be an insult to a Frenchman—but if you beat them with a sword it would be something quite manly. I never heard such nonsense in all my life. They can make a discussion like that last for hours. Music, yes, they know something about music but everything else is play to them."

"You'll never do in Paris with those ideas."

Really he was the kindest of them all. His eyebrows had gone up in a huge arch, making him look like the pictures of Don Quixote, but his eyes were so gentle that one couldn't really laugh at him. She rushed on:

"I don't want to do in Paris. I wish I lived in the country. Surely there is something real there, everyone must be more honest and good, there could never be all this intriguing and lies and—and immorality. It must be—it must be better in the country."

"We're in the country now."

"You don't call this the country? This has nothing to do with the country. It just happens to be far from Paris."

"You are a very thoughtful young lady."

"I have had to think."

Suddenly embarrassed, she bent her head so that her voice was muffled while she continued to clutch the big handkerchief. She had talked too much. If she looked up, she would see the satirical, contemptuous expression which was on every face in this wretched society. One should never show these people the smallest chink in one's defenses. He was quite right when he said they were intelligent. He was one of them himself. But when she forced herself to look up, he had not changed. He was still the same, gentle and kindly and somewhat pathetic because age had slowed him down. She had noticed before that he had an irritating habit of giving a little chirp before he said something he thought profound or important. He did it now, but she was determined not to be impatient with him. She needed to take note of every single person who might possibly be able to help her. This old man would certainly head the list. Her mind began to run ahead to the ways in which he could be useful. After all, he was a cousin and should have some power in the family. He and Father Burke together might be strong enough, if it became necessary, to get her home to Ireland, home to Grand-mère. He could be a refuge. At first she barely took in what he was saying, it so closely matched the ideas that were churning in her head:

"If you like the country, you could come to me. I have a nice place at Angers. It is the country, a country house, smaller than this, about the size of your family house in Ireland. I have never been to Ireland but I remember that your uncle brought a little picture of the house when he came to France. You are right, Hautefontaine is too big. One needs to fill the rooms with guests and then there are too many of them for comfort. In the country we don't have guests."

"Do you live alone, then?"

"No, no. There are my two sisters. They like a quiet life. They never leave the country. They are like you in that."

"But you leave it sometimes?"

"Yes, sometimes, since my wife died, and my daughter is married. It gets lonely. I'd like more company there. Will you come to me?"

"Yes, yes, thank you—"

All at once she felt that she was making a terrible mistake. She was breaking all the rules that the Countess had taught her. It was improper, it was dangerous to have spent so much time alone with a gentleman, however old. She knew those rules. Faintly the sounds of the music came to her from the salon. She stood up, handed him back his handkerchief, which she now realized was the loathsome article that had compromised her in the first place and said clearly:

"Thank you, monsieur. You have been very kind to me. I'm only a silly girl. I'll do better in the future."

He took her hand and held it in his dry grasp, but with an air of respect though he had done it without her leave.

"You can have plenty of time. It's quiet in Angers. You will learn a great many things there."

Then he put his lips down to her hand, tickling her wrist with his prickly mustache, and let her go. She noticed that his pale-blue eyes glistened oddly when he looked up into her face.

With a sense of terror, as if she were being followed by a wild animal, or by a fiend, she walked off down the corridor, wanting to run but now at last knowing that she must keep her dignity. She could feel his eyes on her, though she dared not turn her head even at the end, where the stairs would have made it seem natural. Once out of his sight she fled to her room and lay on her bed, panting, staring at the painted ceiling until it seemed that it would fall on top of her.

Nothing had happened. Then why was she so frightened? They would remember that she was only a child, a foreigner too, one who didn't quite know how to behave in times of stress. But they had all been complimenting her on her accomplishments. They were her cousins, foreigners too in a sense, though they had lived here so long. Perhaps they would make allowances for her. Father Burke—but she had done none of the things he had ordered her to do. Her notebooks were almost blank, all those notebooks in which she was to have worked problems in geometry. And the letters she was to have written in Latin!

She would write to him now, as quickly as possible, and tell him of her terrible danger. But what was it? What could she tell him? Miserably she realized that there was nothing to say, except that she wanted to go home to her grandmother, that she felt surrounded by enemies, that something would have to be done to rescue her before it was too late.

She crawled off the bed and got out her books, spreading

them out on the writing table and looking at them without comprehension. She opened one or two, then realized that at least half a day would be needed in order to retrain her brain to work at all. With determination she sat down and began on Pliny, the calm letter in which he described the ideal life, of carefully balanced reading and conversation and exercise.

At dinnertime she sent Biddy down to say that she could not come, that she had a headache. By five o'clock this was true, and again she lay on her bed and felt pain course through and through her brain while she twisted and writhed helplessly. Biddy brought cold cloths and tried to reduce it, stroking her temples with her gentle fingers, but it was no use. She felt some relief when darkness began to fall and the candles glowed like little suns, each in its own halo. If only André or Robert were here, they would solve everything.

Now and then, when a little remission of the pain let her think, she tried to bring André back as he had so often come to her before, but the attempt only made things worse. Sometimes she imagined that all would still be well, that her stupidity, her independence, her lack of discipline had not been her ruin, but always she quickly realized that she was making no mistake in her prediction of her own fate.

18

She was proved right when the Countess came at last. It must have been at least ten o'clock. The candles had burned quite low. Biddy, exhausted, was sitting at the table with her head in her hands, as if she were reading Pliny. The door opened without ceremony and the fierce little woman was suddenly there, standing by the bed, angry as a wasp, buzzing with temper. Her breath hissed through her teeth between sentences. She seemed not to care about Louise's silence though she asked many questions.

"What have you been doing? Have you taken everything into your own hands? Is this how you return hospitality in your country? Have you learned nothing? Have you opinions of your own? You're making private judgments on all of us. We don't measure up to your standards. We may be cousins but you don't approve of us." It couldn't be true that he had repeated the things she had said, it couldn't be. But he had. "Lies and immorality! Well, miss, you are to be free of it all. He has convinced me. We have had a long discussion. You have accepted him. That will be good enough. It's not how a lady's marriage is made in France but then you don't like our customs."

"Oh, no!"

At this the Countess chose to change her tone, pretending now to be on Louise's side.

"It's good to make your own choice. In our day we never made it. We thought it was so important that we felt we should take advice. Our parents were good enough to be our counselors, failing them, our grandparents. Times have changed.

Young people always know best. My plans for you would not have been any better, perhaps. Probably you never even noticed the gentleman. Perhaps you thought him too young, or too old, or too poor, though he's not as poor as he seems. And then he went to the wars. Perhaps you couldn't wait. Perhaps your blood is too hot."

The Countess seemed to take real pleasure in the misery of Louise's condition, watching her face with curiosity while she spoke, going over to fetch a candle to see her more clearly, ignoring Biddy who was now kneeling on the floor beside Louise, stroking her forehead with her hands as she had done earlier to ease her headache. The Countess said:

"This is May. I have prevailed on him to wait. Ah, you're pleased with that, but it doesn't mean you will get out of it. You have given your promise."

"I have not, I have not!" Louise said wildly, able at last to make some move towards defending herself. "He misunderstood me. He didn't ask me to marry him. If he had, I should have said that he must ask you first. I can't marry him. It's ridiculous."

"I don't find it ridiculous, miss. You have absolutely no money. To find you a husband who would be willing to take you without it would be virtually impossible. You looked to me, perhaps. You may have thought that I would provide for you, or the Archbishop."

"No—no—"

"I'm glad of it." Suddenly she turned on Biddy, plunging towards her with a sharp movement as if she were chasing a cat or a small dog. "Out of the room, you! What are you doing here? Out, out!"

Biddy fled into the adjoining room and shut the door. Countess de Rothe waited until this was done before turning back to Louise, then said, slowly and deliberately:

"You can hope for nothing from me. I have nothing. This house, the Hôtel Dillon in Paris, everything in them too, all belong to my daughter. Both the Archbishop and I are up to our ears in debt. I've lent him money, thousands of francs, and he can never pay it back. He has lent money to Cousin Arthur, my son-in-law, but he'll never see it again unless by a miracle. That shocks you, doesn't it? How do you think we pay for all these balls and parties, all these guests? My daughter pays. We have our incomes also but they're not enough. And there is my granddaughter to think of. She, and not you, is the heiress to all this. If you ever had an idea that you would oust her, you can put it out of your mind."

"No—no—I never had such an idea."

"I believe you. Now you can see that Count de La Touche's offer has come very aptly. I couldn't have kept you here forever. I have launched you into society. That was quite a lot to have done for you. You do see that, don't you? Now you must resign yourself, like every other girl. His first wife was happy enough with him, I believe. He's rich, down there in Angers. He distills his own brandy."

This was said with amazed contempt, and she paused as if to think of the oddity of such behavior before reverting to Louise's problems. "You can consider yourself lucky. He won't trouble you much, once you give him a son, and I'll see to it that you inherit a lot of his property. He must expect to pay something. He has no other heir. His only son was killed in the war in Grenada. His daughter is married near Montpellier. Count de La Touche has a château there too." Then, with the nearest thing to kindness that Louise had ever observed in her, she said: "It's not the end of the world. He's a handsome old man, with good manners for a provincial. After all he is a de La Touche and a cousin, as close to you as I am. You could have done much worse. Try to see it as your chance of freedom. A girl without money, even such a pretty girl as you, can hardly find a husband at all. Now you actually have an offer. I thought you'd never get one. You should be grateful. The way you did it was disgraceful, and I think now that you didn't know what you were doing, but since it's done, accept it."

Louise whispered, "I don't know—I don't know what I'll do."

"You wouldn't try to injure yourself?"

"No." Louise had never thought of such a thing but the notion was interesting. The Countess's momentary uneasiness gave her courage. She said, "That other man—you said there was someone."

"It was nothing, just the beginning of an idea. I hadn't even mentioned it to him. Now it's too late. This will have to do. We'll tell no one, mind, until the very end. I don't want a sensation, nor a scandal. Everything will go on just as usual. Count de La Touche has agreed to this. For a widower of his age it's better. You'll need no presents. He has everything a girl could possibly want." She seemed to see no irony in this statement.

"Can't you see that it's a chance in a lifetime? Have you no sense of responsibility? What about your father? Have you thought of him? Did you expect to be a burden to him again?"

Now the Countess's hands were beginning to twitch as they always did when she was working herself into a fury, and a familiar sharpness returned to her voice.

Louise could bear no more. She forced herself to sit up, then to stand, and found that she was able to think more clearly. She looked directly at the Countess and found that for the first time in her life she was on the point of striking someone. She could not have done it but something may have showed in her eyes because the Countess took a step backward, then said hurriedly:

"You will go on with it. You're not going to try to back out now. It's impossible to change it now. Give me your word that you will go through with it. You have no other choice."

"When?"

She could not bring herself to agree in precise words, but she could see that she had indeed no choice.

"In winter. No one will notice then. It can be here, or in Angers. People won't expect to be invited to the country. Perhaps the Archbishop will agree to marry you."

"Does he know about it?"

"Yes. He sent you his blessing."

She looked around vaguely, almost as if she had brought it in a bag and forgotten where she had put it down. Louise had known that there was no hope of help from the Archbishop and she felt neither surprise nor disappointment. He would probably keep out of her way for the next few days, putting on a preoccupied, distant expression as he did to Madame Dillon whenever she was in bad odor with her mother, waiting for the climate to change. The Countess said:

"It will be better not to speak to him about it. He has so many bigger problems than yours. Your brother, if he had been here, might have been able to do something to find you a husband, but he's too far away. Everything is really the fault of Cousin Charlotte. Count de La Touche is very sympathetic about all that. If you must blame someone, blame Cousin Charlotte and yourself."

"I won't blame anyone."

"Or your mother. She had no sense of business. She should have tried to tie everything up much tighter, not that she would have been able. But she could have tried. Your father, perhaps —it's no use talking about it now. I'll write to him first thing tomorrow. You must have his approval. He will ask if you have agreed to the marriage. He particularly wished that you would marry someone in the family. He should be pleased. I can show you his letter if you like."

"When did he write that letter?"

"When you were coming to France. I got it from Charlotte. It's my authority to find you a husband. Charlotte handed it over to me. Do you understand that? Don't look so bewildered."

"Yes, I understand it."

"Very well, then. I can tell your father that you have agreed. You have not yet said that you do agree. It will be important for the religious ceremony. You must give your consent."

"I give my consent."

"You won't withdraw it? You won't do something silly at the last moment? I don't like your looks, Miss Brien."

"I will not withdraw. I will not change my mind. You may be quite sure of that."

"Good. Then tomorrow you may see your fiancé, in my company. It's very improper for you to see him at all, but I think it will be the best thing in this case. You must never tell anyone how it all came about, nor that you have already spoken to him. If people know that, it will ruin your reputation. He will leave Hautefontaine tomorrow and you won't see him again until the contract is drawn up. He will come up from Angers then and perhaps once more before the marriage. He knows that he has not behaved properly either, in speaking to you himself, and he's ready to fall in with these conditions."

It was then that Louise made the vow that carried her through the next part of her life, that she would not express the smallest doubt or dissatisfaction to anyone, not even to Biddy, concerning her marriage, until it was all over. She would imitate Madame Dillon who sang and played and danced and rode and hunted cheerfully, in the face of death. No one should make her a worse object of gossip than she was already, or than was inevitable when her proposed marriage became known. She knew very well what a spice the details would add to her story. It was fortunate that the Countess wanted to keep them secret too, though she might very well have enjoyed tittering over them with her friends.

Throughout the long summer Louise watched for a break in the Countess's resolve. There was none. She kept the engagement secret, as she had said, until the season was over, even when the men came back from summer maneuvers and the hunting parties, with the Archbishop's pack of staghounds, filled up with bright young men who seemed all determined to practice their wiles on Louise. Not one of them was truly interested in her, but she saw that they preferred the company of the more beautiful girls while they waited for those with the money to make their appearance.

Louise passed as much time as possible with the little girl, Lucy, playing with her as if she were a child too. They spent hours going through huge warehouses off the main courtyard in which the entire contents of a ship from the East Indies were stored. The Archbishop had bought them with a princely gesture a year ago, and having no use for them had put them here. An old watchman was in charge, and on wet days he allowed Louise and Lucy, accompanied by Marguerite, her nurse, and sometimes by Biddy, to play Arabian Nights among them. There were Chinese and Japanese jars and pots and plates and dishes, bales and bales of silk and damask and glazed cotton, rugs and hangings and lacquered chests and panels. Here they could forget the tinkling laughter in the house. All of this property would belong to Lucy, but one day she said seriously to Louise:

"These things are toys. I don't mean to play with toys when I'm grown up. I want to be like you."

"Like me? But I'm playing with toys now."

"Only to amuse me. Inside I know you're different. You're like Marguerite. You're sensible, and you know all sorts of things that I want to know, how to cook, and keep house, and take care of hens, and make butter and look after cows and horses. I'll tell you something." She glanced towards the doorway where Marguerite was sitting knitting a stocking, her smooth head bent over a difficult operation on the heel. "I love Marguerite as much as I love Mama."

"You're not supposed to do that."

"How can I help who I love? All around me I hear them saying that Mama will die. Then I'll have Marguerite."

"You will have me too."

"Yes, I'll always have you. Whenever Marguerite goes home, as soon as she comes back I get her to tell me all about her village, who makes the bread, who shoes the horses, who are the stonecutters and the carpenters and the thatchers and the shoemakers. There are two shoemakers in her village, though it's so small. I know all their names, and their children's names. Now tell me all about Mount Brien."

"It's not anything like as grand as this."

"One of the reasons I love you so much is that you don't like great houses any more than I do. It shows on your face."

"It shouldn't. My manners are not good, I'm afraid."

"I don't like 'good manners' either."

"Why do you want to know about Mount Brien?"

"Perhaps I'll go there some day to see you. I want to know everything. I think we have too much. I think it can't always be like this, people like us having so much and the poor people having nothing. When things change I'll need to know how to sew and keep house, like Marguerite and like you. How did you learn?"

"From watching. And my grandmother taught me a lot of things."

"Tell me about your grandmother. You can begin with her and then go on to all the others."

So for several weeks they refreshed each other, in spite of the difference in their ages, and apart from her enjoyment of the company of this lively, intelligent child, Louise found it a comfort to recall every detail of her life in Ireland for her benefit.

No longer able to confide in Biddy, she avoided her, though she had to admit that plans were afoot to marry her. Biddy's comment was:

"No harm to get away from this crowd. They'd ruin the two of us in no time. Where does he live, your intended? Why doesn't he come courting, like every decent man?"

"I'm not allowed to see him. That's how they do things here."

"It's a very funny way, if you ask me."

"He lives in the country," Louise said, knowing that Biddy would be glad to hear this.

"Thanks be to God. Maybe you'll get your health there. It's a natural life."

No letter came from her father. From time to time she almost fell into believing she would be saved, that her father would refuse his consent and demand to have her sent back, or even placed in a convent for a while. Anywhere, anywhere would do, where she could rest her mind and recover some degree of stability. But gradually she realized that unless her father came in person, nothing could be done for her, and Aunt Fanny would never allow this.

Her feeling of resentment had grown against Count de La Touche since the day of his proposal. In the salon, when she was summoned to see him, he looked quite sheepish and apologetic. She had avoided his eyes and had scarcely spoken a word, and since then had tried not to think of him. Her deepest hatred was reserved for the Countess, who was obviously quite well aware of it but who didn't seem to mind in the least. On the contrary, she was flying high on all the passions that gathered around her head in this house. Louise knew that most of Madame Dillon's friends disliked the Countess too but she would never join in their whispered conversations about her. This isolated Louise still further but she was better pleased, since it left her free to be with Lucy.

Then, on the third of November, the feast of Saint Hubert, even that refuge was taken away from her. The English grooms had been preparing for it for days past, saddles and tack were being polished in the harness rooms, horses shod, young horses tried out, old ones being judged for their fitness to carry older guests. A great feast was prepared for the evening of the great day. Cardinal Rohan's nephew, the Prince de Guémenée, was there squiring Madame Dillon whom he obviously adored, and who looked more beautiful than ever in a dark-green velvet habit and a hat with an ostrich feather that swept her pale cheek. The day began with the Mass of Saint Hubert and the blessing of the horses and hounds by the Archbishop, then the party set off down the valley.

Hundreds and hundreds of peasants had gone ahead to beat out the game. It was perfect weather, crisply frosty but with a clear sun coming up. The colored clothes, the shining horses, the river of hounds, the galloping huntsmen herding the party like sheepdogs, made a splendid picture against the thinning leaves of the forest.

Louise was almost happy today. One of the grooms who liked her, and who always spoke to her in English, had given her a far better horse than the Countess would have allowed. Until the last moment she feared that she would be told to exchange it for a worse one but by the time it was noticed, everyone else was mounted. Lucy's usual pony was not fit that day and she was given another, much bigger animal, on which she paraded up and down before the hunt set off, to the great amusement of the older members of the party.

That horse had never carried a child before. Louise lost track of Lucy, who seemed to be away out in front of the whole group from the beginning. Then, late in the afternoon, when they were all scattered and her own groom was blowing his horn in answer to another at a distance, she saw a slow procession coming towards her. There were four horses, with a litter made of branches laid between them, and on the litter, in great pain, was Lucy. When Louise was close enough to speak to her, Lucy said:

"I fell off that lovely horse. It was my own fault, not his. It was like flying. I made him go too fast. It's my leg that hurts most."

Louise accompanied her home, and that was the last time she was able to be alone with her friend. The guests had found a new toy. Winter was coming on and walks were no longer so pleasant. While her leg mended, Lucy lay in a room where a huge wood fire kept the air warm, and one by one they came to read to her, to dress puppets and give plays with them in a special puppet theater that was wheeled to the foot of her bed, and to carry on their intrigues against a new and amusing background. It was decided that they would all stay until Christmas, and in the last week of November the Countess sent for Louise and said:

"Your father has written at last. The marriage is arranged for the fifteenth of next month."

"May I see the letter?"

"There is no letter, just formal permission. Here it is."

It was there, in her father's handwriting, that he gave permission for the marriage of his daughter Louise to Count Armand de La Touche of Angers and Montpellier, as soon after the date of the receipt of this document as was convenient.

"A letter, a letter," Louise said in a daze.

"There is no letter. Do you doubt my honesty, Miss Brien?"

"Could we not wait until after Christmas?"

"No. This is providential, that we must stay here. We can have the marriage in the house chapel. It's Advent but the Archbishop can give you a dispensation. Would you like to be married in Notre-Dame de Paris, after what you have done?"

"Will Mr. Burke come?"

"I've written to him but I've had no answer."

This was her last hope gone. As for Robert, for all she knew he was already dead.

There was no further question of putting off telling Biddy who the bridegroom was. Her reaction was instant. After one gasp of horror she burst into tears and wailed:

"Was it for that we came all across the wide ocean? For that old fellow? You could have got better than him in Ireland and never left your home, nor I leave my mother. That old fellow is a grandfather, I'd swear."

"Yes, he is. But please, Biddy, don't howl so loud. Someone might come. It's all fixed. I can't do anything about it."

"The old one fixed it, you can bet your boots. And I'd swear he gave her money to do it."

"Biddy!"

"I don't say it would be his idea to do that but it would be hers. The day she scatted me out of the room, I listened at the door, the day she was giving out to you about how poor she is, and the old Archbishop, God forgive him."

"You listened at the door—Biddy, how could you?"

"What else could I do? Didn't I promise Madame that I'd never leave you, not for hog, dog or devil, and I won't, not for any old bitch that was ever born, no matter how high—"

This was too much and Louise had to put a stop to it and make her promise that she would never again use such language about Countess de Rothe.

Biddy herself was frightened at what she had said and apologized over and over, but she did not withdraw her accusation and Louise revolted against any further discussion of it.

As soon as the date for the wedding was fixed, Count de La Touche began to send presents for Louise, lengths of muslin and silk and lace, boxes of jewels, gloves, bonnets, slippers, dozens of things that she had never owned in all her life. The Countess looked sardonically at the things and said she supposed he was getting quite excited about the wedding. Then she began to add some household linen, and brought in her own dressmakers to make some dresses of the new cloth. The wedding dress was white, with white lace ruffles on the sleeves, and there was a white bonnet with long streamers, and a little bouquet of artificial orange blossoms for her hair. A room had to be set aside for all her new possessions, and she was expected to go in there and show them off to each guest in turn. Some added gifts of their own. The whole talk of the bored household was of the wedding. The Countess had been clever, they said, in squeezing the entire trousseau out of old Armand. One had to admire her for it. Though she watched like a cat, Louise saw no sign of derision nor even of pity on any of the faces. Some of the women even seemed to envy her, and presently she realized that the reason was simple: not for an instant did anyone think she loved her future husband. She had gained a new respect in marrying a man who would soon die and leave her rich and her own mistress.

On the wedding day everyone gathered in the salon at noon, then walked in procession to the chapel where the Archbishop was waiting with the parish priest of the village, who was to say Mass. On the steps of the altar Louise saw Count de La Touche for the first time since the day on which the marriage contract had been signed. He had arrived from Angers the day before, but though he had come to the house in the hope of seeing Louise, the Countess had not allowed it. Evidently she still feared that Louise would refuse to go on with the marriage, or perhaps it was another convention.

Louise had not changed her mind. She forced herself to look at him. He had had his eyebrows trimmed and was elegantly dressed in a braided coat, with his wig tightly curled and powdered snow-white. He returned her look with a very uneasy one. It almost seemed that the comedy they were going through was as ridiculous and painful for him as it was for her. As the ceremony went on she barely attended to what was happening. Memories of her grandmother and of her last words to her had flooded into her mind: "Marry for love—don't let them give you away—don't marry to oblige them." These were exactly the things she was doing and now there was no possibility whatever of escape.

19

Angers was a city of bells. One could never forget them since the air one breathed vibrated with their clamor night and day. All conversation had to stop in the marketplace while the nine bells of the Cathedral of Saint-Maurice rent the eardrums. They were immediately followed by Sainte-Croix close by, then by the four bells of the Cordeliers, mingled with the Augustins and the nine small bells of the Jacobins. The single, heavy, plodding bell of the Capuchins, away off in Réculée, could be distinguished in the background.

Every convent and monastery in this most religious city had its own voice, and they were all kept in order by the cathedral clock which struck the hour and half hour with the tune of the hymn to the Virgin: "Inviolata, integra et casta." All through the night, monastery bells rang for the offices at certain hours. By day, as well as Mass and Benediction and Office bells, funeral bells tolled slowly, giving time between the strokes for an Ave Maria, with a longer pause every quarter hour so that one could get through the Miserere. The Angelus rang at six in the morning, at noon and again at six in the evening.

Armand had said he lived in the country. She racked her brains to remember whether he had deliberately deceived her, but she couldn't believe it of him. What he had said was that Angers was the country, not that he lived in the country near Angers. It gave her a headache to think back on such things. In fact his house was on the edge of the town, within earshot of about ten sets of those accursed bells, which whanged in her ears by day and by night until she thought she would go mad.

The house was small compared with Hautefontaine, no more than twenty rooms altogether, with yellowish stone walls and a tiled roof. It was surrounded on three sides by a pleasant little park, with vegetable gardens right under the windows. The fourth side gave on to the street. There were tall trees in the park, and a natural pool where ducks and geese splashed, and where there was a summerhouse to which she used to go with Biddy in good weather to get away from the house. There sometimes, between bells, they could hear jackdaws cawing overhead, almost the same as those around Mount Brien, and sometimes the comfortable cackling of the hens in the farmyard seemed to speak the language of home too.

The journey from Hautefontaine had taken three days. They traveled in a carriage with six horses, Armand and Louise in the most comfortable seats which were at the back, Biddy and Francis, Armand's servant, on the middle seat. Two other servants sat on the front seat, which was as hard as a rock. One of these was Louise's hairdresser, Jean, and he also helped to handle the luggage at the inns. There were three couriers, two who rode beside the carriage and one who went half an hour ahead to see that the road was clear and to arrange for meals and beds. A second carriage had left two days before with the heavy trunks, and with orders for nine fresh horses to be ready at each stage.

Armand had told her that they would arrive in the early afternoon so that she could see the house in daylight, but they were late. It was almost four o'clock before he pointed it out. The outside made a pleasant impression, but once the door clanged shut behind them in the hall, she had a sensation of being closed into a damp trap. She resolved automatically to start curing that at once, with open windows to let in the fresh air. The place seemed stifled with heavy old country furniture, smooth chests, long solid tables and curtains of ancient red damask, but the two liveried servants who waited on them had new, smart suits. She noticed that Armand was watching her, looking from her to the men and back again, to see if she had observed this. She pressed down her irritation and followed him into the long salon off the huge entrance hall.

Two faded old ladies were sitting there, waiting. Both were dressed in black and both wore sad black caps with a little white trimming. The thinner, more sallow one rose and came forward but the other made no move. Armand said anxiously:

"My sisters, Zéphirine and Camille. Zizine, this is Louise."

And he looked from them to her, as he had done with the servants.

The second old lady, whose face was the color of parchment, was struggling to her feet with the help of a cane. The room was bitterly cold. Louise curtseyed in the Parisian manner and saw Zizine's mouth tighten into a thin line of disapproval before she came forward to kiss her on both cheeks. Dry, dry old flesh, half-dead, with an odd vegetable smell—the quick thought was shocking to Louise and she forced herself to hug Zizine warmly and say to the other sister:

"Please don't get up."

Zizine said mournfully, "Poor Lili has such trouble in winter with her rheumatism but she insisted on coming down to see you." Then, with a complete change of tone: "Monsieur, you're late," she said to Armand, who looked crestfallen and began at once to apologize.

"The carriage was perfect when we were leaving Hautefontaine but today one wheel seemed to grate all the time. I couldn't let them drive any faster. Have you been waiting long?"

"More than an hour."

"Well, well, nothing to be done about it, nothing to be done."

He began to make for the door and then recollected Louise, turned back quickly and said:

"Yes, yes, she must be shown her room. Zizine, yes, it will be better if you do that."

Then he was gone. Camille limped out of the salon silently, by another door, without looking back, and Zéphirine led Louise up the main staircase. Through an open door halfway along a corridor they could hear Biddy arguing with one of the servants, saying as they came into the room:

"My lady is not going to spend one night in this room unless there is a fire. It must be lit at once, because it will take hours to get the damp out. You should have had a fire going here for the last week, when you knew she was coming. I don't care where you get the wood—off with you and get some!"

The man came running out of the room, almost colliding with them. He stopped and looked quickly from one of them to the other, then said to Zéphirine:

"May I light a fire, mademoiselle?"

"Ask Madame," Zizine said with a martyred expression, indicating Louise with a limp right hand and then looking fiercely at her toes.

Remembering how she had spoken to Armand downstairs, Louise said:

"Yes, please light a fire. Is there plenty of wood?"

"Yes, madame, plenty of wood."

He scuttled off, his eyes to the ground as if he were afraid of being attacked. Louise examined Zéphirine, trying to discover what was in her mind. Her face was quite blank. Her eyes were glassy and without expression but a slight trembling of the lips showed that something or other was going on in there. What if the old lady were to burst into tears? Appalled at this prospect, Louise put out a hand to touch her sleeve in a friendly gesture. Zéphirine plucked it away as if it were a burr she had picked up on a country walk, snapped her fingers once or twice as if to clean them, reached down to her belt where hung a massive bunch of keys which she undid and held out in an aggressive gesture to Louise. She said in a half whisper:

"Do you want the keys, then?"

"No, no. I don't want to take your place. I'm very young. I have so much to learn."

"My brother's wife always kept them," Zéphirine said, replacing the bunch of keys on her belt.

After a moment Louise said, "Thank you. Is this my room? How pretty it is."

She walked in and looked around, noticing the big window and the seat underneath, with the afternoon sun slanting in on unwashed red velvet walls and bare floors. Already the servant was returning at a run, with a small crate of logs slung between him and another man. Biddy came from the bed, where she had been anxiously feeling the covers as she turned them down one by one, and supervised the laying and lighting of the fire. For perhaps a minute Zéphirine stood at the door watching all this bustle, then she turned silently away. Louise took one quick step after her, crossing the threshold to see her stump off down the corridor.

When the fire was well ablaze, Biddy sent the men away. She shut the door and the two girls looked at each other in alarm. Then Louise said:

"Open a window."

Biddy rushed to do so and the room filled with the sound of bells, beating against their ears, drowning all thought, tormenting them unmercifully until she clapped it shut again. She turned and said:

"Lord God, Miss Louise, have we come to a madhouse?"

"No, no, Biddy, it's only the bells. See, they've begun to ease off already. We'll get used to it."

"This room!" Biddy said, glaring around at it. "Francis told me that no one has used it since Madame died and that's six years ago. The old one was supposed to have it cleaned and warmed and ready but she never gave any orders about it. What a welcome! They'll never see God, any one of them."

Louise did her best to soothe her, sorry that she had seen the business of the keys. Several times Biddy said:

"Mark my words, Miss Louise, you'll have to put up a fight to hold your own in this house."

They had to scramble to be ready for dinner, already delayed. Louise found that some guests had come in honor of their return, several clerics and some neighboring landowners. They were waiting in the salon, glasses in their hands, and they gathered around in a ring to inspect her. Then an old man with an untidy wig said heartily:

"You did well for yourself, old boy. No place like Paris to find the good birds, though you'd think we'd do better in the country."

There was a loud, concerted laugh at this and then several of the guests glanced uneasily at Zéphirine and at the clerics, as if they feared their disapproval. Armand said:

"Thank you, thank you. Not too much of a feast tonight, fish and beans, eh, Zizine? Advent, you know, Advent."

Another guest said to one of the cathedral canons:

"You're keeping an eye on us—we'd be doing the devil and all if you weren't here to watch us."

A burst of strong, barking laughter greeted this remark, and the priest pronounced in a cool, delicate tone, as if he were saying something memorable:

"Fasting is the life of the soul, they say, but a little goes a long way."

Now and then Armand would look around at the company and say:

"Well, well, well, it's good to be at home with old friends again."

At last they moved into the dining room. Louise was glad to get away from all the staring eyes, even for a few minutes. Armand placed her at his right hand, saying to his sister who was about to sit there:

"Now, now, Zizine, time for you to move down. You've had a good run at the top, yes, a good run at the top."

Zéphirine blushed with anger and Louise said:

"Please, mademoiselle, take your usual place."

But she went off to the far end of the table without making any reply. Camille had already shuffled to a chair halfway along at the opposite side. Tears of shame pricked Louise's eyelids but by tilting her head backward she let them dry of themselves.

The meal dragged on. The women spoke very little and she took her cue from them, though she couldn't bring herself to laugh as they did. She looked among them anxiously for a friendly face. The youngest of them looked to Louise almost old enough to be her mother but she seemed the best of them. She was Eve d'Ernemont, and she was escorted by her mother-in-law since her husband was not well enough to go out in company. The other guests called her Fifine. She was very much at home with them all, and especially with Armand, though as she told Louise more than once she was not a native Angevine. Several times during the meal Louise caught her eye, and always met an enigmatic smile, perhaps expressing sympathy for her isolation and her obvious lack of understanding of this kind of company. Old Madame d'Ernemont creaked and groaned and paid no attention to anyone but she made a hearty meal.

Louise had never heard conversation like this before. Every remark seemed to have a set reply and the production of the appropriate one always drew a round of applause as if a great witticism had been uttered. She tried to imagine herself learning this new language. There were proverbs, pieces of folk wisdom, that were quoted as if they were newly invented, and then all except the priests threw back their heads and laughed loudly and rhythmically. After a while she decided that this was what made a happy evening for them, a good laugh, with or without a cause.

When they had eaten the fish and the beans there was a dry

cake with wine, and then they went back to the salon. She stood
a little apart from Armand while he received compliments and
congratulations. She smiled until her cheeks were stiff but said
not a single word, and no one seemed to expect any more of her.
One blessing was that they went away early.

As soon as they were alone together Armand came and put his
hands on her shoulders, looking down at her, smiling comfortably, and said:

"Well, how do you like your new friends? You'll meet others
but these are the closest to me, good, faithful, old friends."

She had to make some answer. She said, "They seem very
simple."

"You found Paris too sophisticated. You said you like country
life."

"I meant country things, horses, cows, forests, quiet places."

"It is quiet here."

She said desperately, "Except for the bells."

"Don't you like them? Don't you like our bells? They're quite
famous, you know, quite famous."

"I expect I'll get used to them."

It was no good. She had made one stupid mistake in Paris and
had gone on to make another and another. Even on the steps of
the altar she could have refused to marry him, if she had been
strong enough. But what was strength? She had plenty of it for
ordinary purposes and she still believed that she could use it
negatively, for enduring. Watching Armand's puzzled expression now, she found herself almost overwhelmed with something
that was much more than mere irritation. She gave him a cold,
hard look, the match of his sister's. He turned away, saying:

"You have been too long in Paris. Yes, that's it, too long after
all. You've been mixing with all sorts of smart people. We're
not like that in the provinces. I don't like comments on my
friends. Some of them are more learned than they look. You're
much too young to speak like that of older people, yes, much
too young." He gave a long sigh. "Well, well, it was to be
expected. Nothing to be done about it, nothing to be done."

And he turned on her the same expression that he had worn
with Zizine earlier. Louise felt her anger burst its bounds. It
had been building up for days, since the day of the wedding,
since the first nights of humiliation and fear and disgust, when

her ignorance had made her do all the wrong things and Armand's impatience had made it all much worse. He hadn't dared to wash himself, lest he catch cold, so that his lovemaking was a stark nightmare, but she had put up with all that. Now it seemed that it was he who had the grievance.

She gasped with fury and began to speak what would have been a tirade of denunciation of him and of his whole household, her cold welcome here, his provincial friends, the misery of her exile from Ireland, the hopelessness of her relations with him, a hundred things that should never be expressed. But Armand had simply turned and trotted out of the room. She could hear him pattering off down the hall. She gave a short, hysterical laugh, then realized that the servants were close by, waiting to clear the salon. A moment later Biddy arrived to take her to bed. She looked at Louise sharply and said:

"For God's sake don't let anyone hear you. We'll all be ruined. Laughing like a jackass all alone in here! Come along now, this moment. You'll be all right once you're in bed."

Louise gave her such a wild look that Biddy grasped her arm and shook her, saying:

"Please, Miss Louise, be good. Oh, I wish Madame was here. What will I do with her at all?"

With an effort Louise recovered herself, the mention of her grandmother forcing her back to sanity. She even managed to smile as she took Biddy's hand in hers and said in quite a normal tone:

"It's nothing. Just those people said so many stupid things, and I couldn't laugh until they had gone away. It's all right now, Biddy. I was very good as long as they were here. Now let's go upstairs at once. Is the fire blazing?"

"Yes, and the whole room looks much better. It's beginning to dry out. In a few days it will be fine, you'll see. I'll get out one of the silk bedcovers when I can get the trunks open—I've forgotten which one they're in but I'll soon find them. It will be a very pretty room. I think you scared off the old one today, Miss Louise. If I'm any judge we won't be seeing too much of her. Francis told me that, and he said it's a pity you didn't take the keys off her when you had the chance. Do you think you'll get another?"

"I can watch for one," Louise said, willing to promise her anything in order to distract her.

The candles shone from their tables and the whole room glowed in their light and in the light of the fire. Fresh wood had just been put on and sparks were flying out into the room. A pretty, dark, young maid with sparkling eyes was standing by the hearth when they came in. Biddy said:

"This is Marie. She's our special maid, for this room only. I left her to keep an eye on the fire. Isn't that grand? She's to do everything I tell her. I never thought I'd see the day when I'd have a maid of my own."

"Who sent her to you?"

"The old one."

"Biddy, you must stop calling her 'the old one.' "

"Yes, you're right. I must give it up. I'll find another name for her."

All the time while she was getting Louise ready for bed, Biddy kept glancing at her anxiously, but Louise had indeed calmed down. Her recent flare of temper had frightened herself. Had she really been on the point of denouncing Armand? It would have astonished him to learn that she had been harboring such thoughts. By his lights she had no right to attack him, nor his friends, nor his way of life. He had been very generous to her. She had had plenty of opportunities to change her mind, weeks and weeks, right up to the day of the wedding, but she had done nothing about it. Everything was her own fault. Escape, escape from Countess de Rothe, Cousin Charlotte, Paris, all the dreadful things that had happened in the last months since she had left Ireland—she had seized the chance to get away from them all, and she had no one but herself to blame.

Desperately, while she lay in the warm bed waiting for Armand to come trotting in, her mind began to explore how it would have been if she had come here with André, how they would have entered the house hand in hand, how he would have shown her the dairy, the henyard, the bakery, the kitchens, the library, the salons. She had no evidence at all that André could love her and yet she felt throughout her being that it could be true. By now, she thought miserably, he had probably forgotten her, so far away and with so many other things to think of. Yes, he would forget her, but she could not forget him. That was an impossibility, like water flowing upward or fish flying. Words of an old song she had heard them sing in the kitchen at Mount Brien ran into her mind:

I wish, I wish, I wish in vain,
I wish I was a maid again,
But a maid again I'll never be
Till an orange grows from an apple tree.

Terrified, she realized that what she was thinking was a sin.
She could be damned to the everlasting flames of hell for it.
The Church said she was to love Armand, but even the child,
Lucy, knew that you can't love to order. Then at least don't
hate: that was the answer. She knew that Armand didn't love
her but the rules were different for men though no one said so.
She would be very quiet, very quiet and good, to use Biddy's
word. She would learn not to speak much—that was one of
Grand-mère's maxims, that when you find yourself among
people who dislike you, it's well to be silent. Then they can't
use your own words against you. You close yourself off from
them. It's as good as building a strong wall.

Tomorrow she would change her life. She would tell Biddy to
put away the more elaborate dresses and she would wear only
very simple ones in Angers. Zéphirine had looked shocked even
at the velvet hood of her traveling cloak when she arrived, and
with more reason at her low-cut dress and pyramid of hair, full
of pearls and flowers, at dinner. Louise had foreseen it—she had
implored Jean not to do her hair as he usually did in Paris and
Hautefontaine. But he had gone on in spite of her. In future
there would be an end to all that. She would learn at least to
smile at their jokes and their vulgar old saws, she would come
to recognize their bells one from another, she would learn the
names of their great families and join in the gossip about them,
the Hullin de la Maillardières, the d'Ernemonts, the Chaus-
sards, the Le Perrochels, the de la Cochetières—she remembered
some of the names already. In a few years everyone would have
forgotten the strange little bird of paradise that old Armand de
La Touche had brought back from one of his trips to Paris. At
best she would be a dove, at worst a crow. That was what Piccini had called her on that fatal day.

20

It was easier than she had thought. There was Mass in the cathedral every morning, then a little housekeeping, or rather watching Zéphirine supervising the household, since she kept the keys. Louise had never seriously tried to get them back. Then she might take a walk if the weather were fine, or sit making lace, as Sophie did when she was agitated, until noon. Visitors came in plenty, most of them clerics who approved of the demure little housewife and who congratulated Armand on his happy choice, as if he had acquired a good dog. Dinner was earlier here and there was no opera nor theater, but always several tables of cards. She saw no one under thirty-five who was not at least a deacon.

As summer came on she began to find out how Armand managed his estates, and discovered that the brandy he made was excellent. It was marketed all over France and was even exported illegally to Ireland. The day he told her that she collapsed with laughter. He said rather stuffily:

"There is not much I can do for my own country. Don't forget, we are all really Irish."

He showed her his little distillery, and she found that he had hired some men from Cognac who had brought their skills with them, and who took pride in the fact that the Angers brandy had a distinctive flavor. Like all the workers on the estates, these men were fond of her because she was able to stand between them and Zéphirine. Biddy was not the only servant who referred to her as "the old one."

Camille counted for nothing, because of her ill health, but Zéphirine was a tartar, ready to sack a man at a moment's notice if he displeased her in any way. One of Louise's triumphs was to set up a little court in which the delinquent servant had to be judged finally by Armand before he could be sent away. This had the good effect of restoring Armand's power so that he almost gave up trotting out of the room, saying, "Nothing to be done about it, nothing to be done."

Armand liked her new way of dressing, her beautiful blond hair flat over her ears, her dresses dark and plain. He said:

"It's more proper now that you're going to be a mother. You look older and more sensible. Zizine says so too. Zizine agrees with me, and she says you should wear flannel petticoats. Have you got enough flannel petticoats? Zizine would have them made for you."

"Thank you, there is no need."

The prospect of the birth always put him into a daze of happiness which he could not forbear from sharing with his old friends.

"See, she's pregnant, my little wife is pregnant," he would say proudly, waving a hand in her direction. "She'll have a son. You can tell by looking at her."

Her smooth, expressionless face completely concealed her boiling anger at their approving looks.

The older women watched their chance until the men were taken up with their own talk, then said:

"Do you get heartburn? That's a sign of a boy. Are your breasts swollen? Do you sleep badly? You must eat for two, or perhaps for three. There are twins in the La Touche family." They cackled for a while over this prospect. "And you must keep old Armand away from the sixth month or you'll have a dreadful time. I'll never forget my Alexandre, it was like being torn in two. They said my screams were louder than the bells. Yes, we all have the same story. Armand won't mind, you may take it from us. He'll have plenty to do. He's never short of what he wants."

"What do you mean? What are you talking about?"

But they looked uneasy then and would tell her no more.

One blessing was that Armand stopped coming to her bed, not waiting for the sixth month. No doubt he knew the superstitions too. He made all kinds of rules for her. She was not to stretch, or run, or turn quickly, or eat certain foods—he had an unending list of taboos for pregnant women, and when she questioned their good sense he was quite put out, saying huffily:

"Don't forget, I have experience of this. And it's very important to me to have a healthy heir."

She needed to rest, she needed to walk in the country, she longed to spend even a few days away from the beastly bells of Angers, so that she could sleep, but Armand said it was impossible for her to leave Angers in her present condition.

"These are women's fancies. The best place for you is at home. You can see, all the women stay at home where they can best be looked after. Dr. Chardin is here to take care of you. Why should you want something different from all the others?"

It was all part of the same trap. The most he would promise was that they would visit the estates at Montpellier later. He said:

"Just have patience until after Christmas, when the baby is born. Then we'll go to Montpellier. Would you like that?"

"Yes, yes, anywhere."

"Well, we'll see. But I always think of Angers as home."

She questioned him closely about his other estates. They were both self-supporting, with forests of good timber, vineyards, toll bridges and rents from various small towns in the neighborhood. The one at Bordeaux was especially beautiful, he said, with a terraced garden that ended in a small lake. In Montpellier the house was good but it was right in the town, in a dark, narrow street. Armand visited it every spring, but otherwise no one used it except Archbishop Dillon. Armand's agent rented it to him for the few weeks he spent in Montpellier every year during the session of the States of Languedoc. The Archbishop was the President of the States, which were papal territory. There was also a Commander of the Province, Count de Périgord, who represented the King at the opening of the States.

"My daughter Helen says it's very grand for a provincial celebration," Armand said. "Perhaps you would like to be there for that?"

"Yes, yes!"

"Of course you would. Young people are never tired of gadding about. My daughter-in-law will come back some day from

Martinique—she may want to live in one of those houses, though I doubt it. She has plenty of places of her own."

"Has she children?"

"A daughter and a son. No need to sound so alarmed. Your children will have the better right to all my property. It's in the contract."

"I was not alarmed. I'd like to meet her someday."

"Why?"

"Why not?"

He gazed at her anxiously but she knew now that he would never interpret her mind correctly. She had merely thought it funny that he should imagine she was worrying about the inheritance of that unknown creature that was jigging about inside her. In her imagination the child was always a girl—if Armand had known that, he would have been really anxious, as he believed that all her thoughts and actions now would affect every aspect of its life.

The doctor agreed with him in this. He was a native Angevin, tall, thin, beak-nosed, yellow-skinned, with a peculiar loping walk said to be caused by his habit of hurrying on foot from one patient to another. Louise had heard that his success in delivering most of the babies in the town over the last thirty years was due to having had his hands blessed by the saintly Abbot of Saint-Lazare. He sometimes seemed to confuse Louise with Armand's late wife, referring to her disordered liver or her rheumatism, but then he always quickly corrected himself, saying:

"Ah, yes, this one will be different."

One evening in early November she was sitting with the two old gentlemen in the small salon that opened off the dining room, the doctor sipping the glass of brandy that was a ritual on each of his visits. Winter had really come now, and it almost seemed that the sun had forgotten to rise this morning. The windowpanes were covered with a leaden light, already reflecting the light of the candles as if it were dark outside, but the whole house had changed and was no longer the gloomy prison it had been a year ago. Fires blazed in all the rooms, and Louise had found a whole store of Turkish carpets in an attic, and had had them laid on the floors. The dark paneling glowed deeply, shining with beeswax. Nursing his glass of warm brandy the doctor said:

"What a cozy room this is, Monsieur de La Touche! I'm not looking forward to going out into the cold. There's a wind off the Loire this evening that would freeze the nose off a brass monkey." They both laughed loudly, of course, though this was one of their standard jokes. Then Armand said:

"My wife must get the credit, Doctor. She has changed the whole house. Her own warm spirit has gone into every part of it."

Louise looked at her toes, accepting the compliment and expecting more of the same from the doctor. Instead he put down his glass with an air of great gravity, straightened in his chair and said:

"There is a theory that a woman should be kept away from domestic things, monsieur, if she is to have a son. She should have been thinking of galloping horses, sword fights, battles, manly things."

Armand said anxiously:

"I've been telling her that, though I haven't gone so far. Do you really believe it?"

"I must believe there is something in it. We know that the body consists of several humors and each of them affects everything we do. Now I don't believe that a fright would be good for her, loud bangings, that sort of thing, though some go so far as to bring their wives to battle so that the unborn child will have a taste for it. But music, domestic affairs, painting, embroidery can only produce girls, all very fine if that's what you want, but it seems to me that you have enough housekeepers already."

Neither of them noticed when she got up and sneaked out of the room. She went upstairs as fast as her heavy body would go and threw herself on her bed, laughing uncontrollably, tears streaming down her cheeks. Biddy leaped up in alarm from her chair by the window, where she had been sewing a robe for the baby.

"Miss Louise! What's happened? Have you got a pain?"

"No, no! Just that it's all so ridiculous. If you could have heard them—if you could have heard—"

By this time she was shrieking with laughter and was quite unable to stop. Biddy shouted for Marie and between them they got her into bed, then Dr. Chardin was standing looking down at her disapprovingly, saying:

"Hysterics! Have you no sense of responsibility to your child?"

But still she laughed, because he had turned into an eagle with a yellow beak and two sharp sets of claws between which he was guarding an egg. His bald head rose and fell at the top. Once she and Robert had seen an eagle when they were riding on the mountains near Oughterard. The country people said eagles stole babies if they got the chance. Was that a baby that he was guarding in the egg? He was always talking about babies. She leaned out of bed to see if the egg were moving, but Biddy and the doctor pushed her back in again. She had to leave them: that was the only thing to be done. She began to walk all the way back to Ireland, by the very same route as she had come, first to Paris, then to Le Havre, then across the water to Kerry, through the house of the O'Connells where all the old people looked at her without surprise. One of them said:

"We knew you would come back. We always knew you would come."

Then there was the long, slow road to Galway, but somewhere along the way a shaft of sense penetrated her mind and she knew she was lying in bed in Armand's house, that the baby was struggling to be born and that she was being told to struggle too. She could hear sharp Angevin voices, full of disapproval, blaming her for not being able to accomplish such a simple task. That meant that the two old midwives had arrived. Was this what had happened to her mother, then? She could hear someone laughing at the far end of the room and a voice said clearly:

"She'll die, just like her mother."

She forced herself to sit up and look at them, and they gazed back at her like children caught at some mischief but with the bodies of old crows, two old crows all in black. She heard Armand's voice at the door, and whisperings, and he went away. Biddy sat beside her, talking gently in Irish to exclude all the strangers who had no business to be there, though she knew they were trying to be kind. Biddy seemed to know much more about what was happening to her than she did herself, and instead of running away in fright at Louise's screams of pain—screams that had nothing at all to do with her and that no lady should utter—she sat there and held her hands and talked sooth-

ingly to her in a language that no one but themselves understood. Even when the eagle and the crows set upon her and
began to tear her to pieces, Biddy was immovable, though they
tried to get her away, out of their way, as they said. The doctor
said at last:

"Leave her there. Perhaps she's doing some good. These
damned little aristocrats are useless when it comes to having
babies."

It would have been a pleasure to slap his face but he moved
away just in time. What had he done with his wig? Poor Dr.
Chardin! Afterwards she was told that when he threw off his
wig it was a sign that the baby was about to be born. Now his
talk with the midwives about wet nurses and clothes for the
baby merely infuriated her. In one of the few gaps between her
fantasies she thought clearly that here was something for the
philosophers of Paris to think about. Was it possible that all
those ladies with their curled lips and painted faces and high-
flown ideas had been through what was happening to her now?
It must be so, but it was monstrous even to imagine it. It
explained why they would never admit young people to their
fraternity—there was something they knew that she could never
have shared until now. Now, now, now she would be a match
for them, if they were ever to meet again.

Towards morning, when her imaginings had become almost
unbearable and strange animals and birds filled the room with
cries and bird whistles, an old priest in a black-and-white habit
came and said prayers over her and she thought: I'm going to
die, then. I didn't believe this would happen to me. It will be
better than what I have now—anything will be better than this.

Blackness came down again, then the worst pain of all, then
total and sudden oblivion, like a blown-out candle.

Her first thoughts on waking were: Why did I have to come
back? It was pleasant, being dead.

The room was very quiet. Biddy was still sitting by her, and
over at the window, where light was beginning to break,
Zéphirine was standing. Biddy leaned over her, looking closely
as if to make sure she was really alive, then said softly:

"Miss Louise, you have a son."

"Where? Are you sure?"

"No mistake about it. They've taken him off to feed him.

He's fat and healthy, thanks be to God. I thought you'd never waken."

Now Zéphirine was coming over to look down at her, taking Louise's limp hand in hers and holding it for a second, saying:

"You poor child, you poor child."

Then she slid away, looking frightened, and went out of the room. Biddy said:

"The doctor is having a sleep. He said she was to call him when you would waken."

"Has she been here all the time?"

"Marie fetched her down from her room a long time ago. The Count's orders. He's in the seventh heaven over the baby."

"In the name of all that's holy, what does he think Zizine knows about babies?"

"Now, Miss Louise, you're not to start laughing again."

They were silent for a while, both thinking of how she had laughed. Then Louise said:

"Who does he look like?"

"Exactly like his father. God forgive me, I was hoping he'd take after your father but he's the spitting image of the Count. All the same I said when I saw him: 'He's like Sir Maurice, that's who he's like.' "

"Then I don't want to see him. Make them keep him away."

It was daylight now, cold white light filling the windows, with a yellowish tinge as if there might be snow. She thought she saw a few flakes fall, with a sidling, insinuating motion. There must be no more of those crazy imaginings. They could only lead to disasters worse than the present one. But what was disaster? And what was truth? In her first letters to her grandmother she had said she was perfectly healthy, that her new life was interesting and kept her busy. Then, equally flatly, she had said that her husband was sleeping with his old mistress again and sometimes with one of the housemaids, but that once she had got used to it she no longer cared. What else was there to say? Truth was in occurrences, not in attitudes and in people. How simple and easy life would be if one could deal only with reality. But when the doctor came in to make sure that she was really alive, she took great care not to look at his feet lest she might see claws.

PART
FIVE

21

André left Providence with Baron Von Closen and the Royal Deux-Ponts regiment on the nineteenth of June. He stood watching the baggage train move out, hundreds of wagons, each pulled by two pairs of oxen and a horse, the wives and children of the soldiers rolling about on the mattresses that topped the loads. Their shrieks of laughter and excitement brought a pain to his heart for their simple happiness, which seemed now denied to him forever.

In his first daze of anger he had scarcely known what he was doing, and he wrote a long letter to Sophie in which he expressed all his horror and disgust at Louise's fate. It never occurred to him to write to Louise's father. His visits to Mount Brien had shown how Sir Maurice was in thrall to the dreadful Fanny, seeming almost afraid of her, as if she had private ways of making him suffer for any sign of insubordination.

Yet André had pitied Fanny. In another household she would have flourished, baking bread, tending the poultry and the dairy, organizing everyone's life, curing minor illnesses with standard remedies—he could imagine a whole, happy background for Fanny, but none of it was possible at Mount Brien. The presence of her sister, brought in for comfort and support, only emphasized the differences between them and the Briens. At the other end of the scale, if Sophie had not been there the Briens might very well have fitted themselves to Fanny's standards and been all the better for it.

He remembered the details of the household very clearly. In his happy prospect of marrying Louise he supposed that he had always had some premonition that this family would be important to him, but he knew now that Sophie was the one who had first attracted him, and Louise, the bright reflection, much later.

He could not understand how Sophie had allowed this misfortune to happen. It was hard to believe that she had not been consulted, and yet her first letter said so. Maurice had taken the whole affair into his own hands and had given permission for the marriage without consulting her at all. André could imagine how this decision had disrupted the peace of the family ever since; Sophie would know how to make her displeasure felt. She said as much in the letter that reached him early in July. She must have replied on the very day that his arrived. Since the summer weather had come, the ships often crossed the Atlantic in less than three weeks.

"Like you," she wrote, "I feel that a terrible wrong has been done, and I have not been able to forgive my son for it. I think that Robert's going off to America was a great blow to him, as indeed it was to me, but I never despair. I prefer to fight back, and so I have told him. I said that he threw Louise to the wolves because of his disappointment in Robert and he has not denied it."

In another place she said:

"I speak very freely to you because I would have welcomed you as my son-in-law." This slip, if it was a slip, amazed him. "Fanny with her usual tact said that Louise has done well for herself since the old man will soon die and leave her his property. Fanny and I have not spoken since then, and I doubt if I will ever be able to bring myself to speak to her again in this life. I have had letters from Louise, from Angers where she is living now. Mr. Burke is in Bordeaux, but he did not come to her rescue as he should have done. Perhaps I wrong him, as he could not do much in face of her father's written permission."

The thin paper seemed to swallow the faintly written words and he had to take it close to the light to make it out. "You will not take offense if I give you advice, as I am much the older. When misfortune falls, it is well to look it straight in the face. Then it can be kept in its place and given its correct name. I shall be glad to hear from you again when you have conquered the worst of your disappointment. Then we shall see what can be done.

"We hear wonderful rumors about America and the brave French army there, but wonder how many of them are true. The poor people here are driven crazy and are talking endlessly about fighting for Irish freedom when the Americans have won theirs. You will find much more courage here than when you were last in Ireland, but I fear it will all lead to terrible things.

"Louise writes that she has settled down in Angers but that it is dreadfully provincial, the people all very respectable on the outside but full of intrigues within. I find that her husband is no better than the next in this matter. She surprised him with one of her maids, not the Irish girl I sent with her but a French one who belongs to the house. He has two old sisters who seem poor company for a young girl. She says she is very well. Do not stop thinking about her. I pray for your own health and safety."

This letter was handed to him early one morning when they had been seven days on the march. The Royal Deux-Ponts had reached North Castle, not far from Long Island Sound, the day before, after a march of twenty-five miles. Even at this early hour the heat was intense but the men were in good spirits, moving precisely and efficiently about t'● business of the camp at the orders of the junior officers. They had marched unceasingly and had every reason to be sulky, but he could hear them whistling and singing as they went about their work. That morning André was to go with Von Closen and a small party to arrange a meeting between Rochambeau and Washington, at last about to join forces. Colonel Cobb, an American who had been sent by General Washington to help them to plan their marches, came with them. Cobb had been with the Deux-Ponts for several days and had brought news of the American army's position.

A few miles to the east they found the American officers at a tiny crossroad inn close to their camp. The place was called White Plains, and was a hilly, sandy, wild place where nothing would grow except heather and thorns. Philipsburg was the nearest village to the camp. The inn was alive with spiders of all kinds, from pale, small ones to black ones as big as sparrows which scuttled at great speed across the floor. The landlord was dreadfully embarrassed about them and kept stamping on them swiftly as they shot past him. Every now and then he said to whoever happened to be nearest to him:

"Must be going to rain, sir. We haven't seen a spider in the house for weeks."

While the Americans went to tell General Washington that they had arrived and to bring him to the inn, Von Closen and André went to have a look at the American camp.

André's first thought was that it would be well if the French soldiers could be prevented from seeing it. The tents were in ribbons, little more than a token shelter from rain or sun, though they were ranged as squarely as if they had been proper bivouacs. There were a great many of them, far too many, it seemed, for the scattered groups of soldiers. The men looked woefully underfed. They were not merely in rags: they were almost naked. They had no shirts, only short, white, fringed cotton jackets and trousers, worn into many holes. Most of them had no stockings and their footgear was of every variety, broken and misshapen with age. Some had cast off their boots altogether. André felt uncomfortable and self-conscious in his smart uniform and shining boots, especially when the soldiers gathered around to admire them as if they were prize beasts.

"My, don't they look fine! If our officers could have gear like that—but they could never wear it with such an air. Turn, sir, and let us see your back. Just as fine, every bit as fine. You don't mind if we speak out, sir, but won't it be warm fighting in those clothes?"

It was all so good-humored that one couldn't resent it, and the fact that the men were not in awe of an officer pleased André so that he answered:

"I'm no warmer than a horse in his clothing. You look mighty comfortable on this warm day."

About a quarter of the soldiers were black, and one of these wriggled his shiny shoulders and said:

"It's all right in summer but we must get this war over before the winter sets in or we'll freeze to death and the enemy can take us away in cartloads."

They had been out on a skirmish the day before and were full of excitement, hoping for more. Walking back to the inn Von Closen said:

"How can they be so cheerful in their condition?"

"They have a cause to fight for, even if they don't all quite know what it is."

"You're a cynic."

"No. But here's proof that men do really rally to a cause."

"Of course they do. You see ours. How could you doubt it?"

"The motives of our army are pretty mixed, if you ask me. The officers are mostly here for the fun, or because they have no other trade, or because they were put into it by their fathers at twelve years old. The men are here for the same reasons but none of them had any choice at all."

"Why are you here?" Von Closen asked, looking at him curiously. "You speak as if you're an outsider."

"I'm here for a cause, I suppose," André said. "The whole world will go the way of America soon. There will be no more kings, or very few, and those who are there will only be ornaments. America has started a hare that will never be caught. I want Ireland to be in the running when the time comes."

"Ah, yes, Ireland," Von Closen said indulgently. "You Irish love your little country, I believe."

"Love is a funny word. At this moment it's more like the feeling you might have for a half-witted sister who needs your protection. Are you married?"

"No, but my fiancée will be waiting for me when I get home. And you? But I've heard the others say that you're married to Ireland. Tell me, why don't all the discontented Irish come to America? It's a free country already, more free than any that I know, even before this war began. Every man is equal. No one bows to anyone else. Once you work the land you're as good as the next. There's no religious persecution. Catholics and Lutherans and Presbyterians live side by side and never persecute each other. Each one goes his own way. It seems to me that the more Irish come here, the better all round."

"Believe me, they've thought of it," André said, "but they don't do well here."

"Why not? Everyone does well here, so far as I can see."

"I don't know whether it's true but I've been told that they drink and fight and don't work hard enough. It could be that they have bad habits, they have so little at home—no one who has not seen the country will believe how bad things are there. The animals are housed better than the peasants."

"That's false economy."

"Yes, and damned uncomfortable for the peasants. You should come there some time. When all this is over we'll raise an army in France and turn our experience here to account by freeing Ireland. Everyone will follow us."

"A rabble, by the sound of them."

"No more a rabble than this army we saw today. All they need is good generals and enough arms, and they'll fight."

"Ask me again when the time comes."

"I certainly will."

"You think that people like General Washington will become the kings of the world?"

"Something like that. Great changes are coming. He would make a handsome king. And what about yourself?" André looked down at Von Closen, delighted with this idea. "You'd make a charming little king."

"I don't think I'd care for it, thank you. I hope King Washington hasn't already arrived."

He came a few minutes after they got back to the inn. They had a quick dinner with him, consisting of ill-cooked pork and beans. The French were shocked at this treatment of the great man but the General only sighed as he studied his plate, before beginning to eat. He had decided to come part of the way next day to meet General Rochambeau and conduct him to the American camp where they could have a long conference. This meant that the Deux-Ponts could rest for a day before starting the short but difficult march to White Plains.

The enemy had retreated back to Manhattan and were as impregnable there as ever. Washington still hankered after an attack there, perhaps because it was the scene of his earlier defeat, but he made it clear that he now completely agreed with Rochambeau that this would be bad tactics.

The four officers and their escort rode back in the cool of the evening to North Castle. Suddenly seized with energy, Von Closen was delighted when they startled a fox on its evening prowl and he made them all give chase. Very soon the fox slipped into the bushes and paused to stare out at them, its little doggy face full of anger. They put the horses to the bushes but they refused, having more sense than their riders. Then the fox silently disappeared, and a minute later it could be seen flying across a piece of open ground, its long feathery tail seeming to carry it off the ground.

Since he had moved to the Deux-Ponts André had lost sight of Lauzun's Legion, though the two regiments were often not far from each other. On the march the Legion was detached from the Deux-Ponts to cover its left flank and to act separately, in conjunction with the American army. Couriers brought news that it had seen some fighting with Tarleton's dragoons and the Hession chasseurs, and had forced them to recross the East River. On the day that they marched from North Castle to White Plains, André met Robert for the first time since the news of Louise's marriage had come. They had struck camp at two o'clock in the morning and by daylight were moving through rough hilly country with narrow, sandy roads which seemed to slide and roll under the tread of the army. The men clambered along as well as they could, often pushing or hauling the wagons with the oxen and the horses.

Getting the wagons into order was the business of the junior officers, and it was extraordinary to see how their efficiency had improved since leaving Newport. They marched out in front, seeming never to tire of encouraging the men, herding them like a flock of sheep or forming them back into lines according to the condition of the terrain. At last they descended a long declivity and debouched onto a better road. Ahead of them they could see some farms, and there, resting on the wild grass, was Lauzun's Legion. They burst into cheers at the sight of the Royal Deux-Ponts, and within a few minutes all the men were trying to find their friends and exchanging details of their marches. André looked for Arthur Dillon and saw him chatting with his cousin Theobald. The horses had been taken out of their little carriage and the two Colonels were stretching their legs and talking to Theobald's son, who was a First Lieutenant.

Then he saw Robert. He was with a small group of young officers, all from the Dillon regiment. André recognized O'Moran and Morgan who were Robert's particular friends in Newport. While he watched, Robert threw back his head and laughed, in that moment so closely resembling Louise that André felt a sudden shock of pain. He took a quick step forward, and then Robert saw him and came running over.

"André! I was looking for you. What has your lot been doing?

We've had a wonderful time. I'm promoted Second Lieutenant. Quick work, isn't it? The Colonel sent for me and told me himself. Good material for an officer, he said, though I hardly know how he found that out. We've been in a battle." He stopped chattering suddenly, then said after a pause: "What's the matter with you? Something wrong? You look like a funeral. Louise? Is it Louise? Is she sick? Have you heard from Paris?"

"She's not sick. I heard only two days ago that she's very well."

"Then what? She refused you? I can't believe it."

"She didn't refuse me. I was too late."

"Too late? What do you mean? They had already promised her? For God's sake. Oh, why did I ever leave her?"

André took him by the shoulder and led him a little apart from the others. The happy boy of a moment ago was gone. Now he looked furious, trapped, almost beyond knowing what he was saying. André said quietly:

"She was already married when my letter arrived."

"Who is it? Who?"

"A cousin you have never met, Armand de La Touche."

"Well? There is more. Go on."

"He's sixty-four. Countess de Rothe wrote to me. I've had a letter from your grandmother too. Armand's son was killed in Martinique or Grenada and he has no heir—Robert! Wait! Robert!"

But Robert had gone running across the ground, uphill, his head down, his arms and legs flying, as if he were being hunted by a pack of dogs. After a second's hesitation André ran after him but he had no hope of catching up with him. Within two minutes, however, Robert threw himself on the ground, out of breath, clutching the grass, beating at it with his fists repeatedly while he lay sprawled half sideways. André came up with him and stood for a moment looking down at him. Then he said quietly:

"I feel as you do but there is nothing to be done. Everything was arranged properly. She had her father's permission."

"She has no father! What right had he to do that to her? Permission! She can't have wanted it, she can't."

"Perhaps she felt it was her duty."

"If she did, it was that old bitch de Rothe who told her to. A heart of stone. Have you ever looked into her eyes? Like lead, like glass—have you ever looked at her properly?"

"I have, in fact. I quite agree with you. But she may have thought she was doing well for Louise."

"No. She wanted to get rid of her. She didn't care a tinker's dam for her. Perhaps the old fellow gave her money—she would take money from anyone. That's what I heard about her since I came out here. Everyone knows her. She's a legend. We should never have left Louise with her."

"I was counting on Madame Dillon to take care of her."

"She's as helpless as Louise. Grand-mère was counting on me to take care of her. It's all my doing."

He turned his face to the ground again but this time heavily, as if his despair were too deep for anger. André said:

"You might not have been able to save her even if you had been there. And she must have given her consent at the altar, else they couldn't have married her."

"That's nonsense—the girls are very well instructed that there's no hope for them if they refuse at the altar. What was the priest doing, I'd like to know? It was his business to find out from her beforehand whether she had given her consent freely or not. But they never do. They play the game along with all the other intriguers. Money—that's all they want, money and position and power, and then more money to keep it up. I wish them all in hell."

"We can do nothing about it."

"That's the second time you've said that." Suddenly Robert sat up and looked at André with a malignant expression. "What do you mean?"

"I mean that it's too late. We must resign ourselves. It's no use fighting it. What else can I mean?"

"If it's no use fighting, why are we out here marching up and down this wild country?"

"That's a different kind of fighting."

"I don't see any difference. One is either a man or a worm. We are alive—we think—we feel. If we don't like something in the world, we go to change it, as we're doing now. Tell me," he said with sudden, intense bitterness, "is this part of getting old?"

"What?"

"This thing that has happened to you. Don't you care enough about her to want to go and get her out of there? Don't you even wish it had all never happened this way? Don't you wish you could go back to Paris when all this is over and find her waiting for you, longing for you, planning for you? I'll tell you something: two days ago when we knew we would join the Americans here, I got permission for six of my men to go back to Newport, gave them horses to ride all the way back to see their sweethearts that they left behind, American girls that they left in Newport. They'll come back, or we'll have to send to fetch them, but no matter what trouble they cause we wouldn't have prevented them from going. They were dying of love. I believe they would have died. And look down the hill, there, where the baggage wagons are. The wives and children of some of our men came all the way out from France with them, or after them, and rode through this beastly heat on those wagons, two hundred miles, from Providence, to be with their men." He glared contemptuously at André. "And you would abandon Louise as if she were worth less than the wives of these poor soldiers, as if she were not worth thinking about any more—"

"I haven't—what are you saying? She's married, I tell you, married to old Count de La Touche."

"I heard. What are you going to do about it?"

"What can I do? You're suggesting something terrible, something much worse—"

"Worse than what? Worse than being taken like a cow to the bull?"

Suddenly André clenched his fist and made a wild movement towards Robert, who quickly twitched himself out of harm's way and lay on his back supported by his elbows, looking up at him with a devilish grin, saying:

"That's better. Taken like a cow to the bull"—he repeated the phrase deliberately, seeming to savor André's anger—"to make a son for an old fool who has no other use for her. Do you think he's faithful to her? Have you ever seen one of that bunch of gentry that was able to stop himself from keeping a mistress or two? That's the game that got me out here. I'm lucky—I know I'm lucky. You're a Frenchman. How can you talk so foolishly? How can you leave her to her fate as if she were an animal going to the slaughter?"

"Be careful what you say about her."

"That rouses you, does it? So it should. Those people in Paris, and their friends down in the country, they're all finished. The games they play will finish them. They're like the Irish land-lords, though they feel so superior. They see nothing beyond their noses. Where is Louise living now?"

"In Angers."

"I bet they're just as bad there."

"That's what your grandmother said, that her husband is no better than the others."

"Already? How does she know?"

"Letters from Louise."

"So I was right. Who was it?"

"Her maid."

"Biddy? I don't believe it."

"Not Biddy. A French girl."

"Then what are you waiting for? How can you wait? I know what I would do if I were you. I would go back to France at the first opportunity and find her, and make her understand that she needn't put up with this life they have arranged for her. You can take her away. Do you want to take her away?"

"Of course."

"Then you have my permission, since you set such store by permissions." He looked at André mockingly. "How soon can you go?"

"You're mad."

"Yes. How soon can you go?"

"I'd hardly get leave of absence now."

"Are you going to ask?"

"I need time to think."

"Why?"

"Your grandmother said in her letter that I should do some-thing about it. She hinted at the same thing."

"Where is that letter?"

"Here in my pocket."

"Show it to me."

"No."

"I thought you wouldn't. She said you should do something about it. That was what she meant. She meant that Louise must not be abandoned. I wonder if she would go out to Angers her-self—I think she may have thought of that. You see, you have her permission too."

"Don't jeer at me."

"Go and take her away."

"It's against the law."

"What we're doing now, at this moment, is against the law of this colony. You're making excuses."

"You have an answer for everything."

"Yes. I could go myself but Louise wouldn't trust my judgment as she would trust yours."

"My head is reeling. What do you want me to do?"

"To go to Angers and take her away, abduct her, if you like. Why can't you understand me? I've said it in every way I know."

"It's a criminal offense. Where should we go? She would be found and brought back, and her last condition would be worse than her first."

"Not if you came out here." Robert laughed. "You see, you're beginning to understand. There is no such thing as law, or truth, unless you want them. You make those things yourself. That's the lesson I learned in Paris. You could come to America. No one would ask any questions. She could be your wife; you could arrive as man and wife."

"It's an abominable idea."

"Have it your own way. You don't really believe it's an abominable idea. I can see your mind working on it. Take time to think—you must, in any case. We're not nearly finished with this war, the Colonel says. Let's not quarrel. You'll come to see that what I'm saying is sensible. You're thinking it over at this moment, aren't you?"

"Yes, yes."

"I knew it. It's written on your face. You'll go back to France —urgent family business, any reason at all—the first moment you can get leave—tell her I told you to go and take her away —I'll give you a letter for her—tell her—tell her—"

Partly to calm him, André said:

"What if she doesn't want to come? What if she's happy enough in Angers?"

"If she were happy, would she have written to Grand-mère to tell about her husband's infidelity? Would she?"

"No."

Robert sprang to his feet and quickly brushed at his sleeve

with his hand, then abandoned the remaining shreds of dry grass that were clinging to his coat. He said:

"It's settled, then. You won't go back on it. It is settled?"

"Yes."

"When?"

"As soon as possible. It will take time to get leave."

"You'll tell me when you're ready to go?"

"Of course, if I can find you."

"Will we be separated again?"

"I think not. So far as I can make out we're going to move together, Americans and French, from now on."

Robert said anxiously, "And we won't quarrel?"

"No. We'll never quarrel."

22

The two armies stayed for several weeks at Philipsburg before moving south. After a few days the American soldiers began to sneak off home. If they were caught, they were brought back and flogged, exactly like the French, though it could have been argued that as volunteers they should have had different treatment. General Washington had to exert all his powers to keep heart in the faithful ones. Dreadful tales came in of atrocities committed by both sides as despair and tension mounted. Washington's own uncertainty showed, in spite of himself, but only in the presence of his senior officers. With the men he was always impressively confident, promising that they would soon be paid, that the war would be over soon and that there would not be another on American soil again until the end of time.

No news came from the Southern colonies, though he sent envoys with letters over and over again to ask what support would be forthcoming if he brought his army to the aid of La Fayette, who was trying with his tiny force to cut off the possibility of Lord Cornwallis's retreat to the Carolinas. This was all the more infuriating since there were reports from various agents that General Clinton in New York and Lord Cornwallis were quarreling with each other. Clinton was refusing to send the reinforcements that Cornwallis wanted, and was even demanding to have three battalions sent back, that he had lent to Cornwallis, in order to strengthen his own position.

Most disappointing of all was the fact that Connecticut had sent only a couple of hundred men instead of the six thousand that had been called for, and even Washington could not make this handful look like an army. Of the two thousand that he had, most were old men or boys, with a great many blacks, but they were absolutely devoted to their General. They were a pathetic sight. When the French officers were invited to review them, no one smiled at their strange appearance.

André saw that there could be no question of leaving for France until this campaign was over. He was constantly in demand as an interpreter between the two armies. On the fifteenth of August, Rochambeau received news from Newport that Admiral de Grasse was on his way from the West Indies with twenty-eight ships of the line, three thousand men, field and siege guns and one million two hundred thousand livres in good French money. He was making for Chesapeake Bay and Rochambeau was to be there on time, with his plan of campaign ready, since de Grasse wrote that he could not stay beyond the fifteenth of October.

Rochambeau summoned André to go with him to tell this good news to Washington, and the two generals settled down to work out their plans in detail. There was to be an end of skirmishes and reconnaissances. Clinton was to be kept in a state of uncertainty in New York, in constant fear of an attack. He was still refusing help to Cornwallis, who had just taken possession of a little town called York in Virginia, and was busy fortifying it. General La Fayette wrote that he believed he could prevent Cornwallis's escape until the French and American armies arrived, but there was a new, desperate note in his words.

An essential part of the plan was that the French commissariat should buy flour and forage, and set up ovens along the right bank of the North River. Spies would instantly take word of this to Clinton, who would see it as fresh evidence that the French were going to attack New York. Meanwhile messengers were to go to Newport with instructions that the fleet, with the guns that had been left behind in its care, was to sail at once for Chesapeake Bay. The two armies at White Plains were to march south as fast as possible and join forces with de Grasse and La Fayette. Their destination was to be kept a complete secret, Washington said, since his men would probably disappear altogether if they knew where they were going.

Though the secret was perfectly kept, both camps suddenly

became like hives of bees about to swarm. Rumors were manufactured out of air and spread with amazing speed. The American camp was a quarter of a mile away from the French and at the far side of a small stream, but the rumors traveled back and forth as if no language barrier existed between them. The strongest rumor was that both armies were to combine in an attack on New York, aided from the sea by the French fleet from Newport. There was talk of a great victory in the south by La Fayette, and another story of his defeat and death. Rain fell in torrents so that it was impossible to work outside, and the men huddled in their bivouacs muttering these strange tales to each other. It was an immense relief when at last the orders came to break camp and move back to North Castle, where a small outpost had been left.

That march back to North Castle turned out to be the worst part of the whole migration. The rain had washed away large parts of the road, which had never been sound in the first place. Dozens of the wagons broke down, or lost wheels, or got stuck fast in the thick mud. It took hours to free them, and they obstructed the road so badly that the rear guard, consisting of the grenadiers and chasseurs of the Deux-Ponts and the Soissonais, with de Lauzun's Legion, had to bivouac for the night after they had covered only six miles.

Soaked to the skin, André walked with de Vioménil and Von Closen and several other officers to a house which showed a light not far from the track. It was a long, low house, a log cabin which had been improved and extended, with a porch that ran along its full length. The rain dripped heavily from the encircling trees. A dog rose up from its place by the door and growled ferociously, then set up a wild and terrifying barking. In a second the door opened and an immensely tall, heavy-faced old man in a deerskin jacket peered out at them, holding an oil lamp high in his hand. He called out in a querulous voice:

"Who is there? Answer, or I'll let the dog loose."

"Thank God he's tied," André said loudly. "May we come in and dry our clothes at your fire?"

"Who are you?"

"French officers on the march. Our men are camped by the roadside."

Behind him he could hear swords cautiously drawn but the old man said:

"Come in, come in. How many are you? This way, this way." He spoke softly to the dog, which instantly stopped its noise. "Come along, don't be afraid. He won't touch you now."

Followed by their watchful servants the officers walked into the house, straight into a big, barely furnished parlor. A small wood fire burned pleasantly at one side. Plain wooden benches were ranged beside it, and a single padded armchair. The long dining table was clear except for a huge Bible with gold-colored clasps. There was no sign of anyone else in the house. He said:

"Alexander Bird is my name. I can't say you're welcome to everything I have because I have nothing to give you."

"We don't need anything," André said, "except to sit at your fire for a while, and if you will allow it, to bring in our supper. We've been a long time without food."

"French, you said? Good. I'm glad to welcome you. You can do something for me after you have eaten."

"Of course."

He piled more logs on the fire which soon blazed up, and they had the intense pleasure of turning before it, watching the steam rise from their clothes, feeling the delightful warmth spread through their bodies. Bird said:

"Why are you marching in this weather? Why didn't you wait until it cleared?"

"That's not how wars are conducted," Vioménil said when André had translated, then waited for his reply to be put into English.

Bird asked in astonishment:

"Is that what he said? It's a mighty funny sound. Is that French? How long will it take him to learn English?"

"I doubt if he'll have time. We hope to finish this war and get back to France in a few weeks."

"You have a fine tongue of English yourself. How come that?"

"I'm more Irish than French. I've been often in America."

"Irish, are you? I know some of them. They fight for the English. But your friends are French. Do you think one of them would cut my hair?"

"I doubt it. Why should they?"

Vioménil said:

"What on earth is he talking about? Cutting hair?"

"He asks if one of you would cut his hair," André said solemnly.

Bird was looking anxiously from one of them to another. Then he said:

"It's not much to ask. The nearest barber is five miles away, and you have seen the condition of our roads. In this warm weather I need to have my hair cut. I should have waited until after you have eaten. Then you wouldn't grudge me this favor."

"I don't think any of us could do it even after supper," André said. "Our servants cut our hair for us. Mine will do it for you, when he comes back. I'll tell him."

"Your servants! You mean those gentlemen who went to get your food?"

"Yes. Mine is quite a good barber."

"Well, we live and learn. I was always told that all Frenchmen are either barbers or fiddlers. Can any of you play the fiddle?"

"I don't think so."

Soon afterwards the servants came back with white bread and slices of beef and bottles of wine, which they laid on the table with their masters' silver and glass as meticulously as if they were serving at home. Bird watched in silence until the officers were sitting down, then said quietly:

"I haven't seen a feast like that ever before. I see you have plenty. May I join you?"

"Of course."

He would not drink wine but filled a glass with whiskey from a small cask that stood on the floor near the fire, turning his back as he did so.

"My own make," he said over his shoulder. "I'm nearly out of it. I can't imagine wasting good grain these days on making whiskey. The soldiers made off with the rest of what I had and I'm making no more until the war is finished one way or another."

"French soldiers?"

"I've seen no Frenchman in all my life until this hour. They were good Americans, they said, fighting for freedom. That's why I keep a dog on the doorstep. We live and learn, we live and learn. General Washington talks of freedom but how is a poor man to buy seed for his farm if all his goods are taken away? I told them that, and they laughed and said they had no money. I didn't laugh. I chased them out of here with my gun. They won't come back, I think."

"When was that?"

"In the spring. We're heartily sick of them and their war in these parts, I can tell you. It's true that things are bad, the taxes would drive a man out of his mind, we never see the people that send out the orders, but if we're going to have people like those that robbed my barns instead, then I'll settle for English rule."

"They won't be the same people. Those were only soldiers."

"Sent by General Washington, they said, but I know he never heard of me. They went off with my whiskey, and my geese and chickens, and they would have taken my cows and my horse only that I hid them. They took my last bales of hay from my barn, and left me with the job of explaining to my cows that they would have to wait for the spring grass to grow. Only that I have good neighbors higher up the mountain, we would all have starved. My son is down in Philadelphia, adding fuel to the fire. If he ever dares to come back, if he puts his nose in here, I'll meet him with a charge of gunshot that will give him something to think about."

"You may change your mind before long," André said. "Perhaps you will be grateful to him some day."

"You think so?"

"Yes. It will all be over soon. Next year you'll see that things will be better. Do you live alone here?"

"Yes, since my wife died. I used to have three slaves but they all ran away to the army with my son. I have a sister in Hartford. She sometimes comes to visit me. They have good land up there, by the river. Here it's too stony. I used to do a lot of clearing but I can't seem to get after it now. Old age is a bad time, young man."

"I know Hartford. It's good land, you say?"

"The best, unless you go south, and that's too hot for me. Why do you ask? You don't look like a farmer."

"I'm a bit of a farmer when I'm in France. I'll go back to it once the war is over."

"Roll on that day. My son wrote that he has a little candle

business now in Philadelphia and he thinks that will be better for him than farming. Nathaniel Bird—you might happen to meet him if you go south. Where are you going now?"

"We're on our way to North Castle."

"That's not where the fighting is. Why don't you go to New York?"

"We follow orders. We do as we're told."

"All armies are the same but they say the French are honest and pay for what they take. I begin to believe it. My son married a Quaker girl. They're honest too, I hear. The soldiers that took my goods said they would make a list and I'd be paid some day. Do you think that's true? Do you think I'll be paid when the war is over? I've heard that General Washington lives like a king. I've heard he'll be a rich man by the end of this, what with his plunder and all. Do you think that's true?"

"Not a word of it. He has lost everything. He can never go home and attend to his plantation. He sleeps out in a tent half the time, to be with his men. General Washington is a truly great man, and as long as I live I'll be glad to have known him."

"Now, now, young man, don't get mad. You say that very warmly. But what is a poor man to think? I've never met him. So you think he's a good man, an honest man? Well, we live and learn. I can believe it now that I've heard it from someone that knows him. Do these gentlemen know him too?"

"Yes, yes, they all know him. They would tell you the same."

"And have they got farms at home, like you?"

"Yes, and houses in Paris too."

"And they left all that to come out and fight for us, so I've heard. Do you think they would mind if I shake hands with them?"

"Not at all. They would be very pleased."

The old man stood up and walked around the table, solemnly shaking hands with each of his guests, to their great delight, finishing with André himself. Then he shook hands with the servants, though he asked anxiously first if they were slaves. André assured him that they were not and Bird said:

"I thought they couldn't be, since they're white men, but things are so strange in other parts of the world, I thought it would be as well to ask. You have black slaves in France, of course?"

"No, just peasants and servants like these."

"It must be hard to work a farm without slaves."

André's servant Pierre cut the old man's hair in the wash house while the officers dozed by the fire. At three o'clock in the morning they were awakened by a courier with a message from Rochambeau that André and Von Closen were to accompany him at once to General Washington's quarters at Peekskill, the little village on the North River where the French army had had its magazine and food depot while they were encamped at Philipsburg. This was far preferable to rejoining the slow-moving army, which was still digging itself out of the mud. They set off within an hour in high spirits, promising Mr. Bird that they would pay him a visit any time they happened to be in the neighborhood.

Von Closen was excellent company. He wanted to see everything and explore everything and assess the early campaigns of the war. At the North River he insisted on going over the forts and drawing maps to bring back to Europe. Then he had to turn aside to see a celebrated waterfall that was only half an hour's ride away, and stop to talk to every farmer about his methods, and compare the breeds of cattle and sheep with those he had at home. Everything interested him and he infected them all with his own enthusiasm.

At Philadelphia he had a glorious time. Rochambeau gave orders that the men were to appear in full dress array for the march through the city, and to achieve this the army halted three miles outside and set to work at getting into perfect trim. On the second day Von Closen and André accompanied Rochambeau and de Vioménil and some other senior officers into the city. They were met and escorted in by a small mounted corps of volunteers, headed by the governor of the state whose name was Reed. At an assembly hall in the city they found de Luzerne, the French ambassador to Congress, with the President and all the notables of the state, waiting to greet them, and then they were taken to de Luzerne's house, where they were treated like kings.

It was marvelous to see how Papa Rochambeau kept himself in the background, making sure that Washington was always the first to be honored, but still he stumped about, shaking hands with everyone, drinking rum punch at the Gentlemen's Club, eating his way through a huge meal at the house of the minister for finance, pretending to drink from his glass when toast after toast was proposed, to victory, to France, to Washington, to Congress, to freedom, to King Louis, only showing his impatience now and then by a tiny twitch of his lips. Once he said under his breath to André:

"Tell the next one that if they want us to win this war we should be on our way now, instead of living it up in this style. They might have given their great general some of the money they're spending on this show."

But when Mr. Reed came up a moment later to ask him to come to dinner the following evening he accepted at once, only asking if General Washington would be there. He was, and the main course was a huge turtle weighing ninety pounds, washed down with good French wine in compliment to the visitors.

The following day, the day before the big parade, the two generals and their officers walked the battlefield of Germantown, six miles outside Philadelphia, and General Washington discoursed on the accidents that had made it a success for him. Von Closen was in his element, asking a dozen questions, all full of the same almost childish curiosity that sent him off to visit museums and shows in every town they passed through. Washington said wearily at last:

"War is a detestable thing. If Cornwallis hadn't made several mistakes, and if he had taken advantage of mine, we should never have won this battle. We'd have been defeated beyond hope two years ago. Instead, he let us have the advantage and now he hopes to get the better of us in return. He sees it as a game. We are fighting for our lives. Dirt, destruction, cruelty, poverty, disease—those are the things that war brings. If every war were a fight to the death, there would be fewer wars. That's a heresy, isn't it, gentlemen?" he said to the young French officers who scarcely knew what he was talking about.

Dinner that day was at the house of the French consul Holker, but Von Closen slipped away with his friend du Bourg to look at yet another museum.

The entry of the French army into Philadelphia had a heartening effect on everyone, both Americans and French. Rochambeau rode at the head of his troops, the bands played, the men marched perfectly, as if they had never in their lives dragged a wagon out of the mud or carried buckets of water to the cooks. The general and his party drew up between the lancers and the hussars of de Lauzun's Legion to salute the members of the Congress and the President, on the balcony of their hall. When they rode past the French embassy André saw that the balcony there was full of ladies, whose loud complimentary comments reached the ears of the officers, making them blush with delight. A moving flash of white caught his attention and he saw that Von Closen, whose part in the ceremonies was finished, had somehow managed to get up there and was chatting to the wives and daughters of the gentlemen of Philadelphia as if he had known them all his life.

During these idle days André found Robert's words repeating themselves endlessly in his mind. Go to Angers, take her away, abduct her if necessary, come back to America as man and wife, like a cow to the bull—whenever he recalled those words, the first that had maddened him into agreement with Robert, he remembered that he had promised to go. As soon as possible, he had said, and he would tell Robert when he was ready.

Before leaving Philadelphia he wrote a letter to Charles Lally, offering to exchange his house and estate at Saint André de Cubzac for Charles's farm and house at Hartford. From that day onward he knew that he would go back to France and take Louise away.

23

The chess game finished at York. Knights, bishops, kings, queens, castles remained on the board. Inside the little town lay a jumble of pawns, several arms and legs, rotting trunks of red-coated bodies lying haphazard, unburied, in the streets or wherever they had fallen. A dreadful stench hung over everything and a few wretched people crept about, handkerchiefs over their faces to keep it out. The houses were gapped or riddled with cannon shot, and the roadways pitted and scarred every few yards, where bombs had fallen. André rode into the town with Colonel Dumas and Von Closen and an escort, to meet the English and collect their prisoners. After a hurried conference it had been decided that the French had better undertake this task, with only Dumas to represent the Americans, some of whom had begun to mutter about reprisals and revenge for the deaths of some of their captured comrades-in-arms. One of these was Colonel Scammell. A story was going around that he had been shot in the back by Tarleton's orders, after he had given himself up. That was more than two weeks ago, and there was no way of knowing whether the story was true. Von Closen said to André:

"These Americans know nothing about the science of war. They've done everything wrong way around. If we had not been here they would have tried to go swarming into York without any preparation, wasting all their men. Now I doubt if they know how to finish a siege either."

He was in impeccable trim for the occasion, not a speck of dust on his uniform, even his horse shining and polished. André said dryly:

"It's easier for us. It's not our war."

"You know," Von Closen said, "Colonel Laurens and some of the others have been saying that the English shouldn't be invited to dinner. I honestly think they imagined we would send Lord Cornwallis and the officers off to the camps with the soldiers."

The disagreements had begun to show almost from the moment when they settled down to the siege. The French followed a complicated set of rules for taking a city, but though they explained them over and over again to the Americans, they could see that they were not understood.

"What's the point of all this?" Laurens said. "Starve them out or bomb them out, one or the other. What's all the fuss about?"

"It works," Vioménil answered patiently. "It keeps order. We don't want to do more damage than necessary."

"They don't worry much about that. They have been raiding and burning for years. Time they got some of the same."

Relations between them were good enough when they were marching from Williamsburg, twelve miles away, for the Grand Approach. The bands played marches, alternately French and American. The sun was blistering hot and the whole column was tormented by mosquitoes and flies, and by a sickly miasma that rose from the swamps on either side of the wretched road. There were thin woods here, which became more dense as they approached York. The French soldiers were in good spirits now that something was about to happen. It had been difficult to keep them in good humor on the long march from the north, but their short stay in Williamsburg had set them up again like new. Still the heat forced hundreds of them to fall out and wait to be picked up by the wagons.

At York there was a week's delay in which the field camp was set up and the soldiers were put to making the baskets to take away the earth from the trenches, and the long, sausage-shaped bags for their defense. When the wagons arrived, four thousand picks and shovels were unloaded and laid in a row ready for action. The engineers had already tested the consistency of the soil and had worked out how many baskets a day could be disposed of by each man. At last, on the evening of the seventh of October, General Rochambeau ordered the chaplain to say the customary prayer for the ceremonial Opening of the Trench. As night fell the work on the first parallel began in total silence, and the American officers said:

"Now that makes sense. That's a businesslike way of going about things."

But they still didn't seem to understand that rules meant order and order meant victory. When the first redoubts were stormed two days later, the Americans ran up and over the defenses like wild animals, instead of waiting for the axmen to come and cut down the wooden posts. General d'Aboville of the French artillery got very worried and gave orders that his men were to be kept as far as possible from the Americans, lest the bad example ruin their training. To counteract this he ordered several displays in which the French could show off their skills to the Americans. The most spectacular feat was when the gunners heated their cannonballs in their ovens, twitched them out expertly with the tongs, then loaded and fired them, aiming at a British ship in the river, and presently the whole camp saw flames rising from the ship which burned for several hours afterwards.

All that was over now. After days of bombardment and a *baroud d'honneur* which showed that he knew the rules too, on the morning of the seventeenth of October, Lord Cornwallis had a drummer boy beat a parley from the highest point of the ruined ramparts of the town. The roar of the cannon was so loud that there was no possibility of his being heard, but beside the little red-coated figure, the watchers could see a soldier waving a white flag. Within five minutes all the guns had gone silent.

The conference in Rochambeau's tent was short and angry. The old man showed less patience than usual, his face constantly flushing with the fever that he had been fighting for several days now. Colonel Laurens and the Marquis de Noailles drew up the articles of capitulation, and as he finished signing the document Rochambeau said loudly:

"I won't have anything but the proprieties. We've had enough irregularity already. Lord Cornwallis has behaved correctly and so shall we. The only thing he failed in was that he didn't wait for the breaching of the ramparts and perhaps he'll tell us his reasons for that. There will be no disorder. We keep our positions, French on the left, Americans in the place of honor on the right. An interpreter will go in with the officers who take possession of the town and make everything plain. They march out in the usual style, drums playing, colors flying, bullet in mouth, Lord Cornwallis rides in front with his second-in-command—"

But when this was translated for General Washington, he absolutely refused to allow it.

"You say he has behaved correctly, sir," he said, "but if I and my men were here alone, Americans only, he would act differently. He hasn't come to sign this paper and I don't believe he'll ride out at the head of his troops either. None of my men could get a sight of him when they were in the town. He treated us with scorn at Charleston, and if he knew the rules he certainly didn't play by them. Sauce for the goose is sauce for the gander, I say. We may meet again at some other city, and we hope that by then he'll have learned a lesson."

"Well, for that reason, perhaps," Rochambeau agreed, but he was obviously put out. "You have some other idea of how we should proceed. What is it?"

"Colors cased, no cannon—we'll go in and get those out ourselves. And I'll have no American marches played by a British band."

"But that is an insult. When we let the defeated army play our marching tunes as well as their own, we pay tribute to defeated courage. They fought valiantly. They are gentlemen."

"I can't agree with you. They haven't treated us by their rules. My men won't stand for it. General Lincoln was at Charleston. He'll tell you how they feel. They forced us then to furl our flags and we were not allowed to play an American march. Furthermore they treated our soldiers vilely when they took them prisoner. Their General Gage revenged himself in Boston by torturing our men, Lord Dunmore in Virginia ordered executions of innocent people, burned out peaceful houses and towns. I tell you, sir, they have done nothing to deserve the treatment of gentlemen."

"It's all true, General," La Fayette said quietly. "It's a different way of making war, not like ours. They had their orders from London, fire and sword, and they carried them out. There must be truth in those stories—I've heard too many of them. They promised a reward to every Indian who would bring in an American scalp—that kind of thing. And you know they deliberately polluted the wells with dead bodies on your route here. They don't keep the same rules. They seem to need to hate the enemy."

"I don't wish my men to hear of such things," Rochambeau said angrily. "We'll do as you say, Monsieur de Washington, but if they play only French marches, it will not look like an American victory."

"I'll tell you what they'll play," General Lincoln said. "They can play one tune of their own, that they're so fond of, 'The World Turned Upside Down.' It seems to me very appropriate."

The other Americans present chuckled but Rochambeau turned away, saying:

"Very well, then. You see to it."

Sickened by the horrors he had seen inside the little town, André rode out at two o'clock by Colonel Dumas's side. The English had made a gallant effort to clean themselves up, and considering how long they had suffered, it was astonishing that they managed to look so spruce. The band marched firmly and played the controversial tune in a spirited, lively way, and the officers stepped out smartly, their faces expressionless. General Washington was proved right. At the last moment Lord Cornwallis refused to lead his own troops, saying that he was sick, but if they felt this as a humiliation they certainly concealed it. They were led instead by Brigadier O'Hara of the King's Guards, who said to André as they began their slow procession between the double line of conquerors:

"Which is General de Rochambeau?"

"At the top, right in front of you."

"There are two. Which is the Frenchman?"

Dumas asked anxiously, "What is he saying? I can't hear him. What's on his mind?"

"Wants to know which is General de Rochambeau."

"Tell him."

"General de Rochambeau is to the left, sir," André said.

Immediately O'Hara put spurs to his horse and galloped forward. André and Dumas followed as well as they could, aware that a sharp hiss had gone up from the Americans drawn up to the right. O'Hara reined in before Rochambeau, drew his sword with a flourish and presented it, hilt foremost. The General gazed at him in amazement for a second, then made a gesture with his elbow so familiar to his officers, in the direction of General Washington. O'Hara paused, he and Washington looked at each other steadily, then Washington said:

"Sir, I can't take the sword from such a worthy hand. General Lincoln will do the honors."

With an expression of fury O'Hara handed the sword to Lincoln, then turned his horse as if he were about to gallop back to the head of his column. He reined in, however, and waited quietly while the English approached and laid down their arms in two piles, placing their cased colors on top.

As the captured army marched back into the town, André saw that some of the younger officers were in tears, though most of them succeeded in keeping their expressions neutral.

While this was going on there were quite loud chuckles from the ranks of the Americans, even one or two catcalls. Washington frowned and glared at them, trying to quell them from a distance, but it was obvious from the slovenly condition of the Americans' uniforms, and by the way they slouched at ease without orders, that no one could influence their behavior on this occasion.

Washington was the only American who seemed to be able to be civil to the English, who had begun to retaliate by making rude gestures in the general direction of the Americans. As clearly as if they had shouted it, their eyes said what they thought of that scruffy army. The Americans growled angrily, and one or two older English officers moved down the line speaking soothingly to their men. By the time the ceremony was over, most of the French officers had begun to mutter too, but their remarks were mostly directed against the Americans:

"Can't they behave like gentlemen? Have they no manners? Did they think we should slaughter all those poor soldiers as soon as we captured them? I shouldn't like to be one of their prisoners."

A story began to go about that the Americans wanted to have Lord Rawdon handed over to them, so that they could make him pay for the atrocities committed by his army in South

Carolina, but Admiral de Grasse had Rawdon safely on his ship and he refused to give him up. Several French officers asked André if this could possibly be true, and he had to hedge endlessly to avoid admitting that it was. Fortunately most of the Americans had no idea of what the French were saying but they could guess a great deal from their looks.

By common consent, there were no Americans present at the dinner that Rochambeau gave for the English officers that evening. When he entered the general's tent, O'Hara looked quickly around, then said as he accepted a glass of wine:

"I see we're to be alone. What a relief! I thought those wild men would fall on us this morning, they looked so fierce."

André translated for Rochambeau:

"The General is sorry that he is not to meet General Washington."

O'Hara gazed at him over the rim of his glass while Rochambeau said:

"It's better to keep our armies separate for the moment. The General sends his respects and hopes you're comfortable."

O'Hara's French was very good, as it happened, and André moved away soon afterwards to attend to other members of the English party. Later he found himself near O'Hara again and managed to say in a low voice:

"You won't give me away, I hope. I answered without thinking. I've spent the day trying to make the lion lie down with the lamb."

"Don't worry. I won't split. Irish, aren't you?"

"French-Irish."

"I'm English-Irish, if you like to call it that. I'm sorry not to meet General Washington, in spite of what I said. I think he's a very fine man, a good enemy, though I'm glad he didn't capture us single-handed. That would be too thick. Well, let's talk of other things. When were you last in France?"

"It's more than a year. I want to get back as soon as possible. I'm going to ask for leave of absence at once."

"You have a wife and children there, I suppose?"

"Not yet."

"You're engaged, then?"

"Yes."

O'Hara drained his glass and waited while a servant refilled it, then said:

"I envy you. God knows where we'll be sent next. We have quite a few Irishmen with us here, in that lot that came out from Cork. Splendid fighters, every one of them, very clever, understand every order at once. We'd never have relieved Fort Ninety-six without them." He laughed. "They should have been here, indeed. They were intended for Lord Cornwallis but Lord Rawdon sent them in the other direction."

"I shouldn't mention Lord Rawdon to the Americans, if I were you."

"No, I suppose not. It's understandable. Privately I can tell you that I thought Rawdon overdid the laying waste. What use is it if you can't get the infantry in? By the time he was finished there was scarcely a village where we could settle comfortably to wait out the winter. I like your French way of doing things better. Don't you have to let your men do some pillaging? I mean to say, how can you stop that? We close our eyes to it unless the stuff should come to the army."

"We don't allow it at all. The General has insisted that we pay for everything." He didn't add that the Americans insisted on being paid, since their experience of being looted by the English.

"Very odd, very peculiar," O'Hara said. "We have a policy of living off the country. It works out better in the end."

As soon as dinner was finished, some of the senior officers set out to pay a visit to Lord Cornwallis in his tent. O'Hara watched them go, then said to André:

"I'm jolly glad they didn't ask me to go along. I'm sick of that fellow and his tantrums. He never stops—he's all over General, every minute and hour of the day." He waved his glass, then drained it. "Now it's my turn to ask you not to give me away. That was the wine talking. For God's sake don't repeat it."

"Of course not."

"He makes me mad, pretending to be sick so as to avoid all this, like a schoolboy. He's no more sick than I am."

"Some of us guessed that."

"You seem much more casual with your senior officers than we are. I see lots of young fellows here hobnobbing with their colonels as if they were their equals. It's very nice but I doubt if we would allow it, unless the junior were a duke."

"Some of them are."

"Oh, I see. And you?"

"Count de Lacy. I hope we'll meet again. I've enjoyed your company."

"I hope so too, but not like this. Your old General, now—he's a character. Well, who knows, some day I may get back to France, not on business."

Two days later André sought out Robert. He found him inspecting the work of a team of soldiers who were filling in the trenches they had dug so painfully such a short time before. They had received a special issue of two days' pay, on Rochambeau's orders, and were very cheerful, joking and laughing as they worked. Stores were being carted out of the town by the Americans and the wagons creaked and rumbled past, loaded with small arms. The American soldiers were better dressed now, since they had found some thousands of uniforms in York and instantly issued them to their own troops. Clouds of mosquitoes hung over the oxcarts and over the men working in the trenches in the late autumn heat. Robert turned quickly at André's approach, saying:

"You've got your leave. I can tell by your face."

"Yes. I'm to go on the *Surveillante* tomorrow with de Lauzun."

"Tell her we talked it over. Tell her it's the best thing, tell her I said she must come away with you. Tell her she's not married at all."

"I'll know what to tell her."

"Don't be angry. You'll need my help, to make her believe it's the right thing to do. I'll give you a letter for her. You can put it into her hands the first time you see her, before you start arguing at all. You will do that?"

"What if she still refuses to come?"

"She must come, she can't stay there now."

"I can't force her. You could do that. I couldn't."

"Why not? I don't see why not."

"She must come freely if she comes with me. If I were to try to force her, it would be as bad as what has been done to her already."

"I'll say that in my letter, then. I wish I could go with you— no, if you fail, then I'll go later. If I hadn't been such a fool, this need never have happened. If I had been there, they couldn't have done this to her."

250

"You might not have been able to do anything."

"I would have killed them, all those old women too, the Archbishop, the whole lot of them, before I'd have allowed it."

"I wonder if you would. One goes along with the customs."

"If you speak like that I won't trust you to carry it through."

"Don't worry, I'll carry it through."

For the rest of the day André walked around as if he were half asleep or ill. The banality of the conversation with Robert had not lowered his mood of excitement. It was as if all of their words had had double meanings. He was going to her, he would take her away, she would be his, the nightmare would be over as if he had never dreamed it at all. He put his hand on the rough table by his camp bed and felt her hand softly under it. He looked towards the opening of his tent and she stood there, smiling at him. When his servant Pierre asked him a question, it was her voice that he heard.

At his age it was ridiculous, he thought from time to time. It was mad to let himself fly at this height over the world, but he did not want to stop. It would be his strength later. When she would see him, she would recognize his power and she would not be able to refuse him. He would force his thought into her mind, so that she would look, and wonder, and see that it was her own.

PART
SIX

24

Louise sat in the window seat of her bedroom, trying to see the summerhouse through the falling snow. She wanted it to be summer, so that she could go there and be alone. In her dream it was all green, the soft grass, the new leaves, the painted posts of the summerhouse where she had sometimes been rather happy a few months ago. Before going out Biddy had wrapped her in a long, feather-filled quilt covered with roses, which curled in and out of the fabric every time she moved. She put out one finger and touched the glazed cloth in the very center of one of the roses. It had a variety of colors like a real rose, like the tiny roses in the hedge at Mount Brien Court.

The huge log fire warmed the whole room and she was quite safe at the window, but Biddy had wanted her to sit beside the fire while she was away. Louise needed to see outside. When the snow ceased to fall, a pinkish glow lay on its surface and the undersides of the branches became intensely black. A light wind blew the thin branches clean, sending the snow scurrying to the ground in puffs. When the bells sounded, their notes seemed lighter, even the cathedral bell, as if its belfry were sinking into the snow and being buried there. Then slowly everything darkened in a cold, ugly light that crept towards the window, first touching the distant roofs, then the trees, then wiping away the pink-white color and replacing it with gray shading into indigo.

The glass of the window beside her felt cold. Now that the room was reflected in it, there was no point in sitting here. The night looked in at her. When she began to unwrap herself the cold struck her at once. She called out angrily:

"Marie! Marie! Where are you?"

Poor Marie came across at once from her chair by the door, where she had been placed by Biddy. She was not to move, not to leave Louise alone for an instant. She was to do her knitting and be quiet, Biddy said fiercely, though Marie was never anything but obedient and well-meaning. The person whom Biddy distrusted was Louise herself, that she would send Marie away as soon as Biddy's back was turned, but Louise had promised to be good too, only asking:

"Why do you have to go out? Why don't you send Marie and stay here with me yourself?"

"I've got to get trimming for my dress. How could I leave it to her? She's only a country girl—she'd bring something outlandish, and once they cut it off they won't change it, as you know very well. And I'd like some fresh air, so I would. I'm stifled in the house, and so are you. An outing would do you nothing but good. That old doctor would like to wait until the baby is walking before he lets you out. It's not natural, it's not right."

Louise began to cry gently, knowing that she was upsetting Biddy but not able to stop herself.

"Take me with you, then."

"Lord God, Miss Louise, I couldn't do that without leave. The Count would show me the door. I'll ask him myself one of these days. If he won't listen to you, maybe he'll listen to me."

Instantly Louise stopped crying and said:

"Yes, do that. He might persuade the doctor, if you ask him."

Something in her tone made Biddy look at her strangely but she made no reply. Louise knew very well why Armand might do something Biddy asked him. He was getting tired of Jeanne, the housemaid he had favored since June, and had hinted that she might be sent away for impertinence soon. Now he had his eye on Biddy. She and Louise both knew it but nothing would make them speak of it. Armand said more than once to Louise:

"Fine little girl, that Biddy of yours. Are there many like that in Ireland?"

Now his eyes followed her everywhere whenever he was in the room, childishly, like a boy watching a puppy. This was something much worse than his taking up again with Fifine d'Ernemont. Louise was not long in Angers before she was told that old story, and realized that the gossips were wondering how long the young Irish wife would be able to keep Armand interested. Once it was certain that she was pregnant, he was back with Fifine in no time, and her horror at his scandalous behavior was secretly mixed with relief that he never visited her bed again.

But this was sinful of her, at least equal to his sinfulness. She should have been seducing him back to his marital obligations. For the life of her she couldn't bring herself to confess this to one of his priestly friends, who came constantly to the house and showered her with blessings against miscarriage and disease at Armand's request. She did go one day, all the way out to Réculée to the Capuchins, and tried to explain the turmoil of her conscience to a weary old priest who said at last:

"Remember that in the end you're only responsible for yourself, for your own soul. God doesn't expect you to change your husband's morals. He will take care of that himself. You're a good child but a woman can only do certain things. Pray for your husband and I'll pray for you."

It was cold comfort at first hearing but after a while something—perhaps the Capuchin's prayers—made her better able to cope with Armand and his friends. Though she had never loved him, a certain tolerant fondness for him had at first made her believe that she might love him in time. Now that was out of the question, but after her visit to Réculée she no longer felt the cold disgust that would have made life in his house a nightmare.

Tatters of the nightmare were still there, however, and it was for this that she wanted to be alone, to examine them hour by hour and try to discover whether she was able to endure them. She could see that Biddy thought she was going mad, especially because she refused to have anything to do with the baby. The wet nurse brought him dutifully every day for her to see, and she glanced at him and away again, but she had never yet lifted him up or fondled him or treated him as if he were really her child. The wet nurse always cooed and rocked the baby in her arms, looking anxiously at Louise as she did so, obviously thinking she was heartless and that she might be moved mysteriously at seeing another woman holding her child, but Louise never would. That child was the cause of all her woes. Her reason told her that it was monstrous to blame him, and she did not blame him, but she knew by some instinctive foreboding that he could be used to make her suffer more, and she felt that she would not be equal to that. In this much Biddy was right. She saw a wild look of terror in Louise's eyes whenever the baby was brought to her, and she thought, rightly, that this was a dangerous and unnatural state of mind for a young mother.

"Can't you take hold of him, and kiss him, or do something for him?" she said to Louise. "What's wrong with you at all? He's a grand little lad. If he was a doll you'd have to like him, and he's your own son. You're sick, that's what it is," she said when Louise made no answer. "You'll be better in a while. I wish to God I had you back in Ireland, and Madame would talk sense to you."

Then Louise was sorry for Biddy and said:

"It will be all right. Just give me time. I must think."

Louise knew that Biddy would never betray her. She never had the smallest fear that she would be carried away or flattered by Armand's attentions. But there were things in Biddy's behavior that had made her uneasy in the last few days, like this walk on a snowy afternoon to buy some trimming for her old dress. What if Biddy were to leave her? What if she wanted to marry someone and go off to live somewhere else? The thought made Louise feel one of those short, sharp flashes of pain in her head that she had been having lately. Marie, settling her in her chair by the fire, looked at her in alarm and asked anxiously:

"Are you all right, Countess?"

"Yes, yes. I'm all right."

Marie backed away, watching her, and took up her knitting again. Then Louise sat quietly, even when Marie lit a candle and when the logs moved slowly as they burned down. When Biddy came into the room some time later she sent Marie away and said:

"Well, you look as comfortable as a grandmother. It's freezing over the snow. You're lucky to be in here, snug and warm." She knelt on the hearth and rearranged the logs, then stretched her hands to the blaze that came up in a moment. Louise sat perfectly still, her hands on the claw-shaped arms of her chair, her eyes fixed on Biddy's flushed face. She looked excited, almost as if she had been running. Curls of her jet-black hair were coming loose from under her cap and her heavy outdoor cloak was awry on her shoulders. There was something, surely there was some reason for her agitation. Francis, Armand's servant? Biddy would have better taste than that. Louise said:

"Show me the trimming."

"It's here, in my pocket."

Biddy took out the little parcel and opened it, showing a length of black braid woven with roses. As she took it from her to admire it Louise felt some warmth go through her, a shiver of returning life, running as lightly as a mouse from Biddy's hand to hers. She leaned out compulsively and took Biddy's two hands in hers, then pressed them against her cheek, saying:

"Biddy, please tell me what is disturbing you. I know there is something, there has been for days past. Is it because I get angry and quarrelsome with you? I don't mean it, you know I don't. I'm weak just now because of the baby, but when I get strong, when summer comes, you'll see it will be better. I'm afraid that you're weak too. If we're both weak, what will become of us? If you leave me, there will be no hope for me at all."

"I'll never leave you." But Biddy turned her back quickly, then stood up and went to get another candle and light it from the first, and brought it to stand on the table beside Louise as if she were going to read or sew. She stood there then, uncertainly, at last saying, "I don't know how to tell it—there's some things too hard for a person to say."

"What? You must say it. The Count?"

"No, thanks be to God. He knows nothing."

"Knows nothing? What have you been doing? You go out, you meet someone. Is that it?"

"Yes, yes, that's it."

"Someone from home? Someone from Ireland?"

"Yes. No, not that."

"Robert? News of Robert?"

Louise rose from her chair, seized Biddy by the shoulders and shook her gently, held her for a second, then moved her hands down Biddy's arms and gripped her by the elbows. Biddy said in a half whisper:

"Yes, news of Master Robert too. Oh, Miss Louise, it's Count de Lacy—he's here in Angers. I've told him that you're sick, and that he can't see you. Every day he tells me to come again tomorrow; he won't let me go. He says he'll wait until you're well again."

"Wait—wait for what?"

"To take you away. Oh, God help me, I should never have said it. I told him I would never give a message like that but he talks and he talks and in the end I do it. I said you're married now and for him to go away. I said you have your child and your duty to your husband and your God, and still he won't go, only always waiting for me and telling me I must come back the next day. He's driving me out of my mind, so he is."

"But you've gone back, every day?"

"What could I do? He's a gentleman, he must get his way. How could I chase him? He might come to the house, he said he would come to the house and ask for you, if I didn't come to him."

"Where do you meet?"

"In the house where he has rooms, right near the cathedral."

"And Robert?"

"Master Robert is well and strong. He left him at the war in America and came home by himself. They were both at that big battle that was won and he was let come home to tell the King. There isn't a scratch on Master Robert. Sit down again this moment or I won't tell you another word."

Louise sat down, obeying automatically, then sprang up to seize Biddy's shoulders again and demand:

"What have you been saying? Is this true?"

"Lord God, Miss Louise, how could I make up a thing like that?"

"Of course not." Louise laughed hysterically, then stopped, shocked at herself, ashamed before Biddy. "Go on. Tell me. You told him to go away."

"Yes, every day I say it to him, and he says he won't go. He put a letter into my hand the second day and I said I would never give it to you, and every day he asks me did I give it yet. Someday I think he'll kill me, but now I suppose you may as well have the letter since you know he's here."

"Yes, yes, give it to me."

"I was going to, this very day and hour. That's why I lit the candle, and you'll sit down, Miss Louise, and you'll do away with it if the Count comes in."

Louise sank into her chair in a daze. Biddy was fumbling in her pocket again, then handing her a letter from Robert, creased and stained from its days in Biddy's charge. She was saying:

"Maybe I should have given you the letter but Count de Lacy said there was something in it about his plan, and I was afraid—"

Absorbed in the letter, Louise barely heard her. Robert, yes, Robert was urging her to leave Armand and elope with André. She had to read it several times before she took that in. He said she was not married at all in the sight of God, and she should go now that she had the chance. She could trust André. They had wronged her, she need never have consented. Armand had no right to keep her since she had been forced to marry him. Robert knew about their father's consent but Grand-mère had not been consulted at all, and she also said that Louise should go with André. Grand-mère! Her letters to Louise were obviously intended for Armand's eye but there had been cryptic passages that might have been intended to convey these thoughts to Louise. She had never properly understood them. Grand-mère had been writing to André ever since Louise's marriage, Robert said. His letter asking for Louise had arrived too late, or so Countess de Rothe said. He had written and asked for her.

Louise lay back in the chair, letting the letter trail from her hand. Seeing that she was finished with it, Biddy snatched it from her and pushed it deep into her pocket again, saying:

"I know what's in it. He told me over and over. Master Robert says you're to go with him. He told Count de Lacy that if he had been here he would never have let you be married. But I'm tired of telling him that it's too late. You can't go. If he had come a year ago, right after the wedding, maybe, or even before you started the baby, but now you can't—"

"Stop chattering, Biddy. When will you see him again?"

"Tomorrow, God help me."

"I'll go with you."

"Oh, Miss Louise, you can't."

"Why not? I'm perfectly well now. It's time I went out. You'll see, I'll arrange it. You've been saying yourself that it's time I went out. Now tell me everything. How does he look?"

"Sure, you remember him well. He's a beautiful gentleman. I won't tell you a thing unless you keep quiet. Your face is red.

Be still. He knew me from the time he saw me in Kerry. He waited for me when I came into the town. I knew him too, the minute I saw him, so I wasn't a bit afraid of him. I thought he was going to ask which was your house because I guessed at once that that was what brought him."

"How did you guess? How?"

"Isn't he your cousin? What else would bring him to Angers but to see you? But he took me into the cathedral the first day, and that's where we had our talk. He didn't come out with it all at once, only asking me first how you were. Then after a while he said he had come to take you away. I said he could not. I took him up to the altar of God and said you're married now, and you have your baby, and your life is here now in Angers with your family. Then he told me he had Robert's letter and I said Robert is not your father, he had no right to say what you're to do. But he kept on asking me to bring you the letter and his message. In the end he let me go but he said I was to come again the next day. It's no wonder I look distracted, it's no wonder you saw it in my face."

"Were you never going to tell me?"

"I was meaning to do it today, but then I was afraid. That's the truth. But it's better this way. If you can come out with me tomorrow you can see him yourself, and tell him yourself, for I know now that he'll never believe me. He'll have to hear it from your own mouth, that he's too late. That's the way of the world. He'll have to swallow the sour drink, like everyone else."

25

Another full day passed before Louise succeeded in getting out of the house. Her mind was in agony. The prison door was open but she was not getting a pardon. If she left, it would be as a fugitive. Her first frantic hope at the prospect of rescue had been replaced with fear, not only of pursuit but of making a mistake worse than the last one. She had accepted Armand with her eyes open, thinking she would be strong enough and that there would be compensations for every one of the obvious drawbacks in her new life. She had been wrong on every count. Why should she be right this time? Perhaps this was another piece of the same stupidity that had led her into her present disastrous position. Biddy with her common sense said it was too late, simply too late, and Biddy was not short of courage. But what if Biddy were taken away from her? And what if Louise were to betray Biddy? A dreadful idea had come to Louise several times lately, that she might strike a bargain with Armand, letting him have Biddy if he would leave Louise alone. It was a monstrous, evil thought but it kept coming back to her, and it proved that she was no better than the other women of Angers, worse than many of them.

Of course if she were to agree to go with André, Biddy would have to come too. If she were left behind, and her part in the plot were discovered or even suspected, she would be tortured, perhaps beheaded. If they were caught as they went, her fate would be the same. Armand would be entitled to put Louise into a convent for the rest of her life, and no one would lift a finger for her. But Biddy would be trodden out of life like a beetle.

So she passed the time in mixed terror and hope, waiting for Armand to come back from a day in the country. She could perhaps have risked going out while he was absent, but he had left instructions with Zéphirine that she was to be kept in her room, almost as if he suspected something. Zéphirine had come very early, before seven o'clock, with this message, staring with her opaque eyes. When Armand came to see her in the evening, Louise said pettishly:

"Why did you say I was to stay in? It was such a lovely day, the sun shining on the snow, and I felt so much better, I would have gone out for a little walk."

"So you feel better? That's good news, yes, good news." He was looking at her in a new, calculating way that frightened her. She had no more idea of what went on in his head now than on the day she married him. She might as well have been a child, or a visitor. She went on without looking at him:

"I'll never be well until I go out. I won't go far, just as far as the cathedral, with Biddy."

He agreed, and some time during sleep her decision was formed without her knowledge. That was how it appeared when she walked through the rooms on her way out of the house at noon the next day. She found that she was appraising them and her own effect on the whole house, in the certainty that she would soon leave it forever. There was nothing here that she would regret. Her mind raced ahead to envisage Armand, back in the charge of Zizine, probably relieved that this foolish phase of his life was over. She remembered a peculiar piece of Galway folklore, perhaps from the islands, a story of a young man who married a beautiful girl from a distant place who stayed for a while and then disappeared. Her husband's story was that they quarreled one day and before his eyes she turned into a fox and ran out the door, and that was the last he saw of her. It was part of a whole complex of stories about foxes, which were said to be evil creatures. Perhaps Armand would make up some such story about her.

She realized that Biddy was watching her anxiously and she tried to speak calmly:

"You told him we would come soon after noon?"

"Yes. He'll be there. He waited all day yesterday, hoping you would come. I told you already, it will be all right."

"Then why do you look so wild?"

"It's you that looks wild. Walk slowly. Keep your eyes down or you'll be noticed. Here, lean on my arm. Your first day out, you're going to the cathedral to thank God for your baby. What could be more natural?"

"Biddy, I'm going to tell him that I'll go with him."

"Oh, God above! What will become of us?"

"We must be careful. If they catch us, it will be the end of us."

"I'm afraid."

"So am I, but there's nothing else to do. Will people see us talking to him?"

"They could, but at this time of the day the church might be empty."

"You go to his rooms."

"That's all right for me. You can't do that. If someone saw you going in they'd put legs under the story at once and send it all over Angers. It would be in the door before you when you'd get home."

"Don't look so excited. People are watching us."

This was said in revenge for Biddy's warning of a moment ago. No one was watching them. The market was just about to finish and the stalls in front of the cathedral were being cleared one by one and loaded on handcarts to be taken away. The stall holders were so busy with their own affairs that they took no notice whatever of the two young women, obviously mistress and servant, wearing heavy, dark cloaks, going into the cathedral to pray.

He was there. She saw him at once, far over on the left-hand side, standing by a pillar, his arms folded, as if he had plenty of time to spare. Apart from him the huge church was empty, but as they came in the sacristan popped out of a door at the top, glanced quickly at the high altar and disappeared again, leaving the door ajar.

Now that she saw him, the reality of what she was doing overwhelmed her. It was wicked, in God's high house, to harbor thoughts of revenge and anger, but she felt that there was no possibility of her forgiving Armand, with his Don Quixote eye-brows and his talk of taking her away to a safe, quiet life in the country. In her youth and ignorance it had never occurred to her at all that he would be unfaithful to her, nor that she would mind if he were. Married women in the country looked satisfied, at peace, not like those fly-by-nights in Paris. So she would be, with Armand, and he had promised her that in so many words. She remembered that she had trusted him because he was different from the other old men. Then he had betrayed her, first with his vulgar, noisy friends, then with Fifine and Jeanne. He deserved her vengeance. She would be revenged. She would take her son with her.

These confused and jumbled thoughts darted like birds through her head. Revenge, pain, the joy of hurting Armand as he had hurt and humiliated her—only for twenty seconds she considered them. They appeared childish and foolish when she dragged them out of their foggy retreat and examined them in the light of common sense. There would be no satisfaction in revenge, only more pain and perhaps even more chains. There is nothing so hard to forget as the pain one gives to others.

André heard their steps. He turned quickly, then came towards them. Louise felt her eyes fill with tears, at this moment when she most wished to be steady. Her weakness was a misfortune. She would not have wept once. But she had been weeping when Armand found her and took advantage of it. The thought calmed her, so that she was able to look directly at André and put out her hand to him, saying in a whisper, because they were in the cathedral:

"Thank you for coming. Thank you for Robert's letter."

"You read it. You know what he wants you to do."

"Yes."

"Will you come with me?"

"Yes, I'll come." She would never be able to take that back. "Where are we to go?"

"To America."

She had not thought of that.

"Can't we go back to Ireland?"

"Not yet. There is an American ship at Bordeaux, waiting for us." How sure he had been that she would come! As if he had read her mind he went on: "If you had refused to come I would have sent the Captain a message to say he should go without us. You have been very ill, Biddy says."

"Yes, after the baby, but I'm well enough now."

"Biddy says you have a son."

"Yes." The time had come to say the next, most necessary thing, which was after all the center of everything. She said it, because there was so little time. "I want to leave him behind."

After a moment he said, "Will you be able to do that?"

"Yes."

"Biddy says you don't care about him at all."

"I do, I do, but he belongs to Armand. He's all that Armand wanted from me. He can have him, then. It's better to leave him, better for everyone. I don't feel like a mother though I suppose I should."

They were no longer whispering. The sacristan popped his head out of the door by the altar and looked at them sharply, like a mouse watching a group of cats, then darted inside again. Biddy was watching too but keeping her distance so that she could not hear their conversation. Aware that she had begun to sound hysterical, Louise said more quietly:

"Biddy says it's too late. She says I should be resigned to my fate and make the best of things. She says there's no way out for me now."

"There is a way out, and you've agreed to it. You read Robert's letter."

"Yes, yes, I'll do as he says. I won't be afraid."

"One thing I must ask you: did you ever love Armand de La Touche?"

"No. How could I? What a funny idea. He never loved me either, except as he might love a good cow on one of his farms. That's how he looks at me, summing me up, working out what I'm worth to him."

"Robert said something like that. Louise, do you think you could love me?"

She looked at him directly, then turned away, saying, "Yes, I could."

"You know that's what Robert wants. He wants us to be married."

"But I'm married already. We can't be married."

"In America no one will know."

She said quickly, "But I don't care about that. I've had two days to think about it and that was enough. Robert says it's not the law of God that I'm to stay with Armand, nor that he has marked me for life so that I can never go to anyone else. I think now that he's right. God help me, maybe I'm a great sinner. I don't know. There are thousands and thousands of things I don't know, but as sure as we're in the house of God this minute I know that I want to go with you. I was afraid when I let them marry me to Armand but I'll never be afraid like that again as long as I live."

In spite of these words, now suddenly she had a moment of panic. Supposing he were to think her unscrupulous, abandoning her husband and her child too easily? According to the ladies of Angers, that was how all men were, pressing you for all kinds of favors, then shocked and scornful if you yielded and gave them. A bunch of those ladies had got her in a corner once, on the same occasion as they had told her that Armand had taken up with Fifine again, and advised her carefully on her own procedure. She was to have an affair of her own, not now but when the baby was born, and they even named one or two men who would be glad to be honored by her.

André said, "Then you won't be afraid of me?"

"How could I be afraid of you? You were always good to me."

Now the sacristan was really watching them, and even took a step forward as if he were going to remonstrate with them for making such a use of his church. Their animated conversation could have nothing to do with prayers. The bells began their clanging at the half hour. Biddy came over to them, saying:

"He's after noticing you, Miss Louise. We must go home. Let you kneel down now and say a few prayers to head him off."

"Yes."

André said, "Biddy, can you come to me at five? It will be almost dark then. I'll tell you what to do."

Louise pulled the hood of her cloak forward to hide her face, then left them together and went towards the high altar and knelt there until Biddy came and touched her shoulder, whispering:

"He's gone. Oh, Miss Louise, we're destroyed now for sure. He says he's taking us to America. I promised Madame that I'd look after you and now look what's happening, leaving your house and your husband and your baby—"

"Never mention the baby again!" Louise said fiercely, rising from her knees and whirling around to face Biddy. "It's no good. He's not mine. He belongs to my husband. That's what he wanted and that's what he's got. Grand-mère said I'm to go with Count de Lacy. It's in Robert's letter. Who am I to trust?"

"I wish he would take us back to Ireland. We should go home."

"He says we can't go for the present. Biddy, I'm in torment too, but I'll get used to it, and so will you, the way we'd get used to a chronic sickness. The day we left Ireland all our misfortunes began. I'm lucky to be able to escape now. Most people would have no hope till death. The baby—I won't think about him now. I know what I'm doing is right. Some day I'll come back and see him, if he's living, and if I'm living. If I stop to think now I'll change my mind. I won't go at all. I'll stay here until I'm an old woman with no teeth and no hair, or else I'll go down some morning early and jump off the bridge into the river. Would that be better? I won't do it. That's for other people but not for me. We should be thankful to have such a good friend to help us."

"He was too slow. He should have married you first, or at least he should have asked for you."

"He didn't know what would happen to me."

She realized now that it was cruel to tell her thoughts to Biddy like this. It could do nothing but harm to the simple, innocent girl, who for all her country wisdom never questioned the laws of the priests nor of the gentry. Even such revolutionary talk as she heard at home was not connected with daily life at all, only with the remote Parliament in Dublin, in which she believed less than she believed in God.

"He was late in asking," Louise said. "I'm going with him now. Perhaps I'm not doing right, but it feels to me as if I'm being rescued at the point of death. We won't talk of that again. Now don't look anxious and worried or they might say I can't go out with you again."

It was almost dark when Biddy set out for André's lodgings and Louise was left shockingly alone with the old fears, which refused to go away. Since the birth of the baby nothing was real, she lived in a false world, like a stage set, a world that could be folded up and put away and forgotten as if it had never been. Even André seemed unreal now. Once she left him she ceased to believe in him. Why should he risk his life and property for her? A sensible man would put her out of his head and find another girl to suit him. He would never travel all across the world to take away one who was already the wife of someone else.

Countess de Rothe would be furious—the notion penetrated into her distracted mind and amused her in spite of herself, before terror took possession of her again.

They were both irresponsible. What if André didn't really love her at all, if he were following a silly dream too, from which they would both awaken and find that they had destroyed one world without creating another? She walked to the window and looked out on the darkening town, lit now by candles and lamps in the windows of the houses. How stable and sure they were! She would give anything in the world for that precious light of peace that can only burn at home, the warm light that perpetually signals love and trust and quiet hope. As these thoughts flowed over her, she remembered André and felt his hands on hers as if he were present in the room. Then all her confusion left her and she knew that what she was about to do was inevitable, and that her doubts and fears were not the reality but the dream.

26

They left Angers just after dark four days later. It had snowed again and the long flight of steps that led up to the cathedral square looked like a smooth sloping street. The people in the houses that opened onto the steps had to use their back doors or else crawl about close to the walls. Firelight and lamplight shone from inside, covering the windows with a moving orange glow. Glancing through one as they passed, Louise saw some children sitting at a kitchen table holding their spoons high and laughing, while their mother ladled soup into their bowls. These were real children, not like her son. She had held him for longer than usual today when the wet nurse brought him, feeling that she should at least try to remember his face. The nurse nodded and smiled encouragingly, obviously hoping that Louise was coming to her senses at last. She felt no attraction to this wizened little creature with a strong look of Armand, but she was glad she did it. Numbed as she was with anxiety, she felt no pain at leaving him. She wanted nothing from Armand, and this child was his property. So she told herself repeatedly, hoping that it was true.

There were few people about on such an evening, though a clear moon and stars foretold that the snow was ended. The dark berline at the door of André's lodgings was the only vehicle in the street. As they approached they could see that the last of the baggage was being strapped onto the top, supervised by the coachman and by André's servant, Pierre. Biddy had a basket and a holdall, but she had been bringing small parcels of things each day and packing them into a trunk which André had given her.

He was watching for them, and hurried them into the carriage at once. A moment later the servants climbed in, the coachman was up and they moved off. In the darkness he took Louise's hand and said in English:

"You left a letter for Count de La Touche?"

She found that she was barely able to speak.

"Yes. We told Marie to say that I'm not feeling well and don't want to be disturbed this evening. Armand went out early to pay visits. He'll have the letter tomorrow." She laughed hysterically. "He'll say, 'Nothing to be done about it, nothing to be done.' "

Only Biddy, sitting stiffly on the seat in front of them, could understand, and she wriggled her shoulders with disapproval. After a moment Louise asked:

"Are we going to travel all night?"

"Tonight we must, except to change horses and perhaps eat something. I sent one of my men out early and he says that the roads are clear from Angers south. After tomorrow we can sleep at the inns. I've dropped hints at my rooms that I'm going to Brest, in case there is a hue and cry. No one will think of Bordeaux."

"I wish we could have gone to another port. You know that Father Burke is in Bordeaux."

"Yes, but he won't see us."

"I'm afraid. I feel as if I've stepped off a roof into space. Your hand holds me up."

"We're going to a safe place. Once we're on the ship you won't be afraid."

"No. Do you know where we're going, in America?"

"Have you just thought of that now?"

"Yes."

"It's a farm, near Hartford, in Connecticut. Cousin Charles Lally has agreed to exchange it for my house at Saint André. We'll stop there so that I can speak to my steward about him."

The servant had been mistaken and the last few miles before the first stage were almost impassable. The horses sweated and pulled frantically and the snow groaned under the carriage wheels. Bright moonlight showed a long, white, vacant country-side in every direction, as far as the eye could see, and no one moving except themselves. At the inn the landlord was amazed that they had been able to come so far.

"But you're safe enough now," he said. "You and your wife and her maid can sleep upstairs. The men can go in the barn. There's plenty of hay there. It's warm and dry. No question of going any farther. Are you mad? The roads are blocked for several miles south, though some say there's a thaw coming. I wouldn't let a dog pass along this road, and my horses are certainly not going. There, that will make up your mind for you. You can't go without the horses. Inside, everyone. We have a good dinner ready, too good for ourselves, but we were going to eat it if no one came. I said to my wife, a good dinner never goes to waste, and she had to agree that we'd eat it ourselves, though she didn't like it. Inside, now, inside."

He almost pushed them through the doorway into the main room of the inn, hot and steaming from the stove at the back. The dinner that was simmering there smelled delightful. The innkeeper's wife said harshly to Biddy:

"You, young girl, take your mistress's things up to the front room. Feel the bed if you like. It's a good one, the very best in the house. They won't be cold. You may make a fire if you like. I would, if I were you. Then you can come down here and help me with their dinner."

Biddy took the lamp she was given and climbed a ladder-like stairs, and they could hear her opening the door of a bedroom. André said:

"Yes, we'll stay, but the moment the thaw comes we must be off."

"What's your hurry?" The landlord was looking at them curiously. "In the middle of winter, no one can be in a hurry."

"We won't move while there is such snow. You're quite right. We were lucky to have got so far. And your dinner—we'll come down and eat that with the greatest of pleasure. We hadn't hoped for such good comfort tonight."

In the bedroom, Biddy had put the lamp on the shelf over the mantel. They looked at each other desperately, André fearing that his mistake was going to destroy them all. What had he done to her, what was he offering her so arrogantly? His company, his love, his so-called protection were all leading her to dangers far worse than any she had yet suffered. Then Biddy gave a quick sigh and said:

"A fire. The old one said we can have a fire."

She hurried downstairs and got one of André's servants busy with logs and kindling, and within a few minutes a fire was hissing and blazing on the hearth. Still in her cloak, Louise stood gazing into the fire, her face lit by the bright flames. Suddenly she whirled around, saying:

"André, come to the fire. Look, it's the most beautiful fire in the world." She took his arm and brought him to stand close by her, then looked into his face as if she were seeing him properly for the first time. "André, how old are you?"

"Twenty-nine."

"So old! That's why you're so wise."

"I don't feel wise," he protested.

"We'll live to be a hundred, won't we?"

"If you like."

"No wonder you're laughing at me. I say things badly. I have a pain, here, around my heart, for all the things that are being done for me. I'm the cause of all this trouble, for being so stupid. I've put everyone in danger, you and Biddy, and the baby—there was no need for any of it, if I had been as wise as you."

"I'm not wise enough."

"Everywhere there were things I could have done, things I barely saw, all around me. Madame Dillon and Lucy needed help from somewhere. I was there and I didn't give it. I wanted to escape. I thought only of myself. Oh, God, how can one be so selfish? I was so critical of them all, I was so righteous and so sure I was better than them, and then I became one of them without noticing what I was doing. I thought of you then, André, even in the church, while I was agreeing to marry Armand, and I made a dream that it was you. That was a crime against Armand. No wonder he was never happy with me. No wonder he always looked at me as if I were a stranger."

"Armand has a bad reputation. You're blaming yourself unjustly."

"Am I? Perhaps about that, but I shouldn't have loved another man while I was married to him."

"You knew you loved me, all that time?"

"Yes. I used to send you messages, from my mind to yours, wherever you were, as if they could be brought by a bird, or by some magic. I knew it was wrong and still I kept on doing it. Afterwards I always felt stronger."

"Perhaps those messages reached me."

He was afraid to tell her of the vision he had seen on her wedding day. She was saying:

"You think that's possible? At the time I hoped they would. Now I don't know what to think. Perhaps I've destroyed us both. I've lost my sense of right and wrong. If Father Burke were here he would say it's my duty to stay with Armand because I promised it at the altar of God. Why should I tell you all this? You might even think I don't love you enough."

"I'll never think that. Come closer. Take off your cloak." He lifted it from her shoulders. "It's ridiculous to blame yourself for the wrongs that were done to you. I know that you love me. I feel it in every part of me. I should never have left you. From now on we'll be together always."

The clatter of a brass gong summoned them downstairs. The landlord sat down with them while Biddy and his wife and Pierre served the dinner, a stew made of some game birds which they couldn't identify.

"You'll never guess, and I won't tell you," he said when André asked him. "Around here we tell no tales. That's how it has to be in my business." He leered at them knowingly, his eyes darting from André to Louise and back again. "You can sleep easy, my lord duke. In the morning when you're on your way south I'll say you went north and I'll laugh myself sick while I watch them take the wrong road."

"Why do you call me duke?" André asked, while Louise bent low over her plate to hide her terror. "I'm not a duke."

"It saves time. I always work from the top down. Don't be offended. We get sharp eyes in my business, I tell you."

But after a while André decided that it was only senseless teasing. Louise was in a panic. Back in their bedroom she kept on saying:

"Perhaps he has been in Angers. Perhaps he has seen me there. We're too near it. André, what will I do if I'm taken away from you again—what will I do?"

She wanted to go on there and then, harness up their own horses and make their way somehow to the next inn, as they had planned to do, and he had to persuade her that this would really arouse all the unpleasant landlord's suspicions. Afraid to sleep, they sat by the fire until just before dawn when they heard a trickling and running of water that filled the air like the twittering of birds. The promised thaw had come. They roused the landlord and were on the road inside an hour, their breath steaming like the horses' breath in the piercing cold, hanging like small yellow clouds against the lamplight.

Now the roads became rivers of mud as the snow melted. Over and over again the coachman had to order the servants down to help move the carriage out of ruts and potholes, invisible in the slush until the wheels sank into them. He had taken two extra horses on traces beside the front pair and these proved their salvation. Two of the postilions rode them and managed to keep all four horses together on the road, even when it seemed that the whole equipage must roll into the ditch. These postilions were also their guides and took them by the worst byroads to avoid the farm wagons which used the high roads. Near the villages things were better, but then the people came to their doors to stare, and Louise was terrified that someone would take the chance of riding off to Angers to find out if a reward were being offered for a runaway wife and her lover. André reassured her as best he could, saying:

"This bad weather is a godsend. It's exactly what we needed. No one will be out, no one will be able to move, until the roads dry up. By then we'll be so far off that they'll never find us."

Then she would relax for a while, until she found at the next inn that people had come in specially to see the gentry who didn't have the wit to stay at home in such foul weather. But the servant who rode ahead always had fresh horses and postilions ready, and the landlords were glad to have any customers at all at this dead time of the year.

On the second day the roads were dry. Clouds of dust filled the air and blew through every chink and cranny of the carriage until their lungs and their eyes were full of grit. No one complained, however, since they felt that anything was better than the snow. As they went farther south André saw that Louise's spirits rose when the sky cleared and the air became warmer. Now and then she and Biddy got out of the carriage and walked or ran on the grassy hills by the roadside, holding hands like children, calling to him to come and join them. The look of terror was gradually leaving her since there was no sign that they were being pursued, and she even said on the third day, before they left the inn in the morning:

"Perhaps Armand was glad to be rid of me. He never liked me, or approved of me, though he used the things he disapproved of to get me for himself." She told him of the time when she had confided her disgust with Parisian society to him, and how he had betrayed her afterwards to Countess de Rothe. "That was why I gave my consent to marrying him, because I had lost all faith. It seems mad now to have given myself over to the very person who had injured me most, but that's exactly what I did."

"Robert couldn't make out why you agreed to it."

"If he had been there, none of it would have happened."

"Do you blame him, then?"

"I have no one to blame but myself. We were a pair of little fools. It was quite easy to deceive us. All those conventions—we thought there was something behind them. It took us too long to see that they were hollow."

He loved to watch her when she was in this mood, her half-closed eyes and lifted chin making her look years older. Abruptly he said:

"Now you look like your grandmother."

"Do I? I'm glad. I'm going to like being old."

"So will I, if you look like that."

"I wish we were going to her. She wrote me such strange letters, trying to tell me that I was not abandoned by everyone. I couldn't understand what she was saying. Armand read all her letters but he could never make them out either. I suppose she was hinting that you might come. She could never say that. I wrote to her about the child, and to say that Armand had gone back to Fifine d'Ernemont. He threw her next letter on the table before me and said, 'Looks as if the old lady is going off her head.' The writing was shaky and the sentences were all unconnected—it did look as if she were wandering in her mind. Then her next letter was quite all right, nothing wrong with it at all."

"Did he open your letters himself?"

"Always, but Biddy sent mine without his seeing them. I hated to deceive him but I had no choice. A letter from Robert made him very angry and he never gave it to me at all. Robert should have been more discreet."

"Then he knew that Robert was angry at your marriage. Was that his only letter to you?"

"I never had another. I thought he had forgotten me. But Grand-mère wrote that you were together all the time. I thought of you both every night before going to sleep. Tell me about the battle. Were you both there?"

"Yes. Arthur Dillon too. All battles are dreadful."

"Were you in danger?"

"No, but some of the junior officers were, Robert and some of his friends. It's always worse for the common soldiers. A couple of hundred of them were killed but they fought well. The English losses were much more, and there were Germans on the English side too. I wish I need never again be in the army, not until the war is for Ireland."

A few miles from Bordeaux they turned off to Saint André de Cubzac. The smooth cornfields were already plowed, and in the neat, bare vineyards all the vines were pruned and staked ready for the spring growth. They reached the little château by a short avenue. It was a plain, long, three-story house of yellow stone with a pergola at one end covered with the bare stems of vines and creepers. Louise loved it at once, and now she had her dream as André, on his tour of inspection, conducted her all over the house and through the stables and the farmyard as well. The steward had been summoned by André's servants, who had evidently told him of their master's adventures, for he looked oddly at Louise, though he treated her as if she were André's wife and the mistress of the house. He was dreadfully disappointed when he was told that they were on their way to America. He said:

"I was hoping you would stay here and take care of the place yourself, Count. It's a long time since there was a family in the house and that's what it needs. Everyone is working well but there's no heart in it. You should go along the road a mile or so and have a look at the house that Count de La Tour du Pin is building. It's like Versailles, they say, though I've never seen that place. There's going to be a gallery along the front, and pillars, and doors opening out of the big salon on the first floor, on to a long balcony. They say his son is looking for a wife and he'll take her to live there. Would you think of building a place like that, sir? The architect comes out from Bordeaux every week to oversee it. That's a house fit for a gentleman."

"I got a fancy for smaller houses when I was in America," André said. "You'll soon have a family here."

As he gave instructions for the Lallys' reception, Louise and Biddy wandered around the house, looking into the bedrooms and sitting rooms, opening the heavy wooden shutters to let in the dusty sunlight. Biddy said:

"I wish we could stay here forever, Miss Louise. It's a house I could love, and we'd all be happy in it. Why did God send us so much misfortune?"

They were afraid to spend the night in Saint André lest they were being followed. Instead, they forded the river and went on to Bordeaux, and put up at an inn far down the Quai des Chartrons. A dismal rain was falling. Thick mist covered the mud flats at the estuary of the river but they could make out the masts of a few small ships far off towards the ocean. Sea gulls cried sharply, swooping around the inn prospecting for food from the kitchen. The sound upset both Louise and Biddy dreadfully, and they stood at the window, their arms around each other's waists, and gazed in horror at the dismal prospect before them. Fortunately André had gone out to find the Captain of the ship, and by the time he came back they were able to look more cheerful.

He brought the Captain with him, an American named Gilbert who was bringing a cargo of nails and small tools to Boston. He made no secret of the fact that he didn't like passengers but that times were too hard to allow him to be particular. If he could get his nails ashore and sell them, he would come back for more and then settle down on Nantucket and go in for whaling. He told them all this over supper, fixing them with big, earnest, brown eyes and speaking very slowly as if he feared that they didn't understand what he was saying. In spite of André's account of the victory at York he refused to believe that the war was over, and kept on repeating:

"Much easier to start a war than to stop one. You'll see, this one won't be over for three years."

At last he went away. The dinghy would come for them at

five in the morning, to catch the tide. It was their last night in France, a moment for rejoicing that their escape was now certain. Louise parted the curtains so that she could see outside. The quayside was desolate and empty of people. Thin moonlight lay on the mud flats and on the dreary water of the river, with black patches where the land stretched fingers out over its leaden sheen.

Without warning, the face of her child appeared before her, so that she gave a cry of pain, like a hurt animal. Instantly André came across the room and took her in his arms. She clung to him, weeping desperately. There was no need to put her grief into words. He understood at once what had happened to her, and he held her quietly for a long time until he could see and feel that she was calmer. Then he said:

"You can still go back if you can't bear it."

"I can't go back. You know I can't. I don't want to. But I didn't know it would be as bad as this."

She could not say another word. From that moment onward she knew that she would never escape. Her son was helpless, unloved, unwanted, but she would never be able to forget him.

27

Ice covered the river and the whole farm was encased in snow when they reached Hartford, but Louise loved it from the first moment.

Their welcome was discouraging, Charles falling into more and deeper fits of gloom as the days went on. It was perfectly clear that he did not want to leave, and if there were any doubt about it Pauline's low-voiced conversations with Louise whenever they were alone would have removed them. She watched until Charles and André went out of the room, exactly like a housemaid waiting to have a conversation with her colleague about their mistress, then said:

"Charles has gone native. He doesn't care for civilized company any more. He just wants to talk to the other farmers about animals and crops and the weather, like the peasants at home. If we stayed here I believe he would forget how to go into a French drawing room altogether. And the children—men don't seem to care about children as women do."

Louise said, "I think Charles loves his children."

Pauline seemed to consider this for a moment, then she changed her tone to a slightly more cheerful one.

"I'm longing to get back to France. Tell me about the house in Saint André."

It was easy to praise it, but then Pauline said:,

"Didn't you want to stay there? I can see that you love it. Perhaps André is doing the same thing to you that Charles did to me: they promise you the moon and then you find out they didn't mean a word of it. André probably told you that America is a wonderful place. All the officers who came to fight here have the same story—it's the land of the free, the great new world where everyone is equal, but I don't like everyone to be equal, and they never are anyway. And now Charles has made it a condition that when we go back we're never to go to Paris. I had to agree, else he would never have consented to go home at all." Now her tone became an impatient whine. "He argues and argues about it. He has lots of reasons. His cousin Thomas Arthur Lally was executed there, for treason or something, Charles says unjustly and perhaps it was. He had lost battles in India and the King should have saved him. Charles goes on and on about it. It's so long ago, 1766—but he says he made a vow that he would never live in Paris again, and he says there will be a war there between the rich and the poor. What do you think of that?"

Louise deliberately simplified her language as if she were talking to a child.

"I've heard that all this talk of liberty will be bad for the poor people in France but I never heard that there will be a war. Aren't you afraid to go home, then?"

"Why should I be afraid? I'll have decent servants again, and proper dinner parties, and be able to get my hair dressed, and see my friends for coffee, and my children will speak good French, and Emilie can have a good governess, a lady, everything that I had myself, and we can find her a good husband when the time comes. Here she might marry anyone at all, a farmer, a woodsman, anyone. Patrick can have a tutor. Perhaps we'll have other children. Tell me all about your wedding. Where did you have it? What did you wear? Did you have a honeymoon? Or did you come straight out here?"

"It was at Hautefontaine."

"You're blushing—you're really in love. I'm not surprised. I would be in love with André if I were married to him. Men like that are very scarce."

The sharp lines around her mouth, the sharp tone of her voice and the way she screwed her eyes up and thrust her chin forward all gave her an unpleasant shrewish look. If André had not warned her that Pauline had to be pitied, Louise would have fled from her company forever. As it was, she said:

"It was nice being married in Hautefontaine instead of Paris. I love to be in the country. Countess de Rothe did everything. My dress was lovely."

"Get Biddy to bring it down. I want to see it."

"I didn't bring it with me."

"Not bring your wedding dress! How could you bear to leave it behind?"

"The ship was so small. Lots of things had to be left behind."

"I'm taking every single thing, all my fur coats and wraps, and my dresses and hats and bonnets. I've hardly worn any of them. They will be right out of fashion but I'll have them remade. I suppose you can still get good bonnet-makers in France. Here you can hardly buy flowers for the bosom of a dress any more. They say there's a shortage of linen because of the war but anyway the women here are savages. They make up flowers out of old linen handkerchiefs but used linen doesn't take the starch properly and they go limp at once. Did you bring some flowers with you?"

"No."

Again that shrewish look, calculating, watching Louise's face coldly, and the comment:

"You may do better than I did. You don't look like an innocent young girl. When I came out here I was so simple, I had no idea what it was like to have a baby and take care of it. I thought everything would be easy. You only had to feed them well and they would be healthy and strong." Then she said hurriedly, "Well, you'll do better than I did."

Louise said, "Emilie and Patrick look very well."

"Yes. Emilie was born in France."

Pauline stood up quickly and walked across the room, then came back to say:

"I'm sorry to be so nervous. I'm sure you think me very rude."

"Not at all. Please don't apologize. Come and sit down. Tell me about the farm."

"I had nothing to do with that, of course, and I advise you to leave it alone. The nigras do everything for you. They can be quite nice and kind, especially Agnes. Tell me more about the wedding. How did André look? We thought he would never marry, then we heard a rumor about a cousin who must have been you. I'm sorry we can't be near enough to each other to be friends. It's such a treat to have another woman to talk to. Charles is no good for chatting. He calls it making conversation. It will all be different when we get back to France. Then I'll never be frightened again."

Louise hoped that she had gone off the subject of the wedding but she came back to it again.

"Who came to the wedding? Were there lots of cousins there?"

"Not many, because it was winter." She described her wedding to Armand, the wedding Mass and feast, all as if André had been the bridegroom and everything had happened a few months ago instead of the year before. Pauline said:

"Tell me about Countess de Rothe. Did you love her? I'm sure she loved you, you're so sweet and innocent." She couldn't have meant to sound contemptuous. "I've never met those Dillons because of being married to a Lally. The Dillons say that all the Lallys are bastards, and they don't like them being friends with Mary Dillon for fear she might leave them her money." Louise noticed that she pronounced "Dillon" in the old-fashioned way, "de Lioune," as the Irish did. Pauline went on: "There are wonderful parties at Hautefontaine, I've always heard. It's not Paris—perhaps Charles will agree to go there. Could you write to the Countess and ask her to invite us?"

"She doesn't like me," Louise said firmly. "You'll do better to make your own approach."

She could see that Pauline thought she was being mean. The whole game was hardly worth it, in any case, because the Lallys would hear all about her escapade the moment they reached France if not sooner. Pauline said:

"Then you had to leave everything and come out here, to please André. Did you ask him to stay for a while and take you to court? That is what I want more than anything in the world. And that's not Paris either—it's Versailles. I'm going to try to make Charles take me there."

"I didn't really want to go to court," Louise said in a last effort to bring Pauline down to earth. "I was at lots of parties in Paris when I came first and I didn't like the people at all, especially the women. They're so artificial, even their fashions show it. I've heard the King and Queen are very simple and put you at your ease, but I would find it all too frightening."

"Yes, I suppose you would."

It was hard to imagine a more unlikely courtier than Charles, with his deerskin jacket and top boots and swinging farmer's gait. On the last days he must have visited his animals a dozen times, inventing one excuse after another to take André out to the stables, repeating himself endlessly in his instructions about their care. He would hold a scythe or a favorite billhook, turning the worn handle lovingly around and around, saying:

"I've had this since we came. We had to make most of our own tools. Well, I know you will take good care of them." Once he said in a dead tone, "She was right, André. The last child died at four months. It's a wonder she's sane at all."

"Charles, I'm sorry."

"I know you are. I hope you have better luck. It's a wonderful life here."

André began to feel like a thief but he could see that Charles was not trying to get out of his bargain. His patience with Pauline was endless. At night, screams and hysterical sobs sounded through the thin wall that separated the bedrooms, and Pauline's tone when speaking to Charles became daily more querulous. The children watched her anxiously and were unnaturally quiet. At last their heavy trunks and baggage were packed and sent off by sledge to Boston, with four servants. Several days later, in a crisp, sunny dawn, the passenger sledge was brought around to the front door. Pauline was in a state of wild excitement, barely containing herself long enough to kiss Louise perfunctorily before hurrying outside and climbing in. Louise stood at the drawing-room window watching Charles wrap her in furs as carefully as if she were an invalid, her children silent and close at either side of her. André was there, looking very strange in a tall cap made of fox fur, helping to buckle the straps, talking to the children, who watched him beady-eyed and unsmiling. Then the two men came back into the house. Charles stood by the blazing log fire in the drawing room, saying nervously:

"I'm sorry you had to put up with so many of her tantrums. She'll be much better once we're on the road. The sledge will come back from Boston in a few weeks. The other one is not quite as big but it will do you until then. We should be taking the less good one but she insisted."

"Charles, please! We're quite content. Don't worry about us. Take care of your family. That's all that matters."

"I feel as if I were leading them into the lion's den. In all my life I have never done anything so stupid. But you're right, there is no help for it."

When he embraced them they saw that he had tears in his eyes. He walked stiffly out to the sledge and got in, the driver instantly cracked his whip over the horses' backs and they glided quietly away, down the hill, across the frozen river to the snow-covered road at the other side.

Now the house felt hollowed and empty. They walked all over it, into every room, feeling like intruders at first and then with a sense of tentative happiness, heightened whenever they encountered Biddy. She was in her element, ordering changes everywhere, especially the moving of André's and Louise's things into the master bedroom. Still Louise felt herself stung from time to time by an old pain, the one she had come to recognize as pain for the loss of her son. Her helplessness made it easier to bear, as did the fact that she suspected that she was already pregnant again, and she hoped that this other child would compensate for the one she had left behind.

It was through Agnes, the main house slave, that she learned of Pauline's misfortunes. Louise noticed that Agnes was not much interested in the preparations for the new baby, and she thought at first that grief for the departed children had upset her. Finding Louise sewing, Agnes would turn away sharply, often with tears in her eyes. It was almost impossible to get her to talk about the baby, even when Louise asked her advice about which room to use for it, which of the slaves was likely to be ready to act as wet nurse, or whether the Lallys had left a cradle in the house that could be used again. Then, on one of the first warm afternoons of May, she was sitting in the garden resting when she saw Agnes come out of the house and set out by a narrow path up the incline beside the kitchen garden. Louise noticed her particularly because she stopped now and then to pluck wild flowers by the side of the path, binding them carefully into a nosegay with grass as she walked along. Quietly Louise stood up and followed her. Agnes was so absorbed that she took no notice. She was crooning softly to herself and swaying from side to side as in a slow dance, sometimes stooping to pick another flower to add to her bouquet. As Louise came closer she could hear the words of her song, repeated over and over:

"Heaven is a beautiful place, I know.
Heaven is a beautiful place, I know.
Mammy coming, Mammy coming with flowers.
Heaven is a beautiful place, I know."

As she got farther from the house she sang louder, no longer concerned that she might be heard, but she never once looked back. At an angle in the path she left it and crossed a meadow, moving a little faster. The cemetery! Louise realized now where she was going. She had been there once with André, a short time ago, when the snow melted and they were able at last to walk the whole of their estate. It was a sad little patch, outlined in rough stones, the graves marked with roughhewn headstones on which often there appeared only a single name—Peter or John or Isaac—names of slaves long forgotten, or remembered no more than a dog would be. On that visit she had noticed a neater, more-cared-for part, but André had made her come away and she had not been able to look at it closely. With a longer distance between them now she saw Agnes make for this plot, where she knelt down and placed her bouquet on one of the graves. Then she suddenly threw herself on her face and lay, twitching, moaning gently, almost appearing to embrace the earth in her anguish. Louise hurried towards her, saying when she was close enough:

"Agnes! What is it? Agnes!"

Instantly Agnes started to her feet, calling out angrily, "Back! Go back! Woman with child must never come here! Back!"

Louise stood her ground, saying, "Yes, I'll go back, but you must tell me whose are those graves."

Agnes brushed off her skirt with her hands, her head bent, then took Louise's arm and led her quickly back into the meadow saying gruffly, "It's Miss Pauline's babies. I must come to them sometimes with flowers."

"Yes, of course. How many babies?"

"Five. They's company for each other." She gave a quick, sideward look at Louise. "Miss Pauline had no luck with babies. No love, no luck. But I loved them all, Agnes loved every one. If I was young enough to be the wet nurse not one of them had died. She sold the wet nurse every time but it was never any different. One of them was my own daughter but she couldn't help it I know."

"Sold them!"

"Yes, ma'am, she did that but it was not their fault. Their own babies didn't die. That was a sign the mothers was healthy, but Miss Pauline said it was a sign they gave black looks to her babies and grudged the milk."

"Do you believe that?"

"No, ma'am, I don't believe it. Didn't I tell you one of them was my daughter? Those women was as sorry after her babies as if they was their own, but they were sold just the same."

"Where did they go?"

"Different farms around, not too far. Master saw to that, because of their husbands. He's always good like that but he picked a couple of bad masters all the same, maybe without knowing it." Suddenly frightened, she asked "Didn't you know about those babies? Didn't you know when you were coming here?"

"Not a word, but it doesn't matter. I would have heard it sooner or later."

"Yes, ma'am, from the neighbors."

"What about their babies? Is it like that with all the people?"

"You mean all the white people?"

"Yes."

"Only with rich folks, them that think it's not fitting for a lady to nurse her own baby."

Agnes muttered these last words with her head bent, as if it were an impertinence.

"Then you think that if Mistress had nursed her own babies they wouldn't have died?"

"How do I know? I said it to her once and I thought she would kill me, she got so mad. She was not a lady you could say much to."

So that was poor Pauline's story, a miserable one indeed. The fashion for natural living had not taken hold until after she had left Paris. It had not reached Angers, and Louise had taken advantage of this to have her son fed by a wet nurse. If Pauline had fed her own, she might have reared them all safely. They had probably died of dirt, and of the diseases the blacks were used to. Louise had already noticed the filth of the Negroes' quarters and was determined to improve them. They reminded her of nothing so much as the hovels on Burke's land in Moycullen.

Later, when she told André about this conversation she asked:

"Did you know about Pauline's babies?"

"Yes."

"Why didn't you tell me?"

"Why should I? Pauline does everything badly. I have no fears for you."

"You're not afraid for the child? You don't think there is something in the air here?"

"I don't believe it. Your children will be quite different."

"Yes, they will be different. I wasn't like this at all before my other child was born. André, what will I do if this one dies, like Pauline's babies?"

"It's a pity you saw those graves."

"They're so near, I was bound to see them sooner or later. I'll forget it now, really I will. I'll put it all out of my head."

But the scene came back to her many times during the following months, haunting her, along with Agnes's murmured song.

Robert came in the middle of June, free of the army at last. He arrived alone, having outridden Martin Jordan several miles back, galloping at top speed so that his horse was covered with lather and stood panting at the front door as if it would drop dead. Louise looked out of the drawing-room window and saw him there, standing beside the sweating horse, looking uneasily towards the door of the house as if he were uncertain that he had found the right place. With a cry of surprise and joy she ran out to the step, paused for one second to look at him, then opened her arms wide and waited for him to run into them. They stood swaying together, weeping and laughing and weeping again, until she held him off at arm's length and looked his face over anxiously, tried to say something and could think of nothing to say. Again she held him close to her and heard him say some words which she barely understood in her excitement. Then André came around the corner of the house in his sleeveless deerskin jacket, carrying a flail that he had been mending. Watching him and Robert embrace each other Louise realized that her brother had really come, that he was really here, and then she could contain herself no longer and burst into childish sobs.

Later in the evening they sat in the parlor reading the letters that Robert had brought. Louise looked up every minute or so, as if she feared he might have vanished. Every time she did this she found that he was watching her too, smiling at their foolishness. He had letters from Sophie and he wanted to see all of Sophie's letters to André and Louise. Sophie was jubilant at the success of their adventure. She had written to Robert:

"Justice has been done at last. I have written a sharp letter to Father Burke, telling him that he failed in his trust. He should have prevented that scandalous marriage by every means in his power. It's not as if I hadn't warned him. He should have gone to Hautefontaine and taken her away. He has replied that he was absorbed in his farming—in the middle of winter!—and that when he woke up to the facts it was too late. Farming! I have told him that he is a priest, not a farmer, and that he has become contaminated by French liberalism."

To Louise she had written:

"After long years of pain, now I am happy, as if I were living my own life over again. It will be a blessed marriage and your children will be born in love. Count de La Touche is furiously angry but we give him no satisfaction. Your father is resigned, as well he might be, since he could have stopped it all at the beginning. Fanny says you have disgraced the family but she is concerned to be revenged for other things. I find that in this part of the world no one knows your story, though no doubt they will hear it eventually. I have warned Fanny not to tell it. There is plenty of other material for gossip without you."

Robert reread the last part of the letter aloud, then said:

"I'm almost sorry for Fanny. She stirs up trouble always. What is that about revenge for other things?"

"The usual battles, I suppose. There are several mysterious things in Grand-mère's letters. I'm sorry for Father Burke. He did try to protect me by making me study but I was idle and lazy. I expect he lost heart."

She looked around the quiet room, lit by several branching candlesticks and warmed by the glowing log fire, since the evenings were still cold. "Paris might as well be on the moon,

Cousin Charlotte's salon, the parties in Cardinal Rohan's, Hautefontaine—Robert, can't you stay here with us? You could have a farm like ours—André will tell you all about it—you need never go back to Paris."

"I've already made up my mind not to go back."

"You'll stay here! André! Robert will stay in America, we'll never be separated again, he can buy a farm near us, we'll be together forever and ever—"

She stopped, seeing his failure to respond to her enthusiasm, then asked anxiously:

"What, then? Where will you go? Canada? It's a much harder life, the climate is savage, everyone agrees."

"Not to Canada either. I'm going back to Ireland."

"Home to Mount Brien?"

"Yes." He lifted his chin and looked at her directly, as if he expected opposition. "Celia and I will be married. Her father will agree. We'll live at Castle Nugent." Louise made no comment, though he was clearly waiting for one. "Grand-mère wrote that Celia's mother died last year, a few months after we left. There will be no one but her father. Papa will help us with plans for the estate and Grand-mère will advise us about the house."

"Is she pleased?"

"She doesn't know my plans yet but she will be pleased."

"You have arranged it all with Celia?"

Instead of replying to this, he said, "Why do you sound so cold? Would you prefer to see me with someone like Teresa?"

Watching the two so similar faces, leaning towards each other, their voices becoming softer and their words faster while they searched each other's eyes, André realized that the words they were using conveyed far less than some other kind of communication that was going on between them, from which he and any other listener would be excluded. He kept perfectly still, and after a long silence Louise said, as if she and her brother had been continuing their conversation, "Yes, you are right. She doesn't like Irish brides but she will make an exception for Celia. Are you sure you love her?"

"More than I knew one could."

"Grand-mère will have an ally against Fanny and Sarah. What about them?"

"All that seems unimportant now."

"From another world, from another life."

"Yes."

"When will you go?"

"July, the second week, from Boston to Le Havre. Then to Ireland when I can get a ship, the O'Connells again, perhaps, or I could risk Galway this time."

"You may have to wait for a ship. You could go to Angers."

"I might be recognized. We're so much alike."

"A dark wig."

"Very well, I'll try it."

Again they paused and gazed at each other, while it seemed to André that a multitude of thoughts crammed the space between them. Then Robert said:

"Yes, I'll do all that, and then I'll write to you and tell you what I have seen."

He stayed with them for three weeks, until the end of the first week in July, when he set out with Martin Jordan on the two-day ride to Boston and the ship that would carry him to France.

PART
SEVEN

28

In the weeks after Robert and Louise went away, Celia sat for hours every day at the sewing table in her mother's room, dreaming of him. She had an exact routine: first she carefully recalled and dwelt for a long time on their first meeting as small children, then she concentrated on each subsequent meeting, its place and occasion and its importance in the growth of their friendship. There were not very many meetings, since her mother had kept her home for any and every reason, and had always specially shortened her visits to Mount Brien Court with a last-minute cry:

"Celia! Be sure to come home early. Other girls may stay late but I need you here. People don't understand that, well-off people like the Briens with plenty of good servants, though it's a mystery how a Catholic is allowed to keep up a place like that—"

The last remark amounted to a threat to the Briens, and to silence her Celia always agreed. Keeping her promise was the heavy price of being allowed to go again. Sophie's scheming further reduced their meetings. It would have been a natural thing for Celia to have been invited to picnics and outings in summer when the whole family took the big boat up the lake to the islands, but Sophie would never have risked letting her be so long in Robert's company.

The miracle had happened all the same. The most exciting part of the dream came when she remembered Robert holding her in his arms that day in the drawing room when he came over to tell her that he was going to France. She had planned none of it. Suddenly and mysteriously and marvelously she had been overwhelmed by her pain and had freely used words that she thought were locked inside her. Her words released his, and suddenly they both knew that they were in love.

It was easy to go over every one of her visits to Mount Brien after Robert had declared his love. She began with her preparations at home, her sometimes false explanations to her mother of why she had to go out, saddling her horse if Mickey was not there to help, her ride down the overgrown avenue and the sharp, glorious gallop along the grass by the roadside to the gates of Mount Brien. Maurice's welcome was an antidote to the black looks of the women, old Lady Brien and those two upstarts, Fanny and Sarah. Maurice was always a perfect gentleman.

Oddly enough the very last time she saw Robert was the occasion whose details she could only remember in patches. After he had brought her to her own front door and they had dismounted, he held her in his arms, then kissed her very gently, his lips clinging to hers for a moment. She couldn't remember going into the house, though the sound of the horse's galloping hooves still echoed in her ears, and his last words:

"I love you, Celia. We must wait."

There the dream stopped, sometimes leaving her with an uneasy feeling that she had said or done something foolish, but she could never remember what it was. From January onward her mother's final illness fully occupied her, and as she sat with her eternal sewing Celia reflected now and then that it would be timely if her mother were to die now. She could feel no affection for her, only a certain amount of pity, and even that had been reduced by years of listening to her complaints. She had an exasperating way of playing with her voice, using special tones to make her wailing demands more effective, drawing out words unnaturally or letting the ends of her sentences trail off in mock helplessness: "Celia, Celia, come, come!" This was on a rising note, then came a groaning sigh. "Come quickly, quick—!" When Celia got up and crossed the room at her usual pace, Mrs. Nugent would look up at her malevolently and say sharply:

"Is that the best you can do? Don't you see that I'm dying?"

Now she really was dying, and when Robert came back there

would be no barrier between them. Her father bumbling uselessly about the place would create no difficulty. He never demanded any attention, disliked it in fact, since he must know that she disapproved of his visits to Mrs. James Burke, where he went and sat in the drawing room every single afternoon. There was no scandal, since he did nothing but gaze, and Mrs. Burke seemed to encourage and enjoy his attention though he was an object of ridicule to the Burke children and the servants.

Mrs. Nugent's death was ugly and difficult. In the last days, at the end of April, while Celia tried to bring her some relief, she found herself increasingly possessed by an urge to run out of the house and leave all the horror behind. Two old women servants took it in turns to help with the nursing, and one of these, Maggie, who had once been the cook, said kindly one day:

"It's harder for you than for us, Miss Celia, if she was never your mother. We see death every day. Let you go out for a while and forget about it. I'll be here saying my prayers. I'll take good care of her. If she asks for you I'll say you'll soon be back. I'll say we sent you off to sleep."

It was a blessing to escape from the house, out into the clear spring morning. It had been an exceptionally hard winter but now it seemed that the green had come sooner than ever. Celia's grandfather, the builder of the house, had taken a fancy to plant a pear tree at the corner of the lawn and now its towering branches were white with heavy blossom. No one knew how to prune it. Some day, she thought, it would fall in a storm and break the drawing-room windows.

She hurried across the weedy gravel sweep and through the gate onto the avenue. There she crossed the stream that separated the home meadow from the avenue, aware that her shoes were already soaked by the long grass and the end of her skirt was heavy with damp. It was cold. She began to say his name over and over, Robert, Robert, Robert, as if she could call him to her, as if he could feel her pain and her need for him over all the miles of land and water that were between them. He should have written to her. By now they must have guessed at Mount Brien that he had not, and that this was why she came uninvited so often, to hear news of him at secondhand. She had not been able to go for almost two weeks now, since her mother's more violent crisis had begun.

In the grip of her tormented mind she began to run across the meadow, joining the avenue where it curved lower down. Here she slowed to a walk, her breath coming so fast that it hurt her, her eyes on the ground as if she feared to fall over some obstacle in her path. At the broken-down lodge the wild, unkempt head of Sally Flaherty showed for a moment in the blackness of the doorway but she disappeared into her rathole again at once. Celia knew that the people in the hovels she passed on her way were watching her, but that they could feel only pity, since they knew all about her mother's illness. She greeted none of them. Even the deceptive sunshine was gone now and a chill wind cut through the thin cloth of her dress. She knew that what she was doing was mad and still she found that she could not stop, not even if she disgraced herself, not even if she lost the last rags of her dignity and reputation.

At the gates of Mount Brien Court she slipped through the wicket without being seen and was off up the avenue at once. A hundred yards on she stopped. A horseman was coming down. She glanced wildly around. The bare pastures at either side offered no cover. She darted onto the left-hand one, then realized the uselessness of it and stopped again, like a frightened rabbit that hears dogs on every side. The horseman was quite close now, trotting easily on the clean gravel. In a daze she was aware that the hooves had moved onto the grass and she lifted her eyes at last and saw that it was Sir Maurice, looking anxiously and kindly down at her. In a moment he had dismounted and was walking slowly towards her as if she were dangerous, trailing his horse by the reins, saying gently:

"Celia, what is it?"

"Everything—everything—"

She could say no more. Tears covered her face but she took no notice of them. She plucked at her cold arms as a light rain began to fall. Maurice dropped the reins quickly, slipped off his jacket to wrap around her, then said:

"Come back to the house with me. You're chilled to death."

"No—no—"

"You needn't see anyone. We'll go in by the back way, to my rent room. There's a fire there. No one will know you're in the house at all. Come along now."

He picked up the reins again and she let herself be coaxed by him to walk back to the house, through the big, neat stableyard where servants looked up but made no remark, through the back entry, past the kitchen, where Maurice called out:

"Patty! A bowl of soup at once in the rent room!"

Then he was leading her into a small paneled room where a turf fire almost filled the hearth, seating her in a leather armchair, kneeling to take off her wet shoes, taking her cold hands and chafing them gently between his, doing every single one of the things that Robert would have done if he had been there. The unexpected kindness so generously poured on her, the warmth of the fire, the quiet of this remote room, all combined to loosen the fearful tensions that had been driving her for weeks past. A glow of pure happiness ran through her. She reached into the pocket of her skirt and found her handkerchief, wiping her face dry and brushing back her lovely dark hair in a series of long, slow movements, then letting her hand fall slowly onto the arm of the chair. She became aware that Maurice was watching her with a peculiar expression but she could not begin to explain herself yet. She felt no embarrassment, he was such a familiar person. She had never been afraid of him.

A kitchen maid brought the soup and she ate it hungrily, every moment feeling a mysterious force of life growing and growing within her. Still Maurice was silent and it was only when she had finished that he said tentatively:

"Now you look better. We haven't seen you for ten days or more."

"My mother is much worse. Dr. Brady says she'll die very soon. I've stayed with her day and night—today I had to get out."

"Of course. Your father told me about it. I was on my way over to see you just now."

"I'd have been glad of your visit."

"I asked him to tell you to come and see us but he said you wouldn't be able."

"When was that?"

"Three days ago. Did he not give you the message?"

"No."

"Of course I should have gone to you at once. I see that now."

"Why? Why should you? Robert?"

"Yes." Maurice spread his hands to the fire as if he were cold.

She had noticed before what broad, strong hands he had, though they were not coarse. He said very quietly, "I'm afraid he has let us all down. He has gone to America with the Dillon regiment."

She was not able to take this in. She said idiotically:

"America? But Robert went to France in January, three months ago." She gazed at him in agony, then whispered, "Did you say America?"

"He's not certain but he thinks the regiment is going to America. There was some scandal, he doesn't say clearly, a duel, a girl, something I never expected from Robert." He had turned away from her now, giving her time to recover. "Louise has written too."

"A girl? What girl was that?"

"His cousin, Teresa. He just says she deceived him. He gives no details."

Slowly Celia stood up, pushing her handkerchief back into her pocket with unnecessary force as if to prove she would not need it. She was not going to weep. It would be more reasonable to laugh. Robert! All her dreaming had been about a ghost, even about someone who had never existed at all. She gave a hard, half-hysterical sob, then clenched her fists, determined not to break down, but then she remembered her last meeting with him, the warmth and safety of his arms around her and the way that his lips had drawn hers to themselves. That was what she could never forget, the prospect opened up of unending happiness and exploration and growing knowledge and trust. It had all been in that single, sincere, loving kiss, far more surely than any words could be.

Maurice had stood up and come close to her, saying anxiously:

"Celia, are you all right? Do you feel faint?"

"No, no—"

"Sit down. Don't hurry away. Wait a while longer. Rest a little."

"Rest!" she laughed bitterly, angrily. "I don't need to rest. You say he let us all down. What did he say about me in his letter?"

"Nothing. He didn't mention you at all."

She had been so sure he had, she had asked so confidently, but she should have known the answer from everything else that Maurice had told her. The whirling in her head was frightening, something quite beyond her experience. She had never fainted in her life but this was a sensation like death must be, a total loss of feeling, possession by an evil nothingness. She groped for the arm of the chair and found that Maurice was holding her up, then lowering her gently into it. After that he knelt on the floor beside her and stroked her hands, then took her pliant head and laid it against his shoulder, holding her close to him. After a long time he said softly:

"I've tried to think hardly about him but I find I can't do it."

"I can't think at all."

"Fanny says she always knew he was weak."

"Fanny is strong herself."

"Yes. She says I'm weak too, that I should cut him off now, never see him again, never have any more to do with him."

"What does Lady Brien say—your mother, I mean?"

"She hasn't spoken to me at all since the day the letter came. She stays in her room. She won't see anyone but Amélie."

"Will your mother cut him off?"

"No. She wouldn't be able to do it either."

"What about me? what am I to do?"

"You'll have to put it all aside, in storage, and learn to love someone else. The second love won't destroy the first. It may even give it an extra dimension."

"Did this happen to you? You speak as if it did."

"Some of it. I didn't have the sense then that I have now."

She said half-hysterically:

"I can't think. How can you talk of second love, as if it were something you could buy in a shop? What's the use of all your common sense when I have such a pain all through me, like a sword piercing my soul? I know now what that means: 'A sword shall pierce through thine own soul.'"

She sprang up and began to pace the little room, two or three steps each way, her hands twitching and clenching each other, her body shaking with dry, painful sobs. She paused by the door and took hold of the handle to open it and flee from the room, then dropped it in despair, realizing that the cage extended in every direction outside. In a half-dream she heard Maurice's voice call her name and she raised her hands to her temples in an effort to shut out the sound. She became aware that he had risen to his feet and was gazing at her with the same anxious look that he had had when he found her on the avenue. She looked at his eyes and saw that they were full of pain, as intense and incurable as her own. He moved a single step towards her, then took her gently in his arms, exactly as Robert had done, and kissed her so gently and peacefully on the lips, drawing them towards his exactly as Robert had done, so that she felt her whole body burn with the same fire that he had kindled. She withdrew after a moment and whispered:

"We loved him, you and I loved him."

Then Maurice held her closer so that her head lay on his shoulder and she let his arms support her. She began to be terrified again. She would have to live for years and years with this pain, she would have to leave Mount Brien now and walk back to Castle Nugent, taking her new pain like a wild animal on a leash, and tie it up and keep it forever and ever. She clutched at him in despair, then felt him gently turn her face to his again, and again with his kisses she experienced a moment of peace. She said:

"I must go back. I have been away too long."

He held her a second longer, then let his arms fall, and they looked at each other sadly, neither able to understand what had happened to them. As she put her hands to her hair and began absentmindedly to tidy it a little, the door opened quite soundlessly and Sarah was there, looking greedily from one of them to the other, then saying:

"Patty told me Miss Nugent came in. She said you were cold and faint. I see you have recovered, Miss Nugent."

Dazed, they turned together to look at her. She walked past them and picked up the little tray with the soup bowl, then backed out of the room, watching them, holding the tray high in one hand. As she closed the door she drew in her breath sharply as if she were smothering a laugh, then she was gone. Maurice said:

"I'll get the phaeton and drive you back."

"Yes. Thank you."

"Wait here. I'll come for you again."

"Yes."

But what if Sarah were to see him go out and come back to torment her? She said piteously:

"Don't leave me—please don't leave me."

"Very well, come with me, then. Don't be afraid."

"I am afraid."

Sure enough, when they passed the kitchen on their way back to the stableyard, there was Sarah slinking like a cat into the dark corridor that led to the front of the house. She half turned, saying softly:

"Taking Miss Nugent home, Sir Maurice?"

"Yes," Maurice said shortly and hurried Celia out into the sunny yard. While the phaeton was being wheeled out and the pony harnessed, he stood in dead silence, holding Celia's arm, his heavy black eyebrows drawn down in fury and his mouth tightly shut.

When they reached Castle Nugent they found that her mother had died in her absence.

29

By the end of that summer of 1780, Maurice and Celia had become lovers. Fanny and Sarah watched their progress with a mixture of gloating fascination and fear. For the first time in her life Fanny was afraid of Maurice and she refrained from scolding and nagging him about Celia as she would have done on any other subject. Neither she nor her sister had the courage to tell Sophie what was happening, and they were very thankful that the old lady had retired almost completely to her sitting room and spent the days writing letters. Throughout the autumn and early winter, in odd corners of the house or in the garden, the two sisters would meet and whisper to each other:

"He's gone to her again. He got the bay horse himself, didn't wait for anyone, just threw on the saddle and the harness, tightened up and galloped off."

"When? When?"

"At two o'clock."

"Perhaps he was going to Galway."

"No. He took the back avenue. He has bought new white gloves and ordered six more pairs from the glovemaker in William Street in Galway."

"How do you know?"

"From Patty, of course. He's her sister-in-law's cousin."

"I saw his new silk scarf. It must have cost a fortune."

"And his boots! Spanish leather, soft as silk. It's dangerous for a Catholic gentleman, going about dressed so fine. Next thing he'll have French broadcloth with gold lace."

"Didn't you know he has ordered it already? A fine new suit. He has! Tailor Cross told me, he went in to Galway, instead of sending for him, thinking we wouldn't find out. Won't we see it when it's ready anyway? Someone will notice he doesn't go out in his ratting clothes now, not fine enough, not good enough for the little Miss Nugent that was his own son's sweetheart."

"The shame, the disgrace of it!"

"Men are all the same, even my lord. What will happen next? A baby, I'll bet my boots. Everyone will laugh. Lady Sophie won't laugh, though."

"She doesn't know. She's too busy now having forty fits over Louise to take a look at what's happening under her nose. They weren't long kicking over the traces, that pair of gentry. Louise's husband-to-be is as old as a field but with bags of money. You'd think she'd be too grand to take him."

"No one is too grand to take money. Miss Nugent has a new dress, black for her mother, of course, but the stuff is too good. I'd like to know who paid for that."

"So would I. Where did you see it?"

"I didn't see it. Katty Joyce told me when she came with the wool. And Pat Cooney said in the kitchen last night that there's a song about the pair of them going the rounds. I heard him when I stood by the door. No one saw me, I was so quiet."

"What is the song? Oh, what is it? Did you hear it? Did he sing it?"

"I heard it but I can't remember any but the first part. I lay awake last night thinking and thinking but I couldn't get beyond the beginning."

"What is the beginning? You do remember it?"

"Yes, yes. It was:

" 'O lie with me, said the fine young man,
And then you may lie with my father.
He'll keep you warm, he'll keep you close,
While I'm gone over the water.'

"There's words in it for the young man's dead mother, the French lady, that she can't sleep easy in her grave, and words for Sir Maurice's mother that she'll die of shame."

"She knows nothing about it, nothing at all."

"You never can tell with that one what she knows."

"She's bound to find out sooner or later."

"Maybe yes, maybe no. Who's to tell her?"

"Not me."

"Nor me. She's black out with Sir Maurice for agreeing to Louise being married to the old fellow. I said it was natural for her to want a bit of high life and that by the sound of him he won't last long, but that only made her as mad as a burned cat. There's no pleasing her."

"But she might get a letter that would tell her all about her fine son."

"Oh. It would have to be the right time, not too soon. Sometimes book learning is useful. You can't write no more than I can."

"It could be done, all the same. There's people who know how to write, that would do it for a consideration."

"But not yet."

"No, not yet."

Gossip flitted up and down the road between Mount Brien Court and Castle Nugent, and of course through Oughterard and Moycullen and Galway, in and out of the houses of poor people and gentry alike. Celia was aware of it but she could not convince Maurice that it was important. He said:

"There have always been stories about us and there always will be. I can't bother with such parochial things. It's not anyone's business."

"They could injure you."

"How? They can put their own houses in order before they begin on mine."

Celia felt humiliated at being associated with the tallywomen and rootless mistresses of the neighboring landlords and their agents, but her own position was in fact a thousand times more disgraceful than theirs. Now and then time stopped long enough for a flash of insight and understanding to penetrate her mind, to tell her that she could break off with Maurice and save herself, but then the pain and sense of loss overcame her again and drove out all reasonable thought. Her perception of Maurice's weakness humiliated her still further. Except in connection with his land and his mill, he seemed to have no interest in anything. He despaired of ever seeing Robert again. Everyone knew now that the Dillon regiment was in America with General Rochambeau's expedition to help the insurgents. They would all be killed. The might of the English army was against them. The offer for Louise by old Count de La Touche was the final blow. He told Celia about it, and about his consent, saying:

"Let him have her. She's ruined anyway. I can do nothing for her. Robert—Louise—my two children are gone. Now I have nothing at all; no one but you, Celia."

Neither of them considered Fanny's three sons as being worth mention.

"Could you not bring Louise home?" Celia asked, horrified at the fate of the girl abandoned as she was herself.

"Home? To Fanny? She's better off with the old man than she would be with Fanny."

And Celia herself was a further barrier. She could see that so long as she was Maurice's mistress, Louise had to be sacrificed. She said:

"Couldn't we go away?"

"Where?"

"Anywhere—London, even Dublin."

"We can't. I have responsibilities here, my mother, Fanny and the children, the farm and the mill and all those tenants—how can you ask such a thing of me? I couldn't live anywhere in Ireland except Mount Brien, without being molested. Don't you know that? As long as I stay here where I'm known, I'm safe, and my family too."

Desperately she said, "But you said you care nothing for them. You said you have no one now but me."

"I must take care of them, all the same. If I were to go away they would have no protection. They would be after them like a pack of wolves."

"Who? Who would be after them?"

"Your Protestant friends."

"God knows they're not my friends."

She dropped the subject then because she knew that what he said was true. Only a year ago her father had tried to get possession of the Mount Brien land under the old law that a Catholic might not make a profit of more than one-third of its value on any farm, but he had been rapped over the knuckles by the Galway lawyer to whom he had hoped to confide his case. The lawyer stopped Celia in Galway and told her about it, saying:

"Tell your father to leave the Briens alone. They have powerful influence everywhere. That law is not meant for people like the Briens. That's for small Catholic farmers and landlords. I gave him a piece of my mind, I can tell you, and you can back me up. I said that if he did a little more supervising at home and less at his neighbors, he'd have money in the bank in no time."

Celia never dared to give the lawyer's message to her father but she had been terribly agitated by the story of his treachery. She had to agree with Maurice now that there was no escape. Still the idea of escape took hold of her. Just after Christmas, when she found that she was pregnant, the idea became an obsession. Now there was no alternative—she must leave home, she could not possibly face the horrors before her. She gasped out her fears to Maurice:

"What will I do? Where will I go? I thought I had had the worst that the world could do to me and now this!"

"What did you expect?" Maurice said, using a new, rough tone that terrified her. "We make love several times a week. Didn't you know this might happen?"

"Yes, yes, but not to me, not to me."

"You should have been more careful."

"Think of what will be said, the Burkes, the Flahertys, the D'Arcys, everyone in Connaught—"

"I didn't know you cared about them. No one else does."

"Your mother—Fanny—"

"It's too late to think of them. Wht does it matter? By now they must have heard all about us."

"I must go away, I must go."

In the old way that she knew, he said, "Would you leave me so easily, then?"

"Easily! Don't torment me."

"It would be like perpetual night. I would die."

"If you loved me you would want me to go."

"I can't let you go. Love! You are my breath, my pulse, my life. If you go away, I will die."

"If I stay here, I will die."

"Go, then," he said in despair. "I can see that you must. Why should you think of me? I've treated you abominably, I've ruined you, I've wrecked every chance you had. That first day,

308

when you were crying in my arms, I should have foreseen all this, but I was thinking only of myself, and of Robert. I wanted you because I loved you and hated Fanny, hated her. That's true, and it has been so for a long time. And it's true too that I loved you, ever since Robert went away, and you used to come for news of him and sit looking so forlorn and nervous. I wanted to put my arms around you and tell you he would never come back, that he cared nothing for you."

"You knew that then!"

"Yes. My mother affected him though I don't believe he knows it. He was to have a French wife. No Irish one would be good enough for him."

"He told me once that she would only approve of a French wife."

"So he knew. I guessed as much. Young people can feel such things, or perhaps she said it, though I told her not to. As you grow older you realize that you don't have to please everyone and you make a better judgment."

"Are you making a better judgment for me when you say I should stay here in spite of everything?" She could not bring herself to mention the baby again; she scarcely believed in it, though it was the cause of her worst terrors.

"No, not a better judgment but the only one possible. What can we do? Nothing will be right. Here I can take care of you. If you go away it will be forever. At best I would see you a few times a year. What use is that to us?"

"I have an aunt in Dublin, my mother's sister. She might let me come to her."

"Go, then, go to her if you want to," he said angrily, but then she wept so bitterly that he had to hold her close to him for a long time and promise that he would never leave her, though it was she who was threatening to leave.

As the weeks went on and the last gray cold sapped the life from everyone, this fearful life kept advancing relentlessly within her. She thought of it as a canker, a disease, incurable and terrifying, and still sometimes a great shaft of light seemed to pierce her so that her whole being was flooded with happiness. When the light faded she was left as before, full of fear, but with a residue of mysterious vitality.

Her father was watching her. Several times she caught him at it, almost as if he knew all about her predicament, but he never said anything to confirm this. He must have heard of Maurice's visits, always in the afternoon when Nugent was away making eyes at Mrs. Burke. Perhaps this was why he kept silent, since she would have an obvious retort. If they met by chance they measured each other cautiously, but she did her best to avoid him.

When she was with Maurice, sometimes she imagined that a miracle would save her and that everything would be all right. She was soothed by his presents, the cloth for two new black dresses which she made up herself to avoid the dressmaker's comments on her changing figure, and a few old necklaces of no great value. He brought these loose in his pocket, pulling them out nervously and putting them around her neck with his own hands, one on top of another, so that she had to lift the beads to look down at them. He said:

"I like seeing you wear them. They're old glass from Venice —bone—amber—nothing much."

He did not say who their original owner was.

During the following months she held them rolled up in her hands or carried them in the pocket of her skirt where no one could see them. After a while she began to play a game in which they were presents from Robert. He appeared early one morning before anyone was about. He stood in the corner of her room, not by the door, and he came towards the bed where she lay half-awake, drowsy, rather high on the pillows because of the baby twitching inside her. He laid his hand on her forehead, then pulled the necklaces out of his pocket and put them around her neck, over her nightdress, and stood gazing down at her for a while until he faded away. He never spoke when he came like that, but there was no need for words between them. She could feel his thoughts go straight into her mind—my love, my dear, my heart, my soul, my darling—and she repeated all those dear words over and over in reply. When he had vanished she didn't want to talk to anyone for hours, so she just lay on in bed, thinking of him, until old Maggie came and forced her to get up.

Maggie was the only one of the servants who knew what was happening to her, though the others may have guessed. At least none of them said anything. No doubt they would have been afraid, and if they knew, they must have been worrying about what would become of them. Their fortunes depended completely on the survival of this ramshackle family, since Castle Nugent was the only Protestant house for miles around where Catholics were employed. The reason was simple: no wages were paid. However a roof and food were certainties, and a place by the fire in winter. Keeping Catholic servants was the final reason why the Nugents were despised by the other Protestant gentry. Maggie was one of the few who remembered that mere shiftlessness was not the reason why they were here. It was John Nugent's mother who began it as a young woman, by taking in four Catholic sisters and training them herself to be passable house servants. She got away with it because she was English, and the servants acquired her accent as far as possible when they spoke in English, as if it were a protective badge of office. Maggie was the last survivor of the original family, but the house and yard swarmed with her cousins and nephews and nieces whose bailiwick Castle Nugent had become.

Maggie realized that something very peculiar was going on in Celia's head. It was bad enough knowing what was happening in her body—she had heard the ballad too and guessed very early that poor Celia was going to pay dearly for her sin. What she had not expected was that the girl would lose her mind. At first Maggie scarcely believed it. Out of charity, for she was long past serious work, she took a tray of tea to Celia's room one day at noon. Celia had not yet come down and Maggie feared that she was about to adopt her mother's wretched habit of lying half the day in bed. She came briskly into the room, saying:

"Now, Miss Celia, time to get up. You wouldn't lounge all day like this if your mother were here. What! In the dark still! Let in the light this lovely summer morning."

Turning back from drawing the curtains she found her eyes held by Celia's, which had a hard glitter, unnatural and disturbing, like the open eyes of the dead. Maggie muttered half to herself:

"God above, girl, what's the matter with you? A fever? Give me your hand."

The hand was cool and healthy but Celia's voice was high, with a crazy chanting rhythm to it:

"He was here, he stood by the window, he came again today, he'll come again tomorrow—"

"Who came? There was no one here," Maggie said in confusion, unable to meet those shining eyes, thinking she was referring to Maurice. Everyone knew he never came until the afternoon and they made sure to keep well out of his sight. A whole new problem would be created if he were to take to coming in the morning. She repeated: "No one came."

"Robert was here, he stood by the window—" She stopped and frowned as if she were trying to remember something, then said in a perfectly normal tone: "You've brought some tea. Thank you, Maggie. Yes, I'll get up now." In a louder tone with a trace of anger she said, "Well? Is there something else?"

"No, nothing else. Do you feel well?"

"Yes, perfectly well. Why shouldn't I feel well?"

The old servant was defeated and went out of the room without another word, but she came every day from that onward, watching for a return of those signs of madness that she had seen on the first day. Once or twice she recognized them in different forms, in staring and muttering and often in a fixed smile directed into a corner of the room, but now Celia had taken to watching her with a crafty expression and she did not say Robert's name again. Sometimes Maggie thought she had recovered, especially when she came down to early dinner at two o'clock, looking neat and fresh in her new black dress that she had been sewing for days and days, but several quick bursts of anger revealed that she was keeping herself in check by force. Maggie made one more attempt to get her to tell what was in her mind. She bitterly regretted it. In the middle of July, when the whole world could see that Celia was pregnant, Maggie brought her noon tray to the bedroom one day and took Celia's hand in hers, saying:

"You need help, my poor child. Don't try to bear it all alone. There's none of us able to do that. Let me get you Dr. Brady—"

She got no further. Celia sat up straight and glared at her wildly, then said:

"Dr. Brady?" She gave a convulsive shiver. "I don't want him. Maggie, I'm going to die. Robert is dead. He comes to me often. He died in America. He's over there now." She nodded towards the corner by the window and Maggie turned instinctively to glance at the empty wall. "I'll be with him forever then but I must wait, he says I must wait." She stopped, gazed blankly at Maggie, then burst into hysterical, racking sobs which gradually became shudders that ran like mice all over her body. Maggie held her in her arms until she was either in a faint or asleep, then withdrew gently and ran downstairs like a woman twenty years younger. There she found Sabina, her cousin who was a housemaid, and said:

"Go to her, go to Miss Celia. Don't let anyone in, no one at all, until I come back."

"What about Sir Maurice?" Sabina asked pertly, and Maggie drew off and slapped her hard on the side of the head.

"No one, I said, no one. If he comes he may wait for me in the drawing room."

"For you!"

Sabina skipped out of the way in case another blow was coming, and made off upstairs.

Maggie had forgotten her, knowing she would do what she was told. She ran to the attic over the kitchen where she slept with the reigning cook, and took her turf-smelling shawl from the peg at the back of the door. Then she set off as fast as she could go, across the fields to Mount Brien Court.

30

Throughout the long hot afternoon Sophie remained at the window of her sitting room, with its view over the front lawn and the avenue, staring, unable to leave it, as if she were an invalid. Since Maggie's visit she had been in a daze. She was taken completely by surprise. Not a word, not a whisper of the gossip had reached her. Maggie was astounded, as shocked at Sophie's ignorance of the story of Maurice and Celia as Sophie was to hear it. She said over and over:

"I'm sorry, my lady, I'm sorry in my heart to tell you this. Sure, I thought you knew all about it, the way you know everything. I'm sorry, I'm sorry."

Sophie got her to go at last, a little calmer, without a single reproach that Maggie hadn't come sooner, with a promise that something sensible would be done for Celia at once.

Her reputation for knowing everything was one of the things that had prevented Sophie from learning what was going on. How could she have missed it? She wasted a lot of time in recalling symptoms that she had misinterpreted, Maurice's new look of health and his new clothes as a sign that the misfortunes of his children had taught him a lesson in courage for himself, the end of Celia's visits as a sign that she had got over her infatuation for Robert, the whispering and muttering of Fanny and Sarah as a sign that they had learned their place at last. She began sentences in her mind but never finished them: "But I thought—" "He should have—" "Why didn't he—" Then she wanted to weep but anger soon disposed of that. It had never occurred to her that Maurice could be reduced to this state by his sorrows. She had thought him too insensitive. What he had done was so low that it was beyond Sophie's understanding.

They're all the same, she said to herself, unconsciously repeating Fanny's comment, even Maurice. He has no family pride, no shame, no sense of his duty to his children or to his name.

Secretly she felt that this was all her own doing. She should have sent him off to the army with the others, out of this damnable country. She would never fully admit that mistake, not even to herself, but it nagged at her mind all the time, interrupting her vaguely forming plans for Celia. It was impossible to apply reason in a case like this. It was a disaster beyond all redemption. Maurice—Robert—every time she thought of them the blood rushed to her head and she felt herself gasp for breath. She should have had it all out with Robert before he went away, she should have made friends with Celia, those times when she came like a lost cat, asking for him. The things she should have done, or would have done if she had had any idea —but it was all useless now.

A child! Whenever she thought of that she felt sick and old and humiliated. This was not a cottier's daughter hired to amuse a bored, rich landlord. The Briens had prided themselves on never doing that sort of thing. A poor man with a handsome wife or daughter had to keep her as well hidden from the big Protestant landlords as the Briens kept their hunters and carriage horses. Maurice had aligned himself now with those dreadful people, dragging the whole family down with him. A decent girl, a neighbor, recently bereaved, in love with his own son— Sophie moaned with pain. Maurice was a fool, as big a fool as his father. That was the other thing she must never say, no matter what the provocation.

Get her out of the country—that was the only solution. Sophie's fingers twitched as if she would seize the girl in her hands and lift her off to some distant place at once, anywhere at all, get her out, get her away. Pregnant? Seven months' pregnant? How far could she travel in that condition? She might die —the evil thought gave Sophie a moment's pleasure and hope before she was revolted by it. She must be taken to a safe place at all costs, at least until the child was born. It was a Brien, after all. But this reflection put Sophie into a new fury. Why should the Briens have to take care of this little trollop, doubly treacherous, doubly despicable, ruining both father and son at one blow? Because if they did not, her common sense told her at once, Celia and her child would live nearby and disgrace them forever. Maurice would continue to visit her, and God alone knew what would happen if Robert came home.

This last thought made her lurch to her feet and begin to walk about the room, but soon she went back to her chair by the window and stared out across the lawn again. It was a glorious July day, the meadows darkening as the tall grass ripened. The birds had gone silent in the heat. In the river field she could see the cows all gathered under the shade of the huge elm tree. As she watched, a group of men and women servants approached them and began to drive them home to be milked. It was strange to see such ordinary things going on while such terrible misfortune enveloped the family. Now she trusted none of them; not one of those servants for whom she had done so many favors had come to her about what was happening, though they had all known about it. Was she so terrifying, or was it that no matter how close you thought you came to these people they would still deceive you? But for Maggie she might not have heard about it until it was too late. If only she could have questioned Maggie further—she felt cheated of the details she longed for. How often did Maurice go to Castle Nugent? How long did he stay? Which room did they use? Did she take him shamelessly upstairs to her own bedroom? Did her father know about it? None of these things was important but the answers would have given some element of reality to the whole story. She could not bring herself to ask Maggie more than one or two questions but had just let her talk on until she had said her say, that Maurice had seduced Celia and that the girl was going out of her mind. The details of her derangement were the worst blow of all.

Sarah missed nothing. She would be certain to have seen Maggie arrive and her snakelike mind would have divined the purpose of her visit. By now, she and Fanny would be muttering in some corner or other. Sophie looked frantically around her room as if she were a prisoner there, locked in by these two harpies. She would have to appear eventually. She set about putting on her usual expression as if it were a dress, walking to the glass to examine her face, raising her eyebrows in a painful attempt to look disdainful, but it was no use. Hurt old eyes looked back at her, frightened and miserable. At that moment one thing became clear to her. She would have to see Celia. There was no alternative. Not a single plan could be made, not a single decision taken, until she had seen her, and talked to her.

The rigid way of life she had adopted made her next move doubly difficult. She never went for drives now, nor called on neighbors. She had forgotten how to ride. The distance was too great to walk. For one minute she considered summoning Celia to her but there were too many arguments against this and besides the girl might not come. At last she realized that only one course was possible. She took a shawl and went downstairs, then around to the stableyard where she ordered the first boy she saw to send out Mike Conran, the coachman. He came running and stared at her in amazement. She said:

"The carriage, at once."

Then she stood while the horses were put in and the huge vehicle creaked out of the coach house where it had lain since Robert and Louise went away. That was the last time it was used, when they drove to Kerry. It had taken a week and more to come back and it had never been the same since that long journey. But she noticed that it had been kept perfectly clean and polished, perhaps for just such an emergency as this, when someone would march out of the house and demand it without warning. He was a good coachman, Mike, like his father before him. His two postilions were well-mounted and smartly dressed, as if they had been ready for orders. Mike was discreet too. He drove the carriage off the cobblestones, helped her in himself and only then asked her quietly:

"Where are we going, my lady?"

"To Castle Nugent."

Instantly she saw that he knew all about Maurice and Celia. They all did, every one of them, except her. She closed her eyes and sat back on the carriage seat, waiting for the horses to move off, then became aware of a commotion in the yard. Anger flared in her at the thought that Fanny might have come out to question her. She knew that her chances of getting away unseen were small. But it was old Amélie's face that appeared at the carriage window, agitated, stuttering:

"Madame—Madame Sophie—where are you going? What, alone? How can you? I'm coming, yes, I'm coming, wherever it is."

She climbed painfully in and fell back in a heap as the carriage moved off. Sophie said sharply:

"You make it sound as if I'm going to the ends of the earth. It's only Castle Nugent, not very far."

Amélie was as ignorant as herself. Sophie watched closely and saw this, and it gave her more comfort than anything else could have done. Amélie's round, honest face was perfectly innocent. If she had been in on the secret too and had kept it to herself, Sophie would have been without a friend in the world. The Irish servants had never made Amélie one of themselves and she had never learned their language. Now in her seventies she did very little work and spent most of her time in Sophie's dressing room going over and over her old clothes, preserving them carefully with tiny, complicated stitches, though none of them would ever be worn again. Sophie asked:

"How did you know I came out?"

"I saw Mademoiselle Sarah watching from the landing window and I came to see what was attracting her."

"Did she say anything?"

Sophie was ashamed of asking the question but she could exercise no restraints of this kind with Amélie.

"She laughed a little, like a mouse squeaking, and said something about 'It has come to this.' What has come? What was she talking about? Is it Robert?"

How could she tell her? She stumbled over various beginnings and at last said only that Celia was to have a child soon and that Sophie was going to offer her help. She could see Amélie's look of confusion, the unvoiced questions to which there could be no answer and finally her decision to ask no more. Sophie sighed deeply and leaned back against the cushions. Amélie's presence gave her courage. From talking to her she had begun to think in French, and this always cleared her head. If she met John Nugent she would give him a piece of her mind that he would never forget, but he was probably at Mrs. Burke's, silly, fat little Mrs. Burke who sent him on messages to the kitchen and made him carry her cushions and rewarded him from time to time with a long, round-eyed, romantic stare. That piece of gossip had reached Sophie fast enough. Why in heaven's name had the other not?

She sat up straight to look through the glass as the carriage turned into the Castle Nugent avenue. A wild-haired, dark-faced old crone peered from the blackened doorway of the castellated lodge, a facade behind which crouched a one-roomed hovel. Dock leaves and nettles grew against it and potato peelings and cabbage stalks littered the space before the door. Mike slowed the horses to a crawl, in fear of the ruts and potholes of the avenue. The grass was tall among the trees at either side, ungrazed, wasted like everything else here. The iron gate at the top was rusted almost to pieces. A horse was walking loose near the front door. It lifted its head and whinnied at the approach of the carriage, then leaped the gate and came trotting down to meet them. Mike flicked his whip at it and sent it galloping back.

As the carriage pulled up before the front door several ragged servants came from around the corner of the house and with wild shouts chased the horse towards the stables. Mike waited for the commotion to die away before opening the carriage door and handing Sophie down. When she was standing on the weedy gravel she hesitated a moment, then said to Amélie:

"Wait for me here, yes, wait. No need to come in unless I send for you."

Maggie had heard their noisy arrival and was standing in the hall behind the manservant who opened the door to Mike's knock. Indeed the whole household must have heard. Feet scurried and there were whispers from the dimness at the back of the hall where a baize-covered door stood partly open. As Sophie came in, Maggie turned and sharply shut it, then came back to elbow the servant aside and say:

"Thank God you came, my lady. Come in here with me."

She led the way into the room to the right of the hall as if she were the mistress of the house. It was a shabby room with faded, chintz-covered chairs, a chaise longue and a spinet whose case had cracked here and there in the sunlight from the tall uncurtained windows. A faint hum of bees came from one corner and Sophie saw honey marks on the wall high up, where they had nested. She said: "I should have come sooner. It has taken me all day to quiet my mind."

"Sit down, my lady. Here, now, in this chair. Rest yourself first."

She placed Sophie in a chair by the huge empty hearth and stood in front of her, unwilling to sit in her presence. Impatiently Sophie said:

"Sit down, Maggie, for heaven's sake. Mr. Nugent is not at home, I hope."

"No. He'll be gone to Mrs. Burke's. You won't mind if I ask where is Sir Maurice?"

"In Cong, I believe, but how should I know where he is? He could be in this house now, for all I know."

"He doesn't come so much lately."

Sophie closed her eyes as if to shut out this new treachery, but then she felt her first trace of pity for Maurice, to her own surprise. She said:

"We don't need either of them. I must see her."

"Yes, my lady."

Maggie had not sat down after all and Sophie felt intimidated by her heavy figure, standing too close. She said:

"Well, can she come downstairs?"

"I'll fetch her to you if I can. Perhaps she won't want to come."

"Then I had better go to her."

"Let me speak to her first."

When Maggie had gone, Sophie sat perfectly still, listening to the soft hum of the bees, her mind a numbed blank. Mike had moved the carriage away from the door, so that she could no longer see it through the windows. Ten minutes passed. She began to think that Celia had refused to see her and that she would have to go up to her room in spite of this. No words would form in Sophie's mind, no way presented itself for starting that extraordinary conversation. To attack her was unnecessary since she was quite powerless, to reason with her was senseless since by Maggie's account she was out of her mind.

Sophie's whole being was filled with dull hatred for the turn that her life had taken, every person she dared still to love destroyed by some inevitable fate, as her children had been destroyed long ago by disease. Maurice was to have restored everything, but now at one blow he had committed the final act of destruction. After this the Briens would never rise again. What life there was left in them was finished now forever.

Sophie was on her way to the door when she heard Maggie's footsteps hurrying along the bare stone floor of the hall. She stood and waited in the middle of the room until the door opened. Maggie was flustered at seeing her there and said at once:

"It's been a long time, my lady, but you can come up now. She wouldn't receive you in her bed. I had to get her up and put her in a chair."

"Can she not do those things for herself? Surely she doesn't need a maid for that."

"Oh, madame, wait till you see her."

Maggie hurried ahead, up the creaking stairs, lit by a high, arched window, past a broad landing whose rotted floor was gone in holes here and there, up a second flight to the main bedroom floor of the house. Dust danced in bars of sunlight that fell through colored glass, red, blue and yellow, making a bizarre pattern on the floor. A door to the right stood partly open as if Maggie had forgotten to close it in her hurry. As she started towards it now, Sophie stopped her, saying:

"I'll go in by myself. Amélie is waiting a long time. Perhaps you could take her into the house."

Maggie hesitated, obviously unwilling to let Sophie go in alone. On an impulse Sophie said:

"It will be all right, Maggie. I'll take care of her."

Then she walked forward into the room, closing the door behind her.

Celia was sitting by the window in a big, low chair, the long, voluminous folds of her black dress covering her feet. As Sophie came in she turned her pale, listless face towards the door, looked frightened for a moment and then drooped her head apathetically. Sophie said quietly:

"How are you, Celia?"

Again she looked frightened, then shook her head as if she had lost the power of speech. Sophie crossed the room and stood in front of her helplessly, her eyes drawn to the curve of Celia's body as if she could see through the cloth to the little body within. Celia spread both hands to cover it in a sudden protective gesture, as Sophie went down on her knees before her, saying:

"I'm here to help you, Celia. That's why I've come. Don't be afraid." She took the girl's hands in hers and felt them wet with her own tears, then brought them to her mouth and kissed them many times, trying to ease the awful lost look that she saw every time Celia raised her eyes. At last Celia said:

"You're crying for Robert, Grand-mère. Then you know he's dead."

"No, my darling, I'm crying for you."

"There's no need. He says I am to wait and we'll be together." She stopped and frowned anxiously. "That sounds wrong. Am I going to die? Yes, that was it. Not here, in heaven. Don't cry, Grand-mère. You look sad that way."

What on earth would she do with her? Sophie looked around wildly, sorry she had dismissed Maggie, hoping she had disobeyed her instructions. There was no one now to help her. A plan that had been forming in her mind came forward as the only possible one. She spoke rapidly, not as if to someone who was half or all crazy but as if she were addressing a perfectly reasonable woman:

"Listen, Celia, you can't stay here any longer. You must let me take care of you. We have another house in Cong, not in the village but in Dooras. You can go there until the baby is born. I'll send an old servant of ours with you—Katta. Has Robert ever spoken to you of Katta? Or perhaps you remember her?"

"Yes, his nurse."

A spark of sense, thank God, Sophie said to herself, and hurried on:

"You'll be safe there until the baby is born, and then you can go away. Would you like that?"

"Yes, yes, anywhere. It's what I want."

But then she stopped and Sophie guessed grimly that she had asked that fool Maurice to take her away and he had refused. What kind of monster would the child of such a pair be? That would be another day's crying. Katta was an inspiration, a genius with babies. Robert and Louise both owed their lives to her. Celia asked in a perfectly reasonable tone:

"When can I go to Dooras?"

"It will take a few days to arrange."

In her relief at Celia's apparent return to normality, Sophie stood up, but she stayed close by her so as still to show friendship. Then Celia said:

"Will Robert find me in Dooras? He'll come looking for me here as usual and I'll be gone."

It was a nightmare from which there was no escape. As long as Sophie stayed with her, Celia's wits seemed to come and go, but in the end she took Sophie's hands in hers and said:

"I do know there is something wrong in my head. There is a pain, and a humming, and I think I imagine things. Can you forgive me?"

"Yes, yes. I've come to take care of you. Now you're not well, but later, when the baby is born, you'll be better."

Almost babbling, she got herself out of the room onto the landing and went to sit on a wide window-seat that looked out over the neglected fields, until Maggie came upstairs to look for her. By then she had recovered enough to be able to stand up and say:

"She has agreed to come away to Cong. I'll send Katta with her, that was nurse .to my grandchildren—why are you staring? What else can I do? She spoke of Robert. I can't help it. There's no one else I can trust."

"Send me with them, my lady. I'm not too old."

"No. Yes—I don't know what I'm saying. Yes, you may go too. I'll send messages at once. I told her it will take a few days. The pear tree needs pruning."

"You're right, it does. It's no one's business."

"What about Mr. Nugent? If he's at home now I should see him."

Suddenly Maggie spat fiercely into her right palm, then rubbed her two hands together, saying:

"The curse of Cromwell on him for a father. May he never die till the house falls in on top of him. Why would you want to see him, or talk to him? He doesn't care a straw for her."

"But she's his daughter."

"You might have to wait for him until the fall of night."

In the end Sophie wrote him a short letter and left it in Maggie's charge. Then she went wearily out to the carriage and was driven home, Amélie silent beside her. Shadows moved behind the windows as they approached the house. She knew she was watched by Fanny and Sarah, perhaps even by Maurice, but she knew too that none of them would dare to question her. She had Amélie bring supper on a tray but then felt that this made her seem defeated. At nine o'clock she went downstairs. The heat of the day lingered in all the empty rooms. Sarah came slinking out of a dark corner in the hall, saying:

"We thought you were not well, madame."

"Where is my son?"

"In the rent room."

Sarah always knew where everyone was. He was there, making up his accounts or pretending to. He put down his quill and looked at her without speaking. She said:

"I went to Castle Nugent today."

"I know. Fanny told me."

"She's very ill."

"Yes."

"I leave your judgment to God. Tomorrow I'll send for Katta and she can take her to Dooras for the birth. Then I'll write to Father Burke and tell him to find her a suitable convent somewhere in Bordeaux, where she can live."

"No!"

"Would you like to keep her, then? Why not bring her to this house? You haven't quite finished destroying her."

Maurice spread his arms forward on the desk, laid his head down on them and wept. She heard his sobs, anguished, painful, tearing at his throat as if he could scarcely breathe. She watched him quietly for a minute or two, then turned and went out of the room.

PART
EIGHT

31

In the middle of November, in 1782, Robert rode over the mountain to see Katta. He knew now that it was not a shorter way but he wanted to follow the track that he and Louise had taken almost three years ago. It was the same kind of day as that one in January, with a hard wind that ruffled the distant lake and wild white clouds giving way now and then to patches of sudden blue. The track had not yet been rutted by the winter rain and in a few places at either side the rushes showed green where they had not yet died.

Presently he passed through the village of hovels high on the mountain. Smoke streamed from the blackened doorways or from the holes in the roofs that served as chimneys. People came running out to see who was there, but this time they recognized him instantly and withdrew again. There was no friendly greeting; no one wanted to speak to a Brien. When he had gone they would probably spend the rest of the day talking about him, perhaps singing the miserable ballad that Sarah had told him about:

> *O lie with me, said the fine young man,*
> *And then you may lie with my father—*

He should know about it for his own protection, Sarah said, and before he could stop her she was quavering out the first lines. Then she saw him begin to blaze with fury and she scuttled away as he lunged towards her. He would not have struck her—it would have been like striking a cat—but it was useful to have terrified her. That was three days after he arrived home, the first day he had been alone with her since he had heard the bare bones of the story of Celia from Sophie. After he had frightened Sarah he got her into a corner of the room and forced more and more information out of her, lifting his fists every time she stopped. Stark fear showed on her face first and then he spotted a gleam of satisfaction and knew it was time to let her go. He had scarcely seen her since. Fanny had kept almost completely out of his way, though he sometimes came upon her herding the three little boys off with significant whispers, as if he were dangerous. Heaven alone knew what she had told them. He was sorry for Fanny, in a way, but he felt nothing but loathing for her sister.

He needed no directions for finding Creevagh this time. He could see the huddle of mud cottages at the edge of the lake long before he came down to the place where the stream had to be crossed. Goats and donkeys were grazing between the houses, and several people were moving about. He flicked at the horse with his whip so that it flew across the stream, then held it in and walked it to Katta's door. He dismounted and threw the reins over the rock by the door, knowing that the horse would not wander.

Katta was standing in the middle of the room. She came forward one step, then covered her face with both hands like a child who believes it will disappear from view as soon as it can no longer see. He came over to her, his three-cornered hat in his left hand, the right free to put around her shoulder in the old affectionate way that she must remember. She peeked at him from between her fingers, and he threw the hat on a stool and pulled her hands aside, saying in Irish:

"Katta, why don't you look at me? If you turn from me, where can I go?"

"I'll never turn from you."

"You were with her. I came to ask you to tell me about it."

"Your grandmother will do that."

"She was not in Dooras. Sarah told me something but not all."

"Robert, how can I tell it? I'm haunted, since that time."

"So am I. It was August, wasn't it?"

"Yes, August Day, the fifteenth, when the baby was born, but she had been in Dooras a few weeks by then."

"Did my father come?"

"How can you ask me that? Haven't you any pity on me?"

"I have, Katta, I have, but I must know every detail of it. How often did he come?"

"Twice. After the second time it was no use. His heart was broken. We could see it, Maggie and myself. When he left her the last time I thought he would die with the pain that was on him."

"Why did he not come again? Why was it no use?"

"Didn't your grandmother tell you?"

"She told me almost nothing. She hardly speaks at all now, to me nor to anyone else."

"Perhaps she will in time."

"Why didn't he come again?"

"She sent him away. The first time, she called him Robert, and was very loving and good, and he thought that would pass and she'd know him again, but when he came the second time she said he was an evil spirit that came to torment her, and she would have no one but Robert, that came every day to see her, and stayed with her, and was the father of her child." Katta gave a wail of anguish, like a sea gull's cry. "Don't make me tell you those things. Have pity on me, and on your father."

"On you but not on him. So then she was alone?"

"What could he do? Maggie and I were with her. He was afraid of doing her an injury. If you saw him then as I did, you'd have pity on him."

"That was Maggie from Castle Nugent who was there, I heard from Sarah."

"Yes, she was with me all the time. Miss Celia was fond of her, and I knew that Maggie used to be called often when she was younger, as a handywoman. She brought the baby, in the end."

"Go on. Why are you stopping now?"

"How can I talk to a young boy about things like this?"

"I'm not a young boy. I've been in the war. I've been halfway around the world."

"It's a pity you didn't stay there. Why did you come back?"

"To marry Celia."

Instantly Katta asked:

"Were you promised to each other before you went away? Lady Brien said you were not. She said it was all in Miss Celia's head and that you could never marry anyway because it's against the law of the land, a Catholic to marry a Protestant."

"Celia didn't know about that law, and Grand-mère knew nothing about Celia and me. When she wrote to me, or to Louise, she said nothing about Celia. You would think she knew nothing about what was happening."

"It's true, she knew nothing until July when Maggie told her, a month before the baby was born."

"She could have written then, she could have told us then, or afterwards. She never said a word."

"About your own father?"

"Yes. It would have been better to hear it from her than from strangers. I got the first stories in France. I didn't believe them, I denied them because I had heard nothing of them from Grand-mère."

"Where did you hear?"

"In Paris, from cousins."

"It would be hard for your grandmother to tell you how her house was brought down."

"Did she go to Cong with you?"

"No, but she went before that, to make sure that the place was in good order. Robert, she did everything for Miss Celia, everything."

"And then she sent her out of the country."

"What else could she do? It was the only safe thing."

"Safe? Why safe?"

"The people were saying she killed the baby—did you not hear that before? Well, that's what was said, and Lady Brien was afraid she'd be brought to court for it, and that no one would believe the baby died a natural death. Robert, I can't tell you any more. My heart will stop. God help us, can't you let it all lie quiet now? What use is it asking all these things? It's more than a year ago, fifteen months ago since it happened. Can't you forget it? Miss Celia is safe and it's all behind her now, and there's no more to be said about it."

"Do you know where she is?"

"No. Somewhere in France. Father Burke took the charge of

her, I think. Lady Brien would never talk to the like of me about that."

"Does my father know where she is?"

"I don't know. We took her to Galway by night and she went on one of the ships that bring the cloth and wine. I asked about it and I was told it was going to France. That's all I know."

"Tell me about the baby."

"No."

"Tell me, Katta, for God's sake."

"It was a girl, very puny, an eight months' child. Maggie said seven would have been better if it had to come early at all. I've always heard that too. It lived a day, long enough for us to get the priest from Cong to give it baptism. It died, the second morning."

"Did she name it?"

"Yes. Louise. Now you're crying. I should never have told you that. No one asked it but yourself."

"She knew what she was doing, then?"

"Once the baby was born she knew everything. That's how it always happens. Once she saw it, her mind cleared like the morning mist, but we wished it didn't because then she nearly died of sorrow. Maggie stayed with her mostly at that time, because she knew her better. It was a month and more before she was well enough to go to Galway. She had to wait there a few days until a ship came in. Maggie stayed with her all that time."

"Where is Maggie now?"

"In Dooras. She would never go back to Castle Nugent and my lady said she can stay in Dooras as long as she likes. She keeps the house, though there's no one there these times but herself, and a man that works around the yard."

"I'll go there now. I can stay in the house."

"Yes. There are beds in plenty."

Katta turned away heavily, wearily. He noticed that she looked much older than when he had seen her last, the white streak now covering half of her jet-black hair. He asked abruptly:

"Where is Matthias? Where is Colman?"

"In the field. The boys too. They left us to have our talk. Una went to the neighbors."

"Everyone knows I'm here, then?"

"Didn't we see the horse coming down the mountain? I wish you could come back happier. Don't quarrel with your father."

"Quarrel! It's beyond that."

"Robert, have no evil thoughts towards him. It was pity for her and grief for you that started it all, as sure as I'm here. Why do you want to know where she is? You wouldn't do her an injury—Robert!"

"I thought of it when I heard first what happened but now I feel differently. I want to know everything that happened. That song—you heard it?" He knew by her face that she had. "Where did it come from? How did the people know that Celia and I were—were—" he couldn't find a word better than Katta's own, "promised to each other?"

"I've heard she used to go to the house to ask about you, and young Lady Brien spoke of it. I think that's how it happened."

It was a moment before he grasped who she meant.

"Aunt Fanny! Of course it would be Aunt Fanny."

"I don't know for sure but I know the song was made up by a man from Galway that she knows well. He makes a lot of songs, especially that kind. I'd swear my oath she doesn't like it no more than you do but that's my guess of what happened."

Robert rode on to Cong, crossing the mountain again by another track to join the main Galway road beyond Oughterard. He galloped the horse until it was in a sweat, then had to stop and water it at Maam Cross before setting off through the wild valley that ended at the top of Lough Corrib. The daylight was fading by the time he reached the fords that let him across to the northern shore. He had trouble remembering the way, having been there so seldom and so long ago. Several times he had to stop and ask the way at cottages where a glimmer of light showed against the darkness. One man said to him anxiously:

"Aren't you afraid to travel alone at this time of night?"

"Is it dangerous? Are there robbers about?"

"Not here, only poachers; they don't want to have anything to do with you. What would robbers live on in these hungry places? But there's the ghosts of the dead, worse than any robbers, and they walk always in November in the dark nights. You can stay with us here and welcome, if you like. We haven't much to give you but you can lie by the fire until the dawn."

The smell that poured out of his cottage was easily identifiable as pigs. Robert said:

"Thank you, I'll go on. It's not far, just beyond Dooras."

"An hour will take you there. Your horse is good. So is your Irish. Where do you come from?"

"Near Oughterard."

"Ah."

Before he could ask any more Robert was on his way. Already since arriving back in Ireland he had developed an extra sense to warn him when someone was going to ask his name. He heard the man shout a blessing after him, to keep the ghosts away.

The Brien house was named, rather too grandly, Dooras Hall. It was a square, plain manor house at the far end of a long field through which an avenue ran uncompromisingly straight. As he rode up he saw that the wide fanlight above the door was lit from within but the windows of the rooms at either side were dark. Maggie probably kept to the back, where the kitchens were. He hitched the horse to a ring on the mounting block and hammered on the door with the handle of his whip. After a while, as he was preparing to hammer again, feet shuffled inside, then a frightened old woman's voice asked:

"Who's there? Is that you, Johnny? Why don't you go to the back?"

"It's Robert Brien, Maggie. Open up!"

He could hear her muttering prayers or curses in Irish as she drew back the bolts. She threw the door wide, then stood looking at him. A lamp with a colored glass globe stood on the hall table and seemed to send a breath of warm air out to meet him. He was filled for a moment with a surprising sense of peace. He said gently:

"I'm tired, Maggie. I've come all the way from Mount Brien today. I want to stay a day or two and talk to you."

"You want to talk about her?"

"Yes."

"Come in, then. It's your house. You have a right to come and go when you like. You need no welcome from me."

"I'd be glad of one all the same."

"What brings you here? Two years ago would have been better."

He stepped into the hall and shut the door quietly. Maggie said:

"There isn't much to eat but you can come to the kitchen if you like. Or I can take it to the dining room."

"The kitchen will be better."

He followed her along the hall, down three steps and into the kitchen, where she found him some cold meat and bread. She watched him eating, sitting in a tall-backed chair to one side of the range, getting up when he had almost finished to draw him a glass of beer from the barrel in the corner. He took it as a sign of friendship and said:

"I stopped for an hour in Creevagh on the way, to speak to Katta."

"Is she well?"

"Well enough."

"Was she friendly to you?"

"Katta is my mother."

"I suppose she is."

"She told me some of what happened to Celia. She said you would tell the rest."

"There's nothing to tell. She had her child, it died and she had to go across the sea for fear of the law."

"You heard that too?"

"There were people that wished her dead. When she lived, they thought of other ways of doing her harm."

"Who were they? Who wished her dead?"

"How should I know?"

"My father?"

"God forgive you, he broke his heart for her."

"My father's wife?"

"I don't know where the story came from. One day there was nothing, the next it was all over Connaught that she killed her child." Her eyes full of angry tears now, the old woman said, "Why are you asking me? It's all finished. I'm trying to forget it. You should try to forget it too. It's the only thing for you now, when you didn't come to her before."

"Am I to blame for everything? Is that what you're saying?"

"There's laws for the gentry and laws for the poor. Maybe you weren't to blame. You were no more than a boy yourself. I have no right to talk to you like this. You led me into it. Your grandmother did what she could as soon as she knew what was happening. I saw her myself, on her knees before Miss Celia. She didn't know I saw; I came into the room after she had sent me away."

"On her knees! My grandmother!"

"Why are you so surprised? Doesn't she go on her knees before God? She knew what to do and she did everything that could be done."

"Everything my father should have done. He came only twice, Katta told me."

"Leave him to God. He could only do harm if he came again."

"Katta said the baby lived for a day."

"What do you know about babies, and you only a boy?"

"It should have been mine."

She made no reply and he knew she was shocked. It was very quiet in the kitchen, one of those still, gray November nights when no sound is heard but the ash falling in the fire and the clock ticking on the wall. After a minute or two Robert said:

"I haven't been a boy for a long time. Tell me what happened after the baby died."

"She lay in bed and we thought she would die too. She looked as if she were asleep but her eyes fluttered all the time under her eyelids. She would eat nothing. Then after a day or two she did sleep, and when we brought her some milk she drank it. Then she asked who was in the house, whether her father knew where she was and a few other sensible questions, and we saw that she had her wits back. Your grandmother sent me a message to say she was to go to Galway when she was well enough but she didn't come again herself."

"Did her father come?"

"No."

"Did she want him to come?"

"She never mentioned him but the one time."

"Maggie, why was the child christened by the priest instead of by the minister?"

"How should I know? She asked for him, and it was easy to find him and bring him over here."

"What is his name?"

"Mr. O'Toole. He lived in Cong, in the village, but he had to go away soon after that because he was not registered. There was information laid about him."

"He wasn't afraid to come?"

"If he were afraid, he wouldn't be in Ireland at all."

"You went with her to Galway, Katta said."

"Yes, at the end of September. We stayed at Mr. Lynch's house in Middle Street, ten days, waiting for a ship to come."

"Was she well at that time?"

"Yes, she got better every day. She was young. The weather was warm almost until the end and she sat in the garden in the sun. I wished she could stay there always, and Mrs. Lynch would have been glad to have her, but there was nothing to be done. She had to go when the ship was ready. The weather was turning black and the Captain wouldn't wait. We got three hours' notice but it didn't matter. I had everything ready for her because we had been waiting for the call from day to day. I went down to the shore with her and watched them row out in the boat, and that's the last I saw of her."

"And my grandmother didn't come to see her in Galway?"

"How could she? She goes out so seldom, those that were after Miss Celia would have found out quickly where she went. And the captains of those ships don't like to be watched. The one that took her away landed a few priests when he came and took on a few boys going to France the way you went yourself. If he thought Miss Celia was being noticed he might have said he wouldn't take her at all. You're trying to blame someone, I can see. Don't blame your grandmother. I did, until I found out that she knew nothing of what was happening. Once she knew, she did everything a person could do."

"Katta said the same."

"Why wouldn't she, and it the truth? Blame yourself, if you like. Miss Celia said to me one night shortly before the baby came that you never wrote her as much as one letter. She was wandering in her mind, and she said it was better that way because you came to see her instead."

"She told you that she saw me?"

"Yes, every day," Maggie said harshly. "It kept her contented and that's all we cared about. We never told her you were not there, and never would be there—" She stopped, perhaps feeling she had gone too far, but Robert was barely listening to her. After a moment he asked:

"Did her father know where she was?"

"If he knew or cared he didn't show it. He was off about his own affairs."

"Does he know where she is now?"

"The only one in Ireland that knows that is Lady Brien. If you want to find it out, you'll have to ask her. It's no use trying to get it out of me because I don't know."

"It's somewhere in France."

"Yes. Father Burke probably knows too but they say he won't come back to Ireland ever again."

He stayed two nights, sleeping in one of the big, cold bedrooms to the front of the house with a view over the leaden lake. The dawns came late, the orange-colored sun forcing its way through black, angry clouds. On the afternoon of the second day Maggie consented to tell him which room had been Celia's, only because he suggested that it was the one where she had put him. She said aggrievedly:

"Do you think I would do such a thing? Here, I'll show you."

She led him through a short corridor towards the back of the house, over the kitchens, to a room that looked into the stable-yard. He walked in and stood looking around, turning slowly, while she watched him from the doorway. He was scarcely aware of her. Here Celia had lived those weeks of pain and fever and bewilderment. Here his own ghost had come to keep her company and here her spirit stayed to tell him of her love, that bewildering, mad love for him that had destroyed her. At last he understood her crime that was really his, her innocence and goodness betrayed by him. Over and over in his mind some illogical words repeated themselves like an incantation: she is gone forever, we are parted forever.

The November afternoon was darkening, the old woman was cold and said in a new, gentler tone:

"Come down, young man, and leave her be. You can do nothing more for her."

"You go down, Maggie. I'll come soon."

But after she had gone he stayed there, his thoughts fixed on that spirit of Celia's that now seemed to fill the room, his mind forming half-finished sentences and odd words, as if she were constantly interrupting him:

"Yes, my love, I should have been here—can you see my tears? —a boy is ignorant—you should have known—worthless, arrogant—I'll find you, my own true love, my only love—I never once truly held you in my arms, never once—are you here, then? If you are here I'll stay forever—it would be easy to die now—in battle I was afraid—but you are alive somewhere—I won't leave you—"

A dizziness in his head forced him at last to realize that what he was doing was foolish, but he stayed on in the room until he was calmer, walking over to the window to look down into the stableyard, lit by cold moonlight. One beam fell across the bed where she had lain. He came back, and put down his hand to touch it, almost as if he were trying to lift it up, then smoothed the quilt gently several times, absently, staring down at the bed, seeing nothing that was there, listening desperately for her voice.

The old woman was coming back. As she shuffled along the corridor carrying an oil lamp high in her hand, he came quickly out of the room, taking the key from the inside of the door. Then he closed and locked it, and put the key in his pocket, saying:

"That room is not to be opened again. I'll take the key with me."

"What will I say to your father if he comes?"

"You can say I gave instructions. But he won't come."

32

The next morning he rode back to Mount Brien. He arrived in the early afternoon, gave his horse to a groom and went through by the back way into the house. Passing by the rent-room door he paused for a moment to listen to the familiar sound, his father endlessly stirring the fire with the poker. He was perfectly sober, though Robert had not thought so when he saw him at this first, his shoulders hunched, his head bent, two hands clasped on the brass knob of the poker and the point stuck into the burning turf, continually moving it from side to side, scratching the hearth through the ashes like a giant rat.

Robert passed on upstairs, the heavy, dead feel of the house already beginning to oppress him. On the landing he paused, then heard the door of Sarah's room close. He crossed the landing and quietly turned the handle of Sophie's sitting-room door. It was locked. He tapped gently and her voice asked:

"Who is it?"

"Robert. Let me in, Grand-mère."

Sweating with anger and embarrassment he heard Sarah open her door again and knew she was standing just inside it, peeping at him. He tapped again and heard Sophie, close by the door, ask:

"What do you want?"

"To speak to you privately."

He heard her turn the key in the lock and he seized the handle at once and marched into the room, saying furiously:

"Did you think we should have our conversation in shouts, through the panel of the door, for Sarah's benefit?"

But he stopped then, because he saw how she had become old and frail, shuffling across the room, back to her eternal seat by the window. She put her hands to her head and said in a querulous tone that he had never heard her use before:

"Please don't raise your voice. Where have you been? I missed you and no one knew where you had gone. I could feel them closing in on me. I thought you had gone for good."

"I went to Dooras. I saw Katta first and then Maggie. I had to go to them because you wouldn't talk to me."

"You're still going on with that? Why don't you forget her and let her be?"

"That's what they said. Out of sight, out of mind, that's the best thing all round. That's what you're saying too."

"Robert, you're getting very nasty."

Before she could sit down he took her by the shoulders and held her firmly, looking down at her, noticing how small she was and how slender the bones under his hands.

"Grand-mère, I don't want to be nasty, but you must tell me where Celia is. She must not be abandoned."

"She's not abandoned. She's well cared for."

"How do you know? Does she write to you?"

"No. Father Burke wrote once and then he told me she was content and safe."

"Is that all she's ever to be? Content and safe?"

"There are worse states she could be in," Sophie said, with a trace of her old temper.

He pressed her down into her chair, then knelt in front of her as he used to do when he was small, and said:

"Grand-mère, for the love of God tell me where she is. If you don't, I must go to Father Burke and make him tell me."

"He won't tell. He has sworn not to. Why do you want to know? Haven't you injured her enough?"

"I want to find her wherever she is and keep her with me for the rest of her life and mine. I want to marry her."

"What makes you think she would consent? Anyway it's against the law for you to marry a Protestant girl."

"What do I care about the law? Plenty of laws have been broken. Does her father know where she is?"

"Of course not. He's a weak vessel, if ever there was one. I'd have been a fool to let him know anything about her."

"Did he know of the story that she had killed her child?"

"How can I tell you that? He had nothing to do with her, nothing at all. That story was started by Fanny."

"Like the ballad."

"What ballad? Is there a ballad? Tell me, tell me!"

"No."

They stared at each other, then Robert said:

"I'm quite determined to ask her to marry me. At least I must do that. Can't you see that it would be right?"

"No."

"How can you judge? How can you decide what to do with her, as if she were your property?"

"You decided that, you and your father."

"Then I'll go to Mr. Burke."

She repeated, "He won't tell. He swore he would not, and he won't."

"I'll go to every house in Bordeaux until I find her. I'll never rest until I see her again."

"You'll get tired of that search."

"Did you know that she had her baby christened Louise by the priest from Cong?"

"I don't believe it." Her face had gone white. "Who told you that?"

"Someone who was there."

"I didn't think to tell them not to speak to you. I'll never tell you where she is. You'll never find out."

"Why do you hate her now?"

"Hate her! Is that what you think? Robert, if you quarrel with me, I'll have no one left to live for. I don't hate her. How could I? She has been destroyed. It's as if she were dead. Can't you see that?"

"It sounds as if she is in a convent. Can't the dead rise again?"

"Yes, in the next life, not in this. I can't bear any more. Why are you doing this to me?"

"For her, for her. I must find her."

"Let me think. You give me no time. You should hate her, if anyone does."

"I did at first but not now. I have no right to hate her."

"You think it goes by right? Well, perhaps so. Most people hate the person they have injured."

"It wasn't I who injured her the most," he said wearily, getting slowly to his feet and gazing down at her. "Or if I did, it was in complete ignorance. You may be right, but I followed your judgment about her before. You didn't say anything to me but I knew what you were thinking, and you were wrong. This time I must follow my own judgment."

"Was I so wrong? Young people are very quick to judge." He could see that he had hurt her deeply but he felt no compunction. "How could I stand by and see this miserable way of life perpetuated in the next generation? Of course I wanted to get you out of it, at all costs."

"Both of us? Louise too? Were you happy with what happened to her?"

"Don't torment me." She moved her head from side to side as if to shake out the agony of her thoughts. "I didn't know what to do. I only know that every single thing in this country is poisoned. There is no order, no honesty, no progress, no ideas, no aristocracy except those dreadful jumped-up adventurers whose fathers and grandfathers made money, who spend their time drinking and fighting and whoring, who hate this country and go off to England at every chance and sit there sneering at their own place and their own people. Those who stay at home are just as bad. Look at Mr. Nugent—look at the Burkes and the D'Arcys—did you want to spend your life with people like that, when you could be with educated people in France?"

She stopped suddenly, then said after a moment: "How foolish that all sounds. I've expressed it badly. You needn't pity me; I've had a useful life and I know it. I'm sorry you don't approve of my judgments but I must make them. You're a man now. You needn't heed me any more. I took care of your girl as best I could and I'll get no thanks for it. You may go back to France and search for her if you like but I won't help you. I'm sorry to part from you like this—"

"No, no, we won't part like this." In a moment he was on his knees again, his head in her lap. After a moment he felt her fingers tickle the back of his neck lightly, once, and he felt certain she would not be able to refuse him. He said softly, looking up at her:

"Tell me where she is. I can have no peace or rest until I find her."

"I'll never tell you where she is, never as long as I live."

"Then I'll go to Father Burke."

"You must please yourself. I trust him not to tell. He has lost faith in you. He won't tell you anything."

"You fight like a good general, Grand-mère. I can't quarrel with you. In York, after the battle, everyone sat down to dinner together. Will you be like that with me?"

"Everyone except the dead soldiers."

"I'll go back to France at once."

"There is nothing more for you here."

"Would you not be glad if I stayed?"

"No. It ruined your father."

"Things like this can happen in France."

"Not quite like this, as I remember."

"Better times are coming for Ireland."

"I'll believe that when I see it."

"I'll come back with Celia, quite soon."

"God forbid. Don't torment me. I'm too old."

It was no use going on with it. He made a few more attempts to get the information he wanted, but she never wavered and he had to give it up.

It was the middle of December, three weeks later, before he found a ship to take him from Galway to Bordeaux. During that time they talked endlessly about Louise, Sophie never tiring of hearing about the Lally farm and the way that André and Louise lived there. The notion of André milking cows amused her so much that she laughed aloud, the first time that he heard her do so since his homecoming. With the same obstinacy as she showed in her refusal to reveal where Celia was, she would not speak of Louise's son in Angers, though Robert had told her that he had seen him. It was as if she were trying to erase that part of Louise's life from existence.

The day before he left, Robert waylaid Mr. Nugent on his way to Burke's, riding his fat old cob with its worn harness, looking more like a journeyman tailor than a country gentleman. The cob halted as if it was glad to rest when Robert blocked the road with his tall hunter. Mr. Nugent looked frightened at first, then assumed an unusually truculent expression. Robert said without preamble:

"I want to tell you that I'm going to ask your daughter to marry me."

"Celia?"

"You have only one daughter."

"I don't know where she is." The expression became petulant, then sly. "You and your family have ruined her between you."

"I know. That's one reason why I want to marry her."

"Compensation?" Nugent laughed, his courage evidently returning. "Well, you may succeed. Don't let me stop you. She has nothing, as you probably know. I doubt if you have much either. I trusted your father. I thought he was my friend."

"Oh, give it up, Nugent," Robert said violently. "No one will be taken in by that line. You neglected her completely. You let her fall into the hands of a scoundrel."

"That's no way to speak of your father."

"You think fathers have rights? I don't agree with you. I was not asking your leave to marry Celia. I was simply telling you my plans and warning you that you had better not interfere."

"Warning me? You are an impertinent young man, doubly, yes, doubly impertinent considering the injury your father did to her. I've sworn never to speak to him again." The cob bent its head and began to crop the grass, edging closer and closer, bending its shoulder blades so that Mr. Nugent was in danger of slipping off. He kicked at it ineptly and it lifted one hind leg as if to dislodge a fly, then went on with its plan of reaching a patch of grass at the foot of the ditch that bordered the road. Its detachment seemed so ridiculous that Robert began to laugh.

Nugent's face turned a peculiar purplish color and his eyes took on a fishlike glaze. "You insult me, yes, you insult me. Do you think I could have stopped her, or that I could have stopped your father? We are a very unfortunate family; we've always been unfortunate and I suppose we'll be so until the end. I don't know why you want to join your misfortunes to ours, but it's none of my business, I'm glad to say, nothing to do with me, nothing at all. Perhaps you think I should have called your father out. Most people would have done that but I don't think it's worth while to get killed for such a cause. Honor? Perhaps you can tell me what that is. Have I got it? Has your father? Have you? If no one has, then why cause all that trouble over something that doesn't exist? You're sitting there high on your horse, laughing at mine—yes, I know that's what you are laughing at, though I could have that horse from under you if I wanted him. You won't do for this country, young man. Patronage will only do so much. You have been too long away, you have French ways and American ways, and you have forgotten what kind of a country Ireland is. If you want to know about Ireland, watch your grandmother. She is a great lady, a great lady, and no one in this whole country will disagree with that." He pulled sharply on the reins so that the cob's head came up, its mouth open and the pinkish tongue protruding in pain. Then it swung out into the road at his wish. "We have no more to say to each other. Let me pass."

"I'm sorry I laughed at you."

"Well, young man, is this another American habit, to apologize? I doubt if it's a French one."

"I don't know where it comes from," Robert said in a low voice. "You're right, I don't know now which is my country, nor which will be."

He stopped, realizing that any further words would only increase the look of contempt on Nugent's face. Without looking at him Robert pulled his horse aside and allowed the cob to pass, then lifted his head to watch it amble off down the road, its rider rolling slightly in the saddle.

33

Robert reached Bordeaux about noon a few days before Christmas. The mud flats at the estuary of the Garonne were a welcome sight. The calm weather that had tempted the Captain to leave Galway had soon given way to violent storms and they were blown miles off their course, losing several days before they were able to turn back.

The Captain was a West Waterford man named Connery who plied regularly between Ireland and France. He was glad of Robert's company, having him to eat with him in his tiny cabin, and he seemed to know everyone in Bordeaux. A Galwayman was the rector there, he said, and he offered to lead Robert there and introduce him, directly they landed.

"Father Martin Glynn from Tuam; maybe you know him already. But what do you want with him? Are you going for a doctor or a priest? Weren't you in the army in America? So I heard anyway."

There seemed to be no one who had not heard. On an impulse Robert said:

"Did you bring out a girl from Galway over a year ago? She came to Bordeaux in the autumn, Miss Celia Nugent."

Connery looked at him oddly, as if he found it obscene of Robert to mention her name at all, but he said politely:

"No, though I know who it was that did. He was lost with his ship the very next voyage, a blasted devil of a winter that took a lot of ships." He was watching Robert with curiosity. "You're following that girl. Well, she got there safe. I can see your heart went cold at the thought of her being on that ship that foundered, but I know she got there safe."

"Do you know where she went, in Bordeaux?"

"I never heard that, but maybe she went to the Lynches. I've often thought that's where she went. They have a fine house on the quayside, fit for the like of her, and it was one of that family that put her on the ship in Galway."

"You know a lot about her."

"Don't be offended, young man. Everyone knows a thing like that, a lady traveling alone, and you far away in America. It was a sad story."

Robert asked, shocked, "Did she not have a woman with her?"

"Not a soul. I heard there was one to go but she got sick at the last moment, and the Captain couldn't wait."

Robert had assumed that Sophie would have sent a maid of her own with her. He had been so sure of this that he had not even asked who accompanied her. It seemed now that everywhere he looked he found more ways in which his family had injured her. The Captain was saying:

"But she was safe as a house. Those people she was with wouldn't touch a hair of her head, once they knew the Briens were her friends."

He seemed innocently to believe this, his honest countryman's face quite without guile, but Robert was sickened at the thought of the extra humiliation and danger to which she had been exposed. If her story were as well known as it appeared to be, there were plenty who would have felt entitled to take advantage of her.

He declined the Captain's help on landing and found his own way into the town, taking two rooms in a small street near the cathedral. They were high up, and looked into the neat, empty gardens of Cardinal Rohan's palace. The landlord found him a servant at once and said that he would have horses and a carriage in a few hours' time. The moment his arrangements were made, Robert set out on foot for the Irish College.

It was quite close, in the rue du Hâ, which was named after the nearby fort. The narrow street was darkening as the winter light faded and lamps were lit already inside the building. He asked at once for Father James Burke but the porter said he was not there. Robert said:

"Then I'll see Father Martin Glynn."

"Oh, you will, will you? Maybe you know him, do you?"

The question didn't seem to need an answer and the porter went off to find the rector. Robert waited in the small, bare room, furnished only with a bench, a battered table and a crucifix on the wall. The cold ate into his bones. There was a musty smell of damp wood and the plaster was cracked here and there with damp. He began to shiver, and realized that he should have stopped to eat something. He felt a strong current of excitement run through him, making him light-headed with hope, the reverse of the ugly despair that had overwhelmed him in Ireland. She was here, somewhere in this town. Soon he would see her, this girl whose essence he had failed to discover for so long, whom he knew now in absence as he had never been able to do when she was near him.

A mad idea came to him that she might be under this very roof but of course that was impossible, with the monastic regime of the college. He tried to imagine how she would look but then fear seized him that she would refuse to see him at all. She had every reason to hate him, or at best to despise him. He sprang off the bench and began to walk around the room, then was suddenly visited with a memory of doing the same for another girl, in another Irish College. The effect was like a cold bath.

He was a weakling, a fool. She must know this by now. Grand-mère was right that his presence here was only deepening the injury he had done to her already. Should he then go quietly away and try to forget her, out of fear and weakness? He could not do it. That hope persisted in spite of all reason. She loved him still; he knew it, he felt it throughout his whole being, as strongly as he had felt it in her room in Dooras.

By the time the rector came in twenty minutes later he was sitting quietly on the hard bench, his hands wrapped in the folds of his cloak for warmth, as immovable as a waiting coachman. The rector was a white-haired man of about sixty with a thin, ascetic face, and the sharp eye of one who is always dealing with the young. He turned this habitual glance on Robert, as if he were summing up his possibilities as a student, but his words were polite as to a grown man.

"I could have come at once. The porter is afraid to disturb me, or says he is. I barked at him once and I've been paying for it ever since. Forgive me—I hope you're not cold. We don't heat much."

"I came to look for Father Burke. I understood he lived here. Can you tell me where to find him?"

"Ah, yes, Burke." The name was evidently not a pleasing one to him. "Yes, he is often here on a visit. He seems to love the place, but he usually lives in his parish. It's Saint Jacques d'Ambès. He'll probably come in tomorrow."

"Is it far to Saint Jacques d'Ambès?"

"An hour's ride or more. It's at the confluence of the Dordogne and the Garonne, near Fronsac, near Saint André de Cubzac. Do you know Mr. Burke well?"

"He was our tutor, my sister's and mine."

"Then you're a Brien."

"Yes."

"I've been to your house. I've met your father. How is he?"

"Very well."

There was no sign that he had heard the story.

"Are you coming to study in Bordeaux?"

"No. I've been to America with the Dillon regiment."

"Ah, a hero. You look too young for that. You're on your way home, then?"

"I hope so."

"You can come tomorrow. When he's in Bordeaux he often comes about noon."

Robert thanked him and left but he did not want to wait on this vague possibility. Night had fallen. Flares lit up the street corners and sentries were visible around the black mass of the Fort du Hâ. A cold rain blew against him on the wind from the river. He felt sickened by the delay, as if it were a bad omen. If he could find her now, while this strength was in him, she would not be able to refuse him. She would recognize it, and pity him. Where could she be? Somewhere in this city, a convent, perhaps. There were several near the cathedral, dark, high walls and shut doors and lightless buildings beyond. Captain Connery had said she might be at the Lynches, who had a fine house on the riverfront. Back at his lodgings he asked the landlord:

"Do you know an Irish family named Lynch who have a house on the quays?"

"Count Jean-Baptiste Lynch, of course. Everyone knows him. He has his own wine business and he takes in others as well."

"Where is his vineyard?"

"Near Saint Jacques d'Ambès."

Feeling himself go weak with excitement and longing, Robert asked casually:

"Can you tell me the exact house? I think I know that Lynch family."

"Your servant will take you there. He knows it well."

The house was far down the Quay des Chartrons, a tall gray house made even darker by the driving rain. The servant was a cheerful young man who did indeed know the house well, having once worked for the family. He was still friendly with one of the other servants and visited him occasionally. Robert asked:

"When did you work at the Lynches?"

"Two years ago; not here but out in Saint Jacques d'Ambès, at the summer house. I got tired of the country—not enough life there for me—but they had no place for me in town."

"Who is in the family? How many people?"

"Every time I looked there seemed to be more of them, five girls, three boys, four aunts, a few uncles, several cousins, a couple of grandmothers, coming and going all the time."

"Coming from Ireland?"

"From everywhere—Paris, Lyons, Marseilles—all over the world."

He had never heard of Ireland.

In his hurry Robert had not considered whether he would be admitted to the house without an appointment. The butler kept him waiting on the steps while he went in to ask. Voices could be heard from beyond the door, a woman's voice, then a man's. Panic seized him. What could he say to these people? How could he explain his intrusion into their house? He began to form sentences about passing through Bordeaux, being Irish, wishing to make their acquaintance, to bring them greetings from Galway, a whole series of approaches which sounded one more impertinent than the other. When the butler came back he said:

"Count Lynch has gone out. You may come tomorrow morning at ten."

Quickly Robert said, "Then may I see Miss Nugent?"

The man looked at him suspiciously, then at the shabby hired carriage waiting in the street.

"I don't know. The master is not here."

He hadn't denied it, he hadn't shown any surprise. She was here, in this house, beyond this door. Desperately Robert said, raising his voice unconsciously in his excitement:

"I've come from Ireland to see her. I must see her. Just tell her I'm here, Robert Brien, of Mount Brien Court."

"You sound like a Frenchman to me; you look like one too."

At the back of the hall someone came out of a room and moved towards them. He couldn't see in the dimness. A stronger wind from the river blew against the globe of the bracket lamp that lit the hall, sending the flame climbing high and wide to the top of the glass. She was there, suddenly illuminated, the white lace at the neck and sleeves of her dark dress showing brightly for a second before the light died down. She said:

"Who is it, Géry? Someone for the Count?"

The butler stood aside, still doubtful, and Robert walked into the hall, standing full under the lamp so that she could see him. She paused, then said quietly:

"Show him into the small parlor, Géry. He's an old friend."

She kept her eyes down and stood very quietly while the butler opened a door to the left of the hall, but her voice had sunk almost to a whisper. He went into the little room and waited for her, touched agonizingly by the words she had used. As soon as the door was closed she stood just inside it, without moving. They looked at each other in silence. Neither was able to make a move towards the other. Her face was paler than he had ever seen it and there was a new sadness in her expression, as if all her experiences had disillusioned her and forced her far into the adult world. There was barely a trace of the impetuous, free country girl whom he had so despised in his stupid youth. He felt himself overwhelmed with pity for her, and an intense love such as he had never conceived of before, even in the haunted room in Dooras. At last he said:

"I was afraid you would refuse to see me."

"No—I would never do that." He noticed now that her voice had changed too, and had become low and calm, not at all as he remembered it. He found her new quiet frightening, and recalled the accounts he had been given of her hallucinations before the birth of her child. He was reassured by the look of understanding and intelligence that met his look. Still something prevented him from going towards her, though his arms ached to take her and hold her close to him. She gave a short sigh, which she controlled at once, then said: "I've wanted so much to see you but I thought I never would again in this life. Then suddenly there you were at the door." Her voice trailed off but she went on after a moment: "I've done great harm to your family."

"You have done harm!" He was shocked into taking a step towards her. "Is that what you think? It's we, my father and I, who have injured you. We can never make amends, we can never hope for forgiveness. I've followed you here to say this to you, but I never dreamed that you had taken on the blame for us. This is the last blow. I'll go away now, if you want me to. I'll leave you and never trouble you again. I look at your face and I can see that you have been in hell. Even if you could ever love me as I love you, all that has happened should be forgotten. You have had too much to bear. We're a cursed family. We bring destruction on everyone we touch. My grandmother was right. She said you should be left in peace. She said we had done you so much harm, and that I could only do more by following you."

Very softly she said:

"I've waited and waited for you. I thought you would never come. If you go away, and if I never see you again, I will die."

Her hands hung loosely by her sides. Quickly he bent and took them in his hands, while he looked closely into her eyes. They were full of tears, and showed a pain and longing that filled him with amazement and anguish. At last he said, shaking his head foolishly as if he could not believe what he had heard:

"Is it possible, is it really true that you love me after all? In Dooras I heard your voice, I spoke to you, I sent my thoughts and my love to you all across the world, wherever you might be. I have nothing to give you, nothing but the bad name we have made for our family, and a wandering life. Is that enough?"

"Robert, I'll go with you wherever you go, I'll live wherever you live, I'll never leave you until I die."

Her voice was so soft now that he barely heard the words, which had an echo of a much older time, as if she were uttering a principle of truth and constancy as much for herself as for him. Very gently he took her in his arms and kissed her on the lips, and felt her heart beat close against his, and knew he had gained the ultimate good at last.